"THIS LIST WILL GIVE YOU A ROUGH IDEA OF THE TARGETS. BY ALLOCATING A PAIR OF WARHEADS TO EACH LOCATION, WE CAN PRETTY WELL GUARANTEE A KILL."

The hushed silence that permeated the room was finally disrupted by Pavl Zavenyagin's strained voice.

"One entry disturbs me, Admiral. Why has Los Angeles been included? I thought we had agreed to spare civilian lives whenever possible."

Stanislav eyed the bureaucrat shrewdly. "In America, the President is the Commander-in-Chief of their armed forces. Thus, it is to our benefit to eliminate him as soon as hostilities are initiated."

"Kill the brain and the arms can't be utilized effectively," interceded Konstantin.

"Precisely, Comrade," said the admiral. "I think a fitting way to begin our little operation would be to explode a warhead directly over the Los Angeles airport just as the President steps forward to welcome our esteemed General Secretary to their country."

COUNTERFORCE
RICHARD P. HENRICK

ZEBRA BOOKS
KENSINGTON PUBLISHING CORP.

ZEBRA BOOKS

are published by

Kensington Publishing Corp.
850 Third Avenue
New York, NY 10022

Second printing: September 1987

Printed in the United States of America
10 9 8 7 6

Counterforce—the nuclear war-fighting strategy of targeting an enemy's military command posts and communications relay stations in order to make a retaliatory strike impossible.

"I am convinced . . . that even one nuclear bomb dropped by one side over the other would result in a general nuclear exchange—a nuclear holocaust not only for our two nations, but the entire world. . . . The starting of a nuclear war would spell annihilation for the aggressor himself."

—Former Soviet Premier Leonid Brezhnev

"I call heaven and earth to witness this day, that I have set before you life and death, blessing and cursing. Choose therefore life, that both thou and thy seed may live."

—Deuteronomy 30.19

Chapter One

A familiar, dreaded growl sounded up ahead, and Konstantin Belchenko instantly froze in mid-step. Intently, he peered through the thick tree line to his left. For the first few seconds, all that he could make out were the shaggy white birch trunks. When the muted grunt repeated itself, Belchenko shifted his line of sight to the section of the wood directly before him. There he spotted the fully grown black bear, furiously flaying at the ground, approximately one hundred meters away.

Aware of the creature's great strength and unforgiving temper Belchenko respectfully kept his distance. Crouching behind a fallen tree trunk, he reached inside the pocket of his greatcoat and removed a compact pair of binoculars. Barely the length and width of his own hand, the powerful field glasses were of German origin. They hardly needed to be adjusted as he brought them to his eyes and focused on the beast blocking his progress. Upon sighting a fist-sized patch of shocking white fur on the bear's right haunch, Belchenko smiled.

"Well, hello Pasha," he whispered to the wind. "It

seems that we are destined to meet once again."

It had been over two decades since Belchenko last set eyes on this particular creature. He would never forget that fateful morning, for he had just returned to these woods of his birth after a year's stay in the jungled hell of Southeast Asia.

How very different were his ponderings at that time. Still guided by the exuberant high hopes of youth, Belchenko had looked to the future with great anticipation. Little did he realize the obstacles that would all too soon strip him of his ambitions.

Today, a more hardened, mature individual watched the huge bear with the white spot on his rump forage among the birches. Like a man reborn, Belchenko now looked at the world with a vision stripped of all illusion. Even nature's basic realities took on a different perspective when viewed in this manner.

One thing that did not change though, was his love for this forest in which he had been raised. The woods outside the small city of Penza were as unspoiled today as they had been over fifty years ago. It was then that his father had been given exclusive use of the stone dacha Belchenko currently occupied. Located 525 kilometers southeast of Moscow on the banks of the Sura River, the cottage served as a welcome second home. Here the great tensions generated in the capital city could be temporarily appeased.

Belchenko had been there for almost a month now. Sent packing from the Kremlin on the insistence of his doctor, the sixty-four-year-old bureaucrat had spent the first two weeks in bed, convalescing from a lung infection that had haunted him all summer. The rest, pure air and hearty country food that his nurse Katrina had prepared for him had certainly done the trick. Already his strength and vitality were returning. For the past week, he had even felt good enough to begin hiking once again.

Well over six feet tall, Belchenko prided himself on his tight stomach and long, slender legs. As a youth, he had enjoyed walking for hours on end. As the gray began painting his ever-receding hairline, his jaunts had gradually decreased in length. Since his sickness he had felt fortunate just to be able to sit outside on a bench in Gorky Park. Belchenko didn't realize how much he missed his hikes until he had resumed them during the past week. Chancing upon the bear this morning was merely an added bonus. Just to wander the thick birch wood, far from the encroaching cries of humanity, was gift enough.

Above him a raven cried harshly, and Belchenko lowered his binoculars to look upward. Here, a small patch of bright blue sky was barely visible, the rest was blotted out by the tall, solid stand of trees. A cooling breeze swept through the forest and the slender trunks swayed in unison like the masts of a fleet of sailing ships. A shower of leaves cascaded from the upper boughs, and once more he was aware of the passing season. The first stirrings of fall were already in the air. Soon the icy winter winds would be upon them. Already the nights were conducive to a roaring fireplace. It wouldn't be long before the hearth would be blazing twenty-four hours a day, seven days a week. Shivering with this thought, Konstantin placed the binoculars back in his pocket and pulled the coat's woolen collar up over his neck. Angling his line of sight back into the woods, he was just able to catch a glimpse of the bear as it ambled off in the opposite direction.

"Goodbye old-timer, until next time," the gray-haired bureaucrat offered softly. "May your hibernation be sound and peaceful."

Aware of the hour, Belchenko turned to retrace the narrow trail that led back to the dacha. With a full, strong stride he proceeded down the dirt footpath, conscious of the endless stands of white birch surrounding him on all sides. A covey of fat quail shot into the air on his right. This unexpected movement was followed by the sudden appearance of a large gray rabbit. Bounding by him in a burst of startled speed, the hare quickly disappeared into the underbrush.

Feeling younger and more energetic than he had in years, Konstantin Belchenko, First Deputy Director of the KGB, pushed himself homeward. With lips tightly puckered, he whistled a spirited folk tune his mother used to sing to him when he was a boy. Even though he hadn't heard the tune in years, the melody instantly came back to him. After repeating the song several times over, he rounded a broad bend and began climbing a steep hill. Halfway up the incline, he stopped whistling. By the time he had reached the summit, a thick line of sweat painted his brow. With lungs wheezing for air, he halted and spat up a wad of viscous white mucus. A sharp pain pierced the lower left portion of his ribcage. Sobered by the gnawing spasm, Belchenko was abruptly brought back to reality. Cognizant of the fact that his ailment was still painfully present, he took a moment to regain his breath before starting on again.

10

The nearby rumbling of cascading waters helped to settle him down. Wiping the sweat from his forehead, he looked out to a scene that calmed him like a strong tonic. Beyond, less than two kilometers distant, was the Sura. Its bubbling blue waters smacked white upon the huge boulders that shaped this portion of the mighty current. Spanning this band of water was a narrow suspension bridge. Barely able to accommodate a single vehicle, the bridge was connected to the opposite bank by a crude earthen roadway. Following this road for another kilometer, Belchenko could just make out the gabled wooden roof of his dacha. A thin ribbon of smoke could be seen rising from the cottage's chimney; Katrina was already preparing for this afternoon's guests.

Gradually, the pain in his left side subsided. Only a few weeks ago this spasm had been his constant companion for hours on end. Surely its quick abatement today meant that he was well on his way to total health. Chastising himself for hiking a bit too far, Belchenko knew that he couldn't afford to get sick again. In the weeks that would follow, his physical well-being had to be assured. The very destiny of the Motherland would depend on his complete awareness.

Merely contemplating the daring plan caused goose bumps to form on his forearms. He'd show those foolish youngsters in Moscow what true leadership was all about! To think that they'd been so totally deaf to his cries for action. After all, what did they know about the teachings of history? Too young to have even fought in the Great War, Viktor Rodin and his followers didn't know the first thing about real struggle. And to think that this spineless idiot was

11

actually serious in his desire to parley with the imperialists! Didn't the General Secretary realize that the capitalists were their sworn enemies? How could anyone in his right mind trust a system whose very survival depended upon decadent greed?

Ever thankful for the invaluable assistance of his two allies, Belchenko knew they'd have just a single chance to stop Rodin before the traitor sold them out completely.

In the next several weeks the plot would be finalized—there would be no time for sickness. Breathing in a deep lungful of crisp, cool air, Belchenko felt his strength return. He made a mental note to limit his future hikes to reasonable distances. Surely this personal sacrifice would pay off handsomely in the long run. In the new world order that would follow, the true principles of Lenin could at long last be applied. Freed from class struggle, the earth's population would finally be allowed to coexist in a society of perfect equality.

Well aware that the first steps to this achievement were already being set into action, Belchenko pushed on. There were still friends to greet and plans to finalize. With fluid, careful steps, the first deputy proceeded down the path leading to the Sura.

The sun was directly overhead when Belchenko arrived back at his dacha. As it turned out, he had no time to spare, for just as he entered the courtyard leading to the cottage, the chopping sound of a helicopter's rotor blades sounded in the near distance. Shading his eyes from the sun's glare, Belchenko looked up and spotted a large vehicle approaching from the northwest. It took only seconds to identify it as a Mil Mi-8 utility chopper. Painted dark green, the helicopter featured a squat, elongated fuselage sporting seven prominent portholes. Beside the last observation window was a red, five-pointed star.

Belchenko was conscious of the powerful downdraft created by the whirling, five-bladed rotor as the Mi-8 circled above the large clearing to the immediate west of the courtyard. Rubbing the debris-blown dust from his eyes, he glanced away as the chopper hovered and slowly descended. The rotors were already spinning to a halt when he crossed through the hedge that enclosed the courtyard.

Cautiously, he looked up in time to see the door, set behind the pilot's side window, pop open. First out the doorway was a smartly uniformed army guard. With eyes set rigidly forward, the young officer snapped a smart salute as a stout, blue-suited individual followed him from the cockpit. Belchenko couldn't help but grin as he took in the familiar mane of unruly white hair and ruddy red face.

Admiral of the Fleet Stanislav Sorokin had been a close friend of Belchenko's for the past forty years. They had fought together in the Great War. Afterward, they shared a mutual talent for self-preservation while assigned to military intelligence under the watchful, paranoid eye of Lavrenti Pavlovich Beria. While Belchenko had continued on with intelligence, Sorokin had applied his considerable talent in a much different direction. Sorokin had been instrumental in the creation of the modern Soviet Navy. From a mere coastal fleet of a few hundred flimsy vessels to a powerful armada second to none, the Soviet Navy could extend its influence on any sea it chose. Sorokin's vision and perseverance had made this dream possible.

Following the portly admiral out of the Mi-8 was the pencil thin, black-suited figure of Politboro member Pavl Zavenyagin. With his ever-present briefcase at his side, Zavenyagin seemed grateful to reach solid ground. He seemed even more fragile than he had appeared last month. Almost completely bald, the thin-boned bureaucrat sported a drooping gray mustache, thick bushy eyebrows and a pair of black, beady eyes. Appearing as if a good wind would blow him away, Zavenyagin seemed insignificant beside the flamboyant admiral. In reality, his position in the Kremlin made him one of the most powerful figures in the world.

Belchenko met his two illustrious guests with a hearty hug and a warm smile. "Welcome to Penza, Comrades. I trust your flight was a smooth one."

"That it was, Comrade," returned the deep bass voice of the admiral. "My only complaint was that they ran out of vodka and herring much too quickly."

"Well, you have nothing to fear here, old friend. I'm certain that you'll find my dacha well stocked for your convenience."

Accepting Sorokin's nod of approval, Belchenko noticed that his companion was looking a bit peaked. "What's the matter, Comrade Zavenyagin? Are you not feeling well?"

Zavenyagin meekly caught his host's glance. "It's nothing, Comrade. I get this way every time I fly. I'll be feeling as good as new in a half-hour or so."

14

"I know what you're going through," Belchenko said. "I get the same feeling when I travel by sea. Stanislav, do you remember that winter storm we plowed through in the North Sea, back in '41? I could have sworn that I was going to vomit out my small intestine."

"Don't tell me that you call that little shower a storm, old friend," the admiral responded with a playful wink. "You should have seen some of the seas that I have crossed in nothing larger than a trawler. The trouble with you two is that you don't know how to properly pacify your stomachs. Try a little vodka and herring next time. That combination never fails to calm the nerves."

Catching Zavenyagin's nauseous wince, Belchenko beckoned to his guests to follow him toward the dacha. As the three passed by the hedge and entered the courtyard, the admiral said, "You're certainly looking fit, Konstantin. How have you been feeling since we last saw each other?"

In answer Belchenko pointed toward a freshly cut cord of birch logs neatly stacked beside the inner fence. "I felled the trees myself. I tell you, Stanislav, I feel like a totally new man."

Examining the line of squarely cut logs, the admiral appreciatively scratched his chin. "Now that's more like the Belchenko I knew in the old days. I was certain you'd lick that infection sooner or later."

"Just be careful you don't overexert yourself," Zavenyagin cautioned. "Less than four weeks ago you were flat on your back with a dangerously high fever. We can't afford to lose you now."

"I was just thinking the same thing earlier," Belchenko said with a sigh. "Perhaps I have been pressing myself these past few weeks, but that just speaks for how well I've been feeling lately. I promise to take extra good care of myself until the operation has been concluded. Speaking of the devil, let's proceed indoors. I've got some exciting news to tell you."

Ten minutes later, the three men were seated in high-backed, red leather chairs, surrounded by the intimate furnishings of Belchenko's well-stocked library. Before them, the fireplace crackled, alive with smoke and flame. A delicate silver serving tray was set up beside the hearth. On its glass surface were a crystal decanter filled with vodka, a samovar of sweetened tea, and a platter of thickly sliced black bread, topped with a mixture of herring fillets, sour cream and chopped onions. Stanislav Sorokin was already on his second helping of both herring and vodka, while Pavl Zavenyagin sipped contentedly on a cup of tea. It proved to be their host who initiated the conversation.

"What is the latest news from Moscow, Comrades?"

"As if you didn't know already," the admiral commented with a wink. "Events are plodding along just as we expected. I imagine you heard that our esteemed General Secretary recently welcomed a U.S. trade delegation of over two dozen 'accredited' individuals. Doesn't Rodin realize that they're nothing but a bunch of CIA spies?"

Zavenyagin sat forward on the edge of his chair. "Yesterday we received the production results from the quarter just completed. For the first time in this century, consumer goods show a healthy increase while military output continues to drop. There is talk on the street that the average citizen is most happy with the bevy of television sets, radios, washers, driers and automobiles now readily available on the open market."

"If the fools only realized they were signing their own death warrants," Belchenko commented dryly. "The imperialists will take this opportunity to flood our markets with their decadent goods. Infected by the greed of possession, our people will soon lose sight of their socialist direction."

"This drop in military outlay has me greatly concerned," the admiral offered between bites of herring. "Just when the Motherland had finally achieved a position of unquestionable superiority, Rodin comes along and negates our advances with a single blow. While we are drowning in consumer goods the West will continue its huge military expenditures until parity is eventually achieved. Our past sacrifices will mean nothing!"

"What is the mood of the Politboro these days, Pavl?" Belchenko asked.

Setting down his tea cup, Zavenyagin's brow tensed. "As before, Rodin's views continue to dominate. Our position will be seriously weakened at the end of this month when Yuri Polnocny retires. The General Secretary will be free to appoint another one of his cronies, and the majority will be clearly his."

"Can the remaining old-timers still be relied upon to support our cause when the time comes?" Belchenko asked.

Zavenyagin did not hesitate to say, "There is no question of their loyalty, Comrade. As long as they remain in office, the better interests of the Motherland will guide their actions. Like ourselves, they too fear the moderate's ways. Unfortunately, their advanced ages make individual dissent difficult."

Belchenko smiled. "Then we'll just have to make the first moves for them. Is the summit still on as planned?"

This time it was the admiral who answered. "As of this morning, things remain on schedule. The meeting in Los Angeles will begin two weeks from tomorrow. I have taken it upon myself to personally be in Petropavlovsk to wish our beloved leader *bon voyage* as he takes off for America."

"Excellent," Belchenko said. "And what of the submarine?"

Sorokin answered while getting to his feet to pour another shot of vodka. "So far, there have been few obstacles. The *Cheka* and the *Vulkan* are presently undergoing joint maneuvers in the North Pacific. This will allow the captains of the two vessels to become more comfortable with each other. Incidentally, we experienced little difficulty in getting our man assigned to the Delta-class boat. His report will tell us just who we can rely on when the going gets tough. Now, Konstantin, what is the nature of this exciting news you are so anxious to share with us?"

Belchenko beamed expectantly. "I'm certain that both of you will be excited to know that, as of yesterday afternoon, one of my most trusted agents successfully infiltrated the Premier's codification staff. In effect, this means the top-secret mechanism needed to unlock the Motherland's nuclear arsenal is now in our hands."

"Then we've done it!" exclaimed a relieved Zavenyagin.

"I'm afraid there's still much more to be accomplished," Belchenko warned. "Yet, knowledge of the daily release code was the obstacle I most feared."

"I concur," Sorokin added. "Without the proper signal our job would have been more difficult than it already is. I commend you on your efficiency, Konstantin. Other than the few logistical difficulties we still have to face, I believe it's time to address the problem of actual targeting."

Belchenko nodded and rose stiffly. Making his way to the right side of the fireplace, he pulled down a large, laminated topographical map of North America. The area shown included a large portion of the Pacific Ocean. Utilizing a pointer, he began talking animatedly.

"Comrades, as we discussed earlier, this is to be a Counterforce attack, intended primarily to take out the imperialists' communications relay stations and military command posts. If all goes as planned, the Americans will be unable to answer with a retaliatory strike. At long last the capitalists will be completely at our mercy. Of course, all this will take place with a minimum of civilian casualties. Stanislav, why don't you begin by explaining just what hardware we have at our disposal."

The admiral finished off his vodka and spoke out clearly. "The primary launch vehicle for the attack will be the *Vulkan*, our latest Delta III-class missile-carrying submarine. This vessel will be loaded with sixteen SS-N-18 Mod 3 missiles. Each rocket will be topped with seven MIRVd warheads capable of eliminating targets over 6,000 miles distant. This will allow

19

us to destroy 112 separate locations."

"By using only a single submarine, won't we be opening ourselves to a needless amount of risk?" interrupted Zavenyagin. "I still feel we should be thinking about sending some ground-based ICBMs to insure the enemy's defeat."

"Your concern is noted, Comrade," the admiral said. "But 112 SS-N-18 warheads will be more than enough to strike the Yankees a crippling blow. Besides being a most effective weapons system, the use of this single submarine will guarantee our anonymity. I can just imagine the logistical problems we would encounter attempting to insure the release of an ICBM. Those characters in the Strategic Rocket Corps have a loyalty all their own."

"Stanislav is correct," Belchenko added. "I thought we agreed on this point weeks ago. Only by keeping our scenario as simple as possible can we hope to succeed. Have you already forgotten our initial agreement, Pavl?"

Zavenyagin blushed and sat back in his chair. "Of course not, Comrade. It's just that I still find it hard to believe that the warheads from one submarine can render the imperialists helpless."

"Don't worry yourself so, Pavl," Belchenko advised. "I, too, had trouble accepting this amazing fact. Yet the crux of the matter is the amount of targets we'll ultimately need to eliminate. I'm certain you'll see by the conclusion of this meeting that the locations that need to be taken out will indeed be destroyed. We'll have more than enough warheads to do the job, without the need for a back-up. Stanislav, why don't you start us off with a list of our primary targets."

Standing up to pour himself another vodka, the white-haired admiral took several seconds before responding. "To guarantee penetration, our first salvo will take out the PAVE PAWS Phased Array Warning System site at Beale Air Force Base, California. With this station eliminated, the United States will be unable to accurately monitor the release of subsequent submarine-launched missiles from the North Pacific basin. "I've taken the liberty of drafting a document outlining the attack format. For security reasons, I'd prefer that the list not leave this room."

Accepting the consenting nods of his colleagues, Sorokin reached into his breast pocket, removed two single sheets of heavy bond paper and handed one to each one of his cohorts.

"This list will give you a rough idea of the targets we'll need to cover. By allocating at least a pair of warheads to each location, we can pretty well guarantee a kill. To eliminate any 'hard targets' such as command posts, which have been buried to protect them from surface blast, ground-burrowing warheads will be utilized."

The room lapsed into silence as Belchenko and Zavenyagin studied the papers just handed them. Both men found their pulses fluttering as their eyes took in the neatly typed columns.

FOR YOUR EYES ONLY
COUNTERFORCE TARGETS

1.) PAVE PAWS radar site; Beale Air Force Base, California

2.) Cobra Dane radar site; Shemya Island,

Alaska

3.) Casino downlink satellite station; Nur-runger, Australia

4.) Satellite control facility; Sunnyvale, California

5.) AT&T switching stations: Lyons, Nebraska; Fairview, Kansas; Hillsboro, Missouri; Lamar, Colorado

6.) NORAD's Cheyenne Mountain Command Post; Colorado Springs, Colorado

7.) SAC headquarters, Omaha, Nebraska

8.) SAC alternate headquarters, Barksdale Air Force Base, Louisiana and March Air Force Base, California

9.) Headquarters, Atlantic Fleet; Norfolk, Virginia

10.) Headquarters, Pacific Fleet; Pearl Harbor, Hawaii

11.) The White House; Washington, D.C.

12.) The Pentagon; Washington, D.C.

13.) Alternative National Military Command Center, Fort Ritchie, Maryland

14.) Controlled Conflict Operational Post, Mt. Weather, Virginia

15.) Alternative Military Command Center, Raven Rock Mtn., Pennsylvania

16.) Satellite downlink station, Buckley Air National Guard Base, Colorado

17.) VLF radio transmitters: Cutler, Maine; Jim Creek, Washington; Northwest Cape, Australia

18.) Enchanced Perimeter Acquistion Radar site; Concrete, North Dakota

19.) Various army, air force and naval bases

located throughout the continental United States and the Pacific Basin (detailed list to follow)
20.) Pindown strike detonated above all ICBM bases
21.) Los Angeles

Konstantin Belchenko completed reading the document first. He looked up and caught the sharp stare of the admiral. The silent exchange was interrupted by Zavenyagin's strained voice.

"This list is most complete, Admiral. One entry disturbs me, though. Why has Los Angeles been included? I thought we had agreed to spare civilian lives whenever possible."

Sorokin eyed the bureaucrat shrewdly. "Your observation is most astute, Comrade. But I'm afraid this is one instance when the loss of innocents can't be helped. For our Counterforce attack to be successful, we must knock out America's command structure completely. We must place them in a situation where there will be no one left alive to order a counterstrike. In America, the President is the key figure in the chain of command. As commander-in-chief of their armed forces, his say-so alone is required to release the missiles. Thus, it is to our benefit to eliminate him as soon as hostilities are initiated."

"Kill the brain and the arms can't be utilized effectively," Belchenko interceded boldly.

"Precisely, Comrade," returned the admiral. "I think a fitting way to begin our little operation would be to explode a warhead directly above the Los Angeles airport, just as the President steps forward to welcome our esteemed General Secretary to his country."

"Brilliant idea!" Belchenko shouted. "In that way we kill two birds with one stone."

"I thought you'd particularly enjoy that little twist," Sorokin said. "Now, Pavl, is that explanation sufficient?"

Zavenyagin shrugged his shoulders and offered no additional comment. Taking this as a cue to move on, Belchenko turned to face the admiral.

"Have you determined a launch position as yet, Stanislav?"

"Good question. In order to be within range of our intended targets, an optimum release site would be somewhere in the North Pacific." He walked to the wall map and pointed to an area northwest of Hawaii. "I'd say the waters north of Midway Island would offer us an excellent location. That's close enough to our home base in Petropavlovsk, and there's plenty of deep water to offer our sub shelter. As the fates would have it, that sector is precisely where the *Vulkan* and the *Cheka* are currently on patrol. Those captains know the area better than their lovers' own curves."

"When are they due back?" Zavenyagin questioned carefully.

The admiral continued to study the map while responding. "They're due back in base by the end of the week. That should give us plenty of time to make the final preparations."

"Comrades, I think that a toast is in order!"

Belchenko's words served to distract Sorokin from his intense inspection of the Pacific. The admiral turned in time to see the first deputy walk to the serving cart and pour three full glasses of vodka. After

24

handing one to each of his fellow conspirators, he raised his own glass and offered a toast: "To the success of Operation Counterforce, and to the glory of the Motherland!"

With a swift twist of his wrist, Belchenko joined his guests by emptying his glass. The chilled vodka was still stinging his throat when Sorokin again filled the glasses and offered his own toast.

"To one unified socialist world free from the greedy spell of imperialist domination! Long live the Rodina!"

Again the glasses were emptied. This time it was Pavl Zavenyagin who shakily stood. Clearly affected by the vodka, he clumsily refilled his comrades' glasses. Raising his own cup before him, he added, "To the workers of the world! Have faith, fellow Comrades, your salvation is imminent!"

Belchenko drained his glass and watched his guests do likewise. Flushed by the powerful liquor, he watched Zavenyagin stumble back into his chair and the admiral turn back to study the wall map. Focusing his own attention on the fireplace, the first deputy centered his thoughts on the blazing birch logs. So intense was their conversation that he had completely neglected to tend the fire. It would need fresh fuel soon before it burned itself out. Aware of the intense orange heat reflected by the burning embers, Belchenko found his thoughts drifting. In the blink of an eye, he soared far away from the somber affairs of state. Even with the fate of the planet in his hands, his concerns centered on a subject far removed from nuclear throw-weights and megatonage. Instead of being cooped up in his library, he wished only to be deep in the birch forest on the trail of Pasha the bear.

That morning, if only for fleeting seconds, he had tasted the fruits of true happiness. Alone in the woods, intoxicated by the crisp fall air, Konstantin Belchenko had discovered a contentment he hadn't experienced since childhood. Far removed from the intrigues of world power, the bear with the white patch on its rump taught him a lesson of a completely different nature. Innocent and unaware, the black bear only knew to feed, to build up its layer of body fat for the long winter that was inevitably coming. It needed nothing more from life than satisfying this basic, instinctual longing.

That was the way to live—in simplicity and innocence. Why must man always strive for that which he can never totally possess? Was this quality innate in all human beings, or was the rage for power a sickness to which he and his type had become addicted?

The fire hissed and crackled, and Belchenko knew that he was too far committed to turn back now. Suddenly conscious of a painful tingling in his lungs, he knew that his next hike would not take place until the new world order had dawned.

Chapter Two

Three hundred and twenty-five miles to the northeast of Midway Island, the Los Angeles-class attack sub USS *Triton* silently drifted one hundred and fifty feet beneath the water's surface. Longer than a football field, and staffed by a complement of one hundred and twenty-seven highly trained officers and enlisted men, the *Triton* was one of the most sophisticated underwater vessels ever put to sea. Packed within its hull was the latest in high-tech machinery. This included a dual set of supersensitive sonar arrays, a powerful nuclear propulsion plant and a wide variety of offensive and defensive weaponry. Primarily designed to hunt down and destroy other submarines and to protect the *boomers* (missile-carrying subs), the *Triton* was also quite capable of striking targets well inland. Such diverse capabilities made it an extremely potent fighting machine.

For two months now, the *Triton* had been on patrol. This extensive tour of duty brought its crew to no exotic ports. In fact, not once during the voyage did the sub even break the surface. Stealth and secrecy were two major elements that guaranteed the vessel's continued existence. The crew were most aware of this fact and accepted their isolation without negative comment.

Captain Michael Cooksey, commanding officer of the *Triton*, was well satisfied with the superb operational capabilities of the equipment and the unequalled competency of his present crew. If all continued smoothly, surely their second battle-efficiency award in a row would be waiting for them at Pearl Harbor. They would be arriving there in less than a week's time.

As usual when a cruise was winding down, Cooksey experienced a touch of depression. After all, these patrols were what he lived for. Having no wife or children anxiously waiting for him in port set him apart from the majority of his crew. Now that he was about to begin his twentieth year of naval service, he knew that the inevitable transfer orders would soon be coming his way. At best, he could hope for command of a destroyer, or even a fleet supply ship. Orders directing him to permanent shore duty would be as good as a commendation to death.

Sprawled out on his narrow bunk, with his hands locked behind his head and his eyes scanning the Spartan contents of his cramped quarters, the captain forced himself to focus on their present mission. The unusual degree of quiet merely emphasized their current situation. Absent was the constant, muted drone of the ship's turbines. In its place, only the hiss of the *Triton*'s ventilation system produced evidence that the vessel was operational.

For twelve hours now they had been drifting, rigged in a state of ultra-quiet. During that time all unnecessary activity was eliminated. Water evaporators were shut down, the garbage disposal system was deactivated, and even the soft-drink machines had been shut off. All men not on duty were sent to their cots as the *Triton* attempted to float noiselessly.

This exercise had a dual purpose. Since anti-submarine-warfare platforms depended largely upon hydrophone listening devices to pick up the sound signature of an approaching vessel, their present state helped to insure their nondetection. As a formidable ASW platform in their own right, the condition of ultra-quiet allowed their own hydrophone operators to receive an uncluttered signal from any advancing naval units.

Using this tactic, Cooksey hoped to pick up the sounds of the American carrier unit he was assigned to intercept. In effect, they were in the midst of a war game, with the *Triton* taking the role of the enemy. If possible, they were to record proof of their interception without the surface fleet knowing the *Triton* was even present. An accomplishment of this difficult task would signal the end of their present patrol.

Since the men were anxious to return to port, they were really putting their hearts into the exercise. The quicker they "tagged" the task force, the sooner they'd be reunited with their long-absent loved ones. The captain hoped that his decision to remain stationary was correct. Although this severely limited the territory they could cover effectively, he had a gut feeling that the surface units would eventually be passing through this area.

Their present position was 32 degrees north latitude, 173 degrees west longitude. To the layman, these coordinates seemed unimportant. Cooksey knew otherwise. No U.S. flagship commander cruising these waters would dare pass up the chance to direct his units over the legendary position know as "Point Luck."

It was at this spot, in 1942, that Admirals Fletcher and Spruance rendezvoused to await the Japanese invasion force headed toward Midway Island. What followed was one of the greatest naval battles of modern times. Eighty-six Japanese warships faced a meager force of twenty-seven U.S. vessels. Amazingly enough, when the smoke cleared not only had the invasion force been turned away, but four Japanese carriers lay on the bottom. Though the U.S. lost the *Yorktown*, and dozens of brave fighter pilots, Pearl Harbor was avenged and the tide of the war had turned.

On several previous occasions Cooksey had commanded his submarine to stop at this site; after explaining its significance to the crew, he would ask for a moment of silent prayer. Other captains were said to do likewise. Traditions died hard in the navy, and Cooksey was gambling that the admiral in charge of the carrier force would take a few minutes to pay his respects, and in the process, teach his men some living history.

Remaining stationary, submerged one hundred and fifty feet beneath the surface, was no easy task. To accomplish this feat they were currently "riding a layer." Since it was impossible for a sub to be so delicately trimmed that it could remain indefinitely static, neither rising or falling, it was necessary to obtain Mother Nature's assistance. In this case, a heavier layer of cooler, more saline water was located. Trimming the sub for a warmer, lighter layer, they were presently balancing on the boundary between the two. The *Triton* could remain in this strata as long as the sea state remained constant and their equipment cooperated.

Cooksey found himself hoping that they wouldn't have to stay there much longer. Rigging for ultra-quiet only produced an additional degree of tension, which was enhanced by their recently concluded two-month patrol period. In times of war, such prolonged isolation would often be necessary. Yet they were merely playing a war game.

The captain stirred uneasily, realizing that his hopes for catching a cat nap had been frustrated. Not that he was ever a sound sleeper. While on patrol, he satisfied himself with barely four hours of shut-eye. That, and an occasional nap, was usually more than sufficient to keep him alert and rested. Lately, though, he had been finding it increasingly difficult to drift off to sleep. Whenever he laid down on his bunk, it seemed that all types of irritating thoughts immediately snapped into his head. When he wasn't worrying about the day he would lose command of the *Triton*, a thousand and one trivial technical problems would haunt him. Too often he would find himself rushing through the sub to check the condition of some insignificant valve, which was usually in perfect condition.

Hesitant to discuss his problem with any of the other officers, Cooksey promised himself he would bring it up during his next physical. Though this would be the logical course of action to take, in reality he doubted that he'd ever have the nerve to make such an admission. Most probably the navy would see his sleeping difficulties as representative of a much deeper psychological disturbance. Such a condition would instantly cost him his hard-won command.

Lately, dozens of cups of extra-strong black coffee had been his savior. When fatigue began catching up with him, a quick caffeine fix had yet to fail. To see him through the watch that would soon follow, the bitter brew would be sorely needed. Try as he could, Cooksey had trouble remembering the last time he hit the sack and had a really sound slumber.

Sitting up with a grunt, he yawned and ran his hands through his brown crew cut. Since he had been dressed in only his scivvies, he reached over and pulled on a pair of dark-blue coveralls. Except for his captain's insignia, he was now dressed exactly like his shipmates.

Walking over to the head, he took a minute to splash some cold water on his face. Although he could feel a line of stubble on his jaw, he decided against shaving. After brushing his teeth, he evaluated his reflection in the mirror.

Though he was well into his forties, he was certain that he could still pass for a thirty-year-old. His lack of facial wrinkles and full head of close-cropped brown hair promoted this appearance of eternal youth. He supposed he owed this to a set of inherited genes. His mother, whom he greatly favored, could easily knock fifteen years off her current age and no one would be the wiser. The single feature that divulged his true age were his eyes. It was here that he was beginning to observe a noticeable change. Slowly but surely, the first hints of crow's-feet were beginning to form beneath his brows. He also noticed that lately his eyes seemed to be constantly bloodshot. And, was it his imagination, or wasn't the bright, vibrant blue gradually fading from his stare?

As if calling him out of a dream, two soft electronic tones chimed in the background, and Cooksey jumped, startled. Realizing that it was only his intercom, he turned to pick up the plastic handset.

"Captain here."

The voice on the other end was deep and tinged by a slight Southern accent. "Sorry to bother you, Skipper, but we're experiencing some problems with the integrity of our ultra-quiet state. Chief Weaver is reporting an unusual ticking noise in the main engine room. The disturbance is loud enough for Callahan to pick up on the hydrophones."

"Any idea where it's coming from?" the captain asked.

"Negative, Skipper. The Chief is currently investigating."

"Sounds like I'd better get down there and give them a hand. Thanks, Mr. Craig."

Cooksey knew that his executive officer wouldn't disturb him unless something serious had developed. Richard Craig had proven himself to be a cool-headed young officer, an XO who could be relied on for quick, precise assessments. Since in times of real combat an unknown noise could jeopardize their safety, the captain was aware of how important it was to find the source of this disturbance and to quickly quiet it.

The engine room was located in the stern half of the *Triton*, two floors beneath Cooksey's quarters. With-

33

out hestitation, the captain guided his solid, six-foot frame down the cramped hallway, so narrow that two men could not pass shoulder to shoulder. Oblivious to the shining banks of stainless steel pipes and the thick cables of exposed wiring that lined the roof of the corridor, he stepped through an open hatch and began climbing down the metal stairway. Faced with another long hallway, he proceeded with quick strides past the crew's mess. Here, he couldn't help but savor the rich, inviting scent of fresh-perked coffee. He noticed at a glance that the majority of green, rubber-meshed tables were empty, then ducked through a pair of open hatchways and descended another flight of stairs. Down there, the distinctive smell of hot oil and warm polyethylene met his nostrils.

A young machinist's mate snapped to attention as Cooksey nodded and passed through still another hatch. Turning to his right, he entered a large, spotlessly clean room. Shiny stainless steel, gleaming white paint, miles of snaking copper tubing and dozens of various-sized gauges lined the walls. Six men were seated at a huge console, scanning the hundreds of dials, gauges and meters that belonged to the nuclear power plant. Here neutron flux, steam pressure, flow rates, liquid levels and various temperatures were monitored. Not stopping to bother the technicians, he opened a sealed hatch and stepped into the main engine room.

Dwarfed by the massive turbine generators, Cooksey spotted Chief Petty Officer Samuel Weaver kneeling beside the main shaft. At his side was a figure that Cooksey immediately identified. The muscular broad shoulders and shiny bald pate could belong to no one else but Chief Peter Bartkowski. Both men were completely involved in their work and didn't notice the captain as he approached them. It was only when Cooksey got within a dozen feet of the two that he realized each man was wearing a stethoscope.

"It's the foward bushing!" the chief boomed excitedly.

Samuel Weaver was quickly at his side. Carefully, he examined with his own listening device the tubular shaft that the chief had been perched before. While Weaver immersed himself in his study, Bartkowski sat up, removed the stethoscope from his ears and only then set eyes on the captain.

"Sorry this took so long, Skipper, but it looks like we've got it licked. Damn bushing must of been packed wrong."

"I knew you'd locate it, Chief. How long will it take you to fix?"

Before Bartkowski could answer, Weaver sat up, noticed the captain's presence, and nervously saluted. "Sorry about this, Captain. Believe me, it's the first we've heard of it. It must have been botched up while we were last in refit at Pearl."

"Easy, Sam," Cooksey advised cooly. "I know you run a taut ship back here. We're just lucky this didn't fail earlier. Can you fix it?"

Chief Bartkowski grinned. "Just give us ten minutes, Skipper. She'll be just as good as new."

"I'm sure she will," said the captain, who was distracted by the soft ring of two familiar tones. He reached over to pickup the intercom and listened to his XO's breathless observation.

"We've got a contact, Captain! Looks like we just

got hit with a pair of sonobuoys topside."

Cooksey let out a relieved sigh. "I'm on my way up, Rich. And by the way, the Chief promises us ultra-quiet integrity in ten minutes. Sound General Quarters. Pass the word by mouth."

By the time Bartkowski and Weaver had concluded their repair of the improperly packed bushing, Cooksey had already taken his command position in the *Triton*'s control room. From his vantage point, directly behind the sonar console, he had a clear view of the various operational stations. To his right sat the two helmsmen, their hands tightly gripping the aircraft-style steering yokes that controlled the sub's direction. Beside them were digital consoles reserved for navigation, engineering, weapons and communications. Each of these stations was manned and ready for action.

At the captain's side stood the *Triton*'s executive officer, Lieutenant Commander Richard Craig. The thin, blond-haired Californian looked like he would be equally at home with a surf board in his hands. Though this was his first stint as XO, he had already gained the respect of the crew. Leaning on the tubular steel railing that separated the two officers from the sonar operators, Craig addressed the red-headed sailor seated to his left.

"What's AUSEX got to say about those sonobuoys, Callahan?"

Petty Officer First Class Charles Callahan held back his response until he finished typing a request into his computer keyboard. "We're still waiting for a response, Mr. Craig. All that we know for certain is that they don't appear to be active arrays."

As the current watch officer in charge of the sub's passive listening devices, Callahan was most familiar with the workings of the so-called acoustic methods of vessel identification. The lightweight, ultra-sensitive headphones he wore were directly connected with the dozens of hydrophone devices attached to the *Triton*'s hull. Although the majority of these powerful, miniature microphones were implanted permanently, several systems were designed to be either towed or to float away from the hull itself. One such system was labeled AUSEX, for Aircraft Undersea Sound Experiment. AUSEX was designed around a neutrally buoyant hydrophone tube that was released on a cable and floated up toward the surface. This allowed any nearby aircraft to be sonically monitored and analyzed.

Callahan was continually impressed with the sophisticated equipment at his disposal. He couldn't help but express his admiration of this gear. As his computer screen lit up, his freckled face beamed.

"We've got a sound signature I.D., sir. Those sonobuoys are the property of a U.S. Navy Kaman SH-2F Seasprite chopper."

"Then we've got them!" the XO exclaimed. "The mother ship has got to be close."

Cooksey reacted calmly. "I'll bet my pension that Seasprite belongs to the carrier task force. Standard operating procedure would have them saturating the ocean with sonobuoys to tag any unwanted visitors. We should be picking up the first of the escorts any minute now."

Not ten seconds passed when Callahan suddenly bent forward and cupped his headphones tightly around his ears. "We're picking up twin screws, coming in from the northwest at approximately 10,000 yards."

"Get us a computer I.D. of the sound signature," the captain ordered.

Efficiently, Callahan typed this request into his keyboard. Several tense seconds passed before the screen lit up with the desired information.

"Big Brother shows an eighty-five percent probability that we've got a Spruance-class destroyer topside."

"That will be the *Eagle*," Cooksey said casually. "I went to school with her present skipper, Jim Powell. The reason we didn't pick her up earlier were those paired LM2500 gas-turbine engines. She's a silent one all right."

Catching his XO's satisfied, boyish grin, the captain wasn't surprised when Callahan excitedly reported that they had several other visitors topside. With exacting precision, the computer identified a Knox-class frigate, a combat stores ship, a Cimarron-class fleet oiler, the Aegis guided-missile cruiser USS *Ticonderoga*, and finally the flagship carrier *John F. Kennedy*.

"Rich, I want you to stow that sound I.D. tape, plus an exact record of our intercept time. The admiral's going to want concrete proof that we were really here."

"Aye, aye, Skipper. Does this mean that we'll be on our way back to Pearl now?"

Cooksey noticed the hopeful tone in Craig's voice. "I guess you're kind of anxious to know if you're a new papa yet. Exactly when was Susan due?"

"Sometime this week, Skipper. But if Susie runs true to form, she'll be late as always. Do you know that she almost missed our wedding? That girl needs an alarm clock glued to her wrist."

Cooksey instinctively checked the large, digital clock mounted in the sonar console. "Give the task force another hour to clear these waters. Then we'll follow in their baffles, all the way back to port. We'll get you back to Hawaii in time, you'll see."

No sooner had these words passed the captain's lips when Petty Officer Callahan said, "We've got an underwater bogey contact, Captain! She's coming in from the south with a bone in her teeth, at nine thousand yards. Awaiting computer verification of the screw signature."

"Could it be one of ours?" the XO asked as he joined Cooksey beside the lucite target-acquisition map next to the sonar console.

Cooksey didn't respond. With searching eyes he studied the gridded, three-dimensional cross-section of that portion of the Pacific basin. The computer-enhanced map clearly showed the *Triton*'s present position, the six ships of the carrier task force presently passing above them, and the rapidly approaching bogey.

"Screw signature doesn't appear to be of Western origin," cried Callahan. "Big Brother is still cross-checking."

"Ping her!" Cooksey ordered, his hands tightly gripped around the railing.

"But the exercise," interjected the XO. "Using active sonar now will clearly give our position away.

39

The task force can't help but know that we're down here."

The captain's face reddened. "I don't give a damn about any friggin' war games! There's a bogey out there headed straight for an intercept with six of our top-of-the-line ships. I've got to know who they are and what the hell they're doing here. Ping them, damn it!"

Not willing to further irritate the captain, Richard Craig held his tongue, while the sonar operator seated next to Charlie Callahan sat forward and switched on the active sonar. A large green cathode-ray screen came instantly alive, as a high-speed pulse of energy surged out of the *Triton*'s huge, hull-mounted sonar transducer. This surge was audible as a quavering note, followed by the plink of a return echo. After this process was repeated, the excited sonar operator reported, "We've got 'em, Captain! Target is moving toward intercept point at a speed of four-three knots. Relative depth is nine-five-zero feet."

With this revelation, Cooksey's face paled. "Only one sub class on this planet can accomplish those specs. Damned if we don't have a Soviet Alfa coming right down our throats. Engineering, prepare the ship to get underway. I'm going to want flank speed. Navigation, plot us a course to intercept that Red bastard. Who the hell does he think he's playing with?"

As the full-throated rumble of the *Triton*'s long-dormant turbines sounded in the background, Cooksey caught his XO's concerned glance. Richard Craig looked younger and more vulnerable than he ever had. Of course, the lad had babies on his mind. Cooksey

40

knew that was a dangerous combination. A lack of total concentration could easily lead to a botched order. The activation of a single wrong valve could easily doom all one hundred and twenty-seven crew members.

If Craig was made out of the right stuff for command, he'd have to get tough fast. Cooksey could think of no better time to see if the young officer was indeed ready. Placing his hand firmly on the lieutenant commander's shoulder, the captain addressed him directly.

"Mr. Craig, even though all the books say the Soviet Alfa can easily outrun and dive the *Triton*, I'd sure hate to just sit here and watch them run under our flotilla like they're doing. I'd like you to take the con and show those Ruskies what the U.S. Navy is all about. We're not authorized to blow them away, but at least we can chase them out of here by putting the fear of God in them. How about it?"

Although Craig's first thought, about the Soviet sub was that it would inevitably delay his reunion with Susie, Cooksey's words redirected his train of thought. Proud that the captain had chosen him to lead the chase, he silently pledged he would do his best to teach the enemy a lesson.

"All ahead, flank speed to intercept point!" commanded the XO, his voice firm with authority.

As the *Triton* trembled beneath him, Michael Cooksey realized that he had made the right decision. Reaching one's mature potential was what these peacetime patrols were all about. Conscious of the stirring around him as the attack team scrambled to accomplish their assigned tasks, he stifled a yawn and

41

concluded that it would take a near miracle to intercept the Alfa before it was long gone from their sector.

Captain Grigori Dzerzhinsky, commanding officer of the Alfa-class attack sub *Cheka*, stood stiffly in the midst of the vessel's attack center. Small and wiry with wavy black hair, the captain found himself quite pleased with his mission's outcome. As always, the *Cheka* was everything he could ask for in a submarine. Faster than the enemy's torpedoes, their titanium-alloy hull allowed them to reach depths of over three thousand feet. No other undersea vessel could attain even a third of that. Dzerzhinsky was equally satisfied with his crack crew. The sixty-man complement went about their jobs like the true professionals they were. In most cases, each was an officer, a Great Russian, and a Party member. Sworn to keep all they witnessed aboard the ship a secret, they pledged their loyalty to him alone. This blind obedience produced a morale and competency level that far exceeded that of any ship of the line.

The light of the attack center was a ghostly red, designed to enhance the brightness of the computer consoles and protect the crew's night vision in the event an emergency forced them to the surface. The only sound audible was the churning grind of turbines as the *Cheka* surged through the icy waters of the Pacific. The carrier task force that they had been assigned to penetrate had long since left their radar screens. He could just imagine the imperialist admirals now, gathered in their luxuriant wardrooms, wondering what kind of vessel could have broken their security perimeter so easily. That would give them something to talk about when they returned to port.

Dzerzhinsky smiled as he attempted to visualize their confused faces. So vivid were his imaginings that he didn't even notice it when the heavy-set, pasty-skinned figure of his *zampolit*, Boris Karpovich, positioned his bulky body beside him.

"So that was the infamous Point Luck," the political officer observed snidely. "It certainly wasn't lucky for the Americans on this occasion. Why, we could have easily wiped out their entire task force before they even knew what hit them."

Dzerzhinsky noticed the smug look of arrogance that painted the *zampolit*'s sweaty face—as if this slob had had any part in the success of their penetration. Knowing that he had to be civil, the captain attempted a forced smile.

"We certainly caught them napping, Comrade *Zampolit*."

"It was more than that," shot back the political officer. "Even if we had advertised our arrival, there would have been nothing that they could have done to avoid us. The *Cheka* proves the superiority of the socialist way of life. Is the imperialist attack submarine still attempting to intercept us?"

"No, Comrade. The Americans wisely abandoned their puny attempt over ten minutes ago. It appears we have these waters all to ourselves now."

"This is a most glorious day. The First Deputy will be most satisfied. Will you join me in my cabin for a toast, Captain?"

Though having to share a drink with Karpovich was not the least bit desirable, Dzerzhinsky knew that he was bound by etiquette to do so. "I would be honored, Comrade. There is a task that I must complete first, then I will be free to join you."

Karpovich's eyes darkened. "What is that, may I ask, Comrade?"

Unable to believe the man's boldness, Dzerzhinsky strained to hold back his rising temper. "The rendez-vous coordinates with the *Vulkan* remain to be final-ized. The presence of that American attack sub forced us to alter our original course. If the imperialists are still in the vicinity, we must be extra cautious so that we don't lead them to one of the Motherland's most advanced strategic-missile firing platforms."

"Of course, Captain," the *zampolit* replied. "I'll be waiting for you in my stateroom."

After wiping his soaked brow with a wrinkled handkerchief, Karpovich turned and disappeared to-ward the sub's bow. Alone once again, Grigori Dzerzhinsky breathed a sigh of relief.

How many times had he questioned the ridiculous necessity of having such an idiot aboard? The *zampo-lit* did nothing but take up valuable space. How he had pleaded with the admiral to allow him to sail without a political officer. Even for a vessel such as the *Cheka*, Stanislav Sorokin wouldn't bend. Know-ing that the admiral's word was final, the captain had reluctantly consented. He would have to put up with the nosey *zampolit* for the rest of the patrol, just as he had put up with so many others on dozens of cruises before. Accepting this fact, the captain took a deep, calming breath and straightened his narrow shoul-ders. With quick, assured steps, he crossed the equip-ment-packed attack center to the digital console reserved for navigation.

In another portion of the North Pacific, three hundred and seventy miles due west of the coordinates known as Point Luck, the captain of the Delta III-class submarine *Vulkan* found himself hunched over the communications panel. Lit by the dim red combat lighting, Petyr Valenko could barely make out the operator's familiar face. From the stream of coded data audible in the distance, the captain was certain that the *michman* was totally immersed in the signal's translation.

Radio messages were rarely transmitted to submarines. Only in matters of utmost urgency would command dare risk exposing their submerged positions. This was especially true of the missile-carrying vessels.

Anxious to know what the jumbled series of dashes, dots, and spaces were all about, Valenko waited expectantly. At least he had one of his best men manning the communications console. The *michman*, Stefan Kuzmin, had sailed with him on three previous patrols. In each instance, his work had been most admirable. As warrant officer, Kuzmin was in the unique position of being middle man between the officers and the enlisted personnel.

Historically, the Soviet Navy had faced a chronic shortage of senior enlisted men. In an effort to overcome this deficiency, and to upgrade the status of a career serviceman, the rank of *michman* was created. Extensively trained in every aspect of the ship's operation, the warrant officer received increased pay, privileges, and eventually an opportunity to be promoted to the officers' ranks.

Having shared many a meal with Kuzmin, Valenko was aware of the young man's innate intelligence. Though he never had the opportunity of extensive elementary schooling, the native Ukrainian was a quick learner. More than that, he was a very likable fellow. When tensions mounted, he could always be relied upon to lighten the situation with a joke or funny comment. Unfortunately, there was no time for pleasantries this evening.

The cryptograph's abrupt silence was followed by Kuzmin's softly spoken words. "That seems to be the extent of the transmission, Captain. We should have a computer translation in a minute or so."

"Any idea where the message originated from?" the captain asked.

Kuzmin looked up from the monitor and briefly caught Valenko's probing stare. "I believe the first call letters belonged to Captain Dzerzhinsky, sir."

Valenko silently absorbed this revelation. If it was indeed the *Cheka* calling, the attack sub was probably relaying to them a set of rendezvous coordinates. This conjecture was verified by the *michman*, who spoke carefully.

"It's an intercept position from the *Cheka*, Captain. We've been instructed to a rendezvous point in the Emperor Seamount sector at dawn."

Hastily checking his watch, Valenko saw they would have plenty of time to reach the spot without demanding too much from the *Vulkan*'s turbines. As he mentally prepared the series of orders that would get them underway, Valenko fielded a brief querry from his *michman*.

"Does this mean that we'll be on our way home now, sir?"

Valenko smiled. "It looks that way, Comrade. We've given the State our two months and then some. I imagine that the crew of the *Cheka* are also anxious to reach port. Captain Dzerzhinsky certainly keeps a taut ship."

"I was surprised when the attack sub left our sector three days ago," Kuzmin observed. "It's unusual to leave us out here unescorted. What do you think they were up to?"

"Who knows?" the captain said cautiously. "With the *Cheka*, almost anything could have been possible. Sometimes I wonder if that crack crew is even working for the navy."

"You and me both, Captain. I've heard tell that Dzerzhinsky has guided his vessel right up to the sub nets at Pearl Harbor. From there he supposedly took pictures of a group of Americans picnicking on the shoreline."

Shaking his head, Valenko grinned. "I bet you can't wait to get back to Petropavlovsk and see that new son of yours."

"I sure can't. Do you realize that next week he'll be six months old? And to think that I've already missed almost a third of life."

"Get used to it, Comrade, or perhaps this line of work isn't for you. And besides, they don't do anything but eat, sleep, and cry the first couple of years anyway."

"Why, Captain, I didn't think you knew so much about babies."

"You'd be surprised, son," Valenko added with with a wink.

Valenko was preparing to leave, to issue the orders sending the *Vulkan* westward, when Kuzmin looked up apprehensively. "Captain, there's one more thing that I'd like to ask of you before we get back to port. Galina and I would like to know if you would do us the honor of being little Nikolai's godfather."

Clearly surprised by this request, Valenko hestitated a second before responding. "It's me who you honor, Stefan. What have I done to be so worthy of this distinction? Why, we hardly know each other."

"Nonsense, Captain. We have sailed three patrols together. Even though we haven't been able to talk as much as I would have liked, your example has meant so much to me. Galina says that you're the father figure I never had to emulate. Whatever the case, we would be proud to have you as our son's guardian."

Veiled by the red combat lighting, Stefan Kuzmin failed to see his commanding officer's cheeks flush. "What else can I say, but that I'll accept."

"Wonderful!" the *michman* exclaimed. He stood to offer the captain his hand. "Galina will be so thrilled. Of course, you'll do us the honor of having dinner at our place when we return to Petropavlovsk."

"You'd better believe I'll be there. Not only do I want to sample some of that good home cooking you're always bragging about, but I'd better check out this boy I'm to be responsible for."

As the two men exchanged a hearty handshake, an observer could indeed have mistaken the figures as father and son. Both sailors were ruggedly built, with similar six-foot-tall frames and handsome Slavic features. Blond-haired and blue-eyed, it was this similarity of appearances that had originally attracted the two to each other.

Valenko broke the hand contact first. "I'd better go and get the *Vulkan* moving. We certainly don't want to stand up the likes of Grigori Dzerzhinsky. Then, if my luck holds out, perhaps the cook will have some stew left over. I haven't eaten since breakfast."

Patting his stomach, the captain pivoted and walked to the navigation station. His mind still reeling with excitement, Warrant Officer Stefan Kuzmin reluctantly returned to the radio console. The man he respected most in the world had not let him down. Perhaps there was a chance they could be real friends after all.

Even though the Delta III-class submarines were among the largest of undersea vessels, with a length of over five hundred feet, extra space aboard the ships was rare. Every corner of the hull was packed with supplies and gear. Even the crew's bunks were "hot," for as soon as one left for his duty station, another took his place in bed. Thus, each section of the sub had a variety of uses. This was especially true in the mess area. Not only was this the place where the one-hundred-and-thirty-two-man crew ate their meals, but it also served as recreation hall, library, barber shop and meeting place.

By the time Captain Petyr Valenko reached the *Vulkan*'s mess, the dozen or so tables here were almost completely empty. With his stomach growling hungrily, he crossed into the galley and intercepted the unchallenged czar of this section of the sub, Chief Cook Anatoly Irkutsk. Known for his volatile temperment, perpetually stained apron and corpulent potbelly, Irkutsk supervised his domain like he owned it. Aware that his bark was worse than his bite, Valenko approached him while he was scraping out the bottom of a badly scorched kettle.

"That's one way to stay physically fit, Chief," greeted the captain.

Irkutsk found little humor in this and responded accordingly. "The damned apprentices the navy gives me are nothing but a bunch of worthless buffoons. I swear that these idiots burn more food than they serve. It's a wonder I can still come up with enough rations to feed the men by the time we reach the end of our patrols. Our larders have never been so empty."

"You'll manage, as always," Valenko said as his stomach gurgled loudly.

Taking this cue, the chief looked up and met the captain's glance. "Missed you at lunch and dinner, sir. I'm beginning to wonder if you'd rather starve yourself than eat my cooking."

"Now, Comrade, you know better than that. Speaking of the devil . . . would you happen to have a leftover bowl of stew and a crust of bread for this starving old man?"

Relishing the moment, the cook seemed to deliberate before answering. "As your good fortune would have it, there's a single portion left. It just happens to be your very favorite, Captain."

Valenko's eyes sparkled. "Ah, you've cooked up some stuffed cabbages! You've made this weary old man's day."

Several minutes later, Valenko sat down at the only occupied table. Nodding toward the solemn-eyed officer who sat sipping his tea, Valenko carefully emptied his tray. With exacting precision, he positioned his dinner before him, careful to use the rubberized matting that kept the plates from slipping in the event of a sudden change of the hull's angle. Enjoying the scent of the steam emanating from the largest of his bowls, the captain broke off a piece of black bread and dipped it in the piping hot sweet-and-sour sauce.

"I tell you, the Chief makes these cabbage rolls better than my own mother. How lucky we are to have such an artist serving us."

As if to emphasize his words, Valenko cut into one of the large balls of cabbage and swallowed down a huge bite. Following this with a sopping piece of bread, the captain saw that his enthusiasm was wasted on his tablemate.

"What's the matter, Senior Lieutenant? Have I done something that has upset you? You look as if you just lost your only friend."

Vasili Leonov, the *Vulkan*'s second in command, merely shook his head despondently and tried to lose himself in another sip of tea.

"I know what it is," Valenko said between bites of fruit compote. "You're in love, aren't you Vasili? I'd bet a month's pay it's that new girlfriend that's got you down."

Astounded, the Senior Lieutenant redirected his dark gaze toward the captain. "Your accurate perceptions shock me, Comrade. I never realized that you were a mind reader."

Valenko cut into another cabbage roll. "That's only

51

one of my many talents, Vasili. You know, I couldn't help but watch you mope around like a sad puppy during the majority of this past patrol. You've got yourself a bad case, there's no doubt about it."

Savoring a bite of cabbage, chopped meat and rice, he continued. "One thing I'll say for you is that you've certainly got excellent taste. I saw you two together, the morning we left Petropavlovsk. My, she's a beauty."

Leonov's sour facial expression lightened noticeably. "If you only knew the extent of her beauty, Comrade. Not only is she the most attractive girl I have ever met, but she's intelligent and a pleasure to be with, also."

"Sounds serious," Valenko observed while chewing on a crust of bread. "Does she realize what being tied down to a submariner would mean? For half the year her bed would be empty."

"Natasha's father is an old navy man himself," Leonov said animatedly. "During the Great War he sailed with none other than Admiral Sorokin."

"You don't say," Valenko commented as he finished off the last of the cabbage rolls. Picking up his mug of tea, he looked the lovelorn officer in the eye.

"Marry her, Vasili. I may not always be right, but I'm never wrong about these matters. Tie the knot when we're home next week. Start yourself a family. I'll envy you all the way to the altar."

Hearing just the words he wanted, the senior lieutenant attempted a smile. "I was afraid that we hadn't known each long enough. We only saw one another less than three weeks."

"That's longer than many," the captain returned.

"Go with your instincts, Comrade. Life is much too short for procrastination."

Sipping his tea contendedly, Valenko could see his advice hit home. Like a new man, the senior lieutenant pushed his chair away from the table and stood triumphantly.

"I feel better already, Captain. You're right—I must go with my instincts. If Natasha will have me, we'll get married at once. I'd be a fool if I thought that I could live without her. How blind I've been!"

Checking his watch, Leonov prepared to exit. "I'm afraid that I'm due up in the control room now. I can't thank you enough for your advice, Comrade. I should have come to you much earlier."

The senior officer pivoted smartly and left the mess whistling a tune from the *Nutcracker*. Petyr Valenko watched him take his leave and stifled a chuckle. Here he was—a godfather and a matchmaker all in the same day. His purpose in the Rodina's navy never failed to amaze him.

After finishing his tea, the captain was preparing to get up and exit himself when a high-pitched, raspy voice greeted him.

"Good evening, Captain. I'm pleased to see that you're the first one here for this week's *komsomol* meeting. It's been much too long since you've given us the honor of your presence."

These shrill words came from Ivan Novikov, the *Vulkan's zampolit*. Not stopping to hear Valenko's response, the short, skinny political officer proceeded hastily across the mess. Reaching the room's far corner, he took up a position before a large, wall-mounted poster of Vladimir Ilich Lenin and began setting up a small lectern.

To Valenko, Novikov always seemed to be puttering around. His constant need to be moving about made the captain nervous. Of course, his very standing as *zampolit* was cause for tension in itself. As the only officer aboard who could directly undermine the captain's authority (in the interests of the Party), Ivan Novikov answered to his own chain of command. Fortunately, the two had yet to seriously tangle. Valenko knew that he was lucky. Many were the tale of political officers who constantly poked their noses into ships' line functions. One good thing about Novikov was that he was satisfied merely to direct the crew's ideological indoctrination and to monitor their political reliability. Propulsion systems, navigational problems and electronic components were of little interest to him. Consigned to making the best of the situation, the captain decided he had better keep up his front of affability. Arming himself with his best diplomatic smile, he crossed the mess to confront the *zampolit* directly.

"Good evening to you, Comrade. Actually, I was just finishing off a late supper. I stood a double watch today and didn't realize that the time was flying by so quickly."

Holding back a forced yawn, Valenko hinted again. "I'll be taking another midnight watch, so I'd better be thinking about getting some rest."

Novikov's head jerked up. "Oh, Captain, you disappoint me. Must you leave already? At least stay for the first half of the meeting. Attendance has been a bit of a problem lately and your presence will be greatly appreciated. And besides, this evening our topic is far from being an ideological one. We will be discussing nuclear warfare strategy."

From the pleading tone of Novikov's voice, Valenko knew he would have trouble getting out of this one. His dilemma was exacerbated as the first of the *komsomol* members began to arrive. Quietly, they took their seats at the tables while the *zampolit* continued readying his notes.

Membership in the *komsomol*, the official Party club, was quite voluntary. It was said to be advantageous for a seaman, or even an officer, for that matter, to attend such meetings. Having the solid support of the party could never hurt come promotion time.

Valenko turned around and noticed that several junior lieutenants had arrived. He nodded politely as their eyes lit up upon identifying him. The majority of the other dozen participants came from the noncommissioned ranks. Unwillingly, Valenko took a seat at the table nearest the lectern. He watched the *zampolit* continue his frantic preparations, and couldn't help but compare Novikov's coloring and facial structure with the representation of the founder of socialism tacked to the wall behind him. Fighting back another yawn, Valenko tried not to think about the comforting shelter of his mattress—when a sweet, familiar odor met his nostrils. The captain swiveled around to see the grinning red face of Yuri Chuchkin. The bearded, heavyset weapons chief, whose habitual, battered briar pipe lay between his clenched lips, slid into the seat beside him.

"Why Captain Valenko, I'm certainly surprised to see you at this friendly little soiree."

"You should talk, Comrade," Valenko retorted. "I

didn't know that they let the likes of you into the *komsomol*. What is this Party coming to?"

Chuchkin let out a deep laugh and the captain was instantly infected by his joviality. The happy-go-lucky weapons chief, who reminded him of the mythical Father Frost, always had that effect on him. His presence would serve to make the evening that much more tolerable.

Valenko fought to control his mirth and moved over to again query the newcomer. "By the way, what *are* you doing here, Comrade Chuchkin?"

Chuchkin took a deep draw on his pipe and released a stream of vanilla-scented smoke. "Why, Captain, didn't you check your ticket stub? I'm tonight's guest speaker."

Again Chuchkin roared with laughter. This time the sharp report of a gavel striking wood redirected their attention to the lectern. All merriment came to an instant end as the *Vulkan*'s *zampolit* coldly greeted them.

"Good evening, Comrades. Welcome to tonight's weekly *komsomol* meeting. I see a few new faces out there this evening. It's always good to have newcomers. The Party shall take note.

"I'm certain that all of you have spotted two esteemed members of our officer corps here tonight. Captain Valenko, all of us are aware of your tight schedule. To give us the honor of your presence is a testament to the great principles of the party that bring us all together."

As Valenko nodded in response to his introduction. Novikov continued. "Tonight, we won't be exploring the lofty theoretical principles that underlay the Rodina's political composition. Rather, we will be discussing much more practical matters. Our country's nuclear war-fighting ability is the deterrent that allows the Motherland to grow and prosper. Without it, the imperialists would run rampant through our countryside, spreading their tired doctrine of decadence and greed.

"To allow us to have a better understanding of the weapons systems that serve to keep the Western hordes in check, Chief Armament Officer Yuri Chuchkin has kindly agreed to say a few words. Comrade Chuchkin. . . ."

To a smattering of polite applause, the corpulent officer stood, straightened his uniform and made his way to the podium. Before speaking, he made extra certain that his pipe was packed, lit and ready for smoking. After completing this ritual, he scanned his captive audience and began speaking.

"Thank you, Comrades. I think that it's only fitting, in this discussion of the Rodina's nuclear war-fighting strategy, that we begin with the *Vulkan*'s responsibilities should the unthinkable come to pass. As you well know, our primary armament takes the form of sixteen SS-N-18 ballistic missiles. These liquid fueled, two-stage rockets features the Motherland's latest technology. The SS-N-18 is the first submarine-launched weapon with post-boost propulsion. Not only does this add significant velocity to the warhead during the final stages of flight, but it also allows the MIRV-bus to readily maneuver.

"The length of each of these missiles is 14.1 meters, with a diameter of 1.8 meters. The warheads rely on inertial guidance, with assistance from frequent stellar observations.

"Each SS-N-18 carries a multiple, independently targetable reentry vehicle, known as a *bus*. This device carries seven separate, two-hundred-kiloton nuclear devices. At the proper time, after the bus has fallen back into the atmosphere, the individual warheads can be aimed at their independent targets. As you know, a kiloton is equivalent to an explosive yield of 1,000 tons of TNT.

"Another remarkable feature of the SS-N-18 is its range of over 8,000 kilometers. Thus, even from our current position, the *Vulkan* could hit targets anywhere in the continental United States. An equally amazing statistic is our payloads' CEP. Circular Error Probable is a measure of a warhead's accuracy. It relates to the radius of a circle into which fifty percent of the nuclear devices are predicted to fall. Extensive tests have shown the SS-N-18 to have a CEP of less than 100 meters. This means that, for the first time, a submarine-launched weapon is able to destroy one of the so-called hardened targets. No longer is the sub force merely a back-up retaliatory system. Today, we have a first-strike ability of unequaled potential."

The unnaturally loud sound of a throat being cleared broke the chief's concentration. Turning his head to check the interruption's source, he saw that the *zampolit* had stood and was rapidly approaching the lectern. He began speaking long before he reached the bearded officer's side.

"This report is extremely fascinating, Comrade Chuchkin, and in much more detail than I was expecting. Your knowledge of the intricate mechani-

58

cal features of the equipment can't be challenged. Yet your assertion regarding the *Vulkan*'s first-strike potential has serious theoretical flaws. I'm certain that all of you are aware of the fact that the Rodina has publicly disavowed any desire to be the first user of nuclear weapons. To even think that the *Vulkan* would be considered in such a role is, therefore, absurd."

Before answering, the bearded chief patiently tamped down the tobacco in the bowl of his pipe, put a match to it, and sucked in a deep draw. "I know nothing of the intentions of the politicians who guide the course of the Soviet Union. All I know is that, from a practical strategic viewpoint, our load of SS-N-18s could singly strike the imperialists a mighty blow. Not even their most sheltered command post would be safe from our reach."

"Enough of such nonsense!" exclaimed the red-faced *zampolit*. "Only the treachery of the war-mongering Americans could push us to such an extreme. We are a peace-loving people. We've more than had our fill of war. First strike intentions have no part in our war plan. This, I am certain of!"

"I beg to differ with you, Comrade Novikov."

These firm words came from the mouth of Captain Petyr Valenko. The political officer could hardly believe his eyes as the captain dared to challenge him directly.

"Why build such super accurate devices such as the SS-N-18 in the first place, if one didn't plan to use them effectively? Certainly, a military strategist must keep his mind open to every kind of attack scenario. To say that the Soviet Union doesn't have a first-strike option is ridiculous in itself."

Novikov's voice trembled angrily. "I repeat, Captain Valenko: it is the policy of the Soviet Union never to be the instigator of a nuclear exchange. Now, if you want evidence of a country gathering itself for a first strike, just look at the United States. Their MX and Trident missile systems, combined with the so-called Star Wars satellite platforms, indicate a clear desire to strike the first blow."

Valenko realized that it was fruitless to continue. The political officer would never open his mind to any expansion of thought. Catching the pleading look of his weapon's chief, the captain vented his tired frustrations with a single, passionate outburst.

"If you ask me, this entire discussion has gotten out of hand. To stand there and say the the Rodina has no plan for a first strike is as foolish as blaming the problem totally on the Americans. The simple fact is that there can be no winner in an extended nuclear conflict, no matter who drops the first warhead. *This* is the concept that the leaders of both sides have to come to terms with.

"The time for name-calling and rhetoric is over. The world's leaders have to face up to their responsibilities. It is their fault that this arms race has gotten so out of control. We have been lucky so far. Over three decades have passed since a nuclear device was last used in warfare. Today, I fear that the odds are turning against us. All it would take is a single, unstable group getting their hands on the nuclear trigger. The sad part is that no matter who was ultimately at fault, the grim outcome would be the same for all of us."

Conscious of the startled silence that met the conclusion of his emotion-filled discourse, Valenko turned and quickly exited the room. Only when he was long gone from the mess area did a nervous rumble of voices break from the *komsomol* members still present.

Ivan Novikov knew it was important that he regain control of his audience at once. There could be no doubting that their captain harbored confused, dangerous thoughts. He would deal with that problem later. Trying to ignore the gleaming eyes of the weapon's chief, who seemed to be enjoying the *zampolit*'s discomfort, Novikov positioned himself squarely behind the lectern and spoke as calmly as possible.

"As *komsomol* members, all of us are aware of the importance of open dialogue. Our esteemed Captain's personal opinions are merely that. For the Party to grow to full maturity, this sharing of viewpoints, no matter how alien, must be allowed. This is the prime difference between the so-called democracies and our glorious socialist system. Each week, our meetings reflect this sharing of philosophies. Now, I think that it's time to return to tonight's intended subject.

"The Party has long realized that only through strength will the imperialists be contained. Yet, what would happen if the Western powers did develop a platform that could knock our missiles from the skies and we were forced to defend the Rodina from direct Western aggression? The following options would then be at our disposal. . . ."

Wishing that he could have followed the captain's lead, the weapon's chief was forced to listen to the *zampolit*'s rambling. It was evident that the man

61

didn't know the first thing about true nuclear warfare. Not having the nerve to excuse himself, Chuchkin surrendered to the solace of his pipe, and a mental recollection of the strange confrontation that they had just witnessed.

Chapter Three

The arctic twilight glowed in ghostly iridescence as two Soviet submarines rounded a breakwater and entered Taliniskaia Bay. Leading the way was the smaller of the vessels. Sporting a streamlined hull, complete with a rounded bridge from which a variety of retractable aerials were extended, the attack sub *Cheka* was making one of its rare surface transits. Following it, nearly one hundred meters off its stern, was the *Vulkan*. Clearly dwarfing the attack sub in length and width, the Delta-class ship was almost twice as large. Characterized by a hunchbacked missile casing, located abaft the angular conning tower, the keeless submersible cut awkwardly through the choppy northern seas. Oblivious to the sickening, rolling pitch of the hull, the submariners inside knew that their home port was only minutes away.

It was at times like this that Petropavlovsk appeared extremely attractive. In reality, the city was an isolated, uncomfortable outpost, perched on the tip of the desolate Kamchatka peninsula. It was home to approximately 200,000 hardy inhabitants, the majority of whom were certainly not there by choice. Pounded by bone-chilling, arctic temperatures, the northeastern Siberian settlement gained its importance as being home to the famed Seventh Squadron, where seventy-five percent of the Soviet Union's Pacific Fleet subs were anchored.

Serving as reminders of their northerly position, a line of scarred icebreakers were the first ships visible as the subs proceeded into the harbor. All too soon the arctic pack ice would be inching its way down the peninsula, and the frustrating, tiring job of keeping an open sea lane would begin. With only a handful of open ports to choose from, this was a most important job. A fleet locked at its berths by ice would do the Rodina little good in times of need.

Petyr Valenko stood in an exposed opening cut into the forward section of the *Vulkan*'s sail. Standing next to him was his senior lieutenant, Vasili Leonov. Both were bundled in fur-lined oilskins. Even with the cover of those heavy coats, they shivered in the icy breeze.

"Just wait until it gets really cold," mocked the captain as he readjusted his mittens and pulled his collar closer to his neck. "Winter isn't officially scheduled to arrive for a full month yet."

"I'll still take this frigid air over the stuffy confines of the sub's interior, any day of the year," Leonov reflected.

Valenko grinned shyly. "You say that now, after being cooped up inside for over two months, but leave you outdoors in these conditions for an hour and you'll soon be begging to come inside."

As if to emphasize his observation, a biting northern gust hit them full in the face. Both men instantly turned their heads downwind in an attempt to escape its piercing effects.

"Who knows—perhaps orders sending us off to the

Mediterranean are waiting in port. Wouldn't you love a honeymoon under the balmy, tropic skies?"

The captain's question produced an instant response from the senior lieutenant. "As long as I'm honeymooning with my Natasha, I'll take it anywhere on this planet. You see, I don't plan to do much sightseeing!"

"No, I guess you don't at that. So, you still have the nerve to go through with it?"

Leonov's eyes gleamed. "Since we last talked in the mess I haven't thought of much else—except my official duty, that is."

Valenko shook his head and grinned. "Well, I wish you all the luck. As soon as we tie up at our pen you may consider yourself temporarily excused from duty. I'll complete the log myself."

"Thank you, Captain!" Leonov said sincerely. Eyes now focused on the rapidly approaching docks, Leonov seemed to be willing them forward. Valenko detached the waterproof intercom and began initiating the complex series of commands that would see them to their proper slot. After passing an anchored trio of Kotlin-class destroyers and a massive Kresta I cruiser, the *Vulkan* began a broad, sweeping turn toward starboard. As they passed by the cruiser's sharply angled bow, Valenko set his eyes on the low profile, concrete-roofed pens that the Seventh Squadron called home.

The *Cheka* could be seen inching its rounded hull into one of the slots closest to the open sea. The *Vulkan*'s berth was three dozen spaces down the line. The majority of these pens were filled with older, Yankee-class and Hotel-class models. Though many of these ships had not been to sea in several months, each of them was fully fit for duty should the need arise.

Five minutes later, the first mooring line was being cinched onto the *Vulkan*'s forward capstan. After making certain that the ship was securely tied, Valenko made his way downstairs. The action there was furious, as the men hastily concluded their duties of buttoning down the sub. Not wanting to get in their way, Valenko proceeded immediately to his cabin. Here he planned to begin work on the report that included a detailed review of the daily events of the last two months. No sooner had he sat at his tiny, wall-mounted desk to begin this chore, when a knock sounded on his door.

"Come in," he said with a touch of annoyance, then lightened as he set eyes on the grinning face of Stefan Kuzmin.

"Sir, I was just reaffirming our date for dinner. Is tomorrow evening at six o'clock all right?"

"That would be fine, Comrade. Where is this place of yours?"

Kuzmin blushed. "I'm sorry. The address is 13 Gorshkov Boulevard. Our apartment is number 301. Bring your appetite."

"That, you can be certain of," the captain said as he looked down at the blank legal pad that lay before him.

The *michman* alertly excused himself. "Well, I won't bother you any longer, sir. Besides, I've got a wife and six-month-old son to see. Good evening, Captain."

With the blond-haired warrant officer's exit, Valenko once again began organizing the series of notes that comprised the *Vulkan*'s informal log. It was his responsibility now to expand on these observations and create a final report. He was just getting through the first week of their patrol when another knock sounded.

"What is it?" Valenko asked with more than a bit of agitation.

The sweet scent of vanilla-soaked tobacco preceded Yuri Chuchkin's entry.

"Sorry if I'm disturbing you, sir," greeted the bearded weapons chief, "but I was just putting together a security roster of all those who will be staying aboard this evening."

"Well, you can count me in there, Chief. I think it's best if I finish up this log while the events are still clear in my mind. Who else is staying?"

Chuchkin pulled the stem of his pipe from his lips before answering. "There's myself, Chef Anatoly, the reactor team and the usual security detail. I thought you'd be interested to know that our good friend Ivan Novikov was one of the first to leave the ship. From the hurried way in which he was moving, our *zampolit* seemed to have a feather up his ass."

Valenko chuckled. "Bet you that he couldn't wait to inform his superiors of the dangerous dissident currently at the helm of one of the Rodina's most powerful weapons systems. I've had run-ins with his type before. He'll get over it."

"I hope so," Chuchkin said. "Otherwise, we'll both end up on icebreaker duty in the Arctic Circle."

"Don't you worry. By the way, why are you staying aboard the *Vulkan* this evening? I'd have thought that you would like to be visiting your mother."

Chuchkin put a match to his pipe's bowl. "That was the plan—until I received a call from logistics informing me to be ready to accept a new load of warheads first thing in the morning. Silly to drive all the way out to her dacha in Malka, only to return in a few hours' time."

"New warheads, you say?" the Captain asked. "I didn't know anything about such a change."

Chuchkin cleared his throat. "Only heard about them myself less than ten minutes ago. I'll try to get wind of exactly what we're taking on from the supply chief. That old Uzbek owes me a few favors. Are you going to be wanting dinner later?"

"Thanks, Comrade, but I think I'll just pick up some cheese and crackers later this evening. I've got more than enough work to keep me busy well into the night."

"Well, if you need anything, just give me a call. Good night, Captain."

"Good night, Chief."

As his heavyset visitor backed out of the room and shut the door behind him, Valenko let out a sigh of relief. Free to return to his work, he stared down at the partially filled pad. Try as he could to return to his original flow of thought, his mind remained locked on a single observation the chief had left with him.

So . . . Ivan Novikov had been one of the first to leave for shore. Was the political officer still upset with that minor confrontation they had the other evening? Valenko couldn't forget how the *zampolit* had hastily averted his eyes from the captain's when they had passed each other a few hours earlier. Why, the man hadn't even returned his simple greeting. Valenko hadn't thought their squabble was that serious. It was more a silly misinterpreting of words than anything else.

Aware of the trouble Novikov could make if he decided to blow their confrontation into a major event, Valenko thought it best to include their spat in his log. A minor addendum would serve to explain what had happened at the fated *komsomol* meeting. Certain that this would clear the air, the captain picked up his pen and once again immersed himself in a re-creation of the patrol just completed.

The next day Valenko was still at his desk. Not even taking time for lunch, he diligently put the finishing touches on his report. When this was finally completed, he felt as if a great weight had been removed from his shoulders. He put the thick stack of legal-sized sheets into a large packet. This pouch would then be messengered over to headquarters, where a squadron typist would get the challenge of converting his scrawled handwriting into legible copy. Quickly now, Valenko changed into a clean uniform, left his quarters and ascended the stairway to the forward entry hatch.

Outside, it was another frigid arctic day. Pulling the fur collar of his greatcoat tightly around his neck, Valenko breathed in the crisp, cool air. Barely lit by the low-rising sun, the sky was a deep blue, with a strata of high-flying, puffy white clouds blowing in from the northwest. Valenko returned the salute of the sentry positioned beside the gangplank and made his way on shore. He was unaccustomed to the feeling of solid ground beneath him and knew it would take a while to feel comfortable on pavement. After all, the constant pitching of the *Vulkan*'s deck had guided his steps for the past sixty days.

Before leaving the pen area completely, he turned to take a last look at his command. Moored securely to its berth, the *Vulkan* appeared a benign behemoth. The sleek, black hull was beginning to show the effects of salt-water corrosion. Splotches of rusty primer could be clearly seen, undercoating the vessel's stern, sail and deck areas. Even though the sub had been completely painted only this past summer, the harsh sea was already leaving its mark. Such was the nature of the element through which they traveled.

A small group of men could be seen gathered beside the humped casing set behind the sail. They were busy repairing a dock-borne loading gantry. Supervising this crew was the bearded, heavyset figure of Yuri Chuchkin. Complete with his faithful pipe between his lips, the weapons chief efficiently orchestrated his men's actions. Feeling he was fortunate to have such an individual aboard, Valenko wondered how the morning's activities had gone. Confident that Chuchkin could handle the loading of the new warheads without incident, the captain took a last look at the crimson hammer and sickle flying from the flagpole. Like a newlywed leaving his bride, he reluctantly pivoted and hastily proceeded inland.

The wharf area buzzed with activity. Dozens of work crews were in evidence, bustling to and from the huge warehouses set up there. Lines of supply trucks cluttered the narrow streets as their drivers impatiently waited for the loading docks to clear. The hum of fork-lift trucks and diesel engines filled the air as Valenko continued down the cracked sidewalk.

Passing through a section of the base reserved for administrative purposes, Valenko noticed an unusually high number of clean-up workers scattered outside the brick office complex. With brooms, rakes, hedge trimmers and even paint brushes in hand, these hard-working souls busily did their duty. Many of them were *babushkas*. These heavyset old women were most comfortable with cleaning; they seemed happy to be doing their day's work for the Motherland and went about their chores industriously.

When Valenko crossed the central parade area he was surprised to find a construction unit in the midst of building a large wooden stage, complete with a huge stand of bench-type bleachers. Other workers were busy implanting several flagpoles in the ground. It wasn't until the captain reached the security checkpoint at the entrance to the facility that he found out what all this unusual activity was for.

"The base is preparing for the visits of both General Secretary Rodin and Admiral Sorokin, Captain," advised the sentry. "They will be arriving here at the end of the week."

Valenko noticed how the young guard's eyes focused on the gold submarine medallion pinned to his collar. Having no need to explain his ignorance, Valenko nodded and signed the register that declared him officially off base.

Petropavlovsk was a sprawling community, comprised of the inevitable conglomeration of ugly, gray high-rise apartment buildings, and quaint, colorfully

71

painted cottages. Spreading out roughly fanlike, with the naval base forming its eastern boundary, the city was known for its widely diverse population, few of whom were actually born there. As is the case with large military complexes throughout the world, Petropavlovsk's unique position created a healthy business climate. Dependent on the city for all types of supplies and services, the base's personnel had developed a good relationship with the local civilians. Thus, Valenko encountered a variety of kind nods and greetings as he entered the city proper.

Shunning the line of taxis that waited outside the guard post, Valenko desired nothing better than a brisk, invigorating walk. The portion of town for which he was headed was less than a mile distant. Turning to the left, he began his way down a six-lane paved thoroughfare packed with bicycles, automobiles and trucks of all sizes. Since he was headed south now, the piercing north wind deflected off his back.

As he merged with the snaking line of commuter foot traffic, he marveled at the mixture of humanity that swirled around him. High-cheeked Mongols and dark-eyed Tartars darted among swarthy Uzbeks and fair-skinned Great Russians. Every element of the Rodina's diverse population seemed to be represented here. Bundled in thick fur coats and wraps of buckskin, ox hide and wool, the hearty population seemed unaware of the bone-freezing chill. To them, this was but another mild fall day in northeastern Siberia.

After passing a huge park filled with immense pine trees Valenko entered the first of the business districts. Here he decided to take one of the narrower side streets. Dozens of simple, one-story structures housed shops primarily set aside to sell foodstuffs. The window of one establishment catering to the fish trade was filled with a single, massive tuna, solidly frozen on a bed of shaved ice. In the shop next door, a bevy of headless, plucked chickens were on display. It proved to be the intoxicating odor emanating from the next store that drew Valenko inside.

Since his youth, the local bakery had been Valenko's favorite store to visit. Tugged along by the patient hand of his mother, he couldn't help but enjoy the sweet, fragrant scent of freshly risen bread and baked pastries. And he still found this perfume irresistible.

Many fond memories rose in his consciousness as he examined the simple shop. Rows of crusty breads were prominently displayed. Some of the loaves were of the darkest brown, while others were created from the purest white flour. Beside this rack was a platter of what appeared to be freshly baked oatmeal cookies. With his mouth watering, he stationed himself in the inevitable line of anxious consumers.

The wait didn't appear to be that bad, and Valenko spent this time watching the bakers as they skillfully plied their trade. Utilizing flat, wooden pallets, they slid the uncooked loaves into the ovens, careful to remove any items that were sufficiently cooked. With his thoughts lost in this simple process, he was conveyed back to reality only by a persistent tugging on his right sleeve.

"Excuse me, young man," greeted the robust, white-haired *babushka* who stood in line behind him. "I couldn't help noticing that you carry no sack to place your purchases in."

Suddenly aware of this fact, Valenko smiled and shrugged his shoulders. "You are most correct, Comrade. I've been at sea so long that I've forgotten what it takes to go shopping on land. I guess that means I can only take what I can presently eat."

"Nonsense," the old woman said firmly. "You're much too skinny already. Take this extra bag that I always carry in case a bargain comes my way."

As she shoved a cotton-mesh string-bag into his hands, Valenko tried to protest. "I won't hear of such a thing," he pleaded.

To this, the *babushka* merely took a step back and shook her head wisely. "Of course you will, brave sailor. You know, my husband was in the navy during the Great War. They say I lost my dearest to a German torpedo, somewhere in the North Atlantic. Just as his sacrifice kept us free, so does your present service. Please do this tired old woman the honor of repaying her gratitude in this very small way."

Touched by these words, Valenko relented. But his response was cut short as a brusque voice shouted out, "Next!"

Now with the means to transport it, the naval officer chose two loaves of black bread, two of rye and one white. He added to this three dozen oatmeal cookies. As the clerk began filling this last part of the order, the *babushka*'s voice once again screamed out.

"Not those cookies, young woman! Give him some from that fresh batch you just took out of the oven. This man you serve is one of our honored heroes!"

Blushing with the compliment, Valenko looked on in amazement as the clerk emptied the cookies she had been loading and began replacing them with those from the upper tray. His astonishment was doubled when the clerk handed him his bag of treasures and then waved away his money. Any protest on his part was deflected by a firm tug on his coat sleeve.

"You deserve only the best," offered the proud *babushka*. "Now, go enjoy the hospitality that awaits you in our humble city."

Knowing nothing better to do but kiss the old lady on each cheek, Valenko grasped the mesh bag after thanking the bakery clerk once again. He left to a chorus of kind grins from those in the line behind.

Once out on the street, a feeling of great inner warmth possessed him. So, his sacrifice was appreciated after all! Fumbling for one of the cherished oatmeal cookies, he became filled with renewed conviction. When serving one's country, a soldier too often forgets his true purpose. The gulf between civilians and the military really wasn't that great after all. Convinced of this fact, he proceeded with a light step, careful to meet the admiring stares of all those he passed.

He was well into his third cookie when a particularly frigid blast of wind sent him reeling. A cold, dark shadow permanently veiled the heavens, and Valenko realized that the short Siberian day was already drawing to a close. Conscious of the passing hour, he knew that there was still one more stop he would have to make before continuing on to Stefan Kuzmin's apartment.

Though he had never shopped in this particular establishment before, he had admired its colorful display windows on several past visits. To reach this spot, he was forced to cross Leninsky Prospekt, one of the cities busiest thoroughfares. The tangle of traffic that he had encountered outside of the base seemed tame compared to the jam of vehicles he now faced. This scene proved that even such isolated cities as Petropavlovsk had their version of the infamous rush hour.

Faced with a seemingly infinite line of trucks, buses and cars, Valenko took his place at the corner with a handful of other pedestrians. Only when the light finally changed in their favor did they dare try to cross. Protected by the two thick white lines of the crosswalk, they bravely moved forward across the eight traffic lanes.

Chilled and anxious to reach his final destination, Valenko led the way. The majority of those who followed were *babushkas* and children. Taking it for granted that he had the proper right of way, the young naval officer hurried to the opposite curb. All seemed clear, when a large black van suddenly shot from the line of stopped traffic. So quick was its approach that Valenko only saw it at the last moment. Spying the vehicle out of the corner of his eye, he could hardly believe it when the driver failed to hit his brakes. The fool was actually accelerating! Was the idiot blind?

For a fraction of a second, Valenko faltered. Standing in the middle of the roadway, with the van hurtling toward him, he could go either backward or forward. Standing where he was would only gain him death. Just as the van's bright lights hit him full in the eyes, he chose the direction in which he had been initially moving. Like a ponderous nightmare, he did all that he could to sprint to the safety of the beckon-

76

ing curb. Fighting his leaden, cold limbs, he summoned that reservoir of strength each of us holds for just such do-or-die emergencies. With long, fluid strides, Valenko leaped toward the safety of the sidewalk. A chorus of blaring horns and shocked screams supported this superhuman effort.

Only when he was firmly behind the safety of the steel signal light did he turn his head and check the van's progress. Just as he did so, the black vehicle whisked by him, only inches away. It appeared as if the madman had been intentionally trying to run him down! Unable to catch sight of the driver or the license number, Valenko felt fortunate just to be alive. Sucking in his breath, he looked up as the van disappeared around the corner and the other pedestrians caught up with him.

"Do you believe that fool?" cried a shocked *babushka*. "The total idiots they allow on the roads nowadays. Just the other day a limousine almost ran me down on this exact same corner."

"Are you all right, Comrade?" offered a fragile, gray-haired old man, who held onto a packed mesh bag much like Valenko's. "Where is the militia when you really need them?"

Thanking the elder for his concern, Valenko offered an explanation. "I guess I was in such a hurry to cross that I failed to see the van miss the light. I'll have to be extra cautious next time."

"That's something each of us needs in abundance these days," returned the old-timer. "The dangers of living in a modern city are just tremendous. You take care, young man."

Accepting this fatherly advice, Valenko pushed on.

As he began his way down the street he desired, he passed by the *babushka* who was still animately conversing with herself.

"That limousine missed me by only inches. Probably some high-brow Party chief was inside, late for a date with his mistress. These days an individual life just means nothing. Now, in the old days, how different things were. . . ."

The old woman's words soon faded as he quickened his pace. Upon rounding the next corner, he found himself sliding uncontrollably on a patch of thick ice. Awkwardly, he caught his balance. Life on land is more dangerous than it is 1,000 meters beneath the sea, Valenko thought. He finally saw the brightly lit windows of the shop he was looking for, less than a quarter of a kilometer distant. He breathed a sigh of relief only upon being certain that the doors to the Pushkin Toy Store were definitely open for business.

Gorshkov Street was located near the large park Valenko had passed on his way from the base. He knew it well, for it was home to a number of naval personnel, especially those with families. Dominated by a dozen rather ugly steel high-rises, the street offered both excellent access to the port facilities and to Petropavlovsk's central park.

By the time he reached number thirteen, Valenko was anxious to gain respite from the biting cold. With numbed feet and hands, he gratefully ducked into the main hallway of the building. Here, relief was almost instantaneous. Luxuriating in the warmth, he was greeted by a wrinkle-faced duty woman.

"Good evening, young man. Can I help you?"

Valenko spotted the woman. She was seated behind a tiny, cluttered desk beside the elevator. "Yes, Comrade, I'm here to visit the Kuzmins."

"Well then, sir, first I'll need to have your name. Are they expecting you?"

Making the most of her lowly position of authority, she eyed the newcomer suspiciously while readying her notebook.

"I'm Captain Valenko, and yes—the Kuzmins' are expecting me."

"Ah, an officer no less," observed the old-timer as she carefully wrote this information down. "Well, enjoy yourself. They are certainly a lovely family."

As he approached the elevator, the duty woman again spoke out. "I'm afraid that lift won't be doing you much good. It hasn't worked properly since the day it was installed. The stairs are right here to your left."

Expecting as much, Valenko found the stairway and began his way up to the third floor. The effects of the biting cold had completely dissipated by the time he reached the door marked 301. He knocked and, almost immediately, the door swung open.

"Captain Valenko?" greeted a tall, attractive young woman, whose exotic, almond-shaped eyes instantly held his stare.

Almost shyly, Valenko nodded. "That's me. You must be Galina. And all this time I thought Stefan was bragging about your beauty."

Guiding a strand of long black hair behind her ear, she responded with a slight blush. "Actually, I'm Ivana, Galina's sister. Does the compliment still stand, though?"

"Of course it does," Valenko said, but his smile revealed a hint of embarrassment.

As she beckoned him inside, he quickly took in the apartment's cramped yet cozy ambience. Serving as a combined living and dining area, the room he entered featured a large sofa, with two stuffed chairs filling the far corner and a fully set dinner table placed before them. Several tasteful landscapes were hung on the walls, while a familiar, haunting symphony echoed from the radio.

"That's Borodin, isn't it?" he asked as he allowed himself to be led toward the couch.

"Actually, it's his Symphony Number Two in B minor," Ivana returned matter-of-factly.

"Ah, In the Steppes of Central Asia," Valenko continued fondly. "It's been much too long since I've heard this piece. As a youth, it was my very favorite."

"As it was mine," revealed his escort, who stood beside him while he took a seat. "In my opinion, very few composers have captured the spirit of the Motherland as well as Alexander Borodin."

He nodded in agreement. "When I was a lad, my father would put this record on the victrola and I would lie there and picture myself riding with the Tartar horsemen."

"To me it has always been the song of the untouched woods and mountains," Ivana countered. "Even on the coldest of nights, I can listen to this piece and instantly transform myself deep into the spring oak wood."

A particularly haunting melody emanated from the speakers, and both listeners silently soaked it in. It was Valenko who broke the spell.

"You know, Stefan didn't mention anything about having other guests present. Where is he, by the way?"

"I'm sorry," Ivana said. "Both proud parents are busy preparing little Nikolai for his first formal dinner party. Actually, Stefan didn't even know that I would be here. I was offered a break in my studies, and took this chance to help my sister out while Stefan was at sea."

"And where are you attending school?"

"At the Institute of Music in Kiev," answered Ivana. "If all goes well, I should be teaching by next spring."

"That is a most admirable profession. I didn't realize that I was sitting here discussing Borodin with an expert."

His remark caused a broad smile to cross Ivana's face. Taking in her natural, innocent beauty, Valenko found his attraction growing. Something in the way she met his attentive stare reflected a mutual feeling. The unexpected cries of a baby sounded, and they both turned in time to see Stefan Kuzmin enter from the adjoining bedroom. Nestled proudly in his arms was a squirming, blond-haired infant, dressed in a navy blue sailor's suit.

"Good evening, Captain," Stefan said excitedly. "I hope we haven't kept you too long."

"Nonsense," said Valenko as he rose from the comfortable couch. "Ivana was being a perfectly charming hostess."

Following Stefan was a thin, attractive woman. There could be no doubt as to her identity. Except for

81

a rather short hair style, her deepset dark eyes and other exotic features were an exact match of the woman who stood beside him.

Stefan Kuzmin gathered them all together and began the introductions. "Galina, at long last you're to meet the man I've told you so much about, our illustrious Captain Valenko."

"That's Petyr to all of you," Valenko instructed. He greeted Galina with a hug and a kiss on each cheek.

"This meeting has been most anticipated by me, also," he added. "Your husband is very proud of you, and rightfully so."

A high-pitched whine of protest followed, and Kuzmin lifted the bundle he had been carefully holding. "No, little fellow, we haven't forgotten you. Nikolai Petrovich Kuzmin, meet your esteemed godfather."

Stefan handed his son to Valenko, who cradled him a bit awkwardly at first.

"Don't be afraid, he won't break," Galina advised.

Not accustomed to handling such a fragile, valuable load, Valenko was a bit uncomfortable. It was only after meeting the youngster's pale blue, inquisitive stare that his apprehensions eased. When the youngster's face lit up with a happy grin and the little fellow cooed a gurgling welcome, the captain instantly relaxed. By the time the first bottle of champagne was opened and the appetizers served, the two were well on the way to becoming the best of pals. Their friendship was sealed when Valenko reached down into his mesh sack and removed a long, rectangular box wrapped in bright red paper. The lad had a great time tearing the wrapping off, but needed his mother's expert hands to remove the gray plastic, cylindrical object securely packed inside of an inner box.

"Why, it's a submarine!" Galina exclaimed as Nikolai eagerly placed its conical hull into his toothless mouth.

"Don't worry, the people at Pushkin's say that it's supposedly child-proof," Valenko said. "It's even guaranteed to crash dive in the bathtub, or your money back."

"She doesn't look like one of ours, Skipper," Kuzmin reflected.

"It better not be," the captain retorted. "Only the greedy Americans would be so foolish as to allow the Japanese to make representations of their latest nuclear craft for children to play with."

"Now, that's enough submarine talk!" Galina said forcefully. "Tonight I would like nothing better than to keep the conversation as far away from your duty as possible. Have you tried the pickled beets as yet? Ivana prepared them from our mother's own recipe."

Taking the hint, Valenko picked up a cocktail fork, speared one of the beets, and chewed it down. "Very tasty. Tell me, ladies, is your mother a good cook?"

"The best," Ivana answered. "Even with her limited supply and budget, Mother could put together a week's meals and never serve you the same thing twice."

Galina continued. "It's a wonder we're both not fat as hogs. Breads and pastries were her specialty."

Suddenly reminded, Valenko reached forward and picked up his cotton sack. "Earlier in the day, I'm afraid I got carried away in the local bakery. Do you think that you could put these loaves to use? With me, they'll only go stale."

He handed the bread to Galina, who checked their composition and beamed. "This is an absolute treasure! Are you certain that you want to give them up?"

Valenko waved away her objection. "Believe it or not, all I wanted was an oatmeal cookie anyway. You know, the clerk there didn't even want to take my money. Since when are naval personnel treated so specially here?"

"You must have gotten lucky," observed Galina. "Most of the townspeople only want our rubles. Half of the time, all we hear is their constant grumbling that we are the cause of the city's pollution and traffic problems. As if Petropavlovsk would be the city it is without the navy's presence. Why, it would just be a backward Siberian outpost without us."

The captain consumed another sip of champagne before answering. "You are probably right. I have been here for several years longer than yourselves and I have watched the city grow as the navy's presence has continually increased. Yet, I could have sworn that I was picking up a new spirit here today. I've never encountered so many friendly strangers before."

"Perhaps they're on their best behavior because of the General Secretary's visit," Galina reckoned. "One thing we know is that the cleaning crews have sure been out in force."

"I couldn't help but notice such crews at the base, also," Kuzmin reflected. "They're painting everything that doesn't move."

"You know, Galina may have hit upon something," Ivana said. "Viktor Rodin's visit here may have opened the townspeople's eyes. Surely they realize how important the navy is to them now. The eyes of the entire world will be focused on Petropavlovsk solely because of this facility's existence. By the way . . . as members of the armed forces, what do you think of the upcoming summit meeting?"

Kuzmin looked blankly at his captain; it was obvious that neither of them knew what she was talking about. Ivana realized this and continued.

"I've forgotten where you've been for the last two months! In a nutshell, about five weeks ago the new American President, Robert Palmer, invited Viktor Rodin to meet with him in Los Angeles. The supposed subject of this summit is the instantaneous freezing of all new strategic missile systems, and the creation of a concrete timetable for the gradual elimination of those nuclear warheads already in service."

"Most impressive," Valenko said thoughtfully.

Kuzmin shook his head in disgust. "If you ask me, it sounds like more imperialist propaganda. Whenever their presidents take office, the first thing they inevitably do is throw the standard olive branch toward the Soviet Union. They may talk peace, but I guarantee you that work on their MX missiles and Star Wars platforms will go on, regardless."

"I beg to differ with you, dear brother-in-law. This may have been the case in the 1960's or 70's, but today a new generation of leaders guides both countries. All over the world, the people cry out for peace. Ridiculously high military budgets have broken the economies of too many nations, and the average citizen has had enough.

"Our General Secretary has voiced his own frustrations. Though he has only been in office a few months more than the new U.S. President, his unprecedented actions are already changing the direction of the Motherland. For the first time ever, defense spending has actually decreased, while consumer expenditures are on the rise."

"It sounds to me like we're asking for trouble," Kuzmin mumbled.

Ivana reacted instantly to this. "That is precisely the paranoid thinking that has gotten us into this mess! We don't need any more nuclear bombs; neither do the Americans. Their people are just as tired of the arms race as ours. Don't forget that Robert Palmer ran on a strong anti-military platform. No U.S. President since Reagan has ever won so decisively. Just give these two dynamic young leaders a chance to meet eye-to-eye. They'll come up with something constructive."

Impressed with Ivana's thoughts, Valenko's attraction to her intensified. "I see that somebody has been doing their political-science homework. For the sake of little Nikolai here, I hope that your optimistic view of world affairs comes to pass, Ivana. Until it does, Stefan and I can only do what we do best to insure this fragile peace."

"Anyone ready for dinner?" Galina asked.

Not hearing a word of protest, she picked up the baby and led the way into the dining area.

Valenko was positively ravenous by the time they sat down at the table. The varied platters of food that soon followed didn't disappoint him in the least. The conversation was of a much lighter nature as they plowed into their borscht. The rich beet soup was another favored recipe of the girls' mother. Valenko found that a spoonful of sour cream perfectly accented the tart, sweet broth. Stefan Kuzmin made certain that the champagne continued to flow. They were well into their third bottle by the time the main course was brought out.

Never had beef stroganoff tasted so delicious. Presented on a platter of wide egg noodles, the meat was tender enough to cut with a fork. Served alongside was a bowl filled with steamed carrots and string beans. It had been much too long since the submariners had tasted fresh vegetables, and the two men joyfully indulged themselves. A cup of strong black coffee and a slice of spicy apple tart completed the feast.

All through the meal, little Nikolai sat in his wooden highchair, content with his bottle and the company surrounding him. By dessert's end, the lad was fast asleep.

While the girls began clearing the table, Stefan volunteered to put the baby to bed. Valenko accompanied him into the apartment's only apparent bedroom. With barely enough room for their own double mattress and a single vanity, they had just managed to squeeze a crib up against the far wall. As he watched the proud papa kiss his son lightly on the cheek and then tuck him in, Valenko found new respect for his warrant officer. Stefan Kuzmin had certainly done well for himself. In such an environment, Nikolai couldn't help but grow into a fine young man.

He held this thought as he seated himself in one of the two chairs set on either end of the couch. The girls were still busy in the kitchen as Stefan rummaged through an antique wooden cabinet and extracted a large bottle and four crystal glasses.

"I hope you have left some room for this cherry brandy. Galina brought it back from Kiev after her last visit."

"Stefan, I don't know where I'm going to put it—but pour away, Comrade."

Both men were totally at ease as Kuzmin raised his glass in a toast. "To my son's godfather—may Nikolai grow up in his likeness."

Not to be outdone, Valenko took a sip of the potent liquor and then offered his own toast. "To my new friends. May health and happiness haunt these walls always."

This time, after the sips were consumed, both men sat back. A moment of contemplative silence passed before Kuzmin anxiously caught Valenko's eye.

"There's something that I think you should know about, Captain. Chief Chuchkin called here earlier, asking if I knew the whereabouts of Senior Lieutenant Leonov. When I explained that I supposed he was with his fiancé, the Chief clued me in on some disturbing news. It seems that Comrade Leonov's girlfriend defected to the U.S. last month with a Western journalist she had been having an affair with. Several of the crew are currently scouring the city to see how Leonov is taking the news."

Valenko winced. "That is a most tragic tale, Stefan, in more ways than one. You see, it was my big mouth that urged Vasili to ask the girl to marry him during this shore leave. The poor guy must be heartbroken!"

"If he knows what's good for him, he'll be drowning his sorrows in a bottle of vodka."

"I hope that's the extent of it," Valenko said. "Leonov's an intelligent fellow, but a little too sensitive. A tragedy like this could knock him completely off balance."

"To the extent of suicide?" Kuzmin asked.

"You never know, Comrade. No pain can be as great as that generated between a man and a woman. I've seen many a brave officer not think twice about risking his life during a patrol, yet simply break apart upon our return after having a spat with his loved one. Sometimes I think that's one of the main reasons I've decided to remain a bachelor all my years."

"Perhaps I should volunteer my own services in tracking Vasili down," Kuzmin offered.

Valenko's response was firm. "Stay home with your wife and son, Comrade. These things have a way of working themselves out."

Lifting his glass, Valenko finished off the fiery spirits. While Kuzmin refilled their glasses, the captain silently cursed himself for getting involved with his senior lieutenant's love life. He had only been trying to do good. Why did these things always have a way of backfiring? His gloomy contemplations were interrupted by the arrival of the girls.

"Hey, you two, why the long faces?" Galina asked. "I bet you've been talking about work again."

"You've caught us out, dear," Kuzmin answered meekly. "We promise there will be no more shop talk."

"If you know what's good for you, you'll keep that pledge," Galina responded. "Now, is the kitchen detail going to have to sit here and just watch you drink that fine Ukrainian brandy?"

"I'm sorry, ladies." Stefan immediately began filling the two empty glasses. While he did so, Ivana nestled herself into that portion of the couch that was situated beside Valenko's chair.

"You wouldn't believe the scene that's visible outside the kitchen window," Ivana said. "I've never seen the snow fall so thickly before."

"Just what we need tonight, a blizzard," Valenko said gloomily.

"Our company isn't that bad, is it Captain?"

Ivana's question was delivered with such innocent spontaneity that Valenko broke out of his sullen mood. As the brandy glasses were passed around, he made the first toast.

"To good food, good friends, and a world filled with peace and understanding."

The brandy was sampled, and while Stefan and Galina discussed Nikolai's feeding schedule, Ivana initiated a conversation with Valenko.

"The trials of parenthood. Actually, little Nikolai is an angel. The dear practically sleeps through the night now."

"I'm certain that Galina appreciates all your help. Have you two always been this close?"

Ivana hesitated a bit before answering. "As the little sister, I was always quite jealous of Galina. We've had our share of spats, but nothing too serious. During school I didn't have much to do with her, except to borrow clothes and make-up. And before long she was married, and here we are the very best of friends."

"That's the way it should be," Valenko remarked, while stifling a yawn. "Being an only child, I wish I could have experienced such a relationship, but it was not to be." He paused, and then said, "I hate to be a spoilsport, but I think I'd better be getting on my way. Paperwork kept me awake most of last night, and all that good food and drink have drained me completely."

Ivana covered a yawn herself. "I guess I'm ready to turn in also. Hold on, and you can walk me downstairs to the apartment I'm staying in."

"I thought that you were staying here."

"I was, but with Stefan's return I just didn't feel comfortable. This place is crowded enough as it is. Fortunately, one of their bachelor neighbors is also a submariner and he's currently out to sea. Galina got the keys from him for just such circumstances."

"What's this about somebody wanting to leave?" Stefan said animatedly. "Are you certain that you don't want one more brandy for the road?"

Valenko stood and the others joined him. "I'm afraid not, Comrade. I can't tell you what a marvelous evening it has been. I haven't had such a good time in years."

"Well, it was a pleasure having you," answered Galina. "Please feel free to make our home yours whenever you so wish."

Kuzmin nodded. "With that blizzard blowing outdoors, you're welcomed to spend the night here. I can personally attest to the comfort of this sofa for sleeping."

"The snows don't bother me, Comrade. In a way, I kind of look forward to walking in the white stuff once again."

"If you change your mind after you poke your head outside, just come back and knock," Galina offered sincerely.

Coats, gloves and hats were produced, and soon

Valenko and Ivana found themselves alone in the hallway. Only when they reached the stairs did the naval officer feel the total effects of the alcohol he had consumed. Slightly dizzy, he halted a moment to tightly grasp the shiny wooden bannister. His escort was in no better shape as she stumbled up beside him. When Ivana hiccuped loudly the two broke up in a seizure of uncontrollable laughter.

"Some example we are to the children of the Motherland," Valenko slurred. "A naval officer and a teacher-to-be so potted they can't even walk down a flight of stairs."

"Speak for yourself, Captain," Ivana retorted. "Didn't you know that it's a scientific fact that women can hold their liquor much better than men?"

Emphasizing this statement with another hiccup, Ivana shakily began to walk down the stairs. Her progress appeared steady until she faltered just as she reached the second floor landing. Keeping her from stumbling was a pair of strong, alert hands. Without a word passing between them, Valenko angled his head down and kissed her full on the lips. A vibrant shock of longing jumped back and forth between them. Impossible to ignore, this heart pounding, instinctive urge was stimulated by passions too-long contained.

"You don't really want to be alone tonight, do you sailor?" Ivana muttered breathlessly.

Valenko answered with another long, electrifying kiss. No more words were spoken as Ivana took his hand and led him to her apartment.

Somehow, they managed to get the door unlocked. Inside it was warm and dark. Neither bothered with switching on lights. Valenko allowed himself to be led by the hand onto a large mattress that lay against the far wall. Needless clothing was tossed to the floor as they both scurried for the cover of the bed's thick, cotton comforter.

Another passionate shock flared as their naked bodies touched and intertwined. Savoring the moment, Valenko allowed his hands to explore those exciting features he had watched all evening. With lips still pressed and tongues probing, his fingers traced the soft yet firm flesh of her breasts. Budlike nipples beckoned to be aroused. With an expert, gentle touch, he did so. Only after leaving them erect and stiff, did he continue his wandering.

A creamy smooth, flat belly led to a pair of tight, squirming hips. Massaging the inner sides of her thighs, a line of goose bumps urged his exploration ever on. The pressure of her lips intensified as his fingers delicately probed the recesses of her womanhood. She needed little priming, for he found these depths wet and hot.

Reaching out with her own hands, Ivana traced the hairy, solid surface of her lover's chest. Her frantic exploration didn't stop until she found her mate stiff and ready. Knowing full well that she was about to be taken by more man than she had ever encountered before, she trembled inwardly. Valenko felt this vibration and knew that the time was right for fulfillment.

Sliding on top of her, he cupped his hands under her buttocks and, with a single plunge of his hips, found his mark. A passionate moan escaped from Ivana's lips as he pushed himself forward and gave her his all. For a fleeting second, neither party moved.

Valenko relished the feel of their initial merger, as the slow grinding of Ivana's hips led him on.

Deliberately slow, he pulled himself back so that his shaft's lips hovered outside the folds of her moist channel. This was followed by another plunge downward. Valenko gradually increased the speed of his rhythm.

Assured by his gentleness, yet clearly awed by his size, Ivana hungrily matched his strokes. Loosened by his penetration, she wrapped her legs around his hips and increased her pumping. All too soon this stroke became a frenzy, and a quivering warmth began rising deep within her. Again she moaned and found herself begging him to take her deeper. Just as he shoved himself to his limit, a fiery, ecstatic warmth shot upward from the pit of Ivana's loins.

Aware of his mate's rousing climax, Valenko abandoned all self-control and joined her. At their moment of climax, their lips again became one. He knew then that their coupling had been most right.

Warm, soothed and satisfied, his new love snuggled up beside him. He was grateful that she didn't need any words to express her satisfaction. As he lay there with Ivana securely in his arms, Valenko was suddenly aware of the distinct, fierce howl of gusting winds outside. Cognizant that he had made the correct choice, he hugged her gently, and within minutes matched the slow, even breaths of her deep slumber exactly.

Chapter Four

Approximately 3,400 miles to the southeast of the Siberian city of Petropavlovsk is the Hawaiian island of Oahu. Like the Soviet city, Oahu gained its primary importance by being home to a huge naval complex. The installation at Pearl Harbor was home port to not only dozens of American surface ships, but also served as headquarters for the Third Fleet's Pacific-based submarines. It was to this spot that the attack sub *Triton* was called to after completing its patrol in the North Pacific.

The morning dawned hot and clear as Captain Michael Cooksey left his command and climbed into the passenger seat of a waiting jeep, parked at the end of the gangplank. Though the *Triton* had arrived there almost twenty-four hours ago, this was the first time that Cooksey had been topside. Invigorated by the fresh, tropical air, he greeted his driver, then sat back for the short ride to Admiral Miller's office.

Cooksey was surprised when the orders inviting him to see the admiral had been received aboard the *Triton* the previous evening. Usually his superiors waited for his final report to be filed before debriefing him. So far, he had only released his preliminary observations of the patrol just completed. Not knowing what was in store, he yawned and took in the passing scenery.

The port area was alive with activity as they crossed its width and began their way up the long, winding roadway that led to the headquarters complex. Thankful for the driver's silence, Cooksey used this time to put the events of the last few days into proper perspective.

Except for the failure to catch up with the suspected Soviet attack sub, the patrol had been a great success. There were no significant equipment difficulties to speak of. Even their interception of the carrier task force had gone as planned.

On a personal level, all that Cooksey could complain about was his continuing problem in getting some decent shut-eye. Since arriving from Midway, Cooksey doubted he had slept more than an hour or two. As usual, when he tried he just lay stiffly in his bunk, his mind going a mile a minute. He knew that he couldn't begin to count the cups of coffee that he had consumed on the way in.

Any irritability on his part was apparently not noticeable to the crew. His conversations with them were brief and to the point, and focused entirely on their immediate duty. As it worked out, the officer he usually had the closest contact with was consumed by worries of his own. For the last few days, his XO had been a bundle of raw nerves. Concerned with the health of his wife, who was due to deliver their first child any moment now, Richard Craig had but one thing on his mind. Fortunately, for the safety of all of them, the exec had been able to sufficiently carry out his varied duties. Of course, he had been the first one off the *Triton*, having learned that Susan had been shuttled off to the base hospital that morning.

Covering up another yawn, Cooksey looked on as they passed through a dual column of majestic coconut palms. The sun felt good on his face, and gradually his inner tension dissipated. His eyes were even beginning to nod shut, when the jeep abruptly braked to a halt. Cooksey fumbled for his I.D. card, so that the alert marine guard would allow them into the command complex that he stood before. The captain's name was noted on a log, and only then were they allowed to proceed.

Headquarters for the Third Fleet was located in a large, three-story, white-brick building. Situated on the summit of a lofty hillside, this location allowed for an excellent view of the port facilities below. As they approached the structure's entrance, Cooksey noticed a wide assortment of differently shaped antennas jutting forth from the tiled roof. Interspersed between these aerials were a pair of massive satellite dishes. Since communications are the eyes and ears of command, Cooksey was aware of the importance of these amazingly accurate and powerful relay systems.

The jeep came to a halt behind a shiny black limousine, with plates identifying it as belonging to the Defense Department. Politely, the driver informed Cooksey that he would be waiting to convey the captain back to his sub. Cooksey thanked the lad, exited the jeep, and made his way inside.

The office of Admiral Broderick Miller was located on the third floor. Although Cooksey had only been called there a handful of times, he didn't need to ask directions to get to the proper door. Taking a second to straighten his uniform, the blonde-haired captain sucked in a deep, calming breath, exhaled slowly and entered.

A good-looking Hawaiian sat behind the reception desk, deeply immersed in the letter she had been typing. Cooksey remembered her from his last visit. The young woman was so wrapped up in her work that he had to clear his throat loudly to get her attention.

"I'm sorry," she blurted with a start. "Captain Cooksey, I'm afraid you caught me in memoland. I'm Lisa, and you're certainly right on time. Can I get you some coffee before you go in to see The Boss?"

"Why, thanks, Lisa, that would be great," Cooksey responded. "Black is just fine."

As she rose, he couldn't help but appreciate her tall, thin figure, and waist-long flowing black hair. It had been much too long since he had seen a woman like this . . . much too long.

When Lisa turned with his coffee in hand, she caught the captain's stare of inspection and smiled. Shyly, Cooksey diverted his glance while taking the enamel mug from her steady hand.

"The Admiral said to show you in as soon as you arrived, Captain. Make the most of the good mood you'll be finding him in. Seems he shot the best round of golf in his life yesterday."

Aware that she could only coax the barest of smiles from the handsome captain's face, Lisa beckoned him to follow her. Efficiently, she approached a pair of polished walnut doors set in the far wall. After knocking on the right side, she turned the handle and signaled Cooksey to enter.

The admiral was on the phone as Cooksey stepped inside. Motioning Cooksey to take a seat, the commanding officer of the Third Fleet continued with his conversation, oblivious to the presence of his newly arrived guest.

Two high-backed leather chairs faced the admiral's desk; and Cooksey chose the one on the left. After seating himself, he examined the office's interior, while the admiral scribbled a long list of coordinates on a legal pad.

Solid, dark-stained wood furniture and plush red leather predominated. One wall was covered by a massive bookshelf crammed with thousands of various volumes. A map rack stood beside it. Cooksey was surprised to find that an intricate map of Midway Island was pulled down and clearly visible. A red grease pencil had been used to circle various locations that lay in the waters to the north of the island. On the wall next to the map rack were over a dozen framed photos, which Cooksey knew were the various ships that the admiral had served aboard. Represented here were vessels ranging from fleet oilers to a destroyer, several World War II-style diesel submarines, and a nuclear-powered aircraft carrier.

The room's only window was a massive affair, set immediately behind the desk. This afforded the admiral an excellent view of the port. A shiny brass telescope sat on a tripod beside it. It was said that Miller often used this scope to watch the sailors down below. It was rumored that many a shirker had been reported from this unlikely vantage point. A golf putting machine, complete with balls, a putter and a spongy green, rubberized skirt completed the furnishings.

Cooksey took a sip of his coffee and looked at the man who sat before him. Well into his sixties now, Admiral Broderick Miller still glowed with an abundance of robust energy. Even though his hair had long turned to pure white, this only gave him an additional degree of distinction. With his skin tanned a golden brown, and blue eyes sparkling, the man seemed a perfect picture of health.

It was hard to believe that this was the same man who had been carried off the flaming deck of the carrier *Yorktown*. For it was during the battle of Midway that the young officer, fresh from the Naval Academy, gained the attention of his superiors. Under the expert guidance of Admiral Spruance, Miller rose quickly in the ranks. Distinguishing himself as a brilliant tactician and competent administrator, he was placed on a variety of ships to accumulate vital experience. This wide range of knowledge served him well in his current post.

The admiral's imploring stare caught that of Michael Cooksey as he silently begged the young officer to have patience. Firmly, he talked into the telephone.

"I understand our time perimeters, Martin, but Friday will be here before we know it. I think it would be best to have all the contingencies thought out well beforehand. A single emergency could have consequences of a most dire nature. Get me that list of the various agencies involved by lunchtime, and by all means get me a copy of that flight plan. I've got to know exactly where that plane is the second it takes off from Petropavlovsk. Thanks for all your help with this, Martin. I'll be talking with you again shortly."

With a sigh of relief, the admiral hung up the receiver, shook his head and addressed his visitor. "Sorry about that, Michael. You know how much I enjoy inter-agency squabbling. That was Martin Lawrence over at State. Unbelievable as it may seem, they want the Third to help monitor the advance of Rodin's plane when it takes off for L.A. on Friday. As if that's all we've got to do."

Pushing his chair back, he swiveled around to take a look outside, while stretching out his cramped, long limbs. This movement seemed to lighten his mood considerably.

"By the way Captain, welcome back home."

"Thanks, Admiral. Is this summit really as serious as it sounds? We just learned of it while we were pulling in yesterday."

"That's right, you were out to sea when President Palmer issued the invitation. You wouldn't believe how quickly this whole thing came down. Sure not like the old days."

"Do you think that it's going to make a difference?" Cooksey asked carefully.

The admiral looked him straight in the eye. "Not as long as they've got vessels like that Alfa pulling hotshot stunts—like the one that you chanced upon at Point Luck. Damned if that kind of thing doesn't get me infuriated!"

"Well, you should have been there watching it all come down," Cooksey said. "The scary thing about it is that they could have done pretty much whatever they wanted with our surface ships, or, for that matter, with the *Triton*."

Broderick Miller's response flowed gravely. "I've read your preliminary, Michael. I can imagine how frustrating it must have been not even having a weapons system capable of running down the bastard. By the way, we've got a definite on that particular bogey. Big Bird had a clean shot of Petropavlovsk when she came waltzing in with a Delta III on her tail. SOSUS confirms that this Alfa and the vessel you went after are the same."

"I can't believe that the President is even bothering to waste his breath with the Soviets," Cooksey said. "Doesn't he know what's going on out there?"

"Well, we certainly send him the reports. Of course, you never know who reads them. I'm still of the opinion that if you've got a chance to open up a dialogue between two new leaders, you've got to do so. Who knows? They might just hit upon something to stop this foolishness. In the meantime, we're going to keep on doing our jobs the best we know how. That was a mighty fine intercept on the carrier task force, Michael. Before that Alfa showed up, our ships didn't have any idea that you were even out there."

Cooksey blushed a bit at the unexpected compliment. "Thanks, Admiral. I'm working with one hell of a fine crew, and our equipment sure can't be faulted."

Broderick Miller stirred anxiously. "Speaking of equipment—how would you like a torpedo that would give the *Triton* an ASW range of 300 miles?"

"That would depend on which science-fiction book I was reading," Cooksey said with obvious disbelief.

"That was *my* exact response when I first heard of

the weapon this spring. I didn't believe the lab people until I read a report of the successful testing of just such a system four weeks ago.

"It's called ASW/SOW, for Anti-Sub Warfare Stand-Off Weapon. Basically, it's a Tomahawk-family cruise missile that can be fired from a torpedo tube. With a range of up to 300 hundred miles, the missile would then drop a Remotely-Guided Autonomous Lightweight torpedo, or REGAL, by parachute. When REGAL hits the water, an acoustic array containing a small computer and a sonar transmitter separates and sinks to a pre-set depth. Meanwhile, the torpedo begins propelling itself in a slow search pattern, awaiting a signal from the sonar array to trigger its advanced-capability motor and run the target through."

Cooksey shook his head in admiration. "I'd say that such a system sounds too good to be true."

The admiral beamed. "Well, believe it or not, two of the prototype ASW/SOW units will be loaded into the *Triton* tomorrow morning. Though still officially an experimental system, I'd say that the Alfa, or whatever else the Soviets may throw at us, has finally met its match."

Expecting a bit more emotion from Cooksey, the admiral watched him stifle a wide yawn. "Are you all right, Michael? You look a bit tired."

Fighting to restimulate himself, Cooksey silently cursed the admiral's awareness. "I'm feeling fine, Admiral. Guess I could have allowed myself a couple of additional hours of shut-eye last night."

"It's more than that," added the hawk-eyed sailor. "You seem tense. Not at all like the old Michael

Cooksey I used to know. What are your plans for your two-week leave coming up?"

Cooksey shrugged his shoulders. "I really didn't have anything set. Just thought I'd hang out around Honolulu."

"If I remember right, you were quite a golfer in your college days. When's the last time you took some time out to hit the old ball around?"

Cooksey had to think a minute before answering. "I don't know, I guess it's been around five years."

"Five years! No wonder you look a bit peaked. Old Doc Miller here has the perfect prescription for charging up that sagging system of yours. Betty and I keep a little place near Princeville, on the northern shore of Kauai. Next door, there's one of the prettiest 36-hole courses that you ever set eyes on. If my memory serves me right, the place is vacant at the moment. You're most welcome to make it your home for the next two weeks."

"It sounds inviting, Admiral," Cooksey said cautiously. "But if the *Triton* is going to be fitted with a new weapons system, I'd better be around for the installation."

"Let your exec handle it," retorted Miller.

"I'm afraid that I couldn't ask that of my XO at the moment, sir. As it looks now, Lieutenant Commander Craig is going to be spending the week in the maternity ward."

The admiral thought a few seconds before responding. "Is Chief Bartkowski still aboard the *Triton*?"

Catching Cooksey's affirmative nod, he continued. "With all of that man's experience, I don't think you have a thing to worry about, Captain. Old Bartkowski can handle those new missiles just fine."

Still conscious of Cooksey's blasé demeanor, Broderick Miller knew that the young officer needed a break to refresh himself. Standing, he decided to play his trump card.

"I wasn't supposed to be letting this out so soon, Michael, but chances are excellent that the *Triton* will be getting its second consecutive battle-efficiency award. You're earned a rest, son, now take it."

Pleasantly surprised by this revelation, Cooksey broke into a warm, satisfied grin. Such awards were all that he and his crew worked for. Their first citation was reason enough for celebration. For them to get two in a row was incredible. Relieved that a lifetime's goal had been more than achieved, he decided that he deserved to give himself a real vacation. Standing, he accepted the admiral's invitation with a smile and a handshake. Who knew—perhaps he'd even be able to get some proper sleep once again.

Twenty-four hours later, Cooksey found himself landing at Kauai's Lihue Airport. Following Admiral Miller's advice, he rented a jeep and was soon barreling along Highway 56 toward the northern edge of the island. Happy to be behind the wheel again, he steered cautiously up the narrow roadway.

The scenery was magnificent, with the crashing Pacific on his right and endless acres of verdant tropical growth to his left. Though the sun had been out in all its glory at Lihue, as he passed through Kilauea the sky clouded up. Minutes later, he was in the midst of a torrential downpour. Just as he thought that he may have to pull off onto the shoulder to let this storm vent itself, the rain stopped, the clouds parted, and blue skies again prevailed. Such cloudbursts were to be expected, for less than ten miles inland was Mount Kawaikini, the wettest known spot on earth.

The jeep's windshield was barely dry by the time he reached the Princeville exit. It didn't take him long to spot the condo in which he would be staying. It was set high on top of a green volcanic bluff, beside the eastern edge of Hanalei Bay. Again he followed the admiral's directions and found the signs that pointed towards the Princeville golf course. Directly opposite the entrance to the club was a private asphalt road, protected by a closed steel barricade. Utilizing his heavy-plastic card key, Cooksey opened the security gate and began his way up the mountainside.

The condo development was comprised of two dozen individual units. Each was two stories high, designed simply from dark-stained native wood. The Millers' place occupied the northern edge of the grounds. This gave him a spectacular view of Hanalei Bay in the front, and a panoramic landscape of lush, tropical mountains behind them. As he parked the jeep, Cooksey could just make out one of the golf course fairways visible down below; a single cart could be seen innocently crossing its length. Anxiously, he switched off the ignition and unloaded his two bags.

The first thing that Cooksey noticed as he proceeded inside was the utter quiet. The second was the moist, heavy floral scent that totally permeated the air.

The interior of the unit was decorated almost

completely with rattan furniture. Huge picture windows dominated the walls, producing a light, airy atmosphere. All he would need now were groceries, and he could pass the two weeks quite comfortably.

A set of golf clubs sat in the hall closet as promised. Since it was still early, Cooksey could think of no better way to spend this first day on leave than to check out this course that the admiral constantly bragged about.

Noon found him at the club's pro shop, signing up for his first round of golf in five years. The metallic clatter of his spikes brought back many pleasant memories, for this was a sport he had enjoyed since childhood. Known as a promising amateur, he had won dozens of trophies during his junior high and high school years. College brought his game to a new plateau when he was named captain of the Citadel's excellent golf team. Always one who thrived on competition, there was even a time when he had toyed with the idea of turning professional, until his naval obligation diverted his talents elsewhere.

Two decades of service, and Cooksey could count the rounds of golf he had played during that time on one hand. He supposed this was due to the fact that his trusty clubs were packed up in his parents basement back in Richmond, Virginia. Yet, he knew that was a poor excuse. The cold truth was that he just didn't allow himself any time for game-playing.

A long-absent surge of excitement possessed him as he introduced himself to the pro and paid his greens fee. As it turned out, there was another single waiting to go and, with Cooksey's consent, a twosome was formed.

His partner was a likeable, bald-headed pediatrician from St. Louis, Missouri. Drawn to Kauai for his honeymoon, this afternoon's game was his first venture away from his new bride. It did Cooksey good to talk with someone not in the service. Introductions were exchanged, their cart was loaded, and by the time the sun was straight overhead they had climbed onto the first tee.

With a bit of apprehension, Cooksey tightened his glove and pulled out the number one wood. The hole was a beauty. It was a par four and appeared extremely unforgiving. The drive would have to carry up a narrow fairway that was flanked by a lake on the right and a sheer, 400-foot drop-off on the left. The doctor hit first and promptly smacked a 200-yard-plus drive straight down the center. After attempting a few practice swings, Cooksey approached his ball. Concentrating on an easy, smooth swing, he hit a sizzler that more than matched his opponent's. A grin of self-satisfaction painted his face as he climbed into the cart and began mentally preparing for the next shot.

Four-and-a-half hours later, the twosome was making a golf date for the next morning as they walked off the eighteenth green. Though his game could certainly use some sharpening, Cooksey had come within three strokes of matching the doctor's par round. True to the admiral's words, the course had been one of the most beautiful and challenging he had ever played. Rolling hills, volcanic promontories, adjoining pineapple fields and thick forests of Cooke pine trees made it a visual paradise. For the first time in months, an entire afternoon had gone by without Cooksey being aware of the passing minutes. Concentration on his game allowed his ponderings to remain far distant from the *Triton* and his duties. The doctor had a great sense of humor, and wasn't a bit inquisitive as to what Cooksey did in the navy. Instead, he chronicled his honeymoon, told various golf tales and gave the captain a comprehensive lesson in the horrors of rising malpractice insurance.

Cooksey decided to drive into town and pick up some groceries before returning to the condo. A nice, thick T-bone steak sure sounded like it would do the trick for the evening. Happy to have a healthy appetite, he made a mental list of the supplies he would need. A walk after dinner would be nice, and then he could settle down with that Ed Beach novel he had been wanting to read for so long. And then—a sound night's sleep. Grateful to have taken the admiral's advice, Cooksey could already feel the tension draining from him. He'd be his old self in no time. Throwing the jeep into second gear, he initiated the long, steep grade into Princeville.

Cooksey's round the next morning was a nightmare. It was at the third hole that his nasty slice reappeared. Six holes later, he was forced to make his way over to the pro shop to replace the dozen balls he had already lost. By the time they reached the fifteenth tee his swing was back in control, but it was much too late to catch the doctor's lead. Beaten by a whopping seventeen strokes, Cooksey humbly said farewell to his partner, who was returning to the mainland in the morning.

That same night, he was searching the condo for a

spike wrench, when he chanced upon a full set of camping gear stashed in a closet. Stored in a blue nylon backpack, the equipment included a sleeping bag, propane stove, canteen, and a myriad of other utensils necessary for a comfortable overnight stay in the wilderness. Supposing that this gear belonged to the admiral's son, Cooksey didn't give it too much thought—until he uncovered a small booklet that lay beneath the toolbox. Entitled *Hiking in Kauai*, it described a variety of excellent hikes into the interior of the scenic island. In college, backpacking had been another of his favorite after-school activities. Weekend treks into the Appalachians were followed by excursions into the Ozarks and Colorado, and even included a week spent roughing it in the mountains north of Banff. Just as exciting as the trips themselves was the time spent preparing for them. This included many hours devoted to devouring guide books like the one he had just uncovered. On a whim, he took it into the kitchen and began reading it over dinner.

One particular hike looked most interesting. Coincidentally, it was the only trip of the dozen offered that was underscored in red by the manual's owner. The 10.8 mile trail from Kee Beech to Kalalau was said to be the most spectacular overnight excursion in all the Hawaiian Islands. The trail started where Kauai's main road, Route 56, ended. That was only seven miles from Cooksey's current location, outside the tiny village of Haena. Accessible only to backpackers, the Kalalau Trail offered verdant valleys, magnificent waterfalls, thick woods of mango, fern and guava, and vistas of the uninhabited north coast that were supposedly unequaled.

Certain that the Millers wouldn't mind if he put this gear to use, Cooksey lugged it into the living room and began making a complete inventory. All that was lacking was a proper food supply. Aware that the store at Princeville had a complete line of lightweight, dehydrated and freeze-dried foods, he decided to visit them first thing in the morning and to bring the gear along with him.

That night, for the first time in months, he slept a sound eight hours. Waking fresh and rested, he made himself a hearty breakfast, crammed enough clothing into the pack to last two days and took off to buy groceries. By 10:00 a.m. he was parked in the lot where Highway 56 ended. Per the recommendation of the guidebook, which he brought along, Cooksey left the jeep unlocked. Local thieves were known to smash a hiker's windows just to check the contents of a closed glove compartment.

The weather was so mild that he stripped off his T-shirt, leaving himself dressed only in khaki shorts and Reebok sneakers. With barely a grunt, he loaded the thirty-five-pound pack onto his back and took off for Kee Beach. Since the trail here was well marked and easy to follow, he spent the first eighth of a mile adjusting his stride to the additional weight. Once that was accomplished, he was able to pick up some speed.

The rudiments of hiking, like golf, are not easily forgotten. Taking care to place his step firmly and not jeopardize his balance, Cooksey soon established a comfortable pace. He couldn't help but feel the alien pressure on his legs and back as the footpath began sloping upward. He knew that he was facing a steep,

111

one-mile climb. To avoid overexertion, he decided to stop approximately every quarter mile to catch his breath and enjoy the scenery.

He took his first rest at a spot where the trail was shaded by a grove of large Kukui trees. Cooksey was able to identify the plant, as well as many other native species, by once again referring to the manual. It was in this manner that he learned that leis were made from Kukui nuts. Its oil could also be burned for light, while its trunk could be hollowed out into an excellent canoe. In the same grove he also located a patch of yellow, lemon-sized sweet guava and the colorful purple plumes of the wild orchid.

A flock of white frigate birds soared up above, and Cooksey looked out to the surging Pacific. How different this view of the sea was from what he experienced six months out of every year. As an explorer of its depths, he almost felt as if the rippling surface belonged to another element altogether. Happy to have his present, solid vantage point, he took one last look at Kee Beach and the Haena Reefs beyond, then turned and continued upward.

It took him a little over an hour to reach this portion of the trail's summit. A thick band of sweat covered his forehead as he peered down into the lush valley that he would presently be penetrating. Here he spotted the plant called the hala. Jokingly referred to as the "tourist pineapple" because of its similar shape to the popular fruit, the hala had a value all its own. Not only were its leaves used for weaving baskets, mats and hats, but its trunk served as an effective pipe to drain the taro fields.

Cooksey's one-mile journey into the Hanakapiai

Valley went much more quickly. It was several degrees cooler down there, as the trail snaked beside a tumbling stream resplendent with stately mango trees, guava and huge Hawaiian tree ferns. A crimson-bodied apapane fluttered its jet-black feathers and lowered its curved, gray bill. Two white-tailed tropic birds sat serenely on a mango branch, their sixteen-inch snowy tail feathers streaming in a gentle breeze.

Conscious of the surrounding paradise, Cooksey unloaded his pack. Before grabbing something to eat, he took a dip in the nearby stream. The water was clear and warm. Close by, a small waterfall cascaded down into a deep, blue pool. Here, for the first time during his hike, he saw another human being.

Floating on her back at the edge of the pool was a young woman. Oblivious to the voyeur watching from above, she lay completely naked. Cooksey could make out a tall, thin frame, bronzed by hours in the tropical sun. From her coloring and features he sensed that she was most likely a native Hawaiian. A wave of long-absent longing rose in his loins and Cooksey guiltily backed away. He had decided long ago that it would be much safer to stay as far away from the female species as possible. He wasn't about to break his promise now.

After picking out a packet of trail mix, he reloaded his gear and began the four-mile trek to Hanakoa. Steep switchbacks dominated the route for a mile as he climbed out of the Hanakapiai Valley. Fortunately, the sun was still at his back and the cooling trade winds helped temper his exertions. The trail gradually narrowed and soon followed a most precipitous slope. It was on such a path that he entered the thickly

113

foliated Hoolulu Valley. Again the temperature dropped as he crossed through forests of fern, kukui, guava, koa and hala trees. Morning glories and mountain orchids splashed the scene with color as thick bushes of ti, the plant out of which hula skirts were made, pushed up in every available open space.

The adjoining valley, the Waiahuakua, was a much broader one. Here he sampled a crisp, juicy mountain apple. Cooksey also sighted his first strawberry, coffee and ginger plants.

At the five-and-a-half-mile marker, he got his first view of the Hanakoa Valley. This broad, terraced depression would be his last reference point until he reached Kalalau Beach. Here he received his first soaking, as a quick-forming tropical downpour drenched him with several inches of cool rainwater in a matter of minutes. Refreshed, he initiated the strenuous, three-hour hike to his goal, 4.8 miles distant.

The character of the landscape changed drastically in the miles that followed. It was much drier, and as the path turned westward, a completely new assortment of vegetation was evident. Desertlike sisal and pink-blossomed lantana shared the banks of the barely trickling streams with dozens of foraging feral goats. The earth was reddish, as if scorched by the fiery sun itself.

There was the distant, muted sound of human voices, and Cooksey caught sight of its source. When he did so, he had to look twice, for approaching him on the trail was a family of backpackers—long-haired father, mother and a ten-year-old son. What caught Cooksey's attention was the fact that each of them was completely naked! He tried not to look so obviously shocked as they passed him displaying broad grins and flashing V-shaped peace signs with their hands. Not knowing what could possibly lay around the next corner, he continued on without complaint.

Twice he had to take long drafts from his canteen before the trail again turned toward the cooling ocean. Here he was afforded a breathtaking view of Kauai's ruggedly beautiful northwestern coastline. This sight alone was well worth his arduous journey. With the sun gradually falling toward the western horizon, the sharp cliffs and rounded valleys stretched out in a seemingly endless, misty procession. This was the type of scene that belonged on a master's canvas, and Cooksey felt humbled in the presence of such raw, natural beauty.

There could be no denying the rapidly passing hour and the tightness gathering in the calves of his legs. It was time to reach his destination and begin setting up camp. Before long the trail began snaking its way down a narrow ridge and Cooksey got his first look at Kalalau. Nearly two miles wide and three miles long, the valley beckoned invitingly. A good-sized stream could be seen smashing its way toward an unspoiled, spotlessly white beach. Like a pilgrim called home from a decade of wandering, he pushed on to this final goal.

It was well into dusk by the time a proper campsite was set up. In order to deflect the incessant wind blowing off the ocean, he chose a site on the opposite side of the remnants of a solid, six-foot-square volcanic stone wall. He barely had time to unload his gear and begin work on dinner before the waning light

115

gave way to total darkness.

Seated on the soft white sand, with his back propped up against the wall, Cooksey gobbled down a meal of chicken, carrots and rice that proved to be quite good for dehydrated food. With the pounding surf surging behind him, he topped off his repast with a dessert of fresh, ripe mango, picked from a nearby grove. With his hunger now temporarily appeased, he stretched out his sore limbs and contemplated the day's activities.

The hike had progressed way beyond his expectations. Bountiful vistas, unlike any he had ever dreamt of, seemingly lay around every corner. Added to this were rarely seen plants and animal life, which could be appreciated in a clean, fresh setting with hints of man few and far between.

Cooksey had forgotten how much his privacy meant to him. Being surrounded by his crewmates, twenty-four hours a day for months on end, afforded him little time for personal contemplation. Though he had left Pearl only three days ago, it felt like weeks. So much new stimuli had been generated during this brief time that his past worries were but hazy shadows of a distant life.

Gazing up into the crystal clear, blue-black heavens, he issued a brief prayer of thanks. With practiced ease, he identified the great box of Pegasus and followed the tail of Pisces to Aquarius's urn. A shooting star shot through Capricorn and triggered Cooksey's imagination.

What had been the prayers of the ancient mariners who had landed on this island thousands of years ago? What had their thoughts been as they looked up

116

into the nighttime heavens to contemplate the wonders of the universe?

The hiker's guidebook had mentioned that Kalalau Beach was one of the first inhabited sites in Hawaii. Here the original Polynesians had built a massive *heiau*, or temple, where they worshipped the magical *menehunes*. For all Michael knew, the wall that he was presently leaning against could be a remnant of such a structure.

A sharp "wolf whistle" pierced the darkness, and Cooksey stirred to the cry of the elepaio bird. Its alien, raspy call was soon swallowed by the hypnotizing sound of the pounding surf. Lulled by this song, he slipped into his double-wide sleeping bag and drifted off into a deep slumber.

Sometime before dawn, Cooksey was possessed by a vision whose source balanced on the thin line between dream and reality. It began with the sound of crackling underbrush waking him. He directed his weary eyes to locate the creature responsible for the disturbance. Softly lit by the glow of the stars, he saw a tall, thin, familiar figure break from the stand of coconut palms. Only when this wraithlike vision calmly entered his campsite did he identify it as the girl he had seen floating in the jungle pool that afternoon. She was still completely naked. He couldn't help admiring her long, silky black hair, pert, dark-nippled breasts, flat stomach and slender legs. His loins ached, and this time he didn't look away as she smiled and continued on toward him.

With his heart beating wildly, Cooksey reached out and guided his phantom lover into the sleeping bag. Afterward, he would never forget the hot, smooth feel of her skin and the sweet, floral scent that permeated her every pore. The only greeting was a silent communication that emanated from her almond-shaped eyes as she expertly peeled off Cooksey's scivvies and positioned herself on top of him. Without a word, he responded to her urgent touch. Her soft lips merged with his as he penetrated her hot depths.

Time came to a standstill. The only thing that mattered was prolonging the pleasure that her touch induced. Thrusting his manhood into her with short, quick strokes, he felt like the hull of a ship plunging through a surging sea.

Nor did it matter when he realized that an unknown number of tiny, dark-skinned figures had totally surrounded them. Again it proved to be the light of the stars that illuminated these wild-eyed miniature humans dressed in shiny grass skirts. Fear and shame were far from Cooksey's mind, for these Lilliputian visitors seemed to sanctify his frantic coupling.

The hint of rising seed increased the rhythm of his thrusts. Unable to hold himself back, he succumbed to a heart-stopping climax. Sleep again clouded his mind, and the last thing he remembered was his lover covering him with a lei of purple orchids. As the first hint of dawn colored the eastern sky, he slipped off into a dreamless slumber, his lips sealed in a satisfied smile.

He awoke to the warming rays of the morning sun. The night's vibrant vision still painted his consciousness with pleasure, but soon the images began to fade. Groggily, he sat up and desperately attempted to hold on to the blissful recollections. Try as he could, his attempts failed. Unable to recall the dream's exact progression, he only remembered that something about it was all too real. It was only then that he turned and laid eyes on the volcanic stone wall that formed his camp's northern perimeter. Etched on this surface were a number of intricate petroglyphs, recognizable now by the light of the sun. The tiny, grass-skirted natives represented in this ancient drawing filled him with a familiar warmth. Looking down to the base of the wall, he spotted a pile of fresh orchid petals, painting a vibrant purple swatch on the pale white sand. Upon seeing this, a vision rose in his mind's eye.

The tall, thin, brown-skinned native had come to him in the night with a single message. The events of the last few days made this lesson obvious. He had been taking his career much too seriously. In the process, he had failed to take the time to rediscover his real self. *Above all, he had to learn to trust his instincts.* There was certainly nothing shameful in experiencing self-pleasure. Life without it would be cold and dry. Revisualizing the exotic ghost who had brought him the key to this secret, Cooksey rose to take a swim and then continue his day's explorations in earnest.

Chapter Five

The morning was gray and frigid as Petyr Valenko returned to the naval base. Oblivious to the drifts of newly fallen snow, many of which were knee-deep or better, he pushed himself forward as briskly as possible. Crews of workers were visible in the streets, busy manipulating their brooms and shovels in an effort to clear the icy precipitation. Little motor or pedestrian traffic was apparent, although Valenko passed a jubilant gang of bundled up children headed into the park with their sleds and toboggans in tow.

The young captain's thoughts were far from the inclement weather conditions as he continued on. The night just passed had been one of the most wonderful, joyous evenings he had experienced in a long time. Except for a brief affair three years ago, no woman had attracted him as Ivana did. She was charming and sensuous, with a keen intelligence and a quick wit. Even though they had known each other for an extremely short time, he could already relate to her as an acquaintance of many years. Of course, mutual physical attraction had a good part to do with their initial relationship.

In the past, when Valenko made love to a woman it too often became but a one-sided operation. He took what he wanted physically and rarely felt any emotional bonds developing. From the moment that he met Ivana, he immediately sensed a difference. Confident and poised, she responded to him as an equal. Just as she satisfied his longings, so he had satisfied hers.

The alcohol had served as the icebreaker; the snowstorm—and the conveniently vacant apartment—had sealed their fates. Their initial lovemaking had served to whet his appetite. Never before had his hunger been so insatiable. All through the night they were linked together. Each time that Ivana shuddered in orgasm, he was wildly driven to give her more. This morning their passion had still been evident. The warm, soft touch of her skin and her sweet, musky scent were still with him when he reluctantly left to fulfill his present duty. Already he was looking forward to the moment of his return.

Aware of an alien soreness in his loins, Valenko grinned as he set eyes on the guard shack perched at the base's entrance. A smile still painted his face as he pulled out his credentials and flashed them before the bored sentry. With a salute, he entered.

Unlike the portion of Petropavlovsk through which he had just passed, the base was alive with activity. Snowplows had already cleared the streets, allowing for a variety of truck and auto traffic. As he crossed the administrative complex, he noticed a large contingent of over a hundred workers furiously clearing the snow from the recently built reviewing stand and bleachers.

He found the going a bit more treacherous in the warehouse sector. There, a thick sheet of ice covered the narrow, dark passageways. Several times Valenko lost his traction and went sliding. One of these excursions landed him hard on his buttocks.

Because of the conditions, this sector held little traffic. Alone in the slippery alleyways, he considered backtracking to follow a safer, yet considerably longer path down to the sub pens. But this was his usual route and the footing probably wasn't that much better elsewhere. The distant cry of a gull and the nearby scent of the ocean called him on.

After crossing a particularly treacherous intersection he had but a single block to go. He moved cautiously down an alley flanked by a pair of huge, corrugated warehouses. An elevated construction scaffold clung shakily to the building on his left. The latticed, steel catwalk had long since been abandoned, its workers waiting for more reasonable weather to complete their tasks. A bone-chilling gust of wind swept up the alley from the sea, and Valenko could hear the rattle of the catwalk's rigging as it scraped up against the side of the warehouse. Ducking his head into the gale, he decided to proceed quickly now, before becoming frozen in his tracks.

Valenko's progress went unimpeded, until a scrambling black cat darted from the shadows to his right, skidded, found its traction and dashed in front of him. Surprised by the unexpected movement, he stopped short, heart pounding. Then he heard an ear-shattering, tearing sound. Glancing upward, Valenko watched in disbelief as the steel scaffolding came away from the building. Instinctively, he dove backward—

just as the catwalk crashed to the pavement. Gasping for breath, he raised his head and saw the smashed and twisted metal beams only inches in front of him. As the debris settled, he saw a bloody black tail amongst the wreckage, and knew that the cat, which had most probably saved his life, hadn't been as fortunate.

Shaken, he looked up and caught sight of the frayed cord to which the catwalk had been attached. It hung from the roof uselessly, swaying in the stiff, frigid breeze. Despite the cold, Valenko's body was covered with a thick sheet of nervous sweat. A ripe candidate for pneumonia, he knew that he had to get to shelter at once. Since there were no apparent witnesses, he decided to push on to the *Vulkan*. There he could take proper refuge and report this near-tragedy to the base authorities. Most aware that the hand of fate had saved him from certain death, Valenko forced down a calming breath of air and continued shakily down the alley.

By the time he reached the pen housing the *Vulkan*, a sliver of arctic sun had broken through the gray bank of clouds. Happy to hear the familiar slapping sound of water against the sub's hull, Valenko anxiously boarded the sleek black vessel. Entering the control room from the forward hatch, he bumped into the bearded weapons chief, Yuri Chuchkin. The plump sailor was sitting before the armament console, the well-chewed stem of his favorite brown briar clenched between his teeth.

"Well, hello, Captain," Yuri said, and he put down a manual he had apparently been studying. "A bit nippy out there, isn't it?"

Valenko answered while slowly peeling off his coat, muffler and gloves. "I'll say, Chief. What's our status?"

"All systems remain operational, Captain. Foodstuffs and other supplies were loaded yesterday without incident before the storm hit. We've also got that load of new missiles stowed away. You won't believe what we've taken on board, why, a good half of those warheads are of the ground-burrowing variety. That's sure a first."

Not giving this revelation much thought, Valenko asked, "Has Senior Lieutenant Leonov shown up yet? I understand that the poor fellow has had his share of problems this shore leave."

Chuchkin said grimly, "We still haven't heard a word from him. You know, I led a bunch of us into Petropavlovsk last night to search for him. We hit Comrade Leonov's place twice, and almost every bar and brothel in town. With that blizzard coming down, we almost froze our balls off in the process. If it wasn't for the vodka, we would never have made it back."

The captain checked his watch. "Thanks for that, Chief. He's still got another hour before being officially A.W.O.L. Let's just keep our fingers crossed and hope he shows up. Now, I'd better get moving myself. I'm sure that you know all about tomorrow's illustrious guests."

Chuchkin's eyes gleamed. "I'll say, Captain. Since word was released yesterday, that's all the crew's been talking about. To think that the Premier of the Motherland and the Admiral of the Fleet will be walking these very decks in twenty-four hours time!

124

This is certainly a proud moment for the men of the *Vulkan*."

"To discuss the final preparations, I'll be calling a meeting of all available hands in the wardroom in an hour's time. This will be the *Vulkan*'s moment in the sun and I want her to shine!"

"Don't worry, Captain. The *zampolit* has already spoken to us once this morning. You know, he's personally supervising the clean-up detail."

"So Comrade Novikov is finally earning his pay," Valenko mumbled. "I'd better see how we stand. See you in sixty minutes, Chief."

"Aye, aye, Captain," Chuchkin said, and he went back to studying his manual.

As the captain proceeded to his cabin, he realized that he had almost forgotten the incident with the catwalk. There promised to be much to do during the next few hours, and he decided that a brief memo covering the collapse would be sufficient. Faced with his present responsibilities, thoughts of the outside world were already dissipating.

This redirection of thought was emphasized as he passed by the wardroom. There, sitting at the table nearest the door, was Ivan Novikov. The political officer was busy whittling a hand-sized piece of wood, while a quartet of conscripts were busy scrubbing the other tables with stiff-bristle brushes. Suddenly conscious of another's presence, the *zampolit* looked up and identified the captain. Valenko could have sworn that the weasel-eyed man actually paled and looked surprised to see him. Valenko noticed that even his adversary's hands were slightly trembling.

This shocked silence could mean only one thing:

The *zampolit*, who had reported their confrontation to command, was probably certain that a new captain would be assigned to the *Vulkan*. Valenko smiled inwardly. Noviko was obviously shaken upon seeing him standing there, his command still firmly in place. The political officer would think twice now before he again challenged the captain's authority.

Valenko's train of thought was interrupted by the approach of a familiar, slovenly dressed, pot-bellied, sour-eyed figure. Only when Chief Cook Anatoly Irkutsk began whining did the captain break his eye contact with Novikov.

"I tell you, Captain, you must do something about the garbage they sent us yesterday. Half of that trash isn't fit for a pigsty. There's cabbage there with worms in it bigger than my little finger. And that meat! I've seen sick horses looking better."

"Easy now, Comrade," Valenko advised calmly. "I'm afraid that you make these same observations every time we restock here. Yet not once have we lost a man to bad food."

"Oh, but this time it's different, Captain! Never have I seen such poor quality. I tell you, someone's making a fortune by selling the food meant for us and substituting this rubbish."

Valenko sighed. "Show me this spoiled food, Chef Anatoly, and I'll tell you if a report to command is in order."

Following on Irkutsk's heels, the captain crossed to the galley, already absorbed by the day's first crisis. Observing his every step with an icy stare of disbelief was Ivan Novikov.

* * *

Forty-two thousand feet above the Sea of Okhotsk, the massive Ilyushin IL-76 jet aircraft belonging to the General Secretary of the Soviet Union soared eastward. One of the largest vehicles of its type in the world, the plane, which was also known as "the flying Kremlin," was jam-packed with sophisticated command and communications gear. Every aspect of Russia's strategic war-fighting ability could be monitored and controlled from there. Thus, it provided a most survivable platform in the event a nuclear crisis demanded the evacuation of Moscow.

On this particular fall morning, the IL-76 was about to complete the first leg of a top-priority shuttle flight. It had just crossed the breadth of the Rodina, and would soon attempt its first trans-Pacific trip, with a final destination of Los Angeles, California.

Sheltered within its comfortable, wide-bodied confines was a hand-picked flight crew, two dozen systems operators and a contingent led by Premier Viktor Rodin himself. His trusted advisory staff of political and military experts were there to provide their expertise, if needed, in the upcoming summit. They sat in a separate compartment located immediately in front of the wing.

The General Secretary was sequestered in his private office, set behind the cockpit. Decorated rather luxuriously for the interior of a plane, this wood-paneled area featured a massive walnut desk and a round conference table. It was at the head of this table that Viktor Rodin was seated. Gazing out of one of the IL-76's few windows, he studied the scenery below.

The morning was proving to be a clear one. Lit by

the weak arctic sun, Rodin was able to get a clear view of the sea. Even from this height, he identified what appeared to be a single destroyer pounding its way westward. Except for this vessel, no other ship was in sight. The monotonous roar of the plane's four Soloviev turbofan engines sounded in the distance and the plane dipped slightly as it passed through an air pocket.

Rodin sat back and caught his own reflection in the window, superimposed on powdery blue Siberian sky. He inspected his perfectly styled, straight black hair. Neatly parted on the side, his hairline had yet to show any sign of receding. Running his hand down his square-cut jawline, the forty-nine-year-old Soviet leader inspected features that only hinted at his Great Russian ancestry. Even with the bushy dark eyebrows and high cheek bones, he appeared much like a Western European. Dressed in his tailored, French-cut suit, he could just as easily pass for the director of a bank—or even a Wall Street broker. His wife always reminded him of this fact, but his good looks certainly didn't hurt when it came to public appearances. This was especially true of his first visit to Europe, where he was surprised to find himself something of a media star. Try as he could to remain humble, he was actually learning to enjoy the constant attention.

The trip to Los Angeles would be his first visit to the United States. Here he planned to use his looks to his best advantage. Aware of American suspicions of the stodgy old statesmen who had previously represented the Motherland, he hoped to gain the trust of the U.S. citizens. Nowhere on the planet were people more media conscious. At the side of their handsome new President, Rodin would look most compatible. Half the battle of understanding would already have been won.

He had spent three weeks extensively preparing for the summit. Yet, more than intricate bargaining, he hoped to be able to explain the general principles underlying his vision. He would leave all the details to his aides. At the moment, it was more important for him and Robert Palmer to know exactly what the other really wanted. Rodin was confident that their goals were the same. It would be their difficult task to tear down the walls of misunderstanding that had separated their two cultures for almost one hundred years. Each leader was already well aware that some of the most perplexing obstacles were to be found inside of their own countries.

Rodin's present visit to Petropavlovsk underscored this fact. They would be landing there not only to refuel, but also to initiate the elimination of just such an interior obstacle. In this case, the opponent was not a Western diplomat, but the Fleet Admiral of the Soviet Union.

Stanislav Sorokin was an already-legendary individual. As the unquestioned father of the Russian Navy, the admiral's vision couldn't be ignored. A lifetime of vigilant public dedication had led to the creation of one of the most powerful fleets ever to sail the seas. Now . . . how did one go about telling such a person that, if all went as planned, such an armada would no longer be necessary?

The time for following the grand old admirals and generals had passed. Today, an enlightened world populace demanded an end to the paranoid military madness that was choking the planet's continued development. Newly elected leaders such as Viktor Rodin and Robert Palmer were the hand-choosen spokesmen of this dynamic generation. It was now up to them to tell the members of their military-industrial complexes that they would no longer have a blank check to play with.

Of course, Rodin knew just what the power-brokers' reactions would be. He therefore moved cautiously in consolidating his power. Otherwise, his policies wouldn't stand a chance. He began his consolidation in the Politboro. This all-powerful committee of thirteen ruled virtually all aspects of the Rodina's direction. Today he could say with confidence that half of the Politboro were solidly behind him. Any time now the remaining hardliners, who were generally well into their seventies, would be stepping down and their replacements would guarantee Rodin a majority. Old age and its resulting ill health were already one of Rodin's best allies. Such prominent figures as Yuri Polnocny and the once-feared Konstantin Belchenko no longer had the stamina to effectively oppose his efforts. The path to nuclear disarmament never looked so promising.

To guarantee the loyalty of the military, Rodin knew that he would have to proceed with utmost care. For that reason, his presummit meeting with Stanislav Sorokin was almost as important as the summit itself. The admiral and his associates had to be reassured that their services would still be vital in the new order to follow. Rodin hoped to paint a picture of a navy without guns. Freed from the wasteful restraints of needless war games and alerts, such a force could concentrate on developing the planet's oceans to their full potential. The source of incredible food and mineral wealth, the oceans could be properly harvested to insure a better life for all.

To Rodin, such a vision made a lot more sense than one predicated on death and destruction. From his window, the Premier caught sight of the western shoreline of the Kamchatka peninsula. The snow-covered expanse was dominated by a thick forest. This was only one tiny portion of the massive Siberian woods over which they had been flying for several hours. Conscious of the utter immensity of the planet itself, Rodin shuddered in anticipation of the greatness that could come from a world in which peace truly prevailed. Without insatiable military budgets to drain them dry, the earth's population would be free to flourish as never before. The hungry would be fed, the cold clothed, the sick healed. Since man craved competition, let the arena be of an economic nature. Though a socialistic order would eventually prevail, there were positive sides to the capitalistic approach that couldn't be ignored. Let the two systems merge, and the result would be a hybrid combining each side's strengths.

Rodin had read several campaign speeches in which Robert Palmer had promoted a similar solution to the earth's problems. Since the American had been elected to his nation's highest office in a landslide victory, the people were ripe for change. The chances for realistic progress had never been better. Both leaders were in the proverbial right place at the right time. By being true to their convictions, they could proceed with that all-important first step—the elimination of all nuclear weapons.

A knock on the cabin door broke through the silence, and the Premier reluctantly interrupted his train of thought.

"Yes?"

The door popped open and Olga Tyumen, Rodin's shapely, blonde-haired personal assistant, entered. She carried a large plastic serving tray, which she placed on the table directly before Rodin.

"I thought some tea and pastries would do you no harm, Comrade General Secretary. After all, you ate practically nothing at breakfast."

Rodin eyed the assortment of cakes, which indeed looked appetizing. With his beloved Anna back in Moscow with their two children, it was now Olga's duty to make sure that he didn't starve himself.

"Thank you, my dear," Rodin said, as he reached for an apple tart. "As usual, I forgot all about my stomach. Would you care to join me?"

Olga smiled and smoothed down her waistline. "I think I'll wait for lunch, sir. I wouldn't want to ruin my diet."

Viktor took a bite of the tart while eyeing her suspiciously. "With a figure like yours, you worry about dieting? Don't you women realize that a man likes a little soft skin around the edges?"

Olga laughed at this and bent to pour him some tea. He couldn't help but admire the ample bust that stretched her blouse taut. Olga Tyumen could leave a married man breathless, a fact that she must have been well aware of.

"And how are my associates handling the flight so far?"

"Most of them have slept all morning. With the time changes and all, one gets most confused.

Rodin sipped his tea thoughtfully. "And how about yourself, Comrade? Are you still anxious to see Los Angeles?"

Olga beamed. "Of course, sir. It's like a dream come true. I can't wait to see Disneyland!"

"Disneyland? Do you mean to say that you're about to travel halfway around the world just to visit a make-believe fantasy world dedicated to a cartoon duck and a mouse?"

Olga blushed. "I'm sorry, sir, but this is something I've wanted to see since I was a child."

"There's no need for apologies," returned the Premier. "I was only playing with you. In a way, I, too, am anxious to see what's so special about this amusement park. I must admit, though, that touring it with the U.S. President will be most unique. If only my children could have been with us. . . . You'll be sure to help me with the proper souvenirs."

"Of course, Comrade General Secretary. I'll be happy to."

The whine of the jet engines changed noticeably as the hint of a pressure alteration pressed on their eardrums. A muted electronic tone sounded, followed by a woman's soothing voice.

"The captain would like to inform you that we are beginning our descent into Petropavlovsk. Please extinguish all cigarettes and fasten your seat belts."

Rodin hastily finished his tart and the tea. Olga stepped forward to remove the tray.

"Thanks for the snack, my dear. I feel better already."

Olga nodded and left the cabin as quietly as she had entered. Viktor Rodin was alone once again. After making sure that his seat belt was buckled, he swiveled around and peered out the window. He saw they were over the sea once again, although this time he knew the body of water to be the Pacific Ocean. As the IL-76 pulled out of a tightly banked turn, he got his first view of the city for which they were headed. Petropavlovsk lay glistening in an ample coat of newly fallen snow. Fortunately, the storm front had long passed and the skies remained clear.

Rodin stirred as a loud, grinding sound beneath them indicated that the landing gear was being extended. The plane slowed as the engines again changed octaves. Still glued to the window, the Premier could now see the first of the port facilities. This included over a half-dozen destroyers, a large missile-carrying cruiser and various support ships. He also spotted the dockside concrete pens where the Third Fleet's submarines were moored. Further inland, they passed over an installation bristling with antennas and radar domes. This all-important site was the heart of the facility. Dozens of individual figures could be seen busily walking to and from this central structure.

And just how would the face of the base change if the summit with Robert Palmer proved successful? Rodin pondered this fascinating question as the airport came into view, opposite what appeared to be a huge, wooded public park. So intense was his train of thought that not even the jolt of the plane's twenty-wheel landing gear biting the pavement disturbed him.

Fleet Admiral Stanislav Sorokin waited impatiently for the glistening, silver-skinned IL-76 to halt before the gate. The command plane had been flying with the benefit of a stiff tailwind and had arrived a good thirty minutes before schedule. Sorokin was pleased with this, for their day promised to be a busy one.

Their first stop, after leaving the airport, would be at the sub pens. Here, the Premier would be escorted on a personal tour of their latest Delta III-class ballistic-missile-carrying sub, the *Vulkan*. Sorokin couldn't help but laugh at the irony of it all. Ignorant of the plan already set in motion, Rodin would be meeting the crew that would soon be responsible for his incineration. If the "man of peace" only knew the ultimate destination of the missiles he would soon be inspecting!

So far, Operation Counterforce was proceeding without serious difficulties. Their only major setback had been the KGB's failure to eliminate Petyr Valenko, the *Vulkan*'s present captain. The hit on Valenko had been ordered following a report from the sub's *zampolit*. Two sloppy attempts on his life had met with no success. The local operatives were far from the professionals who worked out of Moscow, and their incompetency wouldn't be ignored. Yet, it was doubtful Valenko had any reason to believe he hadn't merely been the victim of two unrelated accidents. Whatever, Konstantin Belchenko didn't seem too concerned that the captain remained on duty. A phone call to his dacha in Penza had reconfirmed Belchenko's belief that ways would be found to work around Petyr Valenko.

Sorokin hated having one of his line officers handled in this manner. Valenko had an unblemished service record. He didn't seem to be the type that had strong political convictions, but the admiral couldn't ignore the warnings of the frantic *zampolit*. One more individual would be sacrificed for the good of the masses.

The grinding whine of the IL-76's turbofan engines sounded clearly inside the terminal, and Sorokin walked calmly to the observation window. With his right hand, he vainly attempted to smooth down the wild tufts of thin white hair that never seemed to stay in place. He took a deep breath and prepared to meet the man whom he had already condemned to a fiery death. He looked on as the aircraft slowly pulled up to the terminal, appearing like a ponderous, prehistoric beast. The plane halted, a walkway leading directly into the interior was connected, and minutes later his grinning, youthful guest appeared. With a forced diplomatic smile, Sorokin met the Premier with a hug and kisses on both cheeks.

"Good morning, Comrade General Secretary. Welcome to Petropavlovsk."

Rodin stretched his cramped frame and politely answered, "Thank you, Admiral Sorokin. It's been much too long since I've visited this portion of the Rodina. How have you been?"

"As well as a man of my advanced years can be," Sorokin said without much emotion.

Rodin shook his head. "I just hope that I can remain as active as you when I reach your age, Comrade. I see we've had a little snowstorm."

"It wasn't the first of the season, and it won't be the last," the admiral commented.

"We've been lucky so far in Moscow. The autumn weather has never been so glorious. Of course, now I have the warm, sunny skies of Los Angeles to look forward to."

Sorokin smiled at that. "If you're ready, Comrade General Secretary, I think it's best that we get moving. Our schedule today is a tight one."

"I was expecting as much," Rodin responded, and turned to issue last-minute instructions to Olga Tyumen and the rest of his staff.

Ten minutes later, the Premier and the admiral were cruising down the icy streets of Petropavlovsk. From the spacious back seat of a black Zil limousine, they watched the busy city pass. An awkward moment of silence prevailed. It proved to be Viktor Rodin who cleared his throat and initiated the conversation.

"This city has certainly grown since my last visit. I can attribute the orderliness of this expansion to the navy, Admiral. Your planners did an excellent job of anticipating the future needs of this expanding port facility. As always, I commend you for your foresight."

Sorokin merely nodded at the compliment as Rodin continued. "I have been meaning to meet with you for some time now. As you know, these past two years have been hectic ones for me. Establishing one's power base in the Kremlin can be most tiring, but the effort shall soon pay off handsomely."

Rodin broke off his discourse when the car suddenly skidded on a patch of ice while rounding a broad curve. The alert driver steered into the direction of the skid and soon had the limo back under complete control.

"I imagine that these streets must have been impassable earlier. By the way, are we headed to the base now?"

Sorokin replied flatly, "That we are, sir. Your welcoming speech has been delayed until after your inspection of the *Vulkan*. Since their orders have them sailing on the noon tide, this scheduling change was necessitated."

"There's no trouble with that, Admiral. I'd much rather have the opportunity to meet the brave crew of one of the Motherland's most advanced vessels than hurry off to give one of my infamous speeches."

A shattering *crack* echoed off the window beside Viktor Rodin. Both men instinctively ducked, while the limo swerved and quickly gained speed.

"What the hell?" said the admiral incredulously.

Cautiously, they peeked up and saw the remnants of an icy snowball sticking to the tinted glass.

"Easy, Admiral, it's only a child's errant toss."

Turning in an attempt to get a look at the portion of wooded parkland they were passing, Sorokin cursed. "I'll bet my pension that hooligans were responsible for that so-called innocent snowball. You see, we've had similar problems here before. A squadron of militia will cool their bravado."

Rodin had trouble comprehending the source of the admiral's anger. "Let them be, Comrade. There was no harm done, except a brief scare. Tell me if you weren't tempted as a child to hit just such a target?"

The red-faced commander of the fleet gradually directed his glance away from the woods. "I still think that whoever was responsible should be taught a lesson. The next time, a vehicle could be sent totally

138

out of control. And who knows what deviant behavior this could lead to! The time to stop such foolishness is now, while the perpetrator is still young enough to be taught a lesson."

Shocked by his host's temper, Rodin changed the direction of their pointless dialogue as the naval base came into view. "Ah, I see that we are at the facility already. I had hoped that we could have taken this time to really talk. There are some matters of the highest importance that I must discuss with you. Since my schedule has me tightly booked until tomorrow morning's flight, why don't you come along with me to Los Angeles? The trip over the Pacific will give us an ample opportunity to really get to know each other."

The surprise invitation left the admiral speechless. Ignoring the pounding in his chest, he strove to keep his emotions in check, while pondering the dire implications of such a flight.

Rodin noticed his host's inaction and commented accordingly. "Did you hear me, Admiral? Well—what do you say to being my guest aboard the flying Kremlin? I'll even see about arranging a pass for you to tour Disneyland with us."

Not believing what he was hearing, Sorokin struggled to voice his response. "This invitation is most gracious, Comrade General Secretary, but like yourself, I, too, have a busy schedule. Tomorrow at noon I'm off to Vladivostok, where I'll be inspecting the headquarters of our famed Fifth Squadron."

"Delay it," Rodin said. "Surely you can complete this inspection upon our return. How many opportunities do you and I have to really sit down and empty our hearts? I have much to share with you and I'm sure that you do likewise. No, I insist that you come along."

The limo ground to a halt and, while the driver displayed their entry pass at the guard post, Stanislav Sorokin reluctantly nodded his head.

"I would be honored to accompany you to Los Angeles, Comrade General Secretary," he said gravely.

The Zil had already entered the base by the time Rodin answered. "Excellent, Admiral. I look forward to our chat. Who knows what great ideas you and I will come up with? Why, our flight could change the world!"

If only you knew the validity of that statement, Sorokin thought. He sat back as the young politician picked up the car phone and informed his assistant to begin readying the admiral's travel papers. The familiar base passed in a blur around him as he contemplated the inevitable result of the trip.

The General Secretary had trapped him quite effectively. Even with the powerful clout of his years in the military, one didn't go about refusing the Motherland's chief executive. Any more excuses on his part would only incur Rodin's curiosity. That could be instantly fatal to his dreams. After so many years of self-sacrifice, this final oblation would be well worth the effort. Even if it did cost him his life, Operation Counterforce had to go forth as scheduled. Only in this way would his life's work not be wasted.

Sorokin hardly took notice as the Zil crossed through the base's administrative complex, where the flag-draped bleachers and reviewing stand were set up. Without slowing, the auto continued on past a

140

line of corrugated warehouses and came to a halt outside the concrete pens that housed the Third Fleet's submarines.

Captain Petyr Valenko found himself busy with a seemingly endless series of last-minute details. Not only was he concerned with the upcoming visit by two of the country's most esteemed personalities, but also with implementing the shocking orders he had received barely an hour before. Inside the sealed directive were commands instructing him to take the *Vulkan* back on patrol with the afternoon tide.

His first thought was that there had to be some kind of mistake. Short of active combat conditions, no Soviet warship would be sent back to sea with so little port time. As he thought about it, he realized that he should have read the writing on the wall when they first pulled in to Petropavlovsk. Hardly a day had passed before the dock crew was busy loading a new complement of missiles. And how could he ignore the swiftness with which their foodstuffs had been replaced? Since the orders were signed by the same admiral who would be entering the sub any minute now, Valenko knew that Sorokin could explain exactly what this hasty reassignment was all about. Doubting that he would summon the nerve to make such an inquiry, he decided to play it cool. If the opportunity presented itself, he would present his question as adroitly as possible.

Valenko had used great discretion in relaying the sailing orders to his senior officers. As it turned out, only the recently returned Vasili Leonov took this call to sea happily. The *Vulkan*'s senior lieutenant was apparently anxious for any excuse to get as far away from Petropavlovsk as possible. Valenko couldn't blame the sad-eyed young man for feeling that way.

The red-headed officer had reappeared five minutes before his official leave expired. Sour-faced and uncommunicative, Leonov thanked the captain for his concern, yet begged him not to bring up the subject of his girl's defection. That was fine with Valenko, who wanted only to console his second in command. Leonov was equally tight-lipped with the other men, and the captain watched him guardedly as he performed his duties. Seeing competent work, Valenko was satisfied.

One individual who still concerned him was the sub's *michman*. Stefan Kuzmin had taken the news of their impending cruise badly. Valenko watched the blood drain from his friend's face when he announced the orders in the wardroom. Immediately after the briefing, he took the warrant officer aside to speak with him personally. These were their first words together since the previous night's dinner party. Intimately, Stefan told him of the plans he had made with his family. Many of them included Ivana and Valenko. Mindful of the manner in which the captain had gotten along with his sister-in-law, Stefan spoke as though he and Valenko were already members of the same family.

The captain didn't mind his familiarity in the least. In a way, he felt extra responsible for the *michman*'s peace of mind, and did his best to ease Stefan's emotional pain. The captain's words of assurance rang hollowly. First and foremost, as naval officers

142

their duty was to the Rodina. In this respect, their families were secondary. Certainly this call to sea was unexpected, but every military man knew that a change of plans within the services was as common as spring rain. Above all, they had to grow up and face their responsibilities. Hard as it may seem now, command had to have some sort of extreme need of their services to ask this of them. Besides, the patrol couldn't last long. In another month's time their reactor core was due for replacement. They'd be back in port for a nice long rest within three weeks.

These words had had their desired effect, and Stefan soon accepted their new duty without additional complaint. As Valenko watched the *michman* at work in the control room, he found himself happy with their new friendship. Now, if Ivana only stayed around to greet him on his return, his joy would be complete.

Valenko was in the midst of his final inspection of the *Vulkan* when Lev Zinyakin, the sub's sonar officer, came rushing into the control room. The wide-eyed Lithuanian excitedly addressed Valenko.

"Captain, they're here! The limousine has just pulled up to the gangplank."

Valenko reacted cooly. "Very well. Comrades, please man your stations. Senior Lieutenant, inform the crew to make ready for inspection."

Vasili Leonov clicked his heels, pivoted and depressed a plastic toggle switch set beside the communications console. In response, four muted tones bellowed forth from the sub's public-address system.

Taking a second to make certain his uniform was in order, Valenko positioned himself beside the forward hatchway. Proud of the men who stood beside him, the captain snapped to attention as their first visitor completed the short descent into the sub's interior.

Fleet Admiral Sorokin led the way. The white-haired, hefty figure looked larger than life as he stood there—his medallion-filled, gold-trimmed blue uniform clearly illuminated by the recessed lighting. Before greeting the captain he made certain that his companion cleared the stairway without incident. Only when General Secretary Rodin climbed down the final rung did Sorokin return the captain's salute.

"Requesting permission to come aboard, Captain Valenko."

"Permission granted." Valenko was excited at seeing not only the ruddy, jowled figure of his commanding officer, but also the trim, familiar individual who stood beside him.

The admiral noticed Valenko's stare and wasted no time with the introductions. "Captain Petyr Valenko, may I present General Secretary Viktor Rodin."

Formal as this salutation may have seemed, the immaculately suited statesman stepped forward and warmly shook Valenko's hand. "It is an honor to meet you, Captain. We share much in common, for as a youth I, too, wanted to become a submariner. As it turned out, the Party had other intentions for my services."

Instantly at ease with this guest, Valenko said, "Please feel free to make the *Vulkan* your home. It's not often that we entertain visitors, but we will try our best to make your tour an enlightening one. Shall we start here in the control room?"

"That would be most appropriate," replied the

admiral. "It's about time that I was able to meet some of the men I always seem to be reading such good things about."

Without further delay, Valenko introduced them to Senior Lieutenant Leonov, Warrant Officer Kuzmin, and the various systems operators. Last in line was the *zampolit*. Ivan Novikov remained unemotional while being presented to the Premier, yet seemed noticeably impressed upon meeting the admiral's handshake.

"You don't know what a distinction it is to finally meet you, Admiral Sorokin," the political officer said. "I have read each one of your textbooks, and agree with your theories completely."

"Ah, a fan at last," Sorokin beamed, and allowed himself to be dragged into a discussion of the importance of naval power as an instrument of state policy.

While these two were so preoccupied, Valenko began explaining the purposes of the various consoles surrounding them. The captain could tell by Rodin's questions that he had a quick, probing intellect. Since the Premier had been a member of his high school's DOSAAF (All-Union Voluntary Society for Assistance to the Navy), he had an elementary knowledge of the basics of seamanship. The majority of his inquiries concerned the various sensors and weapons systems the *Vulkan* carried. Whenever possible, Valenko let the officers in charge of the particular area supply the answers.

Premier Rodin smiled with delight when Lev Zinyakin invited him to have a seat at the sonar console. With the aid of a pair of headphones, the General Secretary got an on-the-spot lesson in the detection of underwater targets. This exercise took on added realism when Zinyakin actually turned on their active sonar. When their ping deflected off the flanks of a school of startled fish swimming beneath the hull, Rodin's eyes lit up.

To answer the General Secretary's questions regarding their armament capabilities, the captain called upon the expertise of Yuri Chuchkin. The good-natured weapons chief wasted no time in inviting them to visit the restricted area that comprised the majority of the sub's length.

The journey down to the missile magazine allowed the two V.I.P.s to get a good idea of what life aboard the *Vulkan* was really like. In general, they found the hallways they passed through crowded, yet spotlessly clean. The crew was well behaved and most cordial. Valenko was impressed by the manner in which the Premier stopped to chat with several of the conscripts. Though he might only ask their name and hometown, this jesture proved excellent for morale. When the enlisted men learned that they would be going to sea again in only a couple of more hours, this extra enthusiasm would be most appreciated.

The Premier couldn't help but inquire why the missile compartment was fondly known as the *taiga*. This question answered itself when the locked hatchway was opened and he set his eyes on an immense canyon of green-painted silos. He immediately associated the sixteen launch tubes with the thick trunks of the mighty conifers that occupied the northern regions of the Motherland. They proceeded carefully down the metallic catwalk that separated the tubes into two lines of eight silos. For several seconds, an eerie silence permeated the compartment as both guests

146

contemplated the destructive might stored there.

As they exited, Admiral Sorokin patted the outer walls of the silo marked 1. All too soon he and the Premier would once again be encountering the object stored inside. A chill shot up his spine as he visualized the fiery consumation of that final meeting.

It was during tea in the wardroom that Viktor Rodin formally addressed his select group of tour guides. In a brief speech he thanked the officers for their hospitality and applauded the crew as a whole. He then went on to emphasize the significance of the summit meeting upon which he was about to embark. He left them with a somewhat puzzling declaration that hinted at a possible change in the *Vulkan*'s duty in the years to come.

Astounded by Rodin's audacity, the admiral stood to make some closing remarks of his own. Praising the *Vulkan*'s patrol record, Sorokin stressed the importance of their present duty. Their diligence alone assured the Rodina that the enemy would think twice about starting any surprise hostilities. After thanking them for their sacrifice, the admiral cut his words short after noticing the clock mounted on the galley wall.

Since they had stayed well over their allotted time, the good-byes were short and sweet. As the big-boned admiral led the way out of the forward hatch, Viktor Rodin turned to invite Valenko to visit him in Moscow during his spring leave, if possible. Surprised by the unexpected offer, the captain humbly accepted.

Two hours later, while the General Secretary was immersed in his conciliatory speech to Petropavlovsk's naval hierarchy, the last mooring line was detached from the *Vulkan*'s bow. Without the aid of a tug, the sub reversed the spin of its dual-shaft propellers and backed into the icy waters of Taliniskaia Bay.

It was Captain Valenko who first noticed the empty slip where the *Cheka* had been docked earlier. Feeling they weren't so alone after all, he handed the helm to his doleful-eyed senior lieutenant. Valenko then proceeded anxiously to his cabin to open the second set of sealed orders awaiting him there. Only then would he know where in the world they were presently bound.

Approximately 4,180 miles west of the Kamchatka peninsula, the sun was just breaking the eastern horizon. For Konstantin Belchenko it would prove to be another long day. A ringing telephone had roused him from his warm bed over an hour ago. The first deputy director soaked in the admiral's frantic words and promised to call him back as soon as a solution to the dilemma was worked out. Since the problem was a difficult one, he dressed warmly and decided upon a contemplative walk on the grounds of his dacha.

The air was chilly but fresh as he moved his slender frame outdoors. By the light of the dawn sky, he made his way carefully to the road leading down to the Sura. A crow cried harshly as a rippling northern breeze blew through the surrounding birch wood. As he crossed the forest, the trail gradually widened and he was able to increase his pace. By the time he could hear the flow of crashing waters, his newly circulated blood had warmed his stiff, frozen limbs.

Sorokin's frantic phone call had given Belchenko quite a shock: Viktor Rodin had invited the admiral to accompany him to Los Angeles. The ultimate consequences of such a trip were obvious.

Belchenko's first reaction was that the admiral come up with some kind of excuse to decline this request. But the admiral had already tried that gambit, and every excuse he used had been firmly resisted by the Premier. Not desiring to make Rodin overly suspicious, he had been forced, reluctantly, to agree to go along.

Belchenko walked slowly while his mind raced. The banks of the river were in sight as he followed the trail up to the summit of a treeless hillside. Upon reaching the clearing he was consumed by a fit of violent coughing. Stabbing pains pierced his lungs as he vainly attempted to catch his breath. Only after spitting up a red-speckled mass of congealed phlegm did the choking fit subside.

Whenever he thought he had his sickness licked, his lungs would spasm and tell him otherwise. There could be no ignoring what it meant. Most likely this would be the illness that would take him to his deathbed.

A ray of direct sunlight broke through the misty veil that had settled over the eastern portion of the river valley. A flock of song birds called out behind him. But Belchenko realized that he had no time left for contemplating Nature's bounty . . . or his approaching death.

Years of selfless dedication and hard work were finally about to pay off. Unfortunately, there would be some casualties along the way. Stanislav Sorokin had been right to accept his fate in such an exalted manner. At least he could die knowing that his

149

sacrifice had been for the good of the cause. And what a cause it was!

Peering out over the river valley one last time, Belchenko watched a hawk soaring gracefully above. This successful survivor knew the secret of eternal vigilance. Viktor Rodin and his meek followers were like the hawk's prey. Groveling in the dirt like cowards, those weak fools were about to surrender the fruits of decades of hard work and sacrifice. And for what—a magically transformed world of peace and equality?

Nonsense! Like the snakes they were, the imperialists could never be trusted. Centuries of decadent greed were not about to disappear with the signing of a single treaty. One thing that the capitalists were experts at was taking advantage of those in a weaker bargaining position. Viktor Rodin was merely the answer to their prayers.

Blinded by the illusion of peace, the Soviet Union would disarm itself of its strategic inventory. But the Yankees would make a sham out of their own disarmament. Then, like the Nazi hordes under the madman Hitler, the Americans would pull out the nuclear weapons they had cleverly been hiding. Powerless to respond to such a threat, the Soviet Union would be at the mercy of its sworn enemy.

After Krushchev's bungling of the Cuban missile crisis, Belchenko swore that he would never again allow the Motherland to bargain from a position of weakness. Patriots such as Stanislav Sorokin had helped make this promise a reality. Parity had been achieved, and now the Rodina was even said to have the upper hand. Viktor Rodin wanted to negate their efforts with one simple sweep of his pen.

If it was necessary, then the admiral would indeed have to die in Los Angeles. There was too much at stake to become cowards now.

An intense pain seared his left side, and Belchenko had no doubt that he'd be joining his old friend shortly. They could meet death bravely, knowing that Operation Counterforce would insure the existence of the Rodina for many generations to come.

Chapter Six

Junior Lieutenant Andrie Yakalov's present duty was a dream come true. Since he was a child in the Ukrainian wheat fields outside of Kiev, airplanes had always fascinated him. Just to see aircraft passing in the skies above was enough to thrill him. He would not have believed that, one day soon, his service to the Motherland would find him flying almost five days out of every week.

Long was the road that brought him to his current duty as sensor operator aboard an Ilyushin IL-38 turboprop command plane. Yakalov had consigned himself to the fact that he would most likely follow his forefathers into the wheatfields. Though the youngster dreamed of flying off to foreign lands, he never really thought such an opportunity would come his way. His chance came during his eighth-grade exams. It was at this time that he was found to have unusually sensitive hearing. The school's DOSAAF administrator reported this to Kiev, and several weeks later he received a letter inviting him to enter the Nakhimov Naval School in far-off Sevastopol. Here he would be given further tests and, upon passing them, would be given the opportunity to earn a naval commission. Though he was ecstatic, his parents were somewhat saddened by the fact that they would soon be losing their boy for good. Knowing a rare opportunity when he saw it, Yakalov packed up his few belongings and anxiously initiated the long train ride south to the legendary Black Sea port. Once there, he passed his tests easily and was soon on the way to realizing his dream.

The Il-38 bucked in a pocket of headwind, and the junior lieutenant snapped from his reverie. Still having trouble believing the reality of his present duty, he checked the bank of instruments for which he was currently responsible. Before him were the controls to the plane's sonobuoys, hydrophones, and the magnetic-anamoly detector, commonly called MAD. These sophisticated devices could be utilized to pick up the presence of the enemy's attack and missile-carrying submarines. This was quite an accomplishment, considering their normal cruising altitude was 20,000 feet above sea level.

They were currently over the Pacific ocean, somewhere between Vladivostok, their home base, and the Hawaiian Islands. They had been in the air for over seven hours now, and should be turning back west any moment.

So far, the flight had been an easy one for him. The majority of the patrol had been spent applying the IL-38's other capability, that of a communications relay platform for the Soviet Union's own submarines. The equipment, and the specialist who ran it, were in a separate compartment in the forward fuselage. Since the majority of that gear was top secret, Yakalov was quite happy to stay in his own quarters. One of the first lessons he had learned in Sevastopol was that, to get ahead in the military, one had to learn to mind one's own business.

Where Yakalov really wished he could venture was the cockpit. To him, this was where the action was coming down. He had tried hard to get into the pilot program, but had received one rejection letter after another. It was soon evident that the military wanted him for his ears, not his eyes. He thought it fitting that the tail section of the IL-38 didn't even have a window. This made it easier for him to concentrate with his other senses.

Able to check their course, altitude and airspeed, Yakalov had learned to mentally visualize the scenery that stretched out down below. Efficiently scanning the instruments, his gaze halted on a wallet-sized photograph he had taped to the bulkhead wall. Staring back at him were the figures of his mother, father, and teenage sister as they stood in the fields—the wheat up to their waists. Like looking back at a past life, he pondered the great change in not only his lifestyle, but his entire world outlook.

Farming was an important, noble occupation, but it offered nothing like the opportunities presented to a naval aviator. Already he had seen more of the Motherland than his forefathers had seen in their collective lifetimes. He would never forget the moment that he first set eyes on the Black Sea. Until then, the largest body of water he had seen was the lake where he and his father used to go carp fishing.

Once at the Nahkimov Institute, he had begun meeting lads his own age, the likes of which he never knew existed. Many were from Moscow itself, the sons of high-placed Party bureaucrats. Sophisticated and sure of themselves, they represented an alien world, far removed from the innocent milieu of the wheat fields. What Yakalov lacked in worldlines, he more than made up for in studious application. An avid reader since early childhood, he studied with a zeal that brought him to the upper tenth of his class.

After the completion of his second year of classes, he was given the choice of either duty aboard a ship or one of the new IL-38 flying platforms. Without hesitation, he picked air duty.

His memories of home all but faded as his mind filled with visions of assignments in foreign ports. Rumor had it that crews would soon be chosen for basing in Viet Nam's Cam Rahn Bay facility. Tropical duty was considered the best, not only for the mild weather, but Asia's gorgeous, exotic women. Other scuttlebutt mentioned that Cuba was to be the home of a large IL-38 contingent. That would even be more exciting!

To achieve such an assignment, Yakalov's record had to be spotless. Ever mindful of his still relatively low rank, he was the first to volunteer for unwanted assignments. He made certain that he could be known for his thorough, conscientious work. His effort was paying off, for this flight was his first without a supervisor. He had achieved this level of competency in an unprecedented six months' time after arriving in Vladivostok the previous spring. He was proud of this fact, and surprised when the pilot congratulated him for his achievement during the morning's briefing.

Yakalov had flown with Captain Gregor Silkin on

his last dozen missions. The gray-haired aviator was something of a legend to the younger officers, for he had been the first pilot to land a Yak-36 VTOL (Vertical Take-Off and Landing) jet fighter on the pitching deck of the carrier *Kiev*, in 1976. That Silkin had noticed him was a very good sign, indeed.

Unfortunately, Yakalov had trouble relating to the aircraft's other two occupants. The co-pilot, Senior Lieutenant Martyn Pilyar, seemed cold and distant. The communications specialist, Lieutenant Georgi Romanov, was downright hostile. The man hardly met his glance, as if he were embarrassed to know him.

In Sevastopol, Yakalov had encountered several individuals who seemed most disturbed with his humble origins. His advisor cautioned him that such antagonism would be present throughout his career, for discrimination abounded even in the Soviet Union. This was merely because his parents had not been Great Russian. Thus, he would have to work harder to make up in competence for his lack of the proper ancestors.

If this was the cause of Lieutenant Romanov's iciness, Yakalov knew that he'd have to proceed cautiously. Alienating the man would only lead to getting written up. This was something he had to avoid at all costs. He would keep his relations with the communication's specialist to a minimum and speak only when spoken to.

Again the plane shook in a pocket of gentle turbulence, and Yakalov's eyes went to the digital clock. The return point of their patrol radius was rapidly approaching. In fact, the junior lieutenant anticipated feeling the angled bank of the homeward turn any second now. To occupy his time until the moment came, he decided to have some lunch. A piece of crusty black bread, some fragrant goat cheese and a crispy, green apple comprised his feast. After washing it down with a cup of thermos-hot sweet tea, he burped and once more scanned the instruments. Amazingly enough, he found they were still headed in a northeasterly direction. Checking their flight time, he calculated that even if they turned around right now, chances were slim that they'd have enough fuel to reach Vladivostok. Perhaps Captain Silkin had an alternative destination not on their original flight plan. To double-check this possibility, he decided to chance a call to the cockpit.

Yakalov reached forward to trigger the intercom and, much to his surprise, he found it dead. This discovery disturbed him, and he decided that it would now be appropriate to make his way to the cockpit.

After unbuckling his seat belt, he stood and made his way to the sealed hatch leading to the communications compartment. Not looking forward to an encounter with Lieutenant Romanov, Yakalov took a deep breath and pushed open the doorway. He found the radio expert hunched over the very-low-frequency transmitter. So intense was his concentration that he didn't notice his new visitor until Yakalov had nearly crossed the room's length.

"Get back to your section, Comrade!" Romanov snapped tensely. "You have no business in these parts."

Halted by the stern words, Yakalov stuttered. "I—I—I want to talk to the Captain, and my intercom's not working."

Romanov exploded. "You fool! Don't you realize that we're in the midst of a Red Flag alert? The Captain has no time for your foolish small talk. Now, return to where you belong!"

Yakalov, not used to being spoken to with such rudeness, stood his ground. "Why wasn't I notified of the receipt of such an alert? I still think it's important that I have a word with Captain Silkin."

Impressed with his own bravado, the junior lieutenant resumed walking, oblivious to the radio officer's threats.

"Comrade Yakalov—I'm warning you to halt this insubordination at once!"

His heart pounding, Yakalov boldly opened the hatch leading to the flight deck. He would never forget the sight that awaited him there. Sitting stiffly in his padded leather chair was Captain Gregor Silkin. Staring outward, eyes unblinking, it was obvious that the pilot was dead. Yakalov's glance went from the bloody welt across the captain's right temple to the figure of the co-pilot, sitting calmly beside him. A gloating sneer painted Martin Pilyar's face as a pair of iron hands grabbed Yakalov tightly from behind.

"I told you to mind your own business," Romanov spat. "Now look what your peasant curiosity has led you to."

Ineffectively, Yakalov attempted to break the lieutenant's grasp. "What the hell is going on up here?"

Ignoring him, Pilyar reached forward and switched on the autopilot. "We'll dispose of this fool back in the radio room, Comrade Romanov. Hurry now, we are rapidly reaching the rendezvous coordinates."

Yakalov felt himself being dragged backward. As they reached the communications compartment, a high-pitched squeal sounded from the VLF receiver.

"It's the *Vulkan!*" exclaimed Romanov. "Hold this imbecile while I confirm the release code."

The co-pilot's icy grasp replaced Romanov's. With his arms held painfully from behind, Yakalov watched the radio expert hurry over to the transmitter. Not even taking the time to seat himself, he began signalling a Morse-coded message that Yakalov easily translated:

"Roger, Vulkan, this is May leader. We confirm alert code Red Flag, launch priority one. Release code, Delta-Bravo-Delta-Alpha-one-zero-one-niner-Foxtrot."

Romanov repeated the message; its implications set Yakalov's head spinning. Though the code at that time was different, he had participated in a war-alert exercise once before, and knew that he was hearing orders instructing a Soviet submarine to release its load of missiles. Were they, indeed, at war? Then why had the captain been murdered, and what was the reason for his current criminal treatment? No one in their right minds would deliberately start World War III, would they?

Yakalov trembled with dread as a simple morse-coded response broke from the transmitter.

"Red Flag alert confirmed. Vulkan."

A shout of glee broke from his captors throats.

"The First Deputy will be most pleased," added Romanov. "Now, what should we do with Yakalov here?"

"Whatever we do, it had better be quick," said the

co-pilot. "We've got to get into our parachuting gear. The rendezvous spot is only minutes away."

Romanov removed a hand-sized, hard rubber truncheon from the pocket of his flight suit. Smacking it in the palm of his hand, he approached his prisoner.

"Enjoy the rest of the trip, Comrade Yakalov. There's enough fuel to keep you airborne for another four hours. I'm afraid though that the landing may be a little bit wet."

A malicious gleam poured from Romanov's eyes as Yakalov struggled to free himself.

"You men are mad!" Any further comments from Yakalov were silenced by a painful crack on the forehead. Cold, black unconsciousness followed.

He came to groggily a half-hour later. Beyond the pulsating pain in his skull, the young Ukrainian was instantly aware of a frigid draft. His thoughts still hazy, he rolled over and attempted to orient himself. As the outline of the communications compartment came into focus, his jaw dropped as he saw the plane's forward emergency exit wide open. Satisfied that he had found the source of the draft, he allowed the steady drone of the IL-38's engines to further clear his tangled mind.

The shock of total realization hit him several minutes later. Was it but a horrible nightmare, or had Romanov and Pilyar indeed killed the captain and then issued orders to begin World War III?

His hair was matted with dried blood. Slowly, painfully, he tried to sit up. A wave of dizziness was suddenly compounded by nausea, and for a second he thought he might black out again. Fortunately, his lightheadedness passed and, with an effort, he was

160

able to stand.

His first duty was to close the emergency hatch. Carefully, he proceeded to the open doorway, using the equipment-packed wall of the fuselage to keep him balanced. He peeked outside and took in the vast, surging Pacific below. Thankfully, they were far below cruising altitude, eliminating the need for a pressurized cabin. He hit a button that sent the door slamming shut with a loud hiss.

The quiet was immediate, and it was soon noticeably warmer. Quickly now, Yakalov determined his next priority. Though he would have liked to do something about recontacting that submarine, his continued survival took precedence. Gently massaging his swollen forehead, he made his way to the flight deck.

Gregor Silkin's corpse was a bloody reminder that he had not merely awakened from a bad dream. Seated on the left side of the cockpit, the pilot looked as if he had received his death blow while in midsentence. Trying to ignore his startled, vacant stare, Yakalov positioned himself in the co-pilot's chair. He broke into a cold sweat and fought back panic as he surveyed the complex mass of instruments and remembered that he had yet to take his first official flying lesson!

Thankful for those precious patrols when his curiosity and persistence had drawn him to the flight deck, he was able to identify the altimeter, the horizontal-situation indicator, the air-speed counter and the fuel-quantity meter. He was extra cautious not to disturb the pearl-handled throttle to his left or the flap-control petals, which were recessed into the floor

161

board.

So far, the automatic pilot had done an admirable job of flying the lumbering aircraft. The weather remained clear and the fuel gauge showed at least another hour's worth of available flight time. Yakalov looked out into the vibrant, cloudless blue sky and visualized the moment when the four Ivchenko engines would guzzle their last drop of petrol. Unforgivingly, the IL-38 would plummet into the waiting sea below.

Vainly, the junior lieutenant searched the cabin for any type of manual that could explain the flight systems in greater detail. He grinned sardonically upon uncovering the only printed matter in sight—four dog-eared Swedish porn magazines.

Desperately, he attempted to clear his cluttered mind. There had to be some way out of this predicament. The answer presented itself when a throaty blast of static emanated from the headphones clipped to the left side of his headrest. Of course—he'd use the radio! At least he had had some experience in operating that system.

Fitting on the rubber-padded headset, he easily located the communications panel, set within arm's reach, to his right. Though his knowledge of transmitting frequencies was limited, he did know the band reserved for emergencies. Fighting to keep his hand from shaking, he dialed in the proper wavelength on the digital selector and hit the transmit button. The static immediately stopped its scratchy roar as he spoke into the chin-mounted microphone.

"Mayday! Mayday! This is May leader zero-two-niner requesting emergency assistance. I repeat, this

is May leader zero-two-niner requesting emergency assistance."

He listened intently to the receiving speakers, but heard only a lonely pulse of static. Faced with no alternatives, Yakalov sat forward and again hit the transmit button.

"Skipper, we're picking up some kind of transmission on the international distress band. You'd better take a listen. I think it's Russian."

Lieutenant Bill Todd, pilot of the Grumman E2-C Hawkeye early-warning aircraft, utilized the plane's intercom to reply to his Tactical Coordinator, Mac Arnold. "Roger, Mac. How about playing this call over the system so that we all can have a listen?"

Quick to accommodate his commanding officer, Arnold diverted the transmission so that the entire crew could hear it. It proved to be the co-pilot who identified the distant signal.

"It's Russian all right. The bogey refers to itself as 'May leader zero-two-niner,' and they are indeed requesting emergency assistance."

"Where's that signal coming from?" Lieutenant Todd asked.

Arnold responded instantly. "Our ALF-59 shows them at the limit of our northern periphery, some 500 miles distant."

"Who's working that district for the good guys, Mac?" the pilot queried.

Arnold checked the radar screen. "Tomcat two-zero-zero pulled that duty this afternoon, sir."

Todd's voice boomed with authority. "We'd better

163

pull two-zero-zero off his cap station and have him take a look. Mac, beam this distress call down to the *Kennedy*. I think the Admiral would like to take a listen."

Bill Todd turned off the intercom. The tanned, curly-haired aviator turned to his right and caught the eye of his co-pilot.

"Well, Lieutenant, do you know enough of that Ruskie lingo to try a response?"

The young flyer smiled. "I've been itching to put to use those two grueling years of Soviet language studies at the Academy, sir."

Todd nodded. "Then let's give 'em a jingle. Even without knowing Russian, I'd say that the voice belonging to that plea is damn scared."

The co-pilot selected the proper frequency and spoke fluidly into his chin-mounted transmitter. Thirty seconds later a startled yet clearly relieved response flowed into his headphones. Confidently, he flashed Lieutenant Todd a hearty thumbs-up.

From the tactical data compartment, Mac Arnold listened to the unintelligible transmission and grinned. The Hawkeye was one hell of an aircraft, and he was proud to serve on it. As lady luck would have it, the Russian distress call was picked up at the very limit of their range. Since they were due to swing back to the *John F. Kennedy*, the carrier they were based on, they had received the transmission just in the nick of time. Fondly, he patted the gray-steeled side of the massive digital panel in front of him. Glancing at the green cathode-ray screens that lined its length, he was again impressed by the sensitivity of the 24-foot-diameter radome attached to the top of their fuselage.

Not only could it detect a sea-skimming cruise missile over 115 miles distant, track more than 250 targets simultaneously, and control more than 30 air interceptions, it could also detect radio signals at a distance of over 500 miles. Some controllers even said that the APS-125 could monitor all of the commercial air traffic coming in and out of New York City's three metropolitan airports at the same exact time! Mac always got a kick out of that awesome fact.

To see if he could pick up their bogey's radar signature, he was just giving the plane's over-the-horizon system a try when a familiar, trim officer ducked through the forward hatch. The co-pilot met his nod, then took a seat beside him.

"I'm afraid that we're going to have you earn your keep today, Mac. I need you to tie in with the *Kennedy's* tactical data system. They'll be sending us some info shortly of the highest priority."

Mac entered this request into his computer. While they waited for the monitor screen to flash the requested data, Arnold asked, "Is that distress call for real, Lieutenant?"

The co-pilot hedged his answer. "It sounds like it, Mac. We've got a Tomcat eyeballing them right now."

"What kind of plane is it?" Arnold pressed.

"She's an Ilyushin IL-38—one of the Soviets' big maritime patrol planes. Their primary duty is much like that of our TACAMO C-130, to relay messages to submerged submarines."

"May I ask what the problem is?" Arnold asked discreetly.

The co-pilot paused before responding. "All that I can tell you is that they've apparently got a neophyte up there at the controls. The pilot's dead and there's less than an hour's fuel left. We're bringing the USS *Eagle* in presently to see about picking up any survivors."

"But if there's an amateur flying that plane, what good is a destroyer going to do? Do you really think that a novice could ditch that thing in one piece?"

The co-pilot shrugged. "If I've got anything to say about it, he certainly will. The *Kennedy* is pulling the specs on the IL-38 right now. They're going to send up a diagram of the cockpit controls, and then I get to play angel and talk that scared Ivan down."

"Holy Mother Mary!" Arnold shouted. "This is better than the movies. All that we have to do now is make certain that we write ourselves a happy ending."

As he spoke they saw a flash on the monitor. Both aviators watched as the screen began filling with an intricate sketch of the IL-38's cockpit.

"That's the miracle of modern computers," Mac sighed as the co-pilot cooly studied the diagram.

After patching his headphones into the radio circuit, the lieutenant hit *transmit* and spoke loudly in perfect Russian. "Comrade Yakalov, this is Hawkeye One. I've got the data that I needed. Now, let's see about getting you down. First, we're going to have you head south, so that you'll be within range of the ship we're sending out to pick you up. This won't entail a throttle change, but we are going to have to take you off autopilot. The toggle switch that will accomplish that task is located immediately before you. You'll find it to the left of the round black ball of your altitude indicator. After switching the toggle downward, your next task will be to keep your eyes on the compass that is set beneath the altitude ball. To change your heading to due south, we'll be activating the steering mechanism. When you put your hands on the wheel, do it gently, taking care not to jerk it forward or back."

Watching the lieutenant convey these directives, Mac Arnold had a new appreciation of not only the E2-C's equipment, but also of her crew. If there was anyone who could bring that plane down safely, it would be the men and officers of the United States Navy.

Of course, Arnold couldn't see anything wrong about asking for a little assistance from a higher source. Reaching beneath his T-shirt, he fingered the crucifix that had been handed down in his family generation after generation. To the co-pilot's unintelligible discourse, he added a silent prayer of his own.

The Spruance-class destroyer USS *Eagle* was in the midst of an anti-sub-warfare exercise when it got the call informing them of the approaching IL-38. When notified of their new duty, Captain Robert Powell snapped into action. The gangly Midwesterner hurried from the sonar control compartment set deep in the ship's hull. Quickly, he climbed two banks of steep metal ladders and entered the combat information center. It was from this vantage point that the rendezvous would be coordinated.

The CIC was a dimly lit space, dominated by a massive plotting table. Surrounding it were glowing radar screens, chattering teletypes, several radios and dozens of other pieces of sophisticated gear.

Powell moved to a large, edge-lit vertical sheet of clear plastic. Here he joined his executive officer, who stood before the plotting board with grease pencil in hand.

"What have we got so far, Mr. Morley?"

The XO used a ruler to draw a line from a spot indicating the *Eagle*'s current position to a location in the Pacific due north of them. "Radar's got a good track on the bogey now, sir. Its range is approximately two-eight nautical miles and continuing to close."

"What's its altitude?"

"Five thousand and dropping, Skipper."

Powell responded thoughtfully. "I didn't realize it was coming down that fast. Fuel must be getting critical. Let's scramble our Seasprite and get out there on the double. No telling how that IL-38 is going to handle as it hits the drink."

Two floors beneath the CIC, the destroyer's helicopter crew were in the midst of an early dinner when a tone sounded. The pilot went to a nearby intercom. Air Tactical Officer Gerald Grodsky anxiously shoved another spoonful of mashed potatoes and gravy into his mouth as he watched the lieutenant pick up the handset.

"You'd better get moving on that chicken," Grodsky said to the diver sitting beside him. "I got a feeling that this chow period's about to get an abrupt ending."

"What are you talking about, Grodsky?" the diver asked between sips of hot coffee. "We did our bit for God and country this morning, during that two-and-a-half-hour ASW sweep."

Grodsky had been watching the pilot's expression

as he spoke on the phone, and serenely began wrapping up the two chicken breasts that still lay on his plate. "You'll soon see, my friend."

Seconds later, the flushed figure of the pilot arrived at their table, waving them on excitingly. "Let's move it, gentlemen! We've got ourselves a red alert."

The diver flashed Grodsky a brief *how did you know* look. Pushing their trays aside, they scurried from the mess and headed quickly toward the ship's stern.

Upon first glance, the USS *Eagle* looked sparsely armed. One of America's newest warships, the sleek, modular destroyer's only visible weapons were a pair of 5-inch Mk 45 lightweight cannon mounted fore and aft, and a single ASROC box launcher located forward of the bridge. Most of the ship's offensive capabilities were hidden. They included six torpedo tubes capable of firing both Mk 32 torpedoes and Harpoon missiles, a NATO Sea Sparrow launcher and two Phalanx CIWS gatling guns. Other features included a powerful SQS-53 bow sonar array, a pair of LM 2500 gas turbines, which gave them excellent speed with low noise emission, and, lastly, the ability to carry two helicopters.

The ability to carry its own airborne vehicles was most important. Not only was it necessary for effective anti-sub-warfare operations, it also allowed the *Eagle* to launch its present mission.

The helicopter hangar was located to the rear of the after-funnel uptakes. The *Eagle*'s chopper crew arrived just in time to help the support team slide open the large metal door and tow the Kaman SH-2 outside. The pilot then ducked into the cockpit and activated the Seasprite's two General Electric T58-8F turboshafts. With a staccato roar, the 44-foot-diameter intermeshing rotor blades spun into action. The body of the dark-green vehicle vibrated and the chopper gently lifted.

Gerald Grodsky made his way to the co-pilot's seat while the diver put on his wet suit. As Grodsky buckled in, he turned to his left and asked, "Where the hell are we off to, Lieutenant? I haven't seen you move this quickly since last month's surprise leave came down."

The pilot answered while scanning the instruments. "Hit the chin radar switch and you should be able to see for yourself."

Grodsky reached out and activated the Marconi LN-66HP unit. His monitor came instantly alive and he had no trouble picking out a rapidly approaching, low-flying bogey.

"Whatever it is, it better pull up quick. That aircraft can't be more than two hundred feet above the ocean."

"Do we have a visual yet?" the pilot asked.

Grodsky picked up a pair of binoculars and hastily scanned the northern horizon. His intense survey abruptly halted forty-five seconds later. Focusing on one particular patch of sky to his right, he cried out incredulously, "I can see it! It's a big, old four-engine turboprop job, with a bright red star on her tail. Lieutenant, that poor Russian is headed for a certain appointment with Davy Jones' locker."

"That's the idea," the pilot replied. "Get back and give Simpson a hand with the rescue gear. Our job is to pull any survivors from the drink."

Grodsky could now see the lumbering, silver-skinned aircraft without the binoculars. It continued toward them, a mere one hundred feet from the water's smooth surface. Shaking his head in wonder, he returned to the rear compartment to point out their quarry to the diver.

The Seasprite was still a good thousand yards from the plane when the IL-38's engines feathered to a halt. In response, the aircraft slowly settled downward, skimming, then making contact with the waiting water. Its angle of descent allowed the vehicle to absorb the primary landing shock with its rear fuselage. Only then did the nose pull down, and the wings hit the Pacific, dragging the IL-38 to a frothing halt.

Grodsky had seen several ditchings, but never one so perfectly executed. Inwardly praising the Russian pilot's skill, he slid back the side hatch and began preparing the rescue harness.

Beneath the roar of the Kaman's rotors, he peered down at the choppy sea. They were hovering now, only fifty feet from the downed aircraft, which amazingly enough was still afloat. The wet-suited diver took a position beside Grodsky and both men scanned the plane for any signs of life. Fingers of smoke could be seen rising from the still engines, when suddenly the tail section began sinking.

The diver hit Grodsky on the arm and signaled that he wanted to enter the water. Grodsky signaled him to wait. Until any survivors showed themselves, it would be both useless and dangerous to risk one of their own men.

As the tail continued to sink, the crew of the Seasprite began to fear that their rescue attempt had been futile, when a hatch, set into the IL-38's upper cockpit, miraculously popped open. Each of the naval aviators saw this movement and moved to their action stations. The chopper dipped to a mere twenty-five feet above the surface. The diver cupped a hand over his diving mask and jumped feet first, into the Pacific. Grodsky watched him slice into the ocean, then bob up and begin swimming toward the downed aircraft. Meanwhile, Grodsky began lowering the rescue harness. This sturdy canvas shoulder strap was attached to the Seasprite's powerful winch by a thick, steel cable.

A green, jump-suited figure could be seen now, slowly crawling out of the hatch set into the plane's upper fuselage as the aircraft continued to sink. The entire back half of the fuselage was now underwater; any moment the wings would tip backward and the plane would go down.

Grodsky attempted to urge the man on. With leaden, ponderous progress, the Russian yanked his torso up and kicked his legs free. As he slipped off into the ocean the ship plunged beneath the surface, leaving nothing but a swirling vortex in its wake.

A handful of anxious seconds followed; the survivor was no where to be seen. Had he been sucked down by the plane's maelstrom? The Seasprite's diver was visible, searching the area into which the Russian had jumped. This would be the ultimate tease—to lose him after they had come so close.

The men of the U.S. Navy did not concede defeat easily, and the crew's persistence paid off shortly when a man's head popped to the surface. The diver was quickly at his side. Skillfully, he secured the rescue harness and signaled Grodsky to haul away.

The downdraft of the rotors bit white into the surrounding waters as the winch strained and the cable tightened. Without incident, both men were eventually pulled into the chopper's interior.

Grodsky's concern centered around the Russian. The man was pale and shaking, clearly traumatized by both hypothermia and shock. A bloody gash on his forehead oozed steadily. Grodsky did his best to stem the flow. Then, stripping him of the soaked flight suit, Grodsky covered him up with a thick wool blanket. His trembling soon passed, and a gleam of awareness returned to the survivor's bloodshot eyes. A slight, trembling grin shaped his thin lips as he returned the concerned stares of his rescuers. This feeble attempt at a smile was short-lived, for a wave of tears was soon falling down the man's sharply angled cheeks.

Both Americans looked at each other, unable to comprehend if these were tears of joy or sorrow. Their confusion was increased as the Russian began babbling a simple phrase, constantly repeating it over and over. The diver leaned forward to see if he could make any sense of the strange words which, he supposed, were spoken in the man's mother tongue.

"Grodsky, your people were Russian, weren't they? What in God's name is he saying?"

The ATO, who indeed was of Russian heritage, placed his ear near the man's lips and closed his eyes to aid in concentration. Though it had been many months since he had last heard his Ukrainian grandparents use this very same dialect, the words were easy to translate. Sitting up, he opened his eyes and caught his co-worker's worried gaze.

"Well, Grodsky, can you understand him? What is he trying to tell us?"

The Seasprite's air tactical officer icily replied, "I don't know what the hell it *means*—but he keeps repeating it like all of our lives depended upon it."

"What, for Christ's sake?" shouted the frustrated diver.

The ATO's voice didn't falter. "World War III!"

Chapter Seven

General Secretary Viktor Rodin was satisfied with the progress of his trip so far. Not only did he continue right on schedule, but his meeting with the naval hierarchy in Petropavlovsk had been most unconstrained. Both his major speech and the subsequent conference were completed without incident. An amicable banquet was followed by a welcomed, sound night's sleep. He awoke rested and anxious to get on with the second half of his flight. As always, Olga Tyumen's organizational expertise allowed them to take off with a minimum of delay.

Having Admiral Sorokin aboard the flying Kremlin was a welcomed diversion. For the first two hours of the flight, as the massive IL-76 soared eastward over the blue Pacific, the two men shared tea and a revealing conversation. Rodin was proud of the fact that he had been able to get Sorokin talking about himself. His tongue loosened by the Premier's clever probing, the white-haired admiral gave a detailed review of his naval career. Careful to emphasize the disastrous international implications of a weak Russian Navy, Sorokin explained why command of the seas was so important today.

Currently, the admiral's pet project was the building of the Motherland's first fixed-wing aircraft carrier. Though past Soviet naval tacticians were reluctant to give such ships their due respect, Sorokin felt otherwise. Quick to relate incidents where American carrier groups were of instrumental importance, Sorokin justified his department's current expense requests.

The old-timer's arguments were cleverly presented, and the Premier understood why the man was such a success in his chosen field. Past premiers would have been extremely grateful for his expert advice. Without having to question his motives, they would have felt confident in okaying the admiral's requests without serious objections. Unfortunately for Sorokin, Viktor Rodin was far from being representative of the old leaders.

As he gazed across the conference table at the ruddy-cheeked man opposite him, Rodin considered the manner in which he could most effectively express his personal goals. He knew that he would have to be respectful yet firm. He would have to make the admiral realize that aircraft carrier task forces would be of little value in a world without the constant threat of warfare. In five more hours they would be landing in Los Angeles, and the fated meeting of minds that would ensure global peace would come to pass.

Would the admiral be satisfied with his new position in the world order that was to follow? As guardian of the peacetime maritime realm, he would have tremendous responsibilities. Just as important as his wartime duties, a new front was to be drawn against humanity's true adversaries: hunger, disease, and unrestrained pollution of the world's fragile environment. A man with the admiral's talents for getting things done would be greatly appreciated. Yet Rodin couldn't help but fear that Sorokin was firmly tied to the generation that would label these aims as foolish and naive. Rodin was readying himself for the difficult task of convincing his respected guest that a new, enlightened day had dawned, when a soft electronic tone sounded. Politely, he excused himself to answer the desktop telephone.

"This is the General Secretary."

The voice on the other end was masked by a persistent blast of throaty static. "Sir, this is General Kirovakan at PVO headquarters. We have a satellite transmission for you coming in via the Hot Line from the United States."

Surprised, Rodin took a seat behind his desk and said, "Very well, General. Please be so good as to make the necessary connections."

Over a loud burst of static, Kirovakan responded. "At once, sir. Please hold on while the call is calibrated."

A steady, pulselike hum replaced the crackle of static as Rodin sat back to await his unexpected caller. He had utilized this means of communications only twice before. Once, to receive President Palmer's invitation to visit America, and a second time to accept it. Neither of these calls had been initiated while he was airborne. Rodin sat forward as the line was suddenly activated.

"General Secretary Rodin, this is President Palmer calling from Los Angeles. Can you hear me all right?"

"Yes, Comrade, I hear you fine. I hope that

nothing has occurred to interfere with our meeting."

Rodin looked up in time to see the admiral's reaction to these cautious words. Sorokin's eyes were locked on his own.

"That's something that you'll have to tell me, Comrade Rodin," returned the strong, deep voice of the American President. "Several minutes ago, I received a call from Admiral Miller, Commander of our Pacific Fleet. I'm afraid that he had some disturbing news. Less than an hour ago, a Soviet IL-38 relay plane ditched in the Pacific near Midway Island. A single survivor was picked up by one of our helicopters and transferred to the carrier *John F. Kennedy*, where he is at present."

"I thank you for your cooperation in saving this aviator," interrupted Rodin. "Yet, what does this have to do with our imminent summit?"

"That is the confusing part," the President said. "It seems this survivor was most eager to convey to us information of a puzzling nature. The man swears that he was the innocent victim of a conspiracy that led to the death of the plane's pilot and the abandoning of the aircraft, by parachute, of the two men responsible."

"What kind of conspiracy is this?" quizzed the puzzled Premier.

Robert Palmer cleared his throat. "This particular IL-38's primary mission was to act as a communications relay station between Soviet naval command and your patrolling submarines. According to the rescued airman, minutes before those two men jumped from that plane a signal was apparently sent—informing a submarine called the *Vulkan* that

178

a state of war existed between our two countries." The President paused for a moment, then continued. "This message included a specific missile launch release code, which the survivor swears was received—and subsequently verified—by this very same vessel."

Again Palmer cleared his throat. "I don't have to tell you, sir, that if this is indeed the case, the consequences could be quite disastrous. Please, Comrade General Secretary, I implore you to share with me all that you know of this grave incident. The future of the entire planet is at stake here."

Rodin was speechless. When he finally gathered words for a response, his tone was tinged by disbelief.

"President Palmer, I understand your concern and beg for your patience. As unbelievable as it may seem, this is the first that I've heard of any such episode having taken place. Please excuse me for a few minutes while I contact my staff and get to the heart of this matter. You have my word of honor that I will get back to you as soon as I have a better understanding of just what is going on here."

The American President solemnly agreed to this, and Rodin, thoroughly shaken, broke the connection. For several seconds he merely sat there, eyes transfixed on the blue sky visible outside the plane's windows. Sorokin broke through his confused ponderings.

"What's the matter, Comrade Rodin? You look as if you have just gotten off the phone with the devil himself."

Slowly, the Premier turned his head and met the admiral's stare. "That was none other than President

Robert Palmer. I'm having trouble believing what the man has just told me. Comrade Sorokin, is it possible that one of our relay planes could have inadvertently passed on a set of launch orders to a missile-carrying sub?"

Having expected the worst, Sorokin was prepared. "It is impossible, Comrade! There are just too many safeguards for such a thing to happen."

Rodin responded firmly. "Well, open your mind, admiral, for if what the President relayed to me is true, the inconceivable has indeed come to pass. I need to quickly know the status of the IL-38 relay plane whose morning patrol route took it over the North Pacific. Then get me the exact position of the Delta III-class submarine, *Vulkan*. I would like to talk with its captain, Petyr Valenko, as soon as possible."

Sorokin couldn't believe what he was hearing. Somehow, their plot had failed! To find out what had gone wrong, he knew he would have to play his part straight. He would do what was asked of him and appear genuinely stunned with each successive revelation.

"I will get you that information at once, Comrade," the admiral said as he reached to pick up the phone. While the aircraft's communications operator got him an open line to Petropavlovsk, Sorokin tried a desperate gambit.

"I fear some sort of American trick, Comrade General Secretary. It would be just like the imperialists to create some sort of crisis to justify a strike of their own. I warned you that their pacifist rhetoric was all a clever ploy."

180

Rodin shook his head vigorously. "I beg to differ with you, Admiral. The Americans would have absolutely nothing to gain from such a charade."

"You don't know the Yankee bastards like I do," Sorokin shot back. "They have merely been playing with us all along, probing our weaknesses while preparing their military might for just such a surprise move. Don't forget that it was not long after the signing of the peace pact with Germany that Adolph Hitler commanded his hordes to penetrate the heart of the Motherland. I trust no one, Comrade. This is one lesson that history has taught our people all too well."

The line was now activated, and Sorokin began tracking down the information that Rodin had requested. While he sternly questioned various subordinates, Viktor Rodin watched and considered the admiral's suspicions.

Could it all be some sort of clever ruse on the part of the Americans? Perhaps he *had* been too trusting.

For a moment, Rodin seriously considered ordering the flying Kremlin back to Petropavlovsk. If this were indeed an American trap, each mile they flew eastward would bring them closer to the snare. Yet, what if it weren't? Certainly, President Palmer seemed quite upset. If he had been acting, he had done a most credible job.

As he reflected on the crisis, the Premier realized that if it was legitimate, his greatest nightmare was coming true. The unauthorized use of nuclear arms was every world leader's worst fear. He couldn't ignore the fact that this supposed insurgence had come from the ranks of the navy. His eyes locked on the uniformed, white-haired figure who sat impatiently on the phone before him, Rodin recollected that the Soviet Fleet had once been a hotbed of dissent. It was in 1921 that a handful of naval officers actually took over several battleships to directly express their dissatisfaction with the State. The Kronshradt rebellion had been a black mark on the young revolution's progress. Bloodily quelled, it led to a mistrust that was even evident in the modern navy, in the form of the *zampolits* who still sailed aboard every vessel.

Rodin had taken for granted the loyalties of the military men who served the Motherland. This trust was a part of his character. It was a trait that had been instilled upon him since childhood. Whether or not it was an inherent weakness in his ability to guide the Rodina's future would all too soon be put to a test. He looked on, unblinking, as Stanislav Sorokin cupped the phone's transmitter and pulled it away from his pallid face.

"I have just been in contact with the commander of air traffic control in the North Pacific basin. It seems that one of our IL-38's is indeed overdue. All efforts to contact it have proven unsuccessful."

"And what of the *Vulkan*?" Rodin queried.

"An ELF page is being sent out to them now. Of course, receipt of this message cannot be guaranteed. Land-based contacts with submarines on patrol are minimal at best. That is why we have platforms such as the IL-38s constantly in the area."

"Then launch another one!" exclaimed Rodin. "I must speak to Captain Valenko at once."

Sorokin answered meekly. "I have ordered just

such a flight, Comrade. Unfortunately, the auxiliary aircraft is experiencing engine difficulties. The ground crew is working feverishly to complete the necessary repairs."

Rodin's face flushed as he slapped his hand down hard on the desk. "Get that plane up now, Admiral! Whatever it takes, you must get me in contact with the *Vulkan* immediately. Are there any surface vessels in the area that could possibly make this contact?"

Impressed with the Premier's foresight and a bit shocked by the show of emotion, Sorokin issued a series of inquiries. Minutes later, he responded tersely.

"The Kresta-class cruiser *Natya* is presently in the vicinity of the *Vulkan*'s last known location, Comrade."

"Have them find the *Vulkan* at once!" Rodin shouted. "Then we will use the *Natya* to contact the sub and find out just what is going on down there. And I want a readout of what Captain Valenko was to have done if he *had* received a Red Flag alert. Include a list of targets the *Vulkan*'s warheads were assigned to eliminate."

"You don't really think that the *Vulkan* has received orders commanding it to war, do you?" Sorokin countered.

"I don't know what to think," the Premier replied icily. "My job is to consider all the possibilities."

Sorokin managed a single question. "And what will happen if the *Natya* tags the *Vulkan* and the sub fails to respond to its radio signal?"

The General Secretary answered thoughtfully. "That will depend upon a number of factors, Com-

183

rade. First and foremost is the contents of Valenko's war orders. Second, is the disposition of that spare IL-38. If all attempts at contacting the *Vulkan* are frustrated, and it appears that the vessel is actually going to go ahead with a launch, we will have no alternative but to eliminate the submarine with all due haste."

"You want to sink one of our own subs?" the Admiral cried incredulously.

The Premier did not hesitate to answer. "It's either that, Comrade, or possibly witnessing the beginning of the end of the world!"

Seemingly in response, the flying Kremlin shuddered in the midst of a violent downdraft. As the engines strained to regain the altitude they had so quickly lost, Viktor Rodin reached out to make the inevitable phone call that he had promised on his honor to complete. Still not certain what he'd say to the President, he could only hope that Robert Palmer would trust his sincerity. At the moment, there was little else he had to offer.

Captain Frederick Yerevan, of the Kresta-class cruiser *Natya*, stood alone on the exposed bridge of his ship, oblivious to the icy chill that swept over the North Pacific. Born in Siberia these temperatures, which sent the young conscripts scrambling for cover, didn't phase him in the least. Of course the bellyful of vodka consumed at lunch served to warm him better than the thickest of furs.

Tired of the musty, sweat-scented air of the ship's interior, the captain enjoyed the cold, clean air.

Staffed by a crew of four hundred, the *Natya* was packed from bow to stern. Although a command of such magnitude was good for Yerevan's career, he rather missed those carefree days when he had served aboard boats less than half the *Natya*'s size. One particular command of a Pauk-class attack vessel had been particularly satisfying. With a crew of only fifty, he had spent a free and easy year patrolling the warm, sunny waters of the Black Sea.

That had been a time to cherish, he remembered with a sigh. As the cruiser's hull bit into a large swell, Yerevan instinctively absorbed the brunt of the rolling shock with his knees and peered out at the endless ocean. Somewhere beneath these waters lay the goal of his current assignment.

Barely a quarter of an hour ago, the strange call had arrived from Seventh Fleet headquarters. The directive was short and puzzling. He was instructed to locate and make contact with a Delta III-class submarine, the *Vulkan*. If this vessel was spotted, yet failed to respond to their transmission, they were ordered to launch a pair of SS-N-14s and blow the sub out of the water.

As confusing as this sounded, Yerevan was certain that it was all some sort of weird exercise. Most probably it was tied in with the experimental ASW tracking device presently stored beneath the *Natya*'s hull. Here a sophisticated blue-green laser was currently scanning the seas beneath them. Because such a frequency could effortlessly penetrate water, the oceans appeared virtually invisible. Though still a prototype, such an instrument could revolutionize anti-submarine warfare.

185

Promising as it looked, though, Yerevan wasn't about to rely on that system alone. From the hull, a powerful low-frequency sonar unit pulsed its signals into the depths and awaited the distinctive *plink* of a return. In conjunction with this tested device, the *Natya*'s Ka-25 Hormone helicopter worked the surrounding waters with its dunking hydrophone array. Able to pick up even the most insignificant of sounds, the chopper would know the second a submarine entered the sector.

If the *Vulkan* was anywhere in this portion of the Pacific, the captain had no doubts that his ship would be the one to tag her. Then he would once again radio Petropavlovsk and get a clarification of the confusing orders received earlier.

Totally confident in his crew and the capabilities of his ship, Yerevan decided that it was time to go indoors. With dry lips longing for a taste of vodka, he turned to the entry hatch—just in time to see its steel length abruptly swing open. Out ducked the white-suited figure of his senior officer, a tall, thin Georgian whose high-pitched voice strained the captain's nerves. He greeted Yerevan breathlessly.

"Sir, I have most exciting news. Our Ka-25 has picked up the sound signature of an approaching submarine. A computer analysis of its dual-screw pattern shows it to be one of ours—a Delta III-class. It is currently entering sector two-seven-zero, at a depth of one hundred meters."

Yerevan allowed himself the barest of smiles. "Excellent, Comrade. Be so good as to deploy the towed, variable-depth communications array. What is the depth of the thermocline here?"

"Approximately seventy-five meters, Captain," the alert senior lieutenant, replied.

"Then set the depth of the array at eighty-five meters, and make it snappy!"

The Captain's order was answered with a brisk salute as his second in command pivoted and reentered the bridge. Yerevan followed. The warm, stale air hit him full in the face. Unbuttoning his tunic collar, he strode over to the radio console and studied the various digital band selectors and power readouts. When the panel indicated that the towed array had been deployed, he tapped the operator on the shoulder and addressed him.

"Lieutenant, I am temporarily relieving you of duty. Go get yourself a cup of tea, but be back here in fifteen minutes."

Surprised, the junior officer looked into his captain's eyes to see if this was all some sort of joke. One glance told him it wasn't. Without further hesitation, he rose, handed Yerevan his headphones and turned to exit the bridge.

Yerevan hadn't sat at such a post for much too long. As a cadet, communications had been his specialty, and though the equipment looked vastly different now, the theory was still the same. His orders from command had emphasized the fact that only he was to attempt to contact the sub. It took him several seconds to find and activate the switch that triggered the variable-depth unit. Once this was completed, he fingered the black plastic button of the code transmitter and began tapping out the prearranged message.

One hundred meters beneath the frigid Pacific, the *Vulkan*'s sonar officer, Lev Zinyakin, was busy scanning the surrounding waters using only passive arrays. Though not as accurate as the active system, which sent a pulse of energy surging from their bow, this rig of powerful hydrophones was much quieter. Silence was most important, now that the captain had ordered General Quarters. Though this alert might merely be another of the endless drills, he couldn't ignore the tenseness that possessed the control room.

When Zinyakin focused the listening device on that portion of the sea immediately ahead, a distant, alien tapping sound became audible. Upon verifying that it did not emanate from a lovelorn whale or a hungry crab, he signaled Stefan Kuzmin, seated beside him, to monitor this particular frequency also.

The *michman* focused his hydrophones as indicated. "It sounds like a hailing code! But where in the world is it coming from?"

Zinyakin pressed his own headphones to his ears and increased the amplification of the forward scan to its maximum. "That could be the swish of a variable-depth towed array in the background, Comrade."

The *michman* picked out this characteristic hiss. "I think you're right, Zinyakin. It's at the limit of our range, yet if it is a towed device, there's got to be a surface vessel responsible for it. I'd better inform the Captain."

Petyr Valenko was working at the control room's navigation table with his senior lieutenant when the *michman*'s call reached him. Both men proceeded immediately to the sonar console. Lev Zinyakin provided the initial briefing.

"We believe we've picked up a signal that could be from a towed variable-depth communications array. It's signature is still too faint for full positive identification. That would put it at the limit of our hydrophone range—about ninety kilometers off our port bow."

Valenko put on a pair of auxiliary headphones. It didn't take him long to pick out the distant tapping.

"That sounds like a hailing signal, all right. Senior Lieutenant, what do you think?"

Vasili Leonov took the headphones and placed them on his ears. His observations were voiced listlessly.

"That could be from another ship, Captain, but it's much too distorted to tell for certain. What could we do about it, anyway?"

"For one, we could attempt to answer it," Valenko said.

A high-pitched, raspy voice sounded behind them. Valenko didn't have to turn to identify its source.

"I think that would be most unwise, considering our current orders, Captain," Ivan Novikov said coldly. "You know as well as I that the *Vulkan* is to be involved with no outside communications, except on the authorized ELF bands."

Valenko turned slowly and met the *zampolit*'s piercing gaze. "As the ship's line officer that decision is still mine to make, Comrade Political Officer."

Ivan's eyes narrowed. "Come now, Captain. Both of us know the *Vulkan*'s current alert status. Limit-

189

ing radio contact is standard procedure during such instances."

"I understand that, Comrade. But suppose there is a problem with the ELF channels and a towed array is the only way to reach us. No—under the circumstances, I think a response on our part is most in order. Comrade Kuzmin, I'd like you to see about getting us some more speed. Senior Lieutenant, chart us an intercept point. Lieutenant Zinyakin, stay on those headphones and let me know the second a clear signal is received."

While the junior officers snapped to their duties, the *zampolit* beckoned Valenko to join him beside the vacant weapons console. Novikov's hushed words were delivered with fierce intensity.

"Have you gone insane, Captain? How could you have forgotten the Red Flag alert relayed to us such a short time ago?"

"I have not forgotten about the alert, Comrade," Valenko replied flatly.

"Then why do you so needlessly risk the *Vulkan* by breaking radio silence? As far as we know, we are in a state of war, Captain. Until informed otherwise, we must follow the directives spelled out clearly for each one of us in our sealed operational manuals."

Valenko took in these words and the strained face of the man delivering them. Tired of the *zampolit*'s meddling, he drew in a deep breath and spoke out sharply.

"I'm not denying that the Red Flag alert was received, Comrade Political Officer. I am only exercising a captain's right to seek out confirming orders whenever possible. Surely, this is only another exercise. We shall continue on our present course and close on the source of the transmission. Only after positively identifying it as one of our own ships will the *Vulkan* break radio silence."

Without waiting for a response, Valenko pivoted to return to the sonar station—when a loud explosion sounded from the depths beyond their bulkhead. With this blast, Valenko quickened his stride. As he neared the console for which he was headed, a massive shockwave pounded into the submarine's bow. The deck beneath him shook and the boat shifted hard aport. Struggling to keep his balance, the captain reached out to brace himself against one of the copper ballast pipes. This allowed him to remain upright as the lights flickered and the deck slowly settled beneath him. Quickly, he moved to Lev Zinyakin's side.

"What in hell was *that*, Lieutenant?"

The sonar officer was still rubbing his blast-shocked ears when the captain's question forced him to refit his headphones. Intensely, he scanned the churning seas before them.

"The water's still agitated, Captain, but I can tell you one thing for certain—whatever was towing that communications array was just sent to the bottom by a pair of torpedoes. What's going on out there?"

Unable to respond, Valenko's mind reeled with the implications. He had been certain that this doomed vessel had been a Soviet ship trying to contact them. Yet, why should they be torpedoed? As he desperately tried to reason it out, a raspy, high-pitched voice whispered chillingly in his right ear.

"Now do you doubt the validity of our orders,

Captain? I'm afraid that this is no mere exercise. The power-hungry imperialists have made their long anticipated first strike. We must follow the orders of our operational manual exactly now, to insure that the Motherland is properly avenged."

These apocalyptic words had their desired effect; Petyr Valenko knew that his *zampolit* must be correct. Somehow, the unthinkable had come to pass. Only one thing mattered now, and that was for the *Vulkan* to survive.

The directives contained within the operational manuals of both the captain and the political officer were brief and to the point. In eight hours' time, the *Vulkan* would rise to launch depth and release its load of sixteen SS-N-18 ballistic missiles. Until that fated time, he had to do whatever was necessary to insure the ship's survival.

A meeting would have to be called and the vessel's senior officers notified of their predicament. The thousands of hours of intensive training would at long last pay off. Certain that they would do their duty without question, Valenko turned to call out the series of orders that would take the *Vulkan* deep into the Pacific's silent depths.

Forty-three kilometers northeast of the *Vulkan*, the attack sub *Cheka* floated motionlessly. From the vessel's attack center, Captain Gregori Dzerzhinsky peered through the raised periscope. What he saw sickened him beyond description. Studying the bloody carnage was bad enough; knowing that their torpedoes were responsible for the slaughter tore at his gut.

The sound of the mighty blast had only recently passed, as had the surging shockwave. Yet he couldn't help but visualize the flight of the two torpedoes as they plunged from the *Cheka*'s forward tubes and smacked into the Kresta-class cruiser's midsection.

At least the end had come swiftly for his fellow seamen. One of the torpedoes had struck the *Natya* squarely in its ammunition magazine. Dzerzhinsky had been watching through the periscope as the *Natya* had risen from the water in a plume of flames, cracked in half, and then sank beneath the surface.

Even though the captain was trained to obey without question, this was one order he had carried out with great reluctance. Well aware of the extreme importance of their mission, he still didn't understand why it was necessary to torpedo one of their own cruisers. After all, the blood of four hundred of his countrymen now stained his hands.

A swell smashed into the periscope's lens as the captain continued to look at the handful of wreckage visible topside. From his vantage point he could see the inky oil spill. Floating in this noxious liquid were the remnants of a smashed lifeboat, dozens of empty life jackets and various other debris. As he swept the scene he saw a tableau that would haunt him always. Hugging a large oil drum were three blackened survivors. The captain's throat constricted as he watched several triangular fins vigilantly circling the last living crew members of the *Natya*. Though tempted to send the periscope back into its well, morbid curiosity held him glued to the device as the sharks moved in for the kill.

Though he had never disobeyed an order, he had to fight back the urge to command the *Cheka* to surface and save the survivors. His actions had surely been for the good of the State, but how could he ignore the cries of his conscience? Those were fellow sailors out there, sent to sea by the same authorities who had ordered the release of the torpedoes. As Dzerzhinsky struggled with this moral dilemma, a bass voice boomed out behind him.

"Excellent shooting, Captain. The First Deputy will be most proud."

Sickened by the *zampolit*'s lofty tone, the captain stepped back from the scope as one of the sharks began thrashing the first of its helpless victims. Frustrated and confused, he beckoned the fat political officer to observe the scene topside.

Boris Karpovich peered through the periscope for barely fifteen seconds before quickly backing away. His plump hand trembled slightly as he angled his handkerchief up to mop his sweaty forehead.

"I know these words ring hollow now, Captain, but such sacrifices have got to be made Our very future as a country demands it. Just as millions fell to stop the Nazi barbarians, these men shall be heroes. Believe me, Comrade, it will be well worth it in the end."

Anger swelled as Dzerzhinsky glanced into Karpovich's reddened, beady eyes. What did this pig know of the terrors being experienced by the brave men fighting for their lives on the surface? And what did he know of sacrifice? This slob probably thought

194

that he was doing his part for the Motherland by eating only half a chicken for dinner instead of a whole one. The captain was preparing to give voice to his outrage when the *Cheka*'s senior lieutenant arrived at his side, clicking his heels smartly.

"Captain, I have the results of the remote-controlled hydrophone scan you requested."

Vadim Nikulin's presence immediately diffused the tense situation. The captain relaxed his tightly balled fists and gave his attention to his bald-headed second in command.

"The scan has confirmed the presence of the *Vulkan* southwest of us, some forty kilometers distant. It appears that they had been in the process of significantly increasing their speed to intercept the cruiser when we intervened. As of that moment, their range had kept them from either receiving a clear message or transmitting one of their own."

"Is there any sign that the *Vulkan* knows of our presence?" quizzed Dzerzhinsky.

"I seriously doubt it, Captain. Their sonar remains on passive search, and I believe that they are not yet fitted with the new remote-controlled units as we are."

Dzerzhinsky exhaled a long sigh of relief. "I don't have to remind you, Senior Lieutenant Nikulin, how important it is for us to keep well out of the *Vulkan*'s range. Above all, they mustn't find out that we were responsible for the *Natya*'s sinking. Activate the anechoic sonar masking device, and rig the boat for a state of ultra-quiet. We'll remain here for several hours while the *Vulkan* continues on to its patrol sector."

Again Nikulin clicked his heels, then turned to enforce the orders. When the captain turned to survey the periscope well, he was relieved to find that Boris Karpovich was gone. Not having the stomach to check the fate of the last of the cruiser's survivors, he reached over and hit the hydraulic switch that sent the scope down with a loud hiss.

The captain knew he was fortunate that the senior lieutenant had arrived when he did. Otherwise, he would have said something to the *zampolit* that he might have later regretted. The next few hours would be equally as tense, and it would be best for all concerned if the political officer stayed as far away from the captain as possible. His current duty was difficult enough without having that arrogant slob around to aggravate him.

The *Cheka* had a single, vital mission now, and nothing must get in the way of achieving it. Protecting the *Vulkan* had to be the number one concern of every crew member. It would be a difficult task, but not an impossible one. Invigorated by the challenge, Dzerzhinsky pushed himself to the plotting board. Here he began working on the most efficient course to take them to the *Vulkan*'s preplanned launch site.

Chapter Eight

Viktor Rodin had never been the type of person who was overly worried, yet this long afternoon proved a rare exception. With three and a half hours to go until his plane touched down at Los Angeles, the Premier sat at his desk, picking nervously at a plate of fruit.

Except for the normal sounds of the IL-76 in flight, a hushed silence possessed the cabin. As he had for the majority of the trip from Petropavlovsk, a single individual shared his private compartment. Stanislav Sorokin sat at the conference table, hastily transcribing a coded transmission only recently received from the underground national command center, buried some fifty kilometers from the outskirts of Moscow.

The white-haired admiral looked every bit his age, and then some. Rodin couldn't ignore the strain and anxiety so visible in his companion's face. He had been taking their predicament just as seriously as had the Premier. Of course, he had every reason to: the forces responsible for this current mix-up were under his direct jurisdiction.

Rodin was in the process of slicing into a large

green pear when his desk phone rang. Wiping his hands on a napkin, he quickly picked up the receiver. The sound of static was loud, yet a familiar, strained voice was still audible.

"General Secretary Rodin, this is General Kirovakan. I'm afraid I have most unsettling news. It appears as if the cruiser *Natya* has gone down in the North Pacific with a loss of all hands. Not only have all attempts on our part to reach the ship been unsuccessful, but the results of a recently concluded reconnaissance flight have just reached us. The pilot reports a large oil spill in the sector the *Natya* was to be penetrating. Among the bits of wreckage found floating within this spill was an empty life jacket, with the *Natya*'s name clearly printed on it. As of now, there are no visible survivors."

Speechless, Rodin sat there and digested the tragic report. From the other side of the cabin, the admiral looked up and caught Rodin's shocked gaze. The Premier abruptly diverted his glance back to his desktop. Summoning his inner strength, he found the courage to reply.

"That is indeed horrible news, General. What is the status of the alternative IL-38 relay plane?"

Again Kirovakan's words flowed out somberly. "Five minutes ago, the IL-38 crashed while attempting to take off from Petropavlovsk's airport. All men aboard are believed killed."

A nauseous dread filled Rodin's gut as he spoke quietly into the receiver. "This is a black day, Comrade General. Please continue your efforts to reach the *Vulkan* with the land-based ELF systems. I will get back to you shortly."

The Premier hung up the phone and buried his throbbing forehead in his hands. His was struggling to focus his thoughts when his guest's query broke the stillness.

"What in the name of Lenin has happened, Comrade?"

Rodin lifted his head and somehow found words to answer. "It appears that the *Natya . . .* has been sunk with a loss of all hands."

"That's impossible!" Sorokin cried, his voice trembling.

"Tell that to the reconnaissance pilot who saw for himself what was left of this once mighty warship. There's not even one visible survivor!" the Premier replied icily.

The admiral's face reddened as he sat forward, his eyes wide. "I tell you, it was an American torpedo that took the lives of those four hundred brave men. Open your eyes, Comrade General Secretary, the blame is all too obvious!"

Though it would be easy enough to agree with this observation, the Premier couldn't ignore his instincts. "We still have no direct proof that the United States is involved in this matter. After all, what would they have to gain by all this?"

"An excuse to strike us first with a barrage of nuclear warheads!" Sorokin countered. "This is just the opportunity that the imperialists have been waiting for. Why else have they been spending hundreds of millions of dollars to build such weapons systems as the MX and Trident missiles? If they were such advocates of peace, why build armaments specifically designed for a crippling first strike? Their President

199

Palmer has been cleverly leading us to the gallows all this time."

The IL-76 shook as a wave of turbulence buffeted its fuselage. Rodin grabbed the edge of his desk to balance himself, then attempted a reply.

"It is much too convenient to blame every problem that comes our way on the Americans. I'm still of the opinion that this is all some sort of internal affair. I deeply mourn the loss of the *Natya*'s crew, yet a larger concern faces us at the moment. If, somehow, the *Vulkan* indeed received a proper release code, what are the contents of its captain's operational manual?"

Admiral Sorokin silently cursed the Premier's stubborness. Yet, if he was going to keep the man's trust he would have to answer his every request unerringly. The admiral shakily stood and handed Rodin the results of the coded transmission that he had been transcribing. Rodin anxiously read the report, which was an exact copy of the war orders that were stored inside the *Vulkan*'s safe.

The initial instructions ordered Captain Valenko to run submerged and undetected for a period of eight hours after the receipt of the first Red Flag signal. Only then were they to ascend to launch depth to release their lethal load of ballistic missiles.

Rodin found nothing unusual in such an attack plan. Since submarines had the benefit of being difficult to spot, it was standard procedure to hold back their warheads until after the more vulnerable, land-based ICBMs were released. What he did find disturbing, though, were the contents of the addendum attached to these orders. Starting with the PAVE PAWS radar site at Beale Air Force Base in the state of California, he took in the wide variety of targets that the *Vulkan*'s warheads were assigned to eliminate. These included installations from one coast of the United States to the other. The frightening scope of this attack scenario took on an additional degree of reality as he eyed the last target site listed, the city of Los Angeles. Instinctively, he checked his watch and calculated that in a little over three hours' time he would be landing in this very same metropolis.

Rodin really wasn't concerned for his own life. Of greater importance to him were the millions of human beings such a strike would erase from the face of the earth. And, of course, then there were the hundreds of millions of other lives that were threatened if such an attack was answered.

Sobered by such contemplations, a new sense of urgency underscored his words. "There is one point that I don't understand, Admiral. If I'm not mistaken, the targets for which the *Vulkan*'s warheads are assigned are first-strike sites. Such installations would be eliminated in the first half hour of hostilities. Why would we have this submarine attacking them once again, eight hours later? Surely those targets would be nothing but radioactive craters by that time."

Sorokin stirred, impressed by the Premier's keenness of mind. "I assume that such a redundant strike will merely guarantee that the prime target areas have indeed been destroyed. As you know, those particular sites were chosen by the PVO's computer. The *Vulkan*'s warheads are merely an integral part of the Rodina's attack plan as a whole."

"It's a sad day when the lives of millions rest with

201

the whims of a computer," Rodin observed gloomily. "If you'll be so good as to excuse me, Admiral, I think that it's best if I had some time by myself."

Taking his cue, Sorokin stood and ambled over to the rear doorway. "If there's anything more that you desire to know, Comrade General Secretary, please don't hesitate to call on me. I will continue doing all that I can to determine the true source of our current fix."

As the portly admiral ducked through the hatch and closed it securely behind him, the Premier sighed. Pushing his chair away from the desk, Rodin stretched his tight limbs. Cramped with tension, his muscles ached with a dull, persistent pain. A gnawing discomfort also pierced his forehead. Gently, he massaged his throbbing temples. As the discomfort gradually lessened, a salient thought suddenly dawned: If it hadn't been an American sub that had sunk the *Natya*, could it have been one of their own? And if this was the case, could Admiral Stanislav Sorokin be one of the ringleaders?

Startled by such a speculation, Rodin knew that he was only guessing wildly. The cruiser could have hit a mine—or perhaps there was an accidental explosion inside the ship itself that sent it quickly to the bottom. Combined with the other events of this day, the Premier wished that this had been the case, yet inwardly he doubted it. Somehow he was certain that all the strange happenings were interconnected.

After a slow series of calming breaths, he reached out for a blank piece of paper and a pen. One by one, he listed the series of occurrences that had led to the current quandary. First on the list was President

202

Palmer's call informing him of the downed IL-38 relay plane and the survivor's mysterious tale of mutiny. Had an actual Red Flag alert been transmitted to the ballistic-missile-carrying *Vulkan*?

Could actual nuclear release codes be obtained by an outsider? Though such data was top secret and highly protected, Rodin was certain that no system of secrecy was foolproof.

Of equal importance, was whether or not the American President was telling the truth. Deceit was surely possible, yet the Premier would have sworn that Robert Palmer was a man of his word, with an ultimate goal of world peace exactly like his own. Of course, there was the possibility that the President's military planners were up to something that even Palmer did not know about. Rodin would have to keep his mind open to consider just such a machination.

The idea of returning to Petropavlovsk again crossed his mind, and he reconsidered what such a move would imply. Because of the flying Kremlin's more than adequate staff and command gear, his investigation could be accomplished just as easily here as back in the Motherland. Although he could very possibly be condemning himself to a landing at ground zero, they were already more than halfway to Los Angeles, and to turn back now would be a sign of bad intentions.

Confident that he would get to the crux of this dilemma long before any missiles were released, Rodin considered Captain Petyr Valenko's involvement in the matter. Could the young captain be part of a mutiny? Though they had only met briefly, Rodin had taken an immediate liking to the line officer. The lad was bright and direct. He did not appear as the type to be responsible for such an evil scheme, although Rodin didn't doubt that there were many others in his government capable of such a mad plot. Jealous of his power and fearful of his new ideas, such individuals presented a great threat that had to be respected.

The Premier knew he would have to proceed cautiously and seriously consider the worst-case scenario at all times. The list of targets that lay on his desk were a morbid reminder of the awesome destructive power stored within the *Vulkan*'s missile magazine. As fate would have it, he had inspected that same compartment less than twenty-four hours before. He had no doubts that, if the men he had met there were so ordered, they would carry on with the complicated task of releasing the sixteen missiles without question.

Once more the Premier checked his watch. Subtracting the approximate time at which the *Vulkan* might have received the alert code from the eight-hour hiatus that Valenko's war orders demanded, Rodin calculated just how much time they had left before the first of the SS-N-18s were supposedly to be launched. It wasn't much. His hand trembled as he reached out to activate the red phone.

In another portion of the Pacific, Captain Michael Cooksey's ponderings were of a vastly different nature. His drive had sent his golf ball two hundred and ten yards down the center of the thirteenth fairway. Since the green was still another two hundred yards away, he could do one of two things. If he selected a fairway wood he could probably hit the green, yet risk sending the ball over the volcanic cliff that lay close to the back lip. By choosing a more accurate iron, he could almost guarantee keeping the ball in bounds. Though his chances of hitting the pin would be doubtful, an easy chip shot would accomplish that task more adequately.

Cooksey contemplated his dilemma and choose a two wood. Confident that he was playing his best eighteen holes since college, he decided to go for it all. Besides, a birdie here would place him a stroke under par.

As he pulled the club from his bag, he could think of no other place he'd rather be at that moment. Admiral Miller had been right. The vacation was the medicine that his tired body and soul had demanded. Not only was he sleeping soundly again and feeling like a million bucks, even his golf game was beginning to shape up once more. Life was too short to take it so seriously. He had to learn to enjoy it again before old age and ill health were upon him.

Rediscovering his golf game had helped. The mere enjoyment of walking the lush green fairways, combined with the intricacies of the sport itself, produced a feeling of great happiness. Now, if he could only make this birdie, his joy would be complete.

Cooksey carefully gripped the wood and positioned himself beside his ball. Mental concentration is one of the keys to a successful golf game. Above all, he had to keep his head down, swing easily, and be sure to properly follow through. With these elements in mind, he took one last look at the pin, dug his cleats into the short-clipped grass and swung away.

He could tell by the sound that he had hit it well. Fearful that he had used too much club, he watched the ball shoot forward in a low, whistling arc. His anxieties were negated as the ball bounded onto the green, struck the pin itself, and dropped only a few inches from the cup.

"All right!"

Jubilant and self-satisfied, Cooksey shoved the club back in the bag and was about to enter the cart, when an alien chopping sound caught his attention. From the deep-throated clatter, he knew immediately that it was a military helicopter. Wondering what it was doing in his neck of the woods, Cooksey looked up in an effort to spot it. It wasn't difficult. Soaring in from the pineapple fields to his right was a sleek, white Sikorsky Seahawk chopper. Only a few hundred feet from the ground, the vehicle circled the twelfth fairway and then sped forward. The downdraft from its rotors scrambled Cooksey's hair as the Seahawk hovered over the green for which he was headed. When the swirling giant began gently settling on the grass, Cooksey knew it had come for him.

Conscious that his vacation was over, he watched calmly as the chopper landed on the fairway and its side hatch popped open. A white, jump-suited figure emerged and climbed down onto the grass. This would be the Sikorsky's airborne tactical officer. The rotors continued to whirr as the ATO hunched over and ran toward him.

"Captain Michael Cooksey?"

Cooksey nodded in response and the ATO continued. "I'm Lieutenant Rayford, Captain. Admiral Miller sent us here to taxi you back to Pearl. Sorry to interrupt your game and all, but the Admiral needs you on the double."

From the chopper's rear cabin, Cooksey watched the golf course quickly recede. It was soon out of sight. His fine approach shot and the ball, which still lay only inches from the thirteenth cup, were soon forgotten. Seconds later they were out over the blue waters of the Kauai Channel.

Cooksey was thankful for the ATO's silence as the chopper sped southeast. Closing his eyes, he reflected on the events of the last couple of days. He was in the process of visualizing his hike into the wilds of Kauai's north shore when he felt the Seahawk begin to lose altitude. He glanced outside in time to see Oahu's Kaena Point pass by. Below, the Waianae Mountains were visible. They would most likely follow this range's southern slopes to Pearl itself.

A quarter of an hour later, Cooksey found himself seated before Admiral Broderick Miller. He noticed that the admiral's usually neat desk was cluttered with various reports and an opened map. The senior officer nodded in approval on seeing him and hastily concluded a phone conversation.

"Sure, Martin, of course I understand the time parameters we're facing. Like I said before, all that I can promise you is a total effort on our end. I'll call you as soon as our units are in position."

The admiral appeared tense as he hung up the receiver and greeted the captain. "Welcome, Michael. Sorry to bring you in like this, but I'm afraid I didn't have much choice in the matter. By the way, you look like a different man. I told you that I had the proper prescription to recharge your batteries. Unfortunately, you're going to have to pay the piper now."

Miller stood and walked over to the drawn wall map, which showed a large sector of the Pacific, bordered by the Aleutian Trench to the north, the Kuril Trench to the west, and Midway Island to the south. Using his right index finger, he pointed to the undersea mountain range known as the Emperor Seamount Chain. This subterranean ridge began at Midway and stretched northward for over one thousand miles.

"Several hours ago, a Soviet IL-38 relay plane ditched in these waters. As you know, that particular aircraft is used much like our C-130 TACAMO—it sends command instructions to their submarine fleet. A single survivor was plucked from the seas by a Seasprite and taken to the *John F. Kennedy*. There he related to us news of a most shocking nature. Somehow, a group of mutineers was able to gain control of the IL-38 and relay to the Delta III-class vessel *Vulkan* a set of legitimate 'go to war' orders. By the way, this sub is believed to be the same vessel that you reported contact with at the end of your last patrol. To make matters even more confusing, we've intercepted a Soviet naval transmission believed to be a confirmation that one of their Kresta-class cruisers has gone down in these very same waters. Intelligence believes that what we are possibly witnessing is a mutiny on the part of a select group of high-placed Reds. This plot—if, indeed, it is a plot—was cleverly conceived to interfere with the initiation of the Rodin-Palmer summit."

After checking his watch, he continued. "General Secretary Rodin is scheduled to land in Los Angeles less than two hours from now. I don't have to tell you how news of this conspiracy has gone down in Washington. The Pentagon, State, and the CIA have all been on my back since the moment that Soviet aviator was pulled from the Pacific."

Astounded, Cooksey's response was tinged with disbelief. "Are the Soviet war codes that easily obtainable? And if that Delta received an alert order, why haven't they already launched?"

Broderick Miller moved his dignified frame over to his desk and sat on its forward edge, facing his visitor. "As is the case with any code, no matter how secretive it may be, more than one individual was involved in its creation. This leak was probably at the highest level, confirming intelligence's belief that Kremlin bigwigs are responsible.

"Your second question can be answered by our own war plans. Because of the survivability factor, a good majority of our Tridents are to be held back, to be released several hours after initial hostilities have begun. We believe this is what's happening aboard the *Vulkan*."

"Then you really think there's a Soviet sub out there that could empty its missile magazine any second now?" Cooksey asked incredulously.

"As unbelievable as it may seem . . . yes, Michael, I'm afraid this is the premise on which we must operate."

"Jesus! If I may ask, what are we doing to counter this supposed threat?"

Miller answered without hesitation. "Though we're still hoping that the Soviets will be able to deal with the problem before it gets further out of hand, the

209

President has given us permission to mount an intercept mission of our own. Scuttlebutt has it that the executive order was issued at Premier Rodin's urging. It was from this same source that we supposedly received the *Vulkan*'s patrol sector and its optimum missile-release point.

"We're presently concentrating our ASW operations on the southeast quadrant of the Emperor Seamount Chain. Fortunately, we've still got the *Kennedy* task force out there. We hope to augment their capabilities by calling in every attack sub in the North Pacific."

"How can the *Triton* help?" Cooksey inquired.

The admiral responded matter-of-factly. "As our second consecutive battle-efficiency award winner, I'm counting on your boat to tag those Ruskies first. I've already taken the liberty of sending the *Triton* to sea under the temporary command of Lieutenant Commander Craig. Incidentally, we pulled your smiling XO out of a maternity ward—minutes after his wife gave birth to a healthy, eight-pound boy.

"You'll be taken to a prearranged rendezvous point west of Midway by the same chopper that brought you in. I know this is quite a load to hit you with, but there's no better man I'd rather have out on this job than you, Captain."

Accepting the compliment with a brief smile, Cooksey explored another line of reasoning. "Could this whole thing be a bluff on the part of the Soviets? Could they be planning to use the excuse of a mutinied missile boat to launch a full-scale attack?"

The admiral stood and rubbed the small of his back. "Interesting supposition, Captain, but most doubtful. We've yet to pick up any signs of an alert among their strategic forces. And then there's the momentary landing of the Premier in Los Angeles. That would be a hell of a way to start a war, with your leader at ground zero in the enemy's homeland."

"Who knows—perhaps Rodin is merely playing the part of a sacrificial goat," Cooksey said as he stood to accept his commanding officer's handshake.

"Good luck, Michael. How about sharing a round of golf when this whole fiasco is over with?"

Cooksey answered sincerely. "I'd like that, Admiral. I really would."

"Keep your sensors peeled for that renegade Alfa," Miller added.

"By the way, Admiral, what's the *Triton* to do once we tag this Delta?"

Miller's response was firm. "Unless you hear from me otherwise, blow them away, Captain! You're to go into this just as if a state of war indeed existed."

Cooksey saluted and left the office, with Admiral Miller's final instruction echoing in his head.

Chapter Nine

Deep below the Pacific, the *Vulkan* surged ever southward, its dual shafts propelling it at a speed well over thirty-five knots. Rigged for quiet running, the 509-foot vessel sped ahead in near-total silence; the only sounds it produced were the hiss of the seawater passing through the vessel's missile casing and the popping cavitations on its propellors.

Inside the sub, the crew remained at General Quarters for what they assumed was another one of the endless exercises. But behind the locked doors of the wardroom, a dozen of the ships senior officers sat in rapt attention, their eyes focused on the tall, blond-haired figure who had called them together.

Petyr Valenko stood at the front of the room behind a compact wooden lectern. He spoke forcefully, his words delivered with crisp precision.

"Comrades, as the *Vulkan*'s senior officers, it is my duty to inform you that, at 1330 hours today, I confirmed the receipt of a Red Flag war alert. To my knowlege, this is no mere exercise. You are all aware of the explosion and shockwave that we recently rode out. We believe this emanated from a torpedoed surface ship, which we have yet to positively identify because of a malfunction of our sensor recording equipment. If that action was indeed a hostile move on the part of the enemy, I fear this alert is most real."

Valenko paused briefly to let the information sink in. Shocked expressions proved that his audience had been listening. He cleared his throat and continued.

"I am just as astounded by this revalation as you are. As soldiers, we have been well aware of the possibility of this day. Somehow, we thought it would never come; yet, here we are. No matter who is at fault, you can be assured that the *Vulkan* will do its best to defend the Motherland.

"A Red Flag alert is the ultimate call to war. Because an enemy first strike could knock out command's ability to contact us, the alert itself is all that's needed to authorize a launch. At the receipt of this signal I was required to open the sealed operational manual which is kept locked in my safe. It was at this time that I first saw the *Vulkan*'s war orders.

"Our mission is a simple one. We are to stay submerged and undetected, while proceeding with all due speed to our patrol quadrant on the southeastern edge of the Emperor Seamount. At 2130 hours we will ascend to launch depth and unleash our load of sixteen SS-N-18 missiles. In this manner, the Rodina shall be served!"

As his words rang out, an anxious wave of nervous chatter flowed through the wardroom. Most aware of their concern, Valenko added, "Naturally, your first thoughts must be for the safety of your loved ones back home. As of this moment, I have no idea if nuclear weapons have yet been exchanged. Since this is the case, I have decided to exercise my command prerogative and order the *Vulkan* to attain communication depth at 2100 hours. We will then contact the NAVCOM satellite to confirm that a state of nuclear war exists."

A clamor of excitement spread through the officers as Ivan Novikov rose and spoke out sharply. "But Captain, won't such an ascent needlessly endanger the *Vulkan*? As you've so eloquently stated, the receipt of a Red Flag alert is more than sufficient to warrant a launch. And besides, doesn't the sinking of the ship topside prove that hostilities exist? The imperialist's anti-submarine-warfare tactics are too accurate for us to so needlessly expose ourselves."

A murmur of consenting comments followed. Valenko took in these remarks and said firmly, "It is my command opinion that the risk must be taken. I am not about to commit this vessel's warheads to a conflict that may not even exist. We're talking about the lives of hundreds of millions of people, Comrades. Can we gamble them against the receipt of a single alert transmission? Since there was not even a hint of international crisis when we put to sea, I must insist that this preliminary ascent is warranted."

"But the explosion topside!" whined the *zampolit*. "How can you ignore it?"

"Comrade Novikov, please control yourself. Even if we could confirm that it was one of our ships being attacked, I would still stick firmly to my decision. The loss of a single vessel is one thing, the end of the civilized world is quite another."

Again the nervous sound of chatter filled the wardroom. With a shrug of his shoulders, the political officer reseated himself. The captain watched as Novikov traded a silent glance of concern with the doleful-eyed senior lieutenant, who sat stiffly beside him.

In an effort to regain control, Valenko raised his hands for silence and spoke out loudly. "Until this final confirmation has been achieved, it is my wish to keep knowledge of this alert to ourselves. Only after NAVCOM signals us that a nuclear war prevails will I inform the rest of the crew. I know the hours until that time will be long ones, but I am counting on you to do your duties to the best of your abilities. For the next sixty minutes I will be available in my cabin for any of you with individual questions. That is all."

A second of strained silence followed as Valenko turned toward the wardroom's exit. As he broke the hatch, the sound of the babbling officers rose in crescendo.

Thankful that this dreaded encounter was over the captain quickly proceeded to his private quarters. This took him to the bow portion of the boat, on the deck immediately below the vessel's control room.

His contact with other members of the crew was minimal as he progressed down a narrow, tube-lined corridor, ducked through a hatchway and, utilizing a plastic keycard, entered his locked domain.

Though cramped and sparsely furnished, at least his cabin offered a place to be alone. At that moment he relished his privacy as never before.

The cabin contained a fold-down bunk, a small, wall-mounted desk and a single chair. A simple stool, folded into the wall, was fondly labeled the "hot-seat" by the crew members it was designed to accommodate. There was also a private head that included a metal sink, a toilet and a cramped shower stall.

Conscious of the thick, nerve-induced sweat that stained his khaki shirt, Valenko stripped it off and went to the sink. The cool water felt good on his neck and face. After toweling himself dry, he took a second to examine his reflection in the shaving mirror. It was then he first noticed the pair of red, love bites visible on his neck, just below his right ear lobe. Like returning to a past life, his thoughts flashed back to Ivana and the night of passion from which the marks stemmed.

Had it really been less than three days since they had last been together? Though her image, touch and scent were still fresh in his mind, his responsibilities took precedence over the innocent passions of the senses.

For a second, he mentally recreated their coupling—but instead of experiencing joy, he could only feel the pain of not knowing if his love still lived. If the IL-38's call to action had been legitimate, there was a very good chance that cities like Petropavlovsk had been burned to a crisp during the first minutes of nuclear attack and no longer existed.

In a way, Ivana, her sister Galina, and even little Nikolai would be among the lucky ones. Their deaths would be instantaneous. Vaporized by a flash of superheated fire, there would be little time for either fear or pain. The real losers in a nuclear war would be the survivors. Not only would they have to face the ravages of global radiation poisoning, they would find themselves in a bleak, desolate society with few comforts and little hope for the future. Such a world was not easy to imagine, and Valenko trembled involuntar-

216

ily.

An abrupt knock on the door shattered his macabre train of thought. Remembering his offer to the senior officers, he turned to his bunker to get a clean shirt. As he buttoned it there was a second knock.

"I'll be right there!" Valenko shouted as he hastily tucked in his shirttail. Then he hit the door switch to see which of his senior officers was seeking his advice.

A pair of sour faces met his glance, and a cold heaviness rose in the captain's belly as he identified the waiting figures of Ivan Novikov and Vasili Leonov. Without comment, the gaunt *zampolit* entered first, followed by the senior lieutenant. The door hissed shut and Valenko reluctantly greeted them.

"Yes, Comrades—how can I be of service to you?"

The dark-eyed political officer wasted little time with civilities. "Captain Valenko, have you gone mad? What is this nonsense about you doubting the legitimacy of the Red Flag alert?"

Sensing that he was in for a fight, Valenko answered directly. "I'm not questioning the legitimacy of those orders, Comrade. I am only exercising my right to reconfirm them. Why does this upset you so?"

"Because I can't bare to see this sub sent to the bottom with its load of missiles still aboard!" the *zampolit* shouted. "The Rodina is relying on us to fulfill our rightful duty, and to needlessly risk the safety of this ship is a travesty beyond comprehension."

Valenko looked to his senior lieutenant for support. "Vasili, surely you're aware that a line officer's options include the right to seek reconfirmation of go-to-war orders, if so desired. What is so wrong with this?"

Leadenly, Leonov met his captain's stare. "We are not challenging your right to exercise such an option, sir. What we are questioning are the motives that underline such a decision. Why needlessly risk the *Vulkan* to reconfirm orders that have already been received?"

Shocked by his second in command's obstinance, the captain gathered himself and pressed on. "This doesn't sound at all like you, Vasili. What has happened to the young officer who always promoted a captain's right to interpret his orders as he best saw fit? Since when have you become so narrow-minded?"

"About the same time that you became such a cowardly fool," returned the wide-eyed political officer.

Incensed, Valenko pointed to the door. "I've had enough of your impertinence, Comrade Novikov! Now get out of my sight, before I confine you to your cabin. And you, Senior Lieutenant—I'll be wanting to talk with you privately."

The captain could not believe that his order had had absolutely no effect on the *zampolit*, who stood there unmoving. "Did you hear me, Novikov? I said get out of here!"

In response, the political officer merely shook his head. "Your time for giving orders aboard this vessel are over, Comrade Valenko. For the Rodina's greater interests, I hereby take command of the *Vulkan*."

To back up these bold words, Novikov pulled a chrome-plated pistol from his jacket and aimed it at Valenko's chest.

"What is the meaning of this, Comrade? Put that pistol away and come back to your senses!"

Novikov shook his head and his mouth curled up in a sardonic sneer. "Those are mighty brave words, coming from one who stands on the other end of a gun barrel. Now sit down Valenko, and keep your lips sealed."

From the tone of this delivery, Valenko knew that the threat was real. Reluctantly, he seated himself on the edge of his bunk.

"That's better," the *zampolit* cooed. "Comrade Leonov, I think you had better bind the Captain for his own protection. During the next couple of hours it could prove extremely dangerous for him to get in our way."

Leonov took out a roll of two-inch surgical tape. Wordlessly, he began wrapping it first around Valenko's ankles and then his wrists. As he cut off a strip to cover the captain's mouth, Valenko said desperately, "I still don't understand why you are doing this, Comrades. Surely you must be aware that you can't possibly get away with such a pointless crime."

Without comment, Novikov signaled his fellow conspirator to complete his task. Only after Valenko's lips were tightly sealed did the political officer respond.

"You left me no other alternative, Petyr Valenko. I couldn't possibly stand by and watch you risk this vessel so needlessly. The receipt of the Red Flag alert signaled the end of an era. Cowardly fools like yourself no longer have a place in the Motherland's future. If it were up to me, I would put a bullet in your head and end your misery once and for all. You can thank Comrade Leonov for this temporary stay of execution. Besides, your knowledge of the ship might still come

219

in handy as the time to launch approaches. Hopefully, during those hours that you will have to yourself you will return to your senses. For what we are doing on this fated day is insuring that the Rodina will prevail for the decades of peace that will soon follow."

With the conclusion of his diatribe, Novikov stepped forward and, with a quick snap of his wrist, clubbed Valenko on the side of his head with the butt of the pistol. As the captain fell back onto his cot, unconscious, the *zampolit*'s eyes gleamed in victory.

"Senior Lieutenant, this is a most important moment in the history of the Motherland. The last obstacle to our great dream has finally been overcome. Your unflinching assistance shall never be forgotten. Strange was the hand of fate that led you to our glorious cause. Now come, Comrade. A toast is in order. And then we shall make certain that the *Vulkan* fulfills its rightful place in history."

Without a word of comment, the grim-faced senior lieutenant followed Novikov out into the hallway. Both men turned to their left as the door to Valenko's stateroom hissed shut behind them.

Stefan Kuzmin enjoyed the change of pace that his current duty afforded him. The *michman* would rather be actively involved with a mechanical problem than merely sitting at a console monitoring a bank of instruments. Sensor operations could be extremely challenging, and there was no doubting its importance, yet he'd take his present task over it any day of the week.

Immediately after the *Vulkan* had encountered the

unexpected explosion and resulting shock wave, they had discovered that the hydrophonic recording mechanism wasn't operating properly. Because of this unit's failure, they had been unable to record the sounds the hydrophones had picked up before and after the blast. If the system had been operating correctly, the sounds could have been analyzed by computer, which would have identified the unfortunate vessel that had met its demise topside.

When the system was found to be malfunctioning, Kuzmin immediately volunteered to have a look at it. The senior officer of the deck agreed to this and a suitable sailor was assigned to take over Kuzmin's post at the sonar console.

His trusty tool box at his side, the *michman* squeezed into the cramped compartment where the recording device was stored—between the control room and the sub's bow. The storage cell was packed with various electronic components. Most of this equipment was directly connected to the monitors in the control room. Kuzmin wondered how many of the *Vulkan*'s senior officers even knew that such a receptacle existed.

The warrant officer hooked an electric lantern onto the handle of a vacant storage bracket. The console that he wished to examine lay immediately below. Awkwardly, he went down to his knees. He opened the tool box and removed a set of screwdrivers, then located the metal container where the sonar recorder was stashed. He determined the proper screw size and, after selecting the appropriate tool, began unloosening the metal coverplate. Once this was accomplished, he began his work in earnest.

The device was designed like a large cassette recorder. After confirming that the unit was getting a proper electrical charge, Kuzmin checked the recording heads and then removed the circuitry panel. A tedious test of each individual circuit followed. When this operation failed to show any negative results, he reinserted the panel and took a second to double-check his previous work. From all that he could see, the system should be operating perfectly. On a whim, he decided to check the cassette tape himself. He pulled the thin plastic container off its spools and only then spotted the apparent cause of the malfunction. Somehow, the permanent tape itself had broken.

Dismantling the cassette to resplice the tape would be a most difficult job. Though he never knew of such a component to fail, Kuzmin was confident that he could soon get the whole unit going once again.

Cramped and hot, he decided to work on resplicing the cassette under more comfortable conditions. He pocketed the tape, resealed the recorder, stood, and carefully backed his way out of the narrow cell. As he entered the adjoining hallway, four soft electronic chimes issued from the sub's public-address system. Spurred by the familiar tones, he checked his watch and reaffirmed the completion of yet another work shift.

For four precious hours he would be officially on his own. Conscious of a noisy gurgling in his stomach, he decided that his first stop would be the mess hall. There would be plenty of time to complete his current project after dinner and a sound nap.

The galley area was two floors below. Kuzmin anxiously descended a pair of metal stairwells and turned toward the vessel's stern. After passing that section of the sub reserved for the enlisted men's living quarters, he ducked through an open hatchway and turned into the dining hall.

Being one of the first men there allowed him to miss the long lines that accompanied each meal shift. He picked up a tray and silverware, then proceeded over to the cafeteria-style serving area. Kuzmin nodded to the pot-bellied figure who stood behind two sweaty conscripts who were busy ladling out portions.

"Hello, Comrade Irkutsk. How is the world treating you today?"

Chef Anatoly responded heavily to the *michman*'s greeting. "As usual, I find myself fighting a losing battle. The little food that is fit to serve gets burned by these imbeciles who have the nerve to call themselves cooks. You should just see today's waste! It's going to be the sharks who dine well this evening."

Kuzmin grinned in response to his typical complaint. "As always, you seem to find a way to feed us most adequately, Comrade. What's today's bill of fare?"

Anatoly answered while wiping his hands on his spotted apron. "Sausage a la Baikal, Siberian cabbage and pickled beets. There will be some nice hot rye bread out shortly. You would have had it now, but my assistants here burned the first dozen loaves. Only minutes ago the smoke was so thick that I thought I'd have to call out the fire brigade."

Kuzmin accepted a steaming plateful of food and sniffed at its aroma approvingly. "Well, it sure appears tasty to me. Once more, Chef, it looks like you've accomplished miracles."

"Enjoy yourself, Comrade. Of all those present, it can be said that you are one who has truly earned today's food. Not like the shirkers I get stuck with."

Nodding at this unexpected compliment, Kuzmin picked up his tray and turned to find a table. From the center of the large room, a single diner waved to him. Surprised to find the sonar chief well into his meal, Kuzmin joined him.

"How did you manage to get down here so quickly?" the *michman* asked.

Lev Zinyakin swallowed a mouthful of sausage and said, "You had to be there to believe it, Stefan. Five full minutes before the change of shifts was scheduled, who relieves me, but our own Vasili Leonov."

Kuzmin looked startled. "You mean to say that our esteemed Senior Lieutenant actually took over your watch so that you could break early?"

"As Karl Marx is my witness, so it was. If you ask me, it was the *zampolit* who put the idea in his head. Do you know that Novikov was actually smiling as he made the rounds of the control room? I even heard him tell a joke or two."

"Now that *is* something," Kuzmin said. He cut into his sausage and decided to let it cool a bit before eating. "I wonder what's gotten into those two? Perhaps today's a national holiday that we've forgotten about."

"I doubt that. Although, to see our *zampolit* smiling is reason for a holiday in itself." After consuming a bite of cabbage, he continued. "As usual, poor heartbroken Vasili didn't have much to say as he strapped on the sensor headphones. What followed, though, was most out of the ordinary. Old Novikov himself patted me on the back and complimented me on the splendid job that I was doing. Then the *zampolit* ordered me to 'refresh myself,' as he so tactfully put it. Needless to say, I almost fell over in shock. You can be certain that I got out of there as quickly as possible, before they changed their minds."

"Most amazing," Kuzmin mused as he began to go to work on his beets. "I wonder if the Captain had something to do with it. With this unexpected patrol and all, I've never seen morale so low before. The least the officers can do is be civil."

"That's a thought," Zinyakin replied. "Although I doubt that even Petyr Valenko could cause a smile to cross our *zampolit*'s face if his heart wasn't in it."

"Heart?" the *michman* quizzed playfully. "Since when has our political officer been outfitted with such a human organ?"

Both men laughed and looked up admiringly when one of the cooks dropped off a loaf of fresh rye bread at their table. Kuzmin ripped off the heel, soaked it in gravy, and consumed a healthy bite.

"There is nothing like Chef Anatoly's sausage a la Baikal," he sincerely observed.

After tearing off a hunk of bread for himself, the sonar chief added, "You know, I have it from a good authority that Comrade Irkutsk has a secret source for the sausage's stuffing."

"What's that?"

Relishing the moment, Zinyakin grinned. "My spies tell me that our dear chef stuffs the sausage skins with the remains of those unlucky cooks who have burned their limits on past patrols. Tonight we are probably dining on a poor departed seaman who hailed from the Lake Baikal region. Thus, this recipe's name."

Kuzmin answered his friend with a sarcastic smile. Yet his grin soon faded as his hand went to his mouth and pulled out a long strand of yellow hair.

"See, he was a blond!" Zinyakin exclaimed and shook with laughter as the *michman* loudly belched, then pushed the tray away.

"I'll get us some tea," offered the still chuckling sonar operator.

Distastefully picking his teeth with his fingernail, Kuzmin hastily scanned the rapidly filling room. A line had formed at the serving station. The crowd chatter was unusually hushed in response to the continuing state of General Quarters.

As he surveyed the filled tables, Kuzmin noticed an absence of senior officers. The captain was also nowhere to be seen. Previously, he had done his best to share this sitting with them whenever his duties allowed. Remembering the torn plastic cassette in his pocket, Kuzmin wished that Valenko would appear now, so that he could tell the captain of his finding.

Zinyakin returned with their tea. Over a bowl of fruit compote, discussion turned to their families. Both men proudly displayed the latest pictures of their sons. Since both children were of a similar age, it was hoped that they would grow up together as friends. But if the navy had its way, there was no telling where either of them would be shipped off to next.

Kuzmin left the mess still a bit hungry but in excellent spirits. Without hesitation he made his way to his bunk. Far from being afforded the luxury of private quarters, his position as warrant officer still allowed him a greater degree of privacy than the majority of the enlisted men. Most of the conscripts slept in large communal dorms. Even their mattresses were "hot," meaning that one man slept while another worked.

The *michman* shared his leisure space with a chief petty officer and two first-class petty officers. Though they had no walls between them, a drawn curtain around one's bunk guaranteed privacy. Kuzmin kicked off his shoes and peeled off his uniform. Clothed now in an undershirt and scivvies, he climbed into his bunk, pulled the curtain around him and crawled under the rumpled sheets. As he settled on his back, he burped loudly and again tasted the single bite of greasy sausage that he had consumed at dinner. Three belches later, he silently cursed Chef Anatoly and seriously reconsidered Lev Zinaykin's tale regarding the mysterious source of the sausage stuffing.

Shifting to his side, he attempted to close his eyes, when an alien discomfort began gnawing in his belly. This ache continued to intensify until he found sleep all but impossible. He gratefully remembered the bottle of antacid tablets that Galina had forced him to pack along with his few personal toilet items. He sat up with another burp and reached under his mattress for his leather shaving kit.

The thick white tablets had a gritty, chalky taste, yet he managed to force down four of them. Even then, his stomach still burned. To get his mind off his discomfort, he decided that this would be the perfect time to work on resplicing the broken tape. Since it could just as easily be accomplished in the comfort of his bunk, he reached out for the cassette, grabbed a set of miniature screwdrivers and immersed himself in the job.

The screws that held the plastic tape holder together were tiny. After removing them, Kuzmin took extra care to place them in a spot where they would not get lost. Once the two halves of the cassette were separated, he began the delicate task of splicing together the torn ends of the narrow, plastic ribbon. With steady hands, he used a tiny piece of clear masking tape to do the trick. Careful not to allow the spools to unwind, he screwed the holder back together and wound it tight with his pinky.

With the repair work finished, he decided to listen to the tape and see what it contained. Once again he reached under his bunk, this time removing his prized Sony Walkman, which he had picked up a year ago in Cam Rahn Bay. This device had afforded him hours of listening pleasure, though both prerecorded tapes and batteries were often hard to obtain. Snapping the Walkman open, he pulled out his treasured tape of Tchaikovsky's *Swan Lake* and inserted the tape from the sensor recorder. With the miniature sponge-covered speakers clipped to his ears, he hit the play button and found himself startled by a deafening, grinding roar. Quickly, he reached over and turned down the volume.

Kuzmin was certain he was hearing the explosion that they had monitored earlier. When the sound abruptly ceased, to be replaced by utter silence, he knew that he had reached the spot where the break had occurred. He pressed the stop button and hit rewind.

As the *michman* sat up, he realized that his stomach ache had passed. Gone, too, were all thoughts of sleep. Since it was evident that the recording mechanism had been functioning up to the point of the blast, he was confident that he'd be able to identify the doomed vessel. All he needed was access to the *Vulkan*'s computer.

Kuzmin pulled back the curtain, crawled off the bunk and got dressed. To insure a private work space, he chose the sub's attack center. Located on the floor directly above him, this equipment-packed compartment would only be utilized during the times of actual combat. Here, the *Vulkan*'s various offensive and defensive functions were monitored.

As he had hoped, the attack center indeed proved vacant. After positioning himself before the room's central keyboard, he inserted the cassette tape into the playback mechanism and tapped into the vessel's sensor identification banks. With the assistance of a pair of headphones, he listened to the distant surging that occupied the first half of the tape. Though he was unable to make any sense out of this jumble of noise, the computer had much better luck. When the monitor flashed alive, the *michman* quickly scanned the screen for his requested data.

Propulsion source: Geared steam turbines, 100,000 shp; 2 shafts, 34 knots.

Group Classification: Soviet Kresta-class cruiser.

Sensor Deployment: 1 variable depth communications array.

Kuzmin pushed his headphones closer to his ears as

an alien turbulence sounded above the steady hum of the cruiser's turbines. Again he asked the computer to identify the signature.

Propulsion source: Stored chemical energy.
Group Classification: Soviet SS-N-7 conclusion-tipped torpedo.
Probable source: Alfa-class attack sub.

The significance of this data only sank in when the tape filled with the sound of the massive explosion. The *michman* pulled the headphones off and stared out, wide-eyed. The vessel that had been blasted was indeed of Soviet origin. What shocked him was the puzzling fact that the weapon that had sent it to the bottom was also one of their own. Had a tragic miscalculation taken place topside, or was this attack somehow intentional? Kuzmin knew only one individual who could possibly answer this question. With a determined stride, he took off for the cabin of Petyr Valenko.

The warrant officer barely noticed the sour heaviness that lay in his gut as he traversed the hallway leading to officer country. Not really sure what he had chanced upon, he could only be certain that four hundred of his comrades most likely lay dead in the nearby waters. If this meant that the alert they currently found themselves in was not a mere exercise, and a shooting war actually existed, one question remained: who was the enemy? He was still trying to puzzle it out as he turned down the corridor that brought him to the captain's quarters.

Standing outside Petyr Valenko's door was a grim-faced senior seaman. Kuzmin was shocked to find the sailor with a holstered pistol on his hip.

"Comrade Olenya, what is the meaning of your current duty? Is something the matter with the Captain?"

The big-boned Georgian sentry returned Kuzmin's inquisitive glance with one of bored indifference. "That will be for the *zampolit* to say, Comrade. I've merely been instructed to send all those who desire to see the Captain to Ivan Novikov's cabin."

"What are you talking about, Olenya? Step aside. I have important information for Captain Valenko."

The guard's hand went to his gun as he moved to block the door with his body. "My orders are most explicit, Comrade. Please don't press me to enforce them."

Aware of the man's sincerity, Kuzmin backed off. "Something strange is going on aboard this ship, and I aim to get to the bottom of it. I will be back, Comrade. Of that, you can be assured."

Ivan Novikov's quarters were in an adjoining hallway, and the *michman* wasted no time getting there. He had visited this particular cabin only a handful of times before, yet he remembered those meetings with great displeasure. It wasn't just the hard-edged theories that the political officer was always so quick to promulgate, but rather the man's personality that was so distasteful. Novikov was quick with advice but a poor listener. Too often he sounded as cold as a machine, while reeling off the Party's current viewpoint. There was no doubt that he was but a mouthpiece, with few ideas originating in his own mind.

Kuzmin gathered his nerve and knocked firmly on

the door. Without a word spoken, its length slid open with a hiss. The *zampolit* was seated at his desk. Above him was a large, framed representation of Lenin, the room's only visible decoration. Upon identifying his visitor, Novikov beckoned him to enter.

"Do come in, Comrade Kuzmin. To what do I owe this rare visit? Do you seek Party guidance, perhaps?"

Kuzmin took a step inside, and replied uncomfortably, "No sir. I only desire to have a word with the Captain."

With this, the door hissed shut behind him. The *zampolit* put down his pencil. "Why is that, Comrade *Michman*?"

Noting the undertone of suspicion in the political officer's query, Kuzmin's nerve temporarily faltered. "It was really nothing, sir—just a personal matter that I wished to discuss with him."

A forced smile painted Novikov's narrow lips. "Can't I be of some service to you, Comrade? I'm certain that you'll find me a most worthy substitute."

"Thank you for your offer, but I'd rather see the Captain. Is there something wrong with him?"

"I'm surprised that you didn't notice before," the *zampolit* said smoothly. "The poor man has got an extremely bad fever. The corpsman fears that he's showing the primary symptoms of hepatitis. It was just like our esteemed Captain to want to ignore these danger signs, but I would not hear of it. Senior Lieutenant Leonov was consulted and both of us agreed that Comrade Valenko must get some badly needed rest. I placed the guard outside his room personally, so that he wouldn't be unnecessarily disturbed."

Kuzmin had certainly not noticed any signs of sickness in the captain, and responded carefully. "That was most thoughtful of you, sir. My small problem surely doesn't warrant waking the Captain from his sickbed. I'll handle it on my own."

Novikov looked down at the sheet of paper he had been working on and cooly said, "Isn't this your appointed rest period, Comrade Kuzmin?"

As the *michman* nodded, the *zampolit* continued. "Well, then, get back to your bunk where you belong. We are going to need you rested and alert for the next work shift."

"I was just going back there, sir. I'm sorry if I interrupted you."

"Not at all, Comrade. I only wish you'd have been relaxed enough to share your worries with me. Don't be such a stranger. Your record is good and a visit to one of our *komsomol* meetings will reflect well on you. Remember, the Party is here only to make your toils that much easier."

The political officer hit the door switch as Kuzmin saluted and pivoted to exit. Gratefully, he stepped out into the hallway.

The air seemed fresh and several degrees cooler than the stuffy confines he had just left. As he proceeded down the corridor, he struggled to put his thoughts in order. The *zampolit* was lying—of that he was certain. If Petyr Valenko had hepatitis, he had come down with it within the last couple of hours. Patting his pants pocket, Kuzmin felt the outline of the cassette that had sent him on his journey. Could its mysterious contents possibly have something to do with the confusing encounter he had just experienced? Again, he knew that he could only trust one person's advice.

Picking up an intercom handset, he dialed the captain's room. When there was no answer, he tried reaching Valenko with a general page. Two soft electronic tones sounded throughout the ship. Thirty seconds later, his page was answered by a familiar voice that definitely did not belong to his friend. Breathlessly, Kuzmin disconnected the *zampolit* before he gave himself away.

He was now convinced that he would find something out of the ordinary behind the captain's locked door. Fearful for Valenko's safety, Kuzmin decided that an inspection of his cabin was most necessary. Yet, how could he get past that heavy-handed sentry?

An idea popped into his head as he continued down the corridor separating the officers' sleeping quarters. Just last month he had supervised an inspection of the *Vulkan*'s ventilation system. One of those shafts, which he personally checked, led directly into the captain's room. Accessible from a nearby storage compartment, Kuzmin saw no reason why he couldn't use it to see just what was going on in there. Since the chances of detection were slim, he decided that he had nothing to lose by trying.

The *michman* soon found himself inside a large walk-in closet used to store janitorial supplies. Because of the volatile nature of the cleaning solvents, the room was well ventilated. The air conditioning shaft was set into the upper edge of the wall. It was covered by a flimsy wire-mesh screen. To reach it, Kuzmin had to use a bank of shelves for a ladder.

Using his pocket knife, he loosened the two bottom fastenings that held the grill up. By prying it outward, he was able to squeeze himself into the shaft without completely removing the screen. This was important, as anyone entering the closet would notice a missing cover at once.

Sweating from the effort, he lifted his body into the shaft. He slithered forward to fit his legs in, then crawled backward and refastened the grill cover.

The round metallic shaft in which he now found himself was just wide enough to allow his shoulders room to pass. Forward progress would only be possible by crawling on his hands and knees. He didn't have the benefit of a flashlight and a wall of darkness soon descended. It was impossible for him to gauge his forward progress.

As he pushed himself on, he wondered what he would find at the shaft's end. Perhaps his entire effort would prove to be a waste of time. In a way, he hoped this would be the case, but he seriously doubted it. Petyr Valenko had been fit as a fiddle the last time he had seen him. There was no way the captain could have succumbed to a natural illness so quickly. He had only needed to look into the *zampolit*'s shifty eyes to know that Novikov was lying. Yet, what in the world could he be covering up?

Kuzmin feared the answer to this question. Since sharing the last leave together, the *michman* felt closer to his captain than ever before. Now that Valenko and Ivana had hit it off so well, he was practically a member of the family. Galina had told Kuzmin during the party that the two were attracted to each other, and the next day he had learned just how serious this attraction was. He certainly didn't blame Valenko. Ivana was quite a woman. Not only did she emit a raw sexuality, she was also extremely bright. Her sister had always hinted that it was this above-average intelligence that scared off her suitors, but Kuzmin thought he knew better! She hadn't settled down because she hadn't found a man whom she could call her equal. Surely the captain more than adequately fit this profile. Sorry that their leave had been cut so abruptly, Kuzmin looked forward to their return, when he would once more invite the captain for dinner. With this added motivation, the *michman* scooted forward as quickly as he could.

A blast of frigid air hit his feet, and soon his whole body was enveloped in a chilly breeze, the transfer of which was the purpose of this shaft. When the cold caused painful cramps to develop in his thighs, his progress was all but stopped. Writhing in agony, he reached in vain to massage his muscles. He could only attempt to rub the cramp out against the cold steel of the shaft. Eventually his muscles relaxed and he continued on.

Just when it seemed that he would never reach his goal, a sliver of light beckoned from up ahead. The intensity of the light gradually increased in relation to his forward progress. He had to give his eyes several seconds to adjust to the brightness before he was in a position to see the source of the light.

The ventilation grill was set in the wall immediately above the captain's desk. From this vantage point Kuzmin had an adequate view of the room's interior. It was to the cabin's single bunk that his eyes were drawn. There, laying bound and unconscious on the narrow mattress, was Petyr Valenko.

Angered to the point of desperation, the *michman* snapped out the wire screen's bottom fasteners with the heel of his hand. Oblivious to injury, he tumbled out of the shaft head-first, using the desk to break his fall. Though he was racked with pain, he focused his entire attention on his captive friend.

The warrant officer sighed with relief when his fingers found the captain's pulse; it was weak, but steady. While removing the adhesive tape from Valenko's mouth, Kuzmin spotted a nasty looking red bruise over Valenko's right temple. To halt the spotty flow of blood still oozing from the wound, he used a damp wash cloth as a gentle compress. Then he wet another towel and laid it over Valenko's forehead.

As he unraveled the tape binding the captain's wrists, Kuzmin realized that his friend was stirring. Ever so slowly, the captain's eyes opened. As he struggled to focus, he caught sight of Kuzmin and groggily mumbled, "Stefan? Stefan, what has happened here?"

"Easy now, Comrade," the *michman* gently pleaded. "Give yourself a moment to allow your head to clear. You've got one nasty gash on your forehead."

Kuzmin unraveled the tape that bound the captain's ankles. By the time he was done, Valenko was doing his best to scan the room.

There was a sudden light in his eyes as memory returned, and Valenko gasped, "The *Vulkan* . . . my ship . . . the *zampolit*!"

Kuzmin put a finger to his lips and signaled the captain to be quiet. Then he whispered, "I'm afraid you have a sentry outside your door, Captain. We're

237

going to have be very careful not to draw his attention."

Valenko nodded that he understood and strained to sit up. The *michman* helped him by placing a pair of pillows under his neck.

With frantic urgency, Valenko said, "You've got to help me, Stefan. The *zampolit* and Senior Lieutenant Leonov have taken control of the ship!"

"I figured as much," the *michman* said. "I'll bet this mutiny is related to the sensor tape I just completed analyzing. The hydrophone recording device was *not* malfunctioning, as we had earlier assumed. It looks to me like someone deliberately slit the cassette tape. I can prove not only that the shockwave was caused by an exploding Kresta-class cruiser, but that the weapon that caused the blast was . . . a Soviet torpedo."

Stunned by the disclosure, Valenko's eyes widened. "No wonder Novikov didn't want the *Vulkan* to ascend for reconfirm orders!"

"What are you talking about, Captain?" the confused *michman* asked.

Valenko took a few seconds before answering. "The first thing that you have to know, Stefan, is that the *Vulkan* is under a Red Flag alert. To my knowledge, this is not a planned exercise. As you well know, when such an alert is received we need only concern ourselves with communication attempts on the ELF bands. When Zinyakin picked up that transmission, just before the blast, my gut told me that it was one of our own ships desperately trying to contact us. If it was indeed a Soviet torpedo that took it to the bottom, someone sure went to extremes to make certain that

238

message wasn't successfully transmitted."

Suddenly conscious of the fact that he didn't know the time, Valenko looked at his watch—and issued a long sigh of relief. "Thank goodness there's still time. Our war orders have instructed us to empty our missile magazine at 2130 hours. When I voiced my decision to order an ascent to communication depth at 2100 hours, to receive a final confirmation, the *zampolit* made his move. No war has been declared, they only want us to believe that one has!"

"But why?" asked the stunned *michman*.

"You'll find the answer to your question locked inside the warhead guidance system. If my suspicions are correct, I think you'll find that the set of targets that were originally programmed have been drastically changed."

"In what way?"

"Our previous targets were primarily soft ones—various military and civilian centers on America's West Coast. If hard targets have since been substituted, the *Vulkan* could be the lead element in a surprise, decapitating first strike. To find out for certain, I'm going to need your assistance, Stefan."

"Just name it, Captain. I'm behind you one hundred percent."

"First off," said the captain, "I'm going to want you to tie me up once again. There's no use letting these maniacs know that we're on to them. Then, you're going to sneak back out of here and access that guidance system. Today's code word is *Lake Khasan*. If our targets have been changed, we can be certain of the mutineers' motives. It will be up to you to make sure that our SS-N-18s can't be launched."

"I believe I can get into the missile room without attracting too much attention," the warrant officer said. "Yuri Chuchkin and I are on excellent terms. If I can be there alone for a few minutes, I know of a most accessible circuit panel. A quick slash and the launch-control system will be completely inoperable."

"Excellent! How thankful I am for the bond that brings us together, Stefan. For the sake of little Nikolai and the rest of the children of the world, we mustn't fail. Now quickly, retie these bonds and be off! The seconds to the apocalypse continue to tick away."

Chapter Ten

For President Robert Palmer, the day had already been a most trying one. During the preceding weeks he had looked forward to this afternoon with great anticipation. At last the United States and the Soviet Union could be on their way to a new beginning. The way it was turning out, the present world outlook appeared anything but hopeful.

Palmer reflected on the morning's confusing events as he watched the plane carrying Premier Viktor Rodin touch down on the nearby runway. His vantage point was a private gate, set into one end of Los Angeles airport's international terminal. Standing before a huge picture window, he watched the massive Soviet aircraft hit the pavement with a noticeable jolt. A puff of smoke rose from the landing gear as the brakes were applied, and the lumbering jet coasted to an eventual halt. While it turned to begin the journey back to the terminal, the President mentally prepared himself for the encounter that would soon follow.

At forty-eight, Palmer was one of the youngest Chief Executive's in history. In office for a little over seven months, he had already taken it upon himself to tackle a problem that had been facing the country for almost a century. Soviet-American relations were the paramount concern of the times. This was especially true in the U.S., where citizen involvement had reached an all-time high. Palmer's landslide victory in the recent election proved this.

Running on a platform that emphasized cooperation over confrontation, the young politican had attained the nation's highest office with a clear victory in all but two states. Quite an accomplishment, considering Palmer's previous political experience was limited to a single Senate term.

Graced with the gift of spontaneous rhetoric and movie star good looks, the tall, lanky Midwesterner had a firm understanding of his constituents. Faced with the problems of a spiraling national debt, double-digit inflation and growing unemployment, the public had demanded a change. They were tired of the old-guard politicians who talked at great lengths about the problems but did little to solve them.

Palmer proposed to focus the country's attention on the one issue responsible for the nation's shortcomings. His speeches concentrated on a single fact— because of the needless arms race with the Soviets, the country was experiencing its worst economic difficulties. He promised to cut the massive spending on missiles and other war toys and divert them to other sectors, such as medical research, agriculture and even space exploration. Relieved of its huge military expenditures, he pledged that America would flourish as never before.

Of course, the success of his strategy depended fully upon the cooperation of the Soviet Union. Only with a bilaterial disarmament could such a dream come to pass. Fortunately, the Russian economy was in even worse shape than America's. In a mad rush to obtain military parity with the U.S., the Soviets had promoted military growth as their number one priority. As a result, their consumer hardships had increased. Tired of breadlines, poor quality household goods and other shoddy personal merchandise, the Russian people cried out for change. For the first time since the revolution, angry mobs of dissatisfied Russians roamed the streets of the large cities and demanded a change for the better.

Though the Soviet bureaucracy moved at a ponderous pace, the sudden rise of Viktor Rodin soon brought the changes that the people demanded. Like Palmer, the relatively young General Secretary realized that military spending was draining his country dry. He called for a series of daring, unprecedented economic programs.

Robert Palmer's predecessor in the White House had reacted to Rodin's ascension cautiously. Fearful to take the initiative and open a dialogue with the new Soviet leader, Washington sat back and watched the new Premier consolidate his position with a wary eye. By supporting increased military spending, the previous Administration had made Rodin's job even more difficult. How could he propose cuts in Russia's military establishment when America continued to pump billions of dollars into new weapon systems of their own?

The young contender for the White House realized this dilemma and molded his campaign around it. "Dare for Greatness" was the slogan with which he challenged the American people. Early in the primaries, Palmer announced his desire to meet with Viktor Rodin immediately after he won the presidency. Face to face, the two leaders of the most powerful nations the world had ever known would rationally address the dangerous plight in which they found themselves.

It wasn't long after Palmer had taken the oath of office that his invitation was presented to the General Secretary. Much to the new President's delight, Rodin accepted at once. In response to this, Palmer introduced an immediate freeze on all new weapons development. A day later, the Premier did likewise.

Confident that his colleague's goals and aspirations were like his own, Palmer had spent the past two months preparing for their historic meeting. During that period, a feeling of general euphoria was shared by a majority of the world's population. Encouraged by daily newscasts hinting at drastic results from the upcoming summit, the peoples of the earth had hope that the age of imminent nuclear warfare was finally over.

Robert had awakened this morning feeling strong and self-assured. But then a phone call, relayed to him via the Pentagon, had severely dampened his enthusiasm. The admiral who had conveyed the initial information had related a nightmarish tale of conspiracy, mutiny and the likely threat of a possible Soviet first strike. The President had decided that it was time to initiate a call of his own. Viktor Rodin had appeared genuinely shocked upon hearing Palmer's information.

The Premier's response was strained and confused.

Palmer was certain that the man was learning about the takeover of the IL-36 relay plane—and the subsequent release of launch orders to the *Vulkan*—for the very first time. His decision to continue on to L.A. was most heartening. With a promise to find out just what was occurring aboard the submarine, and to call Palmer back when he had done so, the Premier broke the line.

Palmer had learned the true extent of the crisis when the General Secretary had called back. In a heavy, condescending tone, Rodin confirmed that the *Vulkan* was unable to be contacted. The President could hardly believe it when the Premier asked for American help in tracking down the errant vessel.

A hastily called emergency staff meeting had produced mixed results. As Palmer had expected, his National Security Advisor, Patrick Carrigan, feared some sort of Soviet shenanigans. Distrustful of Rodin's good intentions from the very beginning, Carrigan pleaded with Palmer to cancel the summit and leave Los Angeles at once. To underscore his warning, Carrigan had detailed the incredible destructive power of a Soviet Delta-class sub. Not only L.A., but cities all over the continent would be wiped out if the vessel's missiles were targeted to do so. To insure the country's military command response if the SS-N-18s were released, Carrigan had advised that the U.S. strategic forces be brought to a state of emergency alert.

George Michaelson, the Secretary of State, had taken a much softer stand. Conscious of the ultimate consequences of a Soviet missile strike, he pleaded with the President to proceed with utmost delicacy.

Since all signs pointed to this being an isolated incident, it was their responsibility to help Viktor Rodin resolve the embarrassing situation, whose dire consequences threatened them all. A strategic alert on the part of America would only give the suspicious Russians an excuse to order one of their own. The idea of both countries with their fingers on the nuclear hair-trigger didn't appeal to the Secretary of State at all.

He did, however, agree with Carrigan that Palmer should leave Los Angeles as soon as possible. If the worse-case scenario came to pass, the President had to be far away from any potential target areas.

Robert Palmer concurred with this, and had ordered his E-4B command aircraft known as Kneecap (for National Emergency Airborne Command Post) to be ready for a quick take-off. The converted Boeing 747 was parked in a secured, isolated section of the same airport in which he presently awaited the arrival of the Soviet Premier. Packed with a variety of highly sophisticated communications systems, Kneecap was designed to serve as a survivable flying command post in times of crisis. Its purpose was much the same as that of the mammoth aircraft now nosing into the gate before him.

Taking in the large red star on its fuselage, Palmer watched the plane ground to a halt. So intense was his concentration that Palmer didn't notice the gaunt figure of his National Security Advisor taking a position at his side.

"Well, Mr. President, it appears that Comrade Rodin is right on time for your little party. I still wish that you'd reconsider asking him to board Kneecap

246

with you. There's more top-secret gear crammed into that aircraft than anywhere else on the planet."

Palmer replied without taking his eyes off the IL-76. "Come off it, Pat. What else can I do with him?"

"Leave him in Los Angeles as a hostage until this crisis is resolved," Carrigan stated firmly. "That will give those mutineers something to think about."

"You know that's impossible, Pat. I've waited two long months for this day. I'm not about to go off now and leave the Premier out in the cold."

"I'd say that our current situation warrants some extra thought, Mr. President. I don't think you planned on having a magazine full of SS-N-18s staring us down the throat. Have you given any more thought as to how we're going to respond in the event those missiles are released?"

The President glanced to his right and caught Carrigan's inquisitive stare. "I don't exactly have that many options, do I?"

"You could reconsider issuing that launch-on-warning directive, sir. Clearing our ICBMs out of their silos can save them from certain total destruction."

"Jesus, Patrick, you're not going to start with that again! I've already agreed to your suggestion of bringing our strategic forces up to an alert status of DEFCON 3. With all operational subs out to sea, our B-52s dispersed and all Minuteman crews on alert, I think that's a sufficient show of force at the moment. Remember, this is an isolated threat we're facing, not the whole damn Russian Army!"

Carrigan didn't flinch. "We still don't know that fact for certain, Mr. President. The Russian mind works very differently from our own. Don't forget that we're talking about the best chess players in the world here. I still can't help but smell a trap. Since all that the Soviets respect is a firm show of force in return for any aggression on their part, I've taken the liberty of drawing up a variety of target options. If those SS-N-18s are launched, at least we'll be able to take out an equivalent number of Soviet installations."

"I pray to God that we'll be able to get a handle on this situation long before we're forced to start playing that game, Mr. Carrigan. What's the latest news from Pearl?"

"Admiral Miller reports that our carrier task force is closing in on the coordinates that Premier Rodin gave us. It's spearheaded by the *Triton*, one of our newest attack subs. If the supposed launch position of the *Vulkan* is correct, we should have an intercept within two hours."

A slight look of relief crossed Palmer's face. "I've got a feeling that the U.S. Navy is going to take care of all of our problems for us."

When the cordon of uniformed policemen lining the exit ramp began to stir, the President backed away from the window. "It looks like the General Secretary and his party are on their way down. Come on, Carrigan, at least try to put a neighborly smile on that Irish face. These folks came an awfully long way to see us."

Robert Palmer followed his remark with a playful wink, and his advisor couldn't help but grin in response. Anxiously, both men walked over to greet the group of dark-suited newcomers who were led by the handsome, nattily dressed figure of Viktor Rodin.

As the President approached his Soviet counterpart, he found himself relieved. The sincere warmth that glowed from Rodin's dark, intense eyes couldn't be ignored. They met with a handshake, a hug, and a kiss on each cheek.

"Welcome to America, General Secretary Rodin," the President said. "I can't tell you how much I've looked forward to this day."

"The feeling is mutual, Comrade President," Rodin replied in flawless English. "I just wish that my arrival could have taken place under different circumstances. The plight of the *Vulkan* has cast a dark shadow over this summit of peace."

"That it has. I don't suppose you have any updates on your efforts to reach the *Vulkan*?"

Rodin shook his head gravely. "As before, our navy is still doing its best to reach them. By the way, I would like you to meet the man who is responsible for this effort, Admiral Stanislav Sorokin."

Rodin stepped aside and beckoned into the crowd that had followed him out of the gateway. A heavy-set, white-haired officer stepped from the ranks and approached them.

"President Palmer, this is Admiral Stanislav Sorokin, Commander of the Fleet of the Soviet Union."

The blue-suited naval officer offered the President a cold, emotionless handshake.

Immediately cognizant of Sorokin's enmity, Palmer did his best to break the ice. "It is an honor to meet you, Admiral. I have heard nothing but respectful comments concerning you from my own naval officers. Your foresight and persistent vision are to be admired."

To this, Sorokin merely nodded and did his best to merge back into the crowd from which he had emerged. The admiral's stubborn indifference reminded Palmer of Patrick Carrigan. Though they came from opposite ends of the political spectrum, the two advisors had much in common.

After a quick introduction to the rest of the Premier's staff, Palmer took Rodin gently by the arm and guided him over to an empty corner. "I'm afraid that the crisis aboard your submarine has necessitated a change in our original schedule. I believe it's best for both of us to initiate our meeting in my personal command plane. I have already arranged to have a secured line available for you, connected directly with the PVO underground national command center outside of Moscow."

The Premier noticed the strain visible on his host's face, and answered as openly as possible. "I think that, under the circumstances, this is an excellent idea, Mr. President. There is much that I'd like to share with you, but our privacy and safety must first be assured."

"Excellent," returned a noticeably relieved Robert Palmer. "Because of space limitations, you will be limited to one staff person of your choice. I hope this won't inconvenience you, General Secretary."

"That is no trouble at all, Comrade President. I will have my personal secretary, Olga Tyumen, accompany us. And please, call me Viktor."

Put at ease by his guest's frankness, Palmer managed a gracious smile. "I'll do that only if you will also call me by my first name."

"Robert it is."

The man's charm was infectious. Palmer's instincts said that it was safe to trust the Premier.

"Well then, Viktor, I think it's best if we begin our way over to Kneecap at once."

"Kneecap?"

"I'm sorry, Viktor. That's merely my plane's nickname."

Rodin grinned, then excused himself to inform his staff that he would be leaving them for a while. Stanislav Sorokin took the news with some alarm, and implored the Premier to have a second with him alone. In the privacy of the jet walkway, the two men solemnly faced each other.

"Comrade General Secretary, why must you go up in the imperialist command plane? This whole mess smells more and more like a certain Yankee trap!"

Rodin answered firmly. "I disagree with you, Admiral. Under the circumstances, the President is making the only practical decision. Of course, I'm sorry to have to leave the rest of you in Los Angeles, but that can't be avoided."

"And what if I have news of the *Vulkan*?" implored Stanislav.

"It should be easy enough to reach me, Admiral. The facilities aboard the flying Kremlin should be more than adequate for this task."

"But the Yankees will surely be listening in!"

"That doesn't concern me in the least, Admiral Sorokin. This is a predicament that each side shares equally. Just think how you'd feel if the situation were reversed, and it was one of their Tridents off of our coast. So far, the Americans have been most understanding of our inept efforts to contact the *Vulkan*.

You should be more concerned with your own effort in making certain that this mess doesn't get completely out of hand. I don't know how this cowardly act of mutiny came to pass, but I want it stemmed, and stemmed now! Find me the malefactors, Admiral. Your incompetency so far can't be excused!"

Sheepishly, Sorokin angled his glance down to his feet as the Premier turned to rejoin the American President. Though he fumed inwardly, Sorokin did his utmost to contain his rising temper.

How dare that insolent moron talk to him in that manner! Didn't the fool realize whom he was addressing? The admiral was already serving his country when Rodin was still wetting the bed. Soon Viktor Rodin would know just who the foolish one was!

Even if the Premier missed the warhead that had been intended to take him out, it would already be too late to interfere. The elimination of the imperialist command posts would signal the end of the capitalists ability to defend themselves. The soldiers of the Rodina wouldn't just sit back and mourn the Yankees losses—they would attack and end the American threat forever! Now, if only he could convince the pilot of the flying Kremlin to take to the air, perhaps he, too, could share in the upcoming victory. Stimulated by this thought, his great depression of the last few hours dissipated like a summer fog. Feeling like a condemned prisoner suddenly given a full reprieve, he continued on down the walkway to have a few words with the IL-76's flight crew.

A quarter of an hour later, Viktor Rodin found

himself strapped in a chair in the forward conference room of the aircraft known as Kneecap. More spacious and comfortable than his IL-76 command plane, the E-4B appeared to be a most well designed vehicle. So far, he had seen only the forward portion of the fuselage where the President's private quarters were located. But his host had promised to show him the rest of the plane after their initial meeting was concluded.

Minutes after they entered Kneecap it was taxiing to their take-off position. There was little doubt that the Americans were in a hurry to get airborne. Rodin couldn't blame them. Not knowing exactly when, where, or if the *Vulkan*'s missiles would be released, they could only prepare for the worst. Since he was directly responsible for this tragic mess, the Premier could only express his sincere apologies and do his best to defuse the volatile situation before it was too late.

Only after the plane had attained its cruising altitude did Robert Palmer join him. Though they had met but a short time before, Rodin felt as if they were old friends, reunited after years of separation. As Palmer slipped into a chair on the opposite side of the rectangular walnut table, Rodin did his best to express his true feelings.

"Once again, Robert, I can't tell you how sorry I am for this inexcusable dilemma we find ourselves in. It is my direct responsibility, and therefore I can only plead for your understanding."

"Pleas aren't necessary, Viktor. In a way, each of us equally shares responsibility. Such a crisis was bound to happen sooner or later. Actually, I'm amazed that this is the first time such a horrible thing has come to pass. As holders of the world's primary nuclear arsenals, such a crisis had to be expected as an eventuality. I'm only sorry that you and I didn't meet much earlier. A world without The Bomb would be free from such madness."

"Well said, Comrade," Rodin sighed. "If we can get through this dark day, there will be no excuses for us to delay the immediate banning of nuclear weapons from the face of the planet. I can only hope that we are not too late."

When the plane shook in a slight pocket of turbulence, Rodin swiveled around to peer out a small window. It was a cloudless day; the blue waters of the Pacific were clearly visible, 37,000 feet below.

"Our destiny awaits us beneath those waters, Robert. I feel it's my duty to relate to you a detailed list of the *Vulkan*'s intended targets. Perhaps you might even consider the evacuation of specific locations. Who knows how many lives such an act could save?"

The Premier reached over and handed Palmer a single sheet of lined paper. As the President's eyes skimmed the list, the scope of the potential catastrophe was disturbingly evident. With his voice trembling, he responded softly.

"Do you mind if I give this information to my staff?"

"Of course not, Comrade. This is why I've given it to you. Any other data that you require is also at your service."

The President picked up one of the four telephones that graced the table and punched in a single digit.

"Delores, please have Pat Carrigan see me at once."

As he replaced the handset, he looked up thoughtfully. "I know that nuclear-targeting plans are among the most secretive areas of military operations. Your openness is most appreciated. I hope that the disclosure of such information won't affect the ultimate outcome of this matter. We still have several hours until those missiles are due to be launched. It is imperative that we spend this time wisely. I think that the first step would to be to set up a conference call between ourselves, the Pentagon, and your PVO command headquarters. Our efforts must be coordinated in order to reach the *Vulkan* well before the missiles are released. Have you been able to determine the individuals responsible for the unauthorized release of those launch codes?"

Somberly, Rodin shook his head. "My most trusted aides are currently in the midst of such an investigation. We've only been able to determine that it is attributable to a small group of malcontents. The Soviet Union's military and intelligence arms are just as shocked by this traitorous action as we are.

"Of course, the primary inquiry is taking place among my cryptographic staff. To make certain that other weapons cannot be released, the members of this hand-picked unit were immediately replaced and the launch codes altered. I have authorized the MVD, our internal police force, to initiate a probe separate from that of the KGB to insure a thorough investigation. One thing I guarantee is that the madmen responsible will be uprooted! We shall not rest until this is accomplished."

There was a knock on the cabin door. "Yes, come

in," the President said.

The door swung open and a nondescript, gray-suited, middle-aged man curiously eyed the Premier before addressing Robert Palmer.

"You wanted to see me, Mr. President?"

"Patrick Carrigan, I'd like you to meet General Secretary Rodin." The two nodded leadenly toward each other as Palmer continued. "Pat here is my National Security Advisor. I think that he'd better take a look at this target list before we set up that conference call."

Palmer handed his advisor the sheet of paper. Carrigan remained standing while he read its contents and appeared shaken. His face was noticeably drained of color as he looked back at the President.

"Pretty scary stuff, huh Pat?" Palmer said calmly. "In the spirit of openness and cooperation, the General Secretary has offered us this information. You are free to give it to the Pentagon and to take all necessary precautions—short of full civilian evacuation. One thing I don't want on our hands is a public panic. As is the case in this entire crisis, information will be strictly on a need-to-know basis."

Carrigan responded hesitantly. "Sir, considering that the only major population center listed here is Los Angeles, shouldn't we reconsider evacuation? Even just a couple of hours' notice could save millions of lives!"

"I don't agree with you, Pat. We could lose that many just in the ensuing panic. I've studied all the civil defense manuals and have a pretty good grasp of the problems involved with crisis relocation. We'd need at least a week to properly evacuate the Los

Angeles basin. A couple of hours isn't going to make much of a difference."

This observation was delivered in a flat, grim tone. Palmer's next words were more hopeful.

"Right now, I want all of us to put such thoughts out of our minds. We must instead concentrate on doing everything within our capabilities to stop the *Vulkan* from firing. We're going to need a conference line opened between Kneecap, the Joint Chiefs and the Soviet PVO headquarters. Then, I'm going to want to talk with Admiral Miller. The ball is in Pacific Command's court now. I'm counting on them to end this game with a single shot."

Viktor Rodin watched the President's advisor absorb these words, and could tell that he entertained a solution of a vastly different nature. Like his own Stanislav Sorokin, the man most probably thought that a show of force would be a much better answer to their problem. Thankful to have Robert Palmer for his ally, the General Secretary wondered if his new friend would change his mind once the first of the warheads began dropping on American soil. His stomach soured and he struggled to wipe this line of thought from his consciousness.

Some 2,500 miles away from Kneecap, a Sikorsky SH-60B Seahawk helicopter soared over the Pacific. From its central hatch window, Captain Michael Cooksey peered down at the ocean's surface.

For the last hour, their course had been to the northwest, as they followed the Hawaiian Ridge up toward Midway Island. Cooksey knew these waters well, but not from this particular vantage point. They were passing over a handful of the tiny coral atolls from which the Ridge derived its name. Formed by volcanic activity millions of years ago, the Ridge stretched westward to merge with the Emperor Seamount Chain. Separating these two subterranean features was Midway itself.

So far, the flight had progressed smoothly. The crew of three had been quite courteous, staying mostly to themselves. That was fine as far as Cooksey was concerned. At the moment, he had plenty to think about.

The unexpected trip up from Kauai had happened so quickly that he needed the time alone to put his thoughts in order. His primary concern had been his hasty briefing with Admiral Miller. The Commander of the Third Fleet had seemed unusually tense as he told Cooksey the facts regarding the current crisis.

There was no doubting the seriousness of the situation, especially when the proper launch code had already been conveyed. That such a situation had come to pass did not really shock Cooksey. Having sailed aboard a missile-carrying vessel himself, he knew that the launch of a submarine-based nuclear warhead could be achieved with a minimum of obstacles. This was unlike the release procedure that took place inside an ICBM launch capsule or a strategic bomber. Those delivery systems required the receipt of complex codes before a warhead's triggering mechanism would work. The device that received this code was called a PAL, for Permissive Action Link. It insured that the weapon couldn't be utilized without proper authorization from command.

While visiting a cousin assigned to Whiteman Air Force base in western Missouri, Cooksey had been given a tour of a Minuteman launch capsule. Here he had seen the elaborate safeguard system at work. The process of releasing an ICBM was unbelievably complex. Generally, each two-man launch crew was in charge of ten separate missile silos. When an Emergency Action message or launch order arrived, it had to be decoded and validated. It was then entered into the PAL. Once authorized, each officer would position himself before one of a pair of widely spaced keyholes. The keys had to be turned simultaneously, eliminating the possibility of a launch by a single, renegade officer.

In contrast, missiles launched from submarines had no elaborate PAL devices. Because of the constraints caused by communications difficulties, they could be fired without specific *go codes* from command. All they needed was a single message informing them that a war alert existed. Then it was up to each individual captain to reconfirm that such a state indeed existed and to act accordingly.

Since the same communications restraints limited the Soviets, their submarine-launched missiles were most likely operated in a similar manner. If somehow a war alert had been conveyed to one of their Delta III-class vessels, it was very possible that its skipper thought a nuclear conflict between the two superpowers existed. Whether by intention or accident, a failure to correct this mistake could lead to a most unpleasant outcome. Since the Soviets had so far failed in their efforts to reach the submarine, the U.S. Navy had been called in to do their dirty work.

Cooksey was surprised that the Russians had so openly asked for help. It wasn't every day that the General Secretary of the Soviet Union gave the United States his blessing to blow away one of their most sophisticated strategic plaforms. Something must have occurred inside his own command chain that made contacting the sub an impossibility.

Cooksey was aware of a change in the steady pitch of the Seahawk's rotors. Glancing outside, he saw that they were losing altitude. As he studied the rolling swells, he weighed the *Triton*'s chances of completing its mission.

He really didn't think that locating the Soviet sub would be very difficult. Such ships were large and noisy. If they were where they were supposed to be, the *Triton*'s superior sensors would quickly track them down.

The element that was critical was the time factor. The admiral had given him a rough idea as to when the Soviets were due to launch. Even with the *Triton*'s head start, they would have to proceed with their throttles wide open if they were going to have any chance of reaching the *Vulkan* in time.

He remembered that the *Triton* was now loaded with a new, experimental weapons system that effectively extended their range of attack to a full three hundred miles. The ASW/SOW device could prove crucial to their mission's success.

A coordinated effort on the part of the carrier task force would aid them also. At last report, the *John F. Kennedy* and its escorts were steaming in from the waters northeast of Midway. Their choppers would soon be within range of the southern sector of the

Emperor Seamount Chain. Here they would saturate the ocean with hundreds of sonobuoys. Assisted by ultra-sensitive dunking hydrophones and the ever-probing magnetic anamoly detectors, the helicopters would radio news of a find back to the carrier. The *Triton* would then be informed and a proper kill initiated.

Though it all sounded relatively simple, Cooksey knew that it was an enormous task. If the *Vulkan* wasn't where it was supposed to be, finding it could take days, or even weeks. And even if they were able to tag the sub, there was always the likely possibility that a companion Alfa-attack vessel would be standing by to defend it.

Cooksey stirred restlessly as he recalled their last encounter. It wasn't far from these very seas that the Alfa had shot under the task force at unheard of speeds. He would never forget his feeling of utter frustration as the *Triton* had tried in vain to pursue them, or his exasperation when they realized he didn't even have a weapon capable of touching the Soviet attack sub.

Although not really certain of the Alpha's offensive capabilities, Cooksey knew he was up against a potent adversary. The *Triton* would have to be kept in a state of constant alert to retain the advantage of surprise.

The next few hours proved to be most trying ones. Thankful for a rested body and mind, Cooksey anxiously awaited the challenge. At long last, twenty years of intense study and endless practice exercises were about to be applied. He was feeling most confident that his crew and equipment were the best that the country had to offer when the pitch of the rotors again changed.

Cooksey turned at the sound of movement from behind him, and saw the Seahawk's ATO go into action. The officer was attaching a transfer harness onto the thick, nylon winch cord. Aware of the captain's interest, the airborne tactical officer asked, "Ever go for a ride in one of these little ladies, sir?"

"Not since basic," Cooksey shouted over the din of the chopping rotors.

The ATO smiled. "Well, you have nothing to worry about, Captain. We'll set you down there as light as a feather."

"I'm sure that you will," Cooksey said as the helicopter began a wide-banked turn.

"This must be the place, sir," the ATO observed. "We'd better take a look."

The young officer joined Cooksey at the sliding hatch window. Both men locked gazes on a surging sea that was clearly more turbulent than it had appeared from a higher altitude. White caps topped four-foot swells that constantly rolled in on long fingers from the northwest.

They were only a few hundred feet above the surface now. Cooksey looked down expectantly. A full minute passed, when suddenly he saw a thin line of frothing white turbulence cutting through the green depths. Seconds later, he spotted the tip of a periscope. He pointed it out to the ATO, who reached over and grabbed an intercom. Once the pilot spotted it, the chopper descended still lower.

As the Seahawk made a series of wide-banking turns, Cooksey's eyes remained locked on the sea. Like finding an old friend who has been too-long absent, he watched breathlessly as the top edge of the sub's sail became visible. Next, the sail's two diving planes could be seen. The vessel seemed to remain at this depth for some time, the sail knifing smoothly through the water, when a torrent of crashing turbulence indicated a sudden change. In the blink of an eye, the rest of the three-hundred-sixty-foot-long vessel emerged. As a curl of seawater smashed over the *Triton*'s curved hull, Cooksey beamed with pride.

The intercom buzzed and the ATO answered it, then handed the receiver to Cooksey. The chopper pilot wished him luck, adding that fuel considerations demanded as quick a transfer as possible.

Cooksey thanked him for the lift, and then, with the ATO's expert help, fitted on the shoulder harness. Ready to initiate transfer, the hatch door was swung open and Cooksey was instructed to sit with his feet dangling outside as the chopper positioned itself above the waiting sub.

The sound of whirling rotors was considerably louder now, as the Seahawk continued to descend. Cooksey saw that the *Triton*'s hatch cover had been removed, and two familiar khaki-clad figures were looking up. As he identified his XO and the massive physique of Chief Bartkowski, a wave of emotion swelled in his breast. Like a pilgrim whose long journey had finally brought him home, he muttered a simple prayer of thanks.

"See you around the golf course, Captain," said the ATO as he began working the winch mechanism.

Cooksey flashed him a thumbs-up as the harness pulled tightly around his shoulder blades. Before he knew it, he was suspended outside the hovering chopper. Buffeted by the rotors' powerful downdraft, he shielded his eyes and felt himself dropping.

The accuracy of the Seahawk's crew was perfect—their first attempt brought Cooksey right to the open platform cut into the top of the sub. The chief's massive hands grabbed him securely as the XO hit the harness release lever. The strain on Cooksey's shoulders was instantly relieved.

"Requesting permission to come aboard," Cooksey said with a salute.

"Permission granted," said Executive Officer Richard Craig. For a moment, the three of them watched the sleek, white SH-60B as it sped northeast with a roar.

"I just hope they make it back to the *JFK*," Cooksey said at last. "The way I figure it, those fuel tanks have got to be close to dry. Oh, and by the way Rich—congratulations, papa!"

The XO shook Cooksey's outstretched hand. "Thanks, Skipper. I kind of find it hard to believe myself."

"How's Susan doing?" Cooksey asked.

"At last report she was all smiles, Skipper. Do you know that she waited to go into labor until we had pulled into Pearl? I even got to drive her to the hospital."

"Sorry that we had to drag you away from your new family, but that's the navy."

The XO responded lightly. "I'm fine now, knowing that everything turned out so well. You're sure looking tanned and rested, Captain."

"I haven't felt this good in years. This was the first *R-&-R* that I really enjoyed in too long. Unfortunately, all good things come to an end. What's the status of the *Triton*, Chief?"

Pete Bartkowski, who had been scanning the sea before them, said, "All systems are operational, Captain. Had time to take on a full load of supplies, and also a pair of newfangled, long-range ASW weapons. Lieutenant Spencer has 'em stowed away in the forward torpedo room."

"I think that you'll find some unfamiliar faces aboard, Skipper," the XO added. "Because of the sudden nature of our sailing orders, we had to grab a dozen non-coms off the *Triggerfish*. They're fully competent and seem to have mixed in well with the rest of the crew. Are you going to be able to tell us what this mission is all about now? Our orders didn't say much."

Cooksey's words flowed smoothly. "Believe it or not, gentlemen, the *Triton* is going hunting for a Soviet Delta-class missile sub that is believed to be the victim of a mutiny. We've been called in to eliminate this vessel—at the direct request of their General Secretary. I'll be giving you all the sweet details during the meeting I'd like you to set up in the wardroom. Include all officers and senior chiefs. I'd like this to take place within the hour, so let's get cracking. Will you take her down, Rich?"

"Aye-aye, Skipper," the XO replied. But he couldn't hide his astonishment at the captain's revelations. With a slight shiver, he picked up the intercom and punched in two digits. "Mr. Lawrence, prepare to dive."

Cooksey followed the bulky figure of Chief Bartkowski down the stairway into the sub's interior.

The familiar hum of the *Triton*'s systems surrounded him as he ducked through a hatchway and emerged into the control room. As he examined the equipment-packed compartment and watched its occupants in action, Cooksey knew that he had finally returned home. He watched the diving officer prepare to take them down into their natural element. Beside him sat the planesmen, perched alertly in leather-upholstered chairs, with the rubber steering yoke and plane control sticks well within reach.

Cooksey was scanning the consoles reserved for engineering, sonar, weapons and navigation, when a loud, raucous honk echoed twice. Richard Craig had already sealed the hatch and was in the process of taking a position beside the diving officer. Cooksey remained a detached observer as the diving console's toggle switches were triggered and a series of lights indicated that the valves were opening. Seconds later, the muffled roar of rushing water signaled that the ballast tanks had begun to flood. The stern planes were activated and the *Triton* began to descend.

While the deck began angling downward, Cooksey made his way over to the navigation plotting table. He was in the midst of drawing up a detailed topographical cross-section of the southern portion of the Emperor Seamount Chain when the angle of their descent increased noticeably. Forced to hold onto the edge of the console to keep from falling over, he immediately knew that something out of the ordinary had occurred. Struggling to join his XO, his progress was forced to a halt when the bow began to nose down even more sharply. His thoughts flashed wildly: Had there been a mistake with the ballast calculations?

Perhaps the *Triton* hadn't been sealed properly, and it was the weight of inrushing seawater that was dragging them down to the bottom. One thing he knew for certain was that a dive at this descent and speed would be fatal in a matter of minutes.

Then he heard Richard Craig shout "Hard rise on the stern planes!"

Tense seconds passed, when slowly but surely, their angle of descent lessened.

"Shut all vents!" the XO called out as he made certain that the proper switches were flicked.

Cooksey quickly strode to Craig's side. "Jesus, Rich, what the hell happened?"

It proved to be Dirk Lawrence, their diving officer, who offered an explanation. "It appeared to be the planesmen, sir. I believe they overcompensated for the dive."

To verify this, the three officers proceeded to the diving console. Here they found the two seated seamen visibly shaken. The sweat-stained sailor sitting on the left turned his head and, with voice trembling, sheepishly said, "I'm sorry, sir, but the control stick of the *Triggerfish* has a completely different feel to it."

"It's my fault, Captain," Dirk Lawrence said. "As diving officer, I should have been watching them more closely. I've taken one of those Permit-class subs down myself and can vouch for the difference in plane pressure."

Cooksey looked at his exec and then to his watch. "Well, thank God everything turned out okay. Lieutenant Lawrence, I want you to make certain that all new personnel are monitored closely. Rich, you'd better bring us up to two hundred feet, and then we'd

267

better get going with that officers meeting. We don't have much time."

Confident that this isolated incident would not be repeated, Cooksey excused himself. It had been a long day already, and there was still much more to do. After a quick visit to his cabin and a change into a fresh pair of khakis, he allowed himself the luxury of a cup of coffee and a ham sandwich. By then his XO had called to notify him that the personnel he had requested were present in the wardroom.

As the officers filed inside the wardroom, a rumble of nervous chatter rose from their ranks. Each was aware that the order calling them out of Pearl Harbor was most unusual. When their orders also demanded that they leave without the captain, they knew something deadly serious was up.

Without fanfare, their captain entered and made his way over to the wall beside the wardroom's video screen. As he turned to face his men, the room's only picture could be seen over his right shoulder. It showed a full-length silhouette of the sub plunging into blue depths. Superimposed on it was a lithe Greek god holding a triton-shell trumpet in one hand, and the trident spear of sea power in the other.

Cooksey cleared his throat and spoke distinctly. "Thank you, gentlemen, for your prompt attendance. I'm sure that you're anxious to know about the nature of our present mission, and I'm not going to keep you in suspense any longer. We have been authorized to hunt down and eliminate a Soviet Delta-class submarine, the *Vulkan*. This directive comes from the highest sources, which can be traced all the way back to the General Secretary of the Soviet Union himself.

In effect, we have been asked to do what his navy has failed to accomplish, to stem a mutiny aboard one of their most modern missile-carrying vessels. Since it is feared that the *Vulkan* plans to release its load of sixteen SS-N-18 ballistic missiles once it attains its launch position, we must act with all due haste to cancel this threat. I've drawn up the following map segment to show what we are up against."

As the captain turned to activate the video screen, the wardroom filled with astounded whispers. The babble hushed as the monitor flashed on and Cooksey again addressed them.

"This, gentlemen, is the southern portion of the Emperor Seamount Chain. In order for the *Vulkan*'s missiles to be within range of their intended targets, their release point must be somewhere between this sector and Midway Island. I know this includes a large expanse of territory, and that we are still several hours away, but the task has fallen upon our shoulders and I don't intend to fail.

"Assisting us will be a task force of surface ships currently steaming into these waters from the northeast. This includes the carrier *John F. Kennedy*, the Aegis guided-missile cruiser *Ticonderoga*, and the Spruance-class destroyer, *Eagle*.

"To make the most effective use of this force's formidable ASW capabilities, we will interface with their sensors whenever possible. The *Ticonderoga* has deployed a specially designed low-frequency antenna that will allow them to notify us of any detections. Our helicopters will probably be the first elements to tag the *Vulkan*. As you all know, the Delta-class sub make their own distinctive racket in the water, which should be readily picked up by our dunking hydrophones. The choppers will also enable our forces to cover an extremely large patch of ocean.

"Since the *Triton* is specifically designed to carry out just such a mission, we are being counted on to deliver the fatal blow. To insure this, I'm going to need the help of each of you.

"Lieutenant Weaver, we're going to need every available knot out of our reactor, and then some. For the next couple of hours, I'm counting on maximum speed to bring us within range of our bogey.

"Mr. Callahan, you will have the demanding job of coordinating the sensor interface with the surface fleet. While this is being accomplished, your people will also be responsible for monitoring the *Triton*'s own sensor systems. There is a very good chance that the *Vulkan* is not out here alone. I'm certain that you remember the bogey we encountered during our last exercise at Point Luck. This same Alfa sub was seen escorting the *Vulkan* back to its pen in Petropavlovsk. I doubt if they would send the missile-carrying Delta on patrol without the Alfa along for protection."

A hand shot up in the back of the room and Cooksey signaled a freckle-faced, red-headed officer to stand. "Excuse me, Captain, but tagging the Alfa could pose some serious problems. Not only is its hull coated with an anechoic covering that makes our sonar useless, but she can outdive and outrun us as well. Even if we did manage to pick them up, what could we do about them?"

"Good question, Mr. Callahan. I think Lieutenant Spencer has the answer to that. Lieutenant, are the *Triton*'s most recent additions ready for action?"

Randal Spencer, the ship's weapons officer, stood and answered calmly. "That they are, Captain. If the ASW/SOWs do everything the manual promises, those Ruskies will be fair game. I don't care how fast they're running, but if you can bring them within a 300-mile radius of our forward tubes, I'll do the rest."

This remark brought a surprised comment or two before the captain continued. "Earlier, during a routine descent, the *Triton* was almost involved in a disastrous mishap. A simple mistake on the part of a planesman could have abruptly ended this cruise for all of us. Because we were forced to take on several sailors who are new to our class of sub, I must ask you to keep your eyes peeled for any sign of incompetence. Hopefully, this was an isolated incident, but continued vigilance is necessary.

"Now, if there are no additional questions, you may be off to your stations. I'll kindly ask you to keep knowledge of this briefing to yourselves. An announcement will shortly be made to the rest of the crew. Thank you, gentlemen, and good luck for the hunters!"

To a mild roar of chatter, the officers stood and filed from the room. Cooksey watched the procession and signaled his XO to join him beside the monitor.

"That was an excellent briefing, Skipper," Craig said. "The men were a bit shocked, to say the least."

"Thanks, Rich. I think I got my point across. And I don't blame them for being surprised. I'll never forget that moment when Admiral Miller sat me down and gave me the initial details. To tell you the truth, I still have trouble believing that this thing is really coming down."

271

"Ditto for me, Skipper. The part I'm having trouble with is the fact that the Soviet Premier has actually asked for our assistance. Things must really be out of hand for him to call us in to blow away one of their own subs."

"I've got to admit its one for the books all right. I just hope we don't let them down."

As the captain reached over and turned off the monitor, Craig asked, "Say we don't make it in time, and those missiles get released—what then, Skipper?"

Cooksey reflected a while before answering. "I shudder when I think of the possible consequences, Rich. A magazine full of SS-N-18s can cause one hell of a lot of damage. From their intended launch position, they could probably hit targets anywhere in the continental United States."

The XO's face suddenly paled. "Oh, sweet Jesus! Susan and the baby! They're laying there right at ground zero."

"Easy now, Rich, we've still got a bit to say in the matter."

"Oh, come on, Skipper, you know what an impossible task we face. They could be hundreds of miles away from us right now. And not only are the chances of tagging them slim, but then there's that Alfa to contend with. If we get anywhere close to the *Vulkan*, we're going to have one deadly tiger on our tail!"

Almost fatherly, Cooksey put his hand on his XO's shoulder. "That kind of thinking will only get you an ulcer. It's highly speculative, and self-defeating, too. If that Delta-class sub is there, we're going to take them out. I don't give a damn what they've got

272

between us and them. Nothing is getting in the way of the USS *Triton*!"

These words were delivered with such conviction that the XO couldn't help but lighten. "You said it, Skipper. Let's go get them!"

Playfully, Cooksey cuffed his exec on the side of his head, then pointed to the door. Without comment, Richard Craig managed a brave smile and followed the captain outside.

Chapter Eleven

Deep within the bowels of the *Vulkan*, Senior Lieutenant Vasili Leonov was in the process of inspecting the portion of the sub that held the missile tubes, known as the *taiga*. The cavernous compartment was empty except for Weapons Chief Yuri Chuchkin, who was following Leonov. Their steps echoed off the narrow metal walkway as they passed by the bases of the sixteen missile tubes, placed eight on each side. Beyond, the constant faraway hum of the vessel's engines droned incessantly.

As the senior lieutenant passed the silo marked, 4, he caught sight of a greasy rag sticking out from the silo's support cowling. He halted and studied it with unbelieving eyes. Yuri Chuchkin noticed his distraction and cautiously asked, "Is something the matter, Comrade?"

Leonov pointed to the cowling and replied with a disgusted shake of his head, "Is this the way your men prepare their stations for inspection? Such sloppiness is inexcusable! If the maintenance of the SS-N-18s themselves is as slipshod as this compartment's interior, we'll be lucky to get even a single warhead airborne."

Chuchkin reached out and grabbed the offending rag and briefly inspected its surface.

"I am sorry, sir. It's only a towel used to clean off excess grease from the sealant gaskets. I can guarantee you that the integrity of the missiles is in no way compromised."

"That makes no difference!" Leonov shouted. "Leaving such a rag behind is only indicative of your crew's general carelessness. The simplest mistakes have a way of producing the most dire consequences. Remember this, Comrade, and never let it happen again."

Doing his best to accept the rebuke, Chuchkin lowered his eyes. "You are right, sir. I will speak to the men and get to the bottom of this."

"We must all have pride in our service," Leonov said. "Such careless mistakes should never happen. Now, did you complete the warhead coordinate changes as I requested?"

"Of course, sir. They have been entered into the computer and triple-checked for accuracy."

"Well, check them again, Comrade Chuchkin. A careless mistake in this process could be disastrous."

Chuchkin straightened his shoulders and nodded. "I will do that, sir. I must admit that it represents a radically new set of target coordinates from our previous ones. I imagine it all has to do with those new ground-burrowing warheads that we recently took on."

"That is none of your concern, Comrade." The Senior Lieutenant turned away and continued his inspection.

Further down the walkway, Chuchkin said lightly, "Of course, this coordinate change is nothing but one of those endless alert exercises anyway. Most probably I'll be changing them back within a matter of hours."

"You never know, do you Comrade Chuchkin?"

Shrinking from Leonov's icy words, Chuchkin attempted to change the direction of their conversation. "You certainly gave me a scare back in Petropavlovsk, sir. For a while there, I thought that you might go AWOL."

This unexpected comment caught Leonov up short. Slowly, he turned to face the chief.

"I understand that you were one of those who initiated a search of the city on my behalf. I appreciate this gesture and truly regret that a moment of self-weakness made it necessary. I learned much during this personal crisis, Comrade. You can be assured that it will take more than a woman to divert me from my duty to the Rodina. They are nothing but a bunch of filthy tramps, anyway."

"I don't know if you can go so far as to say that collectively, sir. I must admit that I've had my fair share of female problems, but every once in a while one comes along to make all the bad experiences worth it."

"I guess I'm just waiting for that one to arrive," Leonov said thoughtfully. "Regardless, I want you to recheck those coordinate changes and then speak to your men once more. Instill in them a pride in their duties. Afterward, have them go over this compartment with a fine-tooth comb. I want this all completed within the hour, so snap to it, Comrade!"

Accepting the chief's salute, Leonov hurriedly

checked the remaining silos and then ducked through the hatchway leading to the bow. He continued to complete the second portion of his tour of inspection. Just as important as the missile compartment was that section of the *Vulkan* from which the weapons would be launched, the attack center. Located near the bow, two floors above him, the deserted attack center would soon be alive with frantic action. Anxious for this fated moment to finally arrive, Leonov checked his watch and increased the length of his stride.

As he walked down the cramped corridor he passed that portion of the sub reserved for supply storage. This was not a busy area and his progress was unhindered.

Leonov found himself a bit disturbed that the weapons chief had brought up the subject of his recent troubled leave in Petropavlovsk. He knew that he should have been anticipating such a comment. The good-natured chief had only been trying to lend a helping hand. Never again would Leonov allow his personal life to be scrutinized by his shipmates. This was one painful lesson he had learned all too well.

Though the entire affair had taken place but a few days ago, Leonov felt as if it had happened in a past lifetime. So much had happened since that fated afternoon that the very fabric of his being seemed like it had been torn apart and subsequently resewn. In place of the old self was a new, enlightened being, free from the bonds that had previously tied him down.

The steel-lined innards of a nuclear submarine was a peculiar place to put his life in perspective; nevertheless, Leonov's thoughts had dawned clear and con-cise. How much he had grown in these last few days! It all began when he had learned that Natasha had run off with that American journalist. On his way to buy her an engagement ring, he had made a quick call to her apartment and had learned of her betrayal.

His initial feeling was disbelief. When a call to Natasha's mother confirmed her daughter's actions, Leonov's thoughts turned to hurt, anger and then revenge. He'd track down the two, even if it meant following them to the far corners of the earth. How he relished the moment when he would choke the life from them.

To think that she had chosen a capitalist swine to take off with infuriated him all the more. Could this be the same woman whom he had picked to share the rest of his life? And he had previously prided himself in his knowledge of human nature! Fooled by the ultimate folly, he walked the streets of Petropavlovsk in a daze, totally stunned by his blindness.

With thoughts of naval duty far from his mind, Leonov had looked for solace in a bottle of vodka. Far from appeasing his resentment, the alcohol had only made it worse. To soothe his buried ego, he had picked up a Chinese prostitute. In her shabby hotel room, the hooker had done her best to arouse him. Stripping off her clothing, she revealed a compact, well-formed body. But as she flaunted it before him, a surge of revulsion rose from deep inside. At that moment, having intercourse was not in the least bit desirable. When the prostitute's teases increased, Leonov rose up, totally out of control. For the first time in his life, he savagely beat a woman. The young Oriental was nothing but a sobbing hunk of blood and bruises as he left her, temporarily satisfied that he had somehow avenged himself.

Reality had struck as he hit the icy streets. Sobered by a chilling gust of arctic wind, he could think of nothing but drowning his fears and confusion in more vodka. It was as he stumbled back to the bar that the hand of fate made its move. Blocking his progress on the snow-covered sidewalk was the dark, gaunt figure of the *zampolit*, Ivan Novikov. Though he had never liked this man before, the political officer had proven himself a most willing listener.

Over a cup of steaming hot tea, Leonov had again opened his heart. In the ensuing discussion he learned that he had previously misjudged Novikov. Surely, the middle-aged *zampolit* was wise beyond his years!

The political officer was able to divert Leonov by resurrecting lofty principles and theories that the senior lieutenant hadn't thought about in much too long. What a waste were the selfish ponderings of a single physical being, when the destinies of hundreds of millions of fellow Soviets were so unnecessarily threatened! With precise, eloquent terms, the *zampolit* reaffirmed the ultimate goals of their sworn duties. If everyone with a personal problem had carried on like Leonov, could the Rodina have risen to its current level of greatness? Of course not! There came a time when one had to sacrifice the puny concerns of self and concentrate on the future of the masses. Only in this way could life have a true meaning and purpose.

One socialist world, free from greed and the ceaseless threat of imperialism, was what they were working for. Without such a goal he was better off slitting his wrists, so that he would no longer be a State burden.

There had been a time, not too long ago, when such a lofty, selfless aim had indeed been foremost in his mind. Because his father had been a high-placed Party member, Leonov had been given a complete ideological education. So thorough was his indoctrination that he had even been able to perceive flaws in the lifestyles of his own parents.

The ideals of youth were soon veiled when Leonov was sent to military school. At the Frunze Naval Academy political indoctrination took second place to such complicated technical matters as celestial navigation and nuclear physics. Later courses instructed him in the trade that had filled his life for the last ten years. For an entire decade he did nothing but eat, sleep and dream of submarines. A series of rapid promotions brought him from junior lieutenant aboard a relatively crude November-class vessel to his present assignment. If all continued well, it wouldn't be long until he would be getting his own command. Yet, as the incident with Natasha had proven, all through these frantic times his life had been somehow lacking.

Leonov had assumed this emptiness was caused by his lack of a wife and family of his own. But Ivan Novikov had lifted the blinders from his eyes and shown him that a woman wouldn't be the object to fill this void. Rather, it proved to be his long-dormant political zeal that was to give him new hope and direction.

At Navikov's suggestion, Leonov had accompanied the *zampolit* to Petropavlovsk's Red Banner Naval

Museum. Here, while walking the hallways, deserted except for a large group of curious school children, they studied a pictorial history of the Soviet Navy's long climb to greatness. The chronicle began in the early part of the eighteenth century, when Czar Peter I founded the city of Leningrad at the eastern end of the Gulf of Finland, and built a fleet to fight the Swedes. The armada achieved notable success, yet for the centuries that followed they had few great victories to boast of. This noneffectiveness became most apparent after a humiliating defeat at the hands of the Japanese Navy during the war of 1904.

It wasn't until after World War II that individuals such as Stanislav Sorokin had emerged to lead the ineffective fleet to greatness. Hearts swelling with pride, Leonov and Novikov gazed upon a first-hand account of the ships comprising the current Soviet Navy. Able to hold their own in any ocean in the world, the fleet included a diverse mixture of sophisticated attack and missile-carrying submarines, massive aircraft carriers, heavily armed cruisers, sleek destroyers, and dozens of support vessels and warships of other classes. Almost overnight, the navy of the Soviet Union went from being a mere coastal defense force to the world's foremost naval power.

Leonov was in the midst of expounding on this when Novikov led him into an empty hallway and, in a hushed tone, told him of a conspiracy that threatened the fleet's very existence. His heart pounded as the *zampolit* relayed to him what he knew of General Secretary Viktor Rodin's plans to disband this awesome force once and for all.

Prompted by an insanity that they couldn't begin to

fathom, Rodin actually thought that Russia could disarm itself without fearing a threat from the imperialists. His voice quivering with passion, Novikov swore that all he was revealing was true, told to him personally by various members of the government occupying the highest, most respected offices. The *zampolit* almost broke into tears as he reflected upon the great sacrifices the Rodina had made to achieve this pinnacle of naval success. To strip it bare now, with a mere promise by the Yankees to do likewise, would be the act of a madman! Leonov heartily agreed.

Outside the museum, though the arctic wind still blew in frigid gusts, Leonov hardly noticed the cold as Ivan Novikov revealed an operation designed to defy their Premier's foolish scheme.

Counterforce was a project whose simplistic vision would change the world for all time to come. Well versed in the strategy underlying a surgical nuclear first strike, Leonov shivered in an awareness of the brilliance of the scheme. With a minimum of bloodshed, the earth's population would be free to reap the benefits of a single communist order. Surely, a few casualties now would be nothing compared to the slaughter that would soon follow in the wake of Rodin's sellout.

Without a single misgiving, the senior lieutenant had pledged to aid the *zampolit* in all that he asked. After an oath of secrecy was exchanged, Leonov had followed Novikov into the bowels of Petropavlovsk's KGB headquarters. Here he received an intricate briefing.

As Leonov now climbed the flight of stairs leading

to the *Vulkan*'s attack center, he thought back to these events and shuddered. Before that encounter he had only been half alive. Since then, weak, selfish emotions had been wrenched from his body and buried in the wastes of a past life. Today, it was a new, enlightened Vasili Leonov who walked the sub's deck.

No longer would base emotions get in his way. Now he had a goal to lead him unerringly onward. And how swiftly the attainment of this goal was proceeding! At the moment, only a few short hours stood between the *Vulkan* and its final launch position. Not even the vessel's weapons chief was included in their plotting.

The ultimate test of their power had come when the captain melted right before their eyes. Petyr Valenko was representative of all that was lacking in the officer corps. Unable to comprehend the grandeur of their vision, the captain had attempted a feeble show of resistance. It was because of the weakness of his convictions that he had subsequently failed. Conscious that no further obstacle now lay between them and their great scheme's attainment, the senior lieutenant soundlessly ducked through the attack center's open hatchway.

Leonov quickly spotted a familiar figure hunched intensely over a computer monitor screen in the compartment's far wall. His puzzlement turned to concern as he realized that the console was for the warhead targeting system. Since the *michman* had no business there, the senior lieutenant snuck up behind Stefan Kuzmin and carefully peered over his shoulder. Only after catching a glance of the screen's contents did Leonov break the hushed stillness.

"Interesting reading, isn't it Comrade Warrant Officer?"

Startled, Stefan looked up with a shock. Before he could reply, Leonov said, "Spare me the excuses, Kuzmin. I'm well aware that the material you're reading is of the utmost sensitivity. In fact, there are only three individuals on the *Vulkan* who are trusted with this particular access code. For such a traitorous act, I could shoot you right on the spot. But perhaps you'd like to tell me what this is all about, before forcing me to such an extreme."

Cautiously, Kuzmin turned to meet the senior lieutenant's hard stare. Perceiving that Leonov was too smart for any type of lie, he decided to confront him with the truth.

"I think there's some confusion here as to who's the traitor, Comrade Leonov. You didn't really think that you could get by with this mad scheme, did you?"

"Whatever are you babbling about, Kuzmin? Quit changing the subject and tell me how you got this access code!"

Kuzmin took a deep breath and replied matter-of-factly, "We are most aware of your mutinous desires, Comrade Senior Lieutenant. I am to inform you that you no longer have control of this ship to do as you want."

Leonov took a step backward and stifled a laugh. "So now you're giving me orders, Comrade Warrant Officer? Answer my original question, or risk instant arrest on charges of treason!"

Deciding to go ahead with his bluff, Kuzmin said, "The Captain has informed us where the real source of treason exists. Both yourself and Ivan Novikov are

284

asked to surrender without further violence."

Unable to constrain his rising impatience, Leonov's face reddened. "That's enough of this impertinence! You are to consider yourself under detention. As of this moment, you are relieved of all your duties as warrant officer."

As Leonov reached out to activate the intercom and enforce these orders, Kuzmin stood and knocked his hand away.

"Why, you insolent fool! I'll see you hung for this!"

The Senior Lieutenant moved in to pin Kuzmin down. The *michman* was not about to surrender so easily. Stepping aside, he deflected Leonov's hand with his left forearm, then jabbed him hard in the abdomen with his right fist. The blow temporarily knocked the wind out of Leonov. As he bent over, struggling for breath, his reddened face contorted into a painful sneer. Still gasping for air, Leonov managed to stand and swing out with a series of vicious left jabs.

Surprised by the quickness of Leonov's recovery and his punches, Kuzmin stepped into a powerful right hook aimed squarely at his jaw. Two more punches connected with his mouth and his nose. As blood streamed into his mouth, the *michman* knew he'd have to do something drastic to bring the senior officer down. Since he had always been a much better wrestler than a boxer, he tucked his head down and charged forward.

The attack center's cramped confines served as his ally. In an attempt to step away from Kuzmin's charge, Leonov stumbled over a deck-mounted chair and went crashing to the floor. The warrant officer took immediate advantage and flung himself down on Leonov's stunned body. Rolling him onto his back, Kuzmin was able to pin down his left arm.

Leonov was aware of his desperate situation. In a last-ditch effort to save himself, he reached out with his right hand and blindly groped along the floorboard. He could hardly believe it when his fingers latched onto the cold steel shaft of a large wrench. For once he was thankful for the sloppy incompetence of the crew member who had left the tool there. Utilizing the last of his strength, he swung the wrench upward and cracked its tip into the side of his adversary's head. There was a dull thud and a loud groan as Stefan Kuzmin crumpled to the floor, unconscious.

Leonov hastily pushed the inert body off of his own. Oblivious to a variety of throbbing aches and pains, he managed to stand and briefly scanned the damage done by their scuffle. No equipment appeared disturbed, yet the deck was wet and sticky from the blood that still streamed from the *michman*'s nose and mouth. That could be cleaned up soon enough, and there would be no sign that the battle had ever happened.

The senior lieutenant reached into his pocket and pulled out a roll of white surgical tape. Before applying it to his victim's wrists and ankles, he turned to pick up the intercom. He activated the handset and spoke into its receiver breathlessly.

"Comrade Novikov, it's Leonov. We seem to have one small problem. Stefan Kuzmin has somehow stumbled on to our plans. . . . No, I'm almost certain that this is an isolated case. If you can get down here with a stretcher and blanket, we can wrap up what's left of the *michman* and dump him with the captain. . . . Yes, Comrade, that's an excellent idea. By announcing that both men have come down with infectious hepatitis, who would question a proper quarantine? Please get down here quickly, though."

As he hung up, Leonov exhaled a sigh of relief. Once the warrant officer was stashed away, nothing would stand between them and their goal. With this thought in mind, he bent down and began wrapping Kuzmin's wrists together.

For a full hour, Petyr Valenko waited beside the unconscious body of his friend. Aware of the passing time, he knew that unless Kuzmin came to soon, he'd have to initiate the vital task that still faced them alone.

He had feigned unconsciousness when the *zampolit* and the senior lieutenant had arrived with the *michman*'s bruised body. Thankfully, they had left quickly and Valenko was able to rise and begin ministering to his fallen friend.

Finding Kuzmin's pulse strong and steady, Valenko had unwrapped the bonds and began working on the facial cuts that still oozed blood. The nastiest looking wound was a large, hand-sized bruise that started at the lower left side of Kuzmin's skull and stretched down his neck. Most likely this was the blow that had led to his present comatose condition.

After treating him the best he could, Valenko began his present vigil, ever aware of each passing second. If he was going to act, it would have to be within the hour. He could tell from the loud drone of the

Vulkan's engines, that they were continuing to their launch position at flank speed. The fact that this position was located in the easternmost portion of their patrol sector proved that their targets were not limited to America's west coast. Because of the limited range of the SS-N-18s, each kilometer that the *Vulkan* moved east brought the warheads that much closer to being able to cover the entire continent.

Unable to rely on the help of his crew, Valenko knew that he would have to stop this insanity by himself. Though he would have preferred to have the *michman*'s assistance, it didn't appear that Kuzmin would be able to rise to the occasion.

Valenko reflected on the great responsibility that rested on his shoulders and inwardly trembled. To fail would mean the possible loss of untold millions of innocent lives. Though he had some knowledge of the assumed effectiveness of a surgical nuclear strike, he doubted that the West would be totally decapitated. Surely portions of their command and communications systems would still remain operational. Infuriated by this unwarranted attack, the Americans would strike back with every warhead they could muster. Their Trident submarines alone contained enough destructive capability to give the Motherland a fatal blow. Since these vessels were extremely difficult to track down, they could lie in waiting for months, biding the moment until revenge would be theirs.

Try as he could, Valenko failed to determine the motive that had inspired such a crazed scheme. The Premier had come out strongly against any first use of nuclear weapons. Valenko had met him only a few days before. Not only did Viktor Rodin seem to be a man of his word, he also appeared to be sincere about his present mission. Hadn't the summit with the American President been convened to make such an attack even more of an impossibility? And why time this blow to coincide with the General Secretary's visit to America?

There was no doubt that a dangerously sick minority was responsible. Most likely holding high positions in the seat of the government, these conspirators genuinely believed that Rodin was the traitor for sincerely desiring peace.

Valenko had long ago come to terms with the awesome killing potential inside of the *Vulkan*'s missile magazine. A trained, loyal warrior, he swore to protect the Rodina without undue questions. As he viewed the current situation, there was little doubt that the Motherland's most dangerous enemies were inside the *Vulkan*'s hull. No matter the risks, he had to stop them before the peace of the entire world was needlessly threatened.

Again he checked his watch and realized it was time to move. As he splashed cold water on his face, Valenko was aware of a stirring in his bunk. Quickly, he looked back into the cabin's interior. Meeting his hopeful stare, was a dazed but conscious Stefan Kuzmin. The captain ran to his side as the *michman* struggled to sit up.

"Easy now, Stefan. You took quite a blow."

Valenko caught the warrant officer as he fell back dizzily.

"What happened, Captain?" Kuzmin said weakly.

"The Senior Lieutenant and the *zampolit* brought you in about an hour ago. I don't know what hit you, but for a while there I was afraid that you'd never snap out of it."

Gradually, Kuzmin's eyes focused. "An hour ago, you say? Have they released the missiles yet?"

Relieved that Kuzmin's concussion wasn't as serious as he had feared, Valenko helped him sit up. "No, Comrade, we still have at least sixty minutes before the *Vulkan* reaches the launch point."

"Then we still have time to stop them," Kuzmin said with a bit more strength. "I pulled up the information that you asked for, and first-strike targets have indeed been selected. Leonov caught me in the attack center. I'm afraid he knows that we're on to them."

"You've done your job well, my friend. Now, it's up to me to make certain that those SS-N-18s go nowhere."

"Oh, but Captain, you've got to let me help you!" the *michman* pleaded as he struggled to stand. Caught by a wave of dizziness, he was forced to reach out and steady himself against the wall.

"Nonsense, Stefan. You are in no shape to leave this room."

Ignoring Valenko's pleas, Kuzmin took a deep breath and stood up straight. This time, his balance remained steady.

"It will take more than a little knock on the head to keep Stefan Kuzmin down," he said as he gently rubbed the left side of his neck. "So you really think that it's not too late to stop them, Captain?"

Realizing the warrant officer's stubbornness, Valenko grinned. "We can do it, Stefan. Don't forget—there's that new godchild of mine who I swore to protect."

"Well then, what's the plan?"

Valenko turned and pointed to the air-conditioning ventilation screen. "The way I figure it, we'd better not count on the crew for any help. Who knows what the *zampolit* and the senior lieutenant have been feeding them? That means that we're on our own. Are you certain that you want to go through with this, Stefan? That trip down the shaft is hard enough uninjured."

Kuzmin managed a smile. "I wouldn't miss this trip for the world, Captain."

Valenko smiled in return. "If you're really capable, I certainly won't turn down the help. Between the two of us we'll have double the chance of succeeding. I think it's better if we split up. Would you like to have a go at cutting the fire-control system?"

"I sure would," Kuzmin affirmed.

"Good. You hit the *taiga*. I'll go forward. Each of us is only going to get a single chance. We've got to make it a good one."

Once more Valenko checked his watch. "We'd better be going, my friend."

Fully alert now, the *michman* pivoted and began his way over to the wall-mounted shaft, with the captain close on his heels.

For Seaman Third Class Valeri Balashikha, the day was turning out to be a most confusing one. It was at times such as these that the nineteen-year-old, dark-eyed Uzbek cursed his misfortune at having been drafted into the navy. Not only was his current duty ridiculously monotonous, but his commanding officer was in the foulest of moods. This was most unlike the weapons chief. In the past, Yuri Chuchkin had been someone whom the young conscript respected. Always fair with both his praise and complaints, the chief had been more like a friend than a superior.

But forty-five minutes ago, Chuchkin had called together the twelve seamen who were assigned to the *taiga* and had chewed them out. Never had the seaman heard such words come from the previously good-natured chief. After it was pounded into their ears what a bunch of idiots they were, the men were given their orders. Not only were they to repeat the same tasks that were concluded several hours before, but this time they were to scrub down the magazine with three times the effort! Balashikha knew that the military had strange ways, but this was too much.

He had received the worst assignment of all— degreasing the launch tube sealant gaskets. Not only was the work boring, it soon got one covered from head to toe with foul-smelling, slimy grease. Even as a child, getting dirty had driven the fastidious Uzbek crazy. Not one to go sliding in the mud with his fellow playmates, he preferred to stay clean and dry. This was a delight to his mother, who always commented on what an easy child he was to raise.

He would never forget how she broke out in tears when he had received the orders sending him to Sevastopol. Father took it all in stride. Having served in the navy himself, he promised his son that the three years would go all too quickly. Wait till he visited his first exotic port—that would make the training all worth it.

Neither father nor son could have foreseen that Valeri would receive duty aboard a missile-toting submarine. In a way, the assignment was a compliment. Only the most intelligent and promising conscripts were trained for the undersea service. Certainly, the job was of extreme importance, but it would bring them to no foreign ports. Submerged beneath the sea for months on end, the submariner learned to share what little vacant space there was with one hundred and thirty-two fellow sailors.

After a while, this crowd got on Balashikha's nerves. He was even forced to share his own bunk. The Siberian who was presently using the mattress was a foul-smelling creature. Raised on goat's milk and venison, he apparently didn't know what it was to shower or wash one's uniform. The odor wasn't very conducive to a sound sleep.

Valeri had completed servicing eight of the sixteen missile tubes. The thick, black grease had already spotted his clothing and gotten under his fingernails. Though he had another eight tubes to go, he stopped to wipe his hands clean for some temporary relief.

He sought some solvent and a clean rag from the storage closet in the *taiga*'s rearmost corner. It was unlikely that anyone else would be there. Still, he feared the possibility of bumping into Chief Chuchkin. In his current mood, there was no telling what he'd do to Valeri if he caught him there.

The cool, creamy solvent effectively stripped the grease from his hands. Feeling like a new person, Valeri went on to find a clean rag. As he reluctantly prepared to return to the launch tubes, he heard someone approaching. Alertly, he hid behind the door and cautiously peeked through the crack to see who it was. He was totally surprised to find the quickly moving figure of *michman* Stefan Kuzmin.

The blond-haired warrant officer was known to be quite personable, although Valeri had had little contact with him. Seeing the *michman* here was shocking, but not because it was a part of the ship restricted to those who worked there. Rather, it had to do with the recent announcement by the senior lieutenant. An unusual broadcast had informed the crew that both the *michman* and their captain were being quarantined with infectious hepatitis—an extremely contagious liver disease.

If this was the case, what was Stefan Kuzmin doing here in the *taiga*? Valeri could think of only one thing: Somehow, the *michman* had escaped his voluntary confinement and was wandering through the ship completely delirious with fever.

Fearful for his health, Valeri Balashikha instinctively held his breath. He peeked out to make certain that the warrant officer had passed, then sprinted toward the intercom. The seaman third class exhaled only after making certain that the *Vulkan*'s senior lieutenant was personally on the other end of the line.

Chapter Twelve

"All stop! Callahan, she's all yours."

Michael Cooksey's orders barked out loud and clear. In response, the *Triton*'s propulsion shaft came to a halt and the sub glided forward in almost total silence. The sonar officer took advantage of this quiet to fully concentrate on the vessel's sensors.

The sub was using a tactic called *sprint and drift*. In order to cover as much territory as possible, the sub would sprint at all-out flank speed for a period of time. Then the captain would call for the engines to halt and the drift portion of the operation would begin. Because the sound of their own engines would be absent, it was at this time that the sensor operators would have their best chance of picking up the signatures of any nearby bogeys.

As Charlie Callahan and his two assistants leaned over their monitor screens, the captain and his XO positioned themselves behind the brass railing set to the rear of the sonar station. Both officers looked on as the headphoned sensor operators activated the tools of their trade. These included a wide array of powerful hydrophones mounted on the ship's hull. Such sensitive microphones could pick up the most minute sounds, from the click of a tiny crab to the mournful cry of a passing whale. In the midst of the ocean's natural symphony, the relatively loud, alien noise produced by a manmade device was hard to miss.

Callahan and his crew also had the use of a towed-array sled that was reeled out from the *Triton*'s stern. This not only carried hydrophones, but also a thermometer capable of determining unnatural changes in the ocean's temperature. Such an anamoly would be produced when a passing sub stirred up a layer of water from a different depth. This could be of extreme significance, since the temperature of seawater drops at least one degree centigrade with each meter of depth.

Also in front of the men was a large glass screen belonging to the ship's BQQ-5 active sonar system. Mounted in the sub's bow, it transmitted a concentrated acoustic pulse into the surrounding waters. In the headphones, this pulse was recognizable as a quavering note, followed by the distinctive *plink* of a returning echo. The presence of any alien object crossing in the path of the surge would be instantly reflected back to the operator. One of the drawbacks to this device was that the hunted can detect an active sonar transmission earlier than the hunter can pick up the target.

Aware of each passing minute, Cooksey studied the sensor crew at work and stirred impatiently. Beside him, Richard Craig pulled a handkerchief from his pocket and mopped a line of sweat from his forehead. Both men looked on hopefully when Callahan suddenly bent forward and pushed his headphones closer to his ears.

"I've got one of the task force's choppers, Captain! The signal from the interface with the *Ticon-*

deroga is weak, but it sounds as if their dunking hydrophones have tagged something."

"Have the computer boost the signal to maximum and filter the resulting distortion. Then maybe we'll have something to run a signature I.D. on," ordered the captain. He then turned to address the *Triton*'s navigator. "Smitty, how far are we from the *Ticonderoga* now?"

Chief Petty Officer Warren Smith looked at his plotting table and said, "They're approximately eight-five nautical miles to the northeast, sir."

As Cooksey chewed this over, Callahan spoke out excitedly. "I've made the boost and Big Brother has been most cooperative. It's a bogey submersible, all right! Jesus—even from this distance you can hear it churnin' up the water something fierce. Still waiting on that positive I.D., sir."

Cooksey reached out to put on an auxiliary set of headphones. It didn't take him long to pick out the characteristic hissing sounds produced by a myriad of collapsing air bubbles generated at the swirling tip of a submarine's propeller. Cooksey managed a relieved smile as he pulled off the headphones and handed them to his XO.

"We've got the bastard, Rich! I just know it's that Delta."

The exec put the phones to his ears and heard the alien racket for himself. "Whatever it is, it sure has a bone in its teeth. What's next, Skipper?"

Cooksey's eyes remained locked on the computer monitor screen as he replied, "First, we wait for a definite verification indicating that we've tagged the right sub. Then, we'll a need a targeting solution.

We're well within range of that new ASW/SOW device. I'd like to get close enough to them to use our active sonar."

"But won't our ping give us away?" the XO asked.

"That's the way I want it, Rich. It's time to let that Soviet captain know he's been tagged. Maybe then he'll have serious thoughts about continuing with this madness."

A full minute of silence had passed when the computer monitor unexpectedly flashed to life. All eyes were on the green-tinted screen as it printed out the following:

Sound I.D.: tip-vortex cavitation
Source: dual propellor shafts powered by pressurized water reactor (60,000 shp.)
Origin: Seventy-six percent probability, Soviet Delta III-class submarine.

"I knew it!" Cooksey said, and playfully patted the back of the red-headed petty officer seated before him. "Good job, Callahan. Let me know when we're within range to hit them with active."

Turning from the sonar console, the captain addressed his exec. "Let's move it, Rich. All ahead flank to intercept point. I'll take care of getting Mr. Spencer and his gang ready."

By the time Cooksey had moved to pick up the intercom handset, the *Triton* was already reawakening. The distant groan of the sub's propulsion unit was followed by a noticeable surge of forward movement. Steadying himself against the bulkhead, Cooksey spoke crisply into the intercom.

298

"Mr. Spencer, this is the captain. It's time for your bunch to earn their keep. Ready that ASW/SOW in number one tube. You'd better load two Mark-48 ADCAPs for good measure. Do you still have that MOSS decoy available? . . . Good, we just might need it. Hold tight and we'll be getting you a targeting solution. This is finally going to be a real one, Lieutenant. Good shooting!"

The captain disconnected the line and turned to watch the control room's staff in action. Confident of their abilities, he crossed over to the plotting board. Now would begin the complex process of stalking their prey. Compass and ruler in hand, Cooksey drew up an intricate topographical cross-section of the southernmost section of the Emperor Seamount Chain.

Cruising in the waters to the immediate north of the USS *Triton*, the *Vulkan* plunged ever eastward. From the sub's missile compartment, the roar of its twin-shafted engines echoed with a persistent whine. Oblivious to the racket, Stefan Kuzmin carefully crossed the *taiga*'s length. He didn't stop until he reached the room's rearmost corner. Here, situated beside launch tube number one, was the steel-plated electrical box that he sought. Six screws held the galvanized cover that protected the fire-control system's fragile interior components. To remove them, the warrant officer needed a screwdriver that he hoped to appropriate from a tool box in an adjoining storage space.

Kuzmin's head pounded with a continuous, throbbing ache as he peered into the storage space and found no tool box. Cursing the missile crew's incompetence, he began searching for it elsewhere. Though he never did find the box itself, he eventually located a tool that would do the job.

The task of removing the screws took longer than he would have liked. Plagued by a shaky, sweat-stained hand, the *michman* did his best to concentrate on the job. He had to kneel down to get to the pair of screws that were placed on the cover's bottom. Not only did his bruised body hurt from the after-effects of his fight with the senior lieutenant, the concussion he had suffered was causing blurred and double-vision. To compensate, he did his best to keep the head of the screwdriver steady with touch alone.

An eternity seemed to pass before the bottom two screws were finally removed. Standing up to reach the other four, he found himself swept by waves of nausea and dizziness. Flushed and lightheaded, Kuzmin struggled to remain standing with a superhuman effort. Slowly, he regathered his composure. Pushed onward by the overriding importance of his present mission, he did his best to get back to work.

With Petyr Valenko's apocalyptic warning still ringing in his ears, the *michman* successfully removed the two screws that bolted down the cover's sides. Only the top two remained. He was well on his way to pulling one of these out, when the screwdriver popped out of his wet grasp.

"Damn it!" Kuzmin was once more forced to kneel down to find the errant instrument. Again he was possessed by a wave of dizziness as he dropped to his hands and knees. With sweat rolling down his

300

forehead in thick waves, he searched the floor in vain.

"For the sakes of Galina and Nikolai, you've got to be down here somewhere!" he pleaded as he groped about like a blind man.

Frustrated, tired, his body racked with discomfort, Kuzmin momentarily halted his frantic pursuit when the sound of footsteps echoed in the distance. Desperately now, he turned to search the floor beside the launch silo—and found his fallen tool. Without hesitation he rose to complete his task. Fortunately the dizziness was gone, and Kuzmin soon found himself with one screw to go. He angled the tip of the screwdriver into the screw's head and was in the process of twisting it loose, when the bright beam of a flashlight cut through the darkness. This was followed by the *zampolit*'s strained voice.

"Comrade Kuzmin, please show yourself! We know that you are here. You must stop this foolishness at once!"

Frantically, Kuzmin hurried to remove the last obstacle, but his shaking hand slowed him considerably. As he struggled for inner control, the sharp voice of Vasili Leonov rang out behind him.

"There he is—behind number one! He's at the fire-control panel!"

Realizing that he wouldn't have time to finish, the *michman* ducked for cover behind the missile tube. Squeezing himself down the narrow metal catwalk between the silos and the hull, he tried to lead his pursuers away. He made it nearly halfway down the compartment's length before a flashlight beam caught him in the back.

"Comrade, he's up by number four!" Leonov shouted, and then proceeded to follow the same precarious route that the *michman* had taken.

Sensing his pursuit, Kuzmin turned for the central catwalk that lay before the fourth and fifth tubes. He reached this walkway just as the beam of a flashlight caught him full in the eyes. Temporarily blinded, he stumbled back toward the rear of the compartment.

"Hold it there, Kuzmin," called the *zampolit.* "My aim is most unerring!"

As if to emphasize the warning, Kuzmin heard the distinctive click of a pistol's hammer being cocked. Reluctantly, he halted beside the second tube.

By the time he had regained his breath, both the political officer and the senior lieutenant stood before him, gloating.

"Good try," Novikov observed wryly. "But I guess that you just didn't have it in you. Now, prepare to die, fool."

Slowly, deliberately, the *zampolit* raised the short barrel of the compact pistol. Conceding his untimely death, the *michman* sighed. He faced his executioner, unflinchingly, when suddenly the compartment was filled with a firm, deep voice.

"What the hell is going on here?" boomed Yuri Chuchkin as he ducked into the compartment from its rear hatchway. He saw the bruised *michman* and the two officers who faced him, and said incredulously, "Are you mad, Comrade? Put that pistol down at once! An errant bullet down here can sink us in the blink of an eye!"

Cognizant of the truth of the chief's warning, Novikov lowered the pistol and handed it to Vasili

Leonov.

"Now, will someone kindly tell me what the meaning of all this is?" the astounded chief asked.

Novikov attempted an explanation. "Thank goodness that you got down here to assist us, Comrade Chuchkin. We were just going to call for help. As we announced earlier, the *michman* here is the victim of a horrible fever. So crazed is he that, when we found him, he was in the process of sabotaging the fire-control system."

A look of doubt crossed the chief's face as he hastily scanned Kuzmin's blank expression, then turned to check out the fire-control panel. It didn't take him long to spot the loose screws lying on the floor.

"Is this the truth, Stefan?" the chief said incredulously.

The warrant officer responded with defiance. "Yes, Yuri—I was trying to disable the launch system, but I wasn't prompted by any ridiculous fever. It was from our Captain's own mouth that the orders sending me on this desperate task originated. The *Vulkan* has been the subject of a mutiny, my friend. The two men who stand before us want nothing else but to use our SS-N-18s to initiate World War III!"

"Oh, come now, Comrade Kuzmin," the *zampolit* interrupted. "Please spare us any more of your twisted fantasies. Do you have any doubts, Chief, that what you are hearing is the product of a sick, feverish mind?"

Chuchkin looked again into the *michman*'s bloodshot eyes and silently implored his old friend for some kind of reassurance. "I must admit that this is a most bewildering predicament. I'm afraid only one man aboard can sort this thing out. It is imperative that I be allowed to speak with the Captain."

This time it was the senior lieutenant who responded. "That is an impossible request, Chief. You heard my announcement earlier. Our esteemed Captain is in no shape for idle conversations. Right now, he's fighting for his very life. As is my duty, I am in command here. So, without further delay, you will please give us a hand in restraining our poor *michman*. That is, unless you're afraid of catching the virulent, infectious strain that he presently carries."

The chief took several steps forward, putting him almost opposite Kuzmin. He examined his shipmate and had to admit that he looked far from normal. Not only was he slovenly dressed and unusually dirty, but there could be no ignoring the thick patches of sweat that stained his shirt and still dripped from his forehead. The warrant officer did appear sick, yet could even a fevered delerium prompt him to take such a grave action as attempting to disrupt their launch-control system? He responded accordingly.

"I'm in no way doubting your authority, Comrade Leonov, but because of the serious nature of this disturbance, I would still like to see the Captain, no matter how ill he may be."

Novikov's face reddened with anger. Before he could voice his displeasure, the compartment filled with the dreaded sound of a loud, hollow ping.

"It must be the Americans!" Leonov cried. "We've been found!"

Making the most of this moment of shocked stillness, Kuzmin snapped into action. Though he hated to do it, he reached over and, after grabbing hold of Chuchkin's left arm, swung the portly chief into the path of his two adversaries. The resulting chaos was all that he needed to sprint the dozen meters that separated him from the fire-control panel. With his bare hand, he began stripping the already-loosened remaining screw. After a few turns it popped free, and with eager hands he went to rip off the metal cover plate. Just as he wrenched it free from its base, a stabbing pain thudded into his back and sent him tumbling to his knees. As the plate he had been holding crashed to the floor, he looked back over his right shoulder and saw the ornate hilt of the *zampolit*'s carving knife protruding from his rib cage.

Even as his life force streamed from him, Kuzmin reached up in a last attempt to get to the now-exposed circuitry. Inches away from his goal, a searing pain forced his hand downward. As he vainly fought the black, spinning veil that rose in his consciousness, his inner sight began focusing on a magnificent glowing light brighter than any he had ever seen before. He only surrendered to its shimmering radiance after identifying the voice that called him homeward. With a longing smile, he went to his final sleep picturing the angelic face of his beloved Galina.

"We've got a return, Captain! We've got them!" From the opposite end of the control room, Cooksey looked up from the plotting table and shouted, "Give us a range, Callahan."

"Bearing, three-four-zero, sir. Range, six-three nautical miles."

Cooksey reached out and marked the spot with red grease pencil on the map's glass projection screen.

"Shall we launch the SOW device, Skipper?" his XO asked.

With his eyes still locked on the map, Cooksey said, "Let's give them another minute to change their course, Rich. They know we're out here now. If they have any second thoughts at all, now's the time to express them."

The sixty seconds passed like an eternity for Cooksey. Surprised to find himself hesitant to give the order to send the Soviet sub crew to their deaths, he remembered the admiral's firm reply when he had asked Miller what they were to do once the Delta was tagged. "Blow them away," the admiral had ordered, just as if a state of war indeed existed. With this directive in mind, Cooksey said, "Mr. Callahan, ping them again and give us a course update."

Callahan triggered the active sonar unit, and once more a powerful pulse of acoustic energy streamed from the *Triton*'s bow.

"Course remains due east, Captain. Range extended to six-five nautical miles."

Cooksey turned to face his XO. "Let's rub them out, Rich. Get me Spencer on the phone."

The exec picked up the handset on his left and activated it. When he was certain that the proper party was on the other end of the line, he handed the receiver to the captain.

306

"Mr. Spencer, prepare a final targeting solution—sonar has got the coordinates," Cooksey said grimly. "Let's see what that new-fangled weapon we took on is made of."

To this, the weapon's officer responded apologetically, "I'm afraid that's going to be impossible at the moment, Captain. We're showing a failure in the SOW device's acoustic array system. We've got it pulled apart and are checking it now."

"I should have expected that," Cooksey said. "This new stuff is too damn complicated. Ready a pair of old-fashioned Mark-48 Advanced Capability torpedoes. The targeting angle is good and I don't foresee any outside difficulties."

But, from the sonar console across the room, Callahan shouted, "Captain, we've got ourselves another bogey, bearing zero-one-zero. Relative range roughly seven-eight hundred yards. I believe I heard torpedo doors opening! Where in the hell did they come from?"

"It's the Alfa!" Cooksey cried. He spoke rapidly into the receiver he still held. "Mr. Spencer, belay those launch orders. I hope to God you've still got that Mk-70 loaded. Prepare the stern tubes and stand by for action."

Then Cooksey put down the handset and barked, "Rich, sound General Quarters. Mr. Lawrence, take us down, crash dive! Engineering, I want flank speed!"

Sharp tones sounded throughout the *Triton*, sending the crew scurrying to their action stations as the sub's planes bit into the surrounding water. Their angle of descent increased sharply, sending the vessel plummeting downward as the crew did their best to brace themselves.

With a tight grip on the plotting board to keep his balance, Cooksey watched his men struggle to remain at work and prayed that his desperate maneuver was successful. As his compass and ruler slid off the table and fell to the deck, he mentally calculated the odds and knew that they were far from being in his favor.

Only seconds before, they had been on the attack. Now they were running for their lives.

Captain Grigori Dzerzhinsky, of the Alfa-class attack sub *Cheka*, beamed with delight as his senior lieutenant informed him of their target's hasty dive. As if this pathetic move would save them, Dzerzhinsky mused while relishing his moment of supreme power. Feeling like a cat playing with a doomed mouse, he watched his men—seated alertly at their stations—anxiously awaiting his next command.

Dzerzhinsky was aware that time was on their side. The longer they could keep the Americans running, the closer the *Vulkan* would be to its final launch position. Of course, destroying the imperialist vessel would be the easiest way to remove this final obstacle. He was in the midst of deciding which weapon he would use to finish them off, when a dreaded, familiar voice sounded from behind.

"Whatever is the matter, Captain? What is the meaning of this delay in eliminating the Yankee attack sub?"

The *zampolit*'s concerned words did little to arouse the captain. "Perhaps you would like to take command of the *Cheka*, Comrade Karpovich. Let's see how you would handle the attack."

Dzerzhinsky watched with disgust as the pasty-skinned political officer nuzzled up beside him. "I only wish that I were more fully trained to do so, Captain. Shouldn't we at least be continuing our pursuit? Even the men are confused by our present inaction."

"That's funny, I haven't heard a complaint yet," Dzerzhinsky said as he calmly looked at his watch.

Frustrated by the captain's restraint, Boris Karpovich nervously asked, "At least tell me why you didn't release the torpedoes when we had them dead in our sights."

Dzerzhinsky realized that the whining political officer would pester him endlessly until his curiosity was satisfied. "Comrade Karpovich, if the Americans had remained stationary for ten more seconds, they would no longer be a concern for us. Their sudden crash dive has forced me to drastically change our attack plan. No use wasting two homing torpedoes that would only get lost in the swirling clutter produced by their emergency descent."

"But won't we certainly lose then now?" continued the tense *zampolit*.

"Lighten up, Comrade," the Captain responded. "Must you always worry so? If you'd only trust in my ability, you'd soon find out that we're only waiting for the water to clear before going down to finish them off. They aren't going anywhere that we can't reach them."

Karpovich wiped his soaked forehead with a crumpled handkerchief. "For a second there, I actually thought that you were letting the Americans go free."

"Now why in the world would you think that, Comrade?" the captain asked with a puzzled frown.

The political officer wiped his sweaty neck. "I guess I'm just getting to be a paranoid old fool, Captain. The operation is so close to it's completion that I just can't bare to see something go wrong now."

"Well, you'd better learn to relax, Comrade, or we'll be picking you up from the deck after a heart attack someday. Just think—then you'd never see the new world order take shape."

Without excusing himself, Dzerzhinsky walked over to the sensor console. There, seated beside the two regular operators, was Senior Lieutenant Vadim Nikulin. With headphones clamped securely over his shiny bald skull, Nikulin was concentrating on the sonar monitor when the captain nudged his arm.

"Well Vadim, what do our Yankee friends have to say for themselves?"

The senior lieutenant pushed back his headset and said, "They certainly left a knuckle in the water when they initiated that crash dive, Captain. Never before have I witnessed such a speedy descent."

"Their commanding officer's a sharp one all right," Dzerzhinsky agreed. "A good captain trains his crew to be an extension of himself. Unfortunately, there are some situations from which even the most skillful of crews cannot extricate themselves. Shall we go down and teach our nosy friends a lesson?"

Nikulin's eyes narrowed as the fat figure of the

zampolit squeezed up beside the captain. Dzerzhinsky sensed him and said, "Comrade Karpovich, you will be happy to hear that we have decided to put the imperialists out of their misery once and for all. Now, if I were you, Comrade, I'd find something sturdy to hold onto. The ride that's going to follow could get a little rough."

Boris Karpovich heeded the captain's warning and hurriedly stepped back to brace himself on the steel railing that enclosed the periscope well. Satisfied that they would finally be on with the hunt again, he listened as the captain delivered a series of complex diving orders. Seconds later, the *Cheka*'s engines roared and the deck dipped precariously forward.

It took all of Karpovich's strength to keep himself upright as the sub dove deeper into the ocean. At the same time, he watched Grigori Dzerzhinsky stand behind the seated helmsman, keeping his balance with but a single hand. It was at moments such as this that the *zampolit* admired the captain. Appearing completely at ease, the captain alertly shifted his weight to compensate for each new pitch of the deck. In the midst of all this, he continued giving orders.

Proud of Dzerzhinsky's skill, and that of his fellow crew members, Karpovich felt more confident. No enemy could escape the *Cheka* once a blood trail had been scented. Certain of this fact, he pondered the strange road that had brought him there.

Far from the intrigues of Moscow, his experiences aboard the attack sub gave him a whole new perspective on life. Not only was the environment alien, the men surrounding him were unlike any individuals he had ever met before.

As a junior member of Konstantin Belchenko's personal staff, Karpovich was afforded an inside look at the forces that ran their government. It proved to be during Viktor Rodin's phenomenal rise to power that he had become disillusioned and had written an impassioned letter to Belchenko. Never would he forget the one-on-one meeting that followed. Not only did his superior listen to his thoughts, Belchenko even agreed with him on many points. This was especially in the area of international relations with the West.

Four meetings later, the first deputy had shared with him a fictional scenario of the operation that was to become known as Counterforce. Impressed with its scope and solidly behind its motives, Karpovich had been invited into Belchenko's inner circle. The legendary figures with whom he was soon meeting included Admiral Stanislav Sorokin. In fact, it was at the admiral's invitation that Karpovich had begun the intensive training for his current assignment. And here it was, only months later, and the dream of Counterforce was now a reality.

Karpovich took strength from his realization as the *Cheka* canted hard on its side. Though his shoulders strained with pain and his stomach roiled, he dared not protest. For how often did one actually get to see the hand of destiny unfold?

In the dark, cold seas beneath the advancing Soviet attack sub, the USS *Triton* continued its frantic plunge. With an outside pressure of over three hundred and fifty pounds per square inch, the vessel's valves, seals and other vulnerable fittings strained to the breaking point. Ever conscious of the great pressure was the *Triton*'s crew. This was especially evident inside the control room. Here, the tension took the form of strained, concerned expressions and a deathlike silence. The unnatural quiet was broken only by the distant rumbling of the propulsion unit, the creaking strain of the hull itself, and the muted voice of the diving officer as he read off the depth.

"We're breaking one thousand feet, Captain."

Cooksey stood at the officer's side and nodded somberly. As he watched the digital depth meter, a series of soft, electronic tones diverted his attention to the compartment's interior. Richard Craig picked up the intercom. The XO spoke into the receiver, listened for a moment, then dropped the handset to his side and addressed the captain.

"Skipper, it's Chief Weaver. He's got a minor seal failure in the engine room and is requesting permission to shut down the main turbine to initiate repairs."

"Absolutely not! They're going to have to hold on a bit longer."

As the XO conveyed his response, the diving officer called out, "Eleven hundred feet, sir."

Cooksey nervously shifted his weight. Around him the bulkhead seemed to moan in protest and the intercom sounded again. Once more the exec answered it.

"Skipper, it's Chief Bartkowski. We're taking in water from the galley. Seems that the garbage disposal is backing up on us."

313

"Well, have the Chief patch it up the best he can! Damn it, Rich, we're at war here."

"Twelve hundred feet," called the diving officer.

Cooksey's shirt was matted with sweat as his eyes went back to the depth counter. For the first time in days, a throbbing ache began rising in his forehead. He massaged his temples the best he could.

Damage control reported five more leaks as they passed the eighteen-hundred-foot mark. The strain on their welded hull was just as great as the tension inside as the *Triton's* exec made his way to the captain's side.

"Skipper, we've just about hit our depth threshold. Surely you're not thinking of outdiving the Alfa. With that titanium hull of theirs, they've got at least a thousand feet on us."

Cooksey ignored his exec's pleas; his eyes remained riveted on the depth counter. At a depth of eighteen hundred and fifty feet, he said, "Okay Rich, we'll have it your way. Remove the diving angle! Full rise on both planes. Back emergency. Blow the forward group. Vent forward tanks when you get an up angle!"

In response, both planesmen pulled back hard on their control sticks. As the sub's angle slowly changed, the *Triton* groaned in protest. Only when the rest of Cooksey's orders were carried out did the 6,900-ton vessel stop its descent. After checking the depth counter, Cooksey ordered, "All stop! Rig for ultra-quiet."

A series of muted electronic chimes sounded through the sub. This was followed by a distant whirring rumble as the ship's single propellor shaft spun to a halt.

Except for the occasional creak of their hull, all was silent as Cooksey moved over to the sonar console. Joining him behind its red-headed operator was the XO. Richard Craig's face was etched with relief as he followed his captain's example and clipped on a pair of auxiliary headphones.

"We've lost them, Captain!" Vadim Nikulin said incredulously. "There's absolutely nothing out there!"

"Open your ears, Comrade!" Dzerzhinsky shouted from the other side of the attack center. "A vessel of that size doesn't just disappear."

Since the *Cheka* was still in the midst of a full diving angle, it took some effort for the captain to reach his senior lieutenant. By the time he reached his side and put on a pair of headphones, another figure had joined them.

"What has happened, Comrade?" asked a concerned Boris Karpovich.

Completely ignoring the *zampolit*, Dzerzhinsky reached up and turned the volume of their hydrophones to maximum intensity. For a full minute he continued listening, then yanked off the headset and addressed the helmsman.

"What is our present depth?"

"Five hundred and ninety meters, sir," the helmsman responded without hesitation.

"Secure from the dive," the captain ordered.

The *Cheka* shuddered as its bow planes bit into the icy water. Slowly but surely their diving angle decreased.

"Stop all engines! Rig for silent running!" Dzerzhinsky added as he remounted the headphones. Before he could clip them securely over his ears, the *zampolit*'s voice rang out loudly.

"But, Captain—why just sit here, still in the water, while the Americans continue to make good their escape? Certainly, you're allowing them to get away."

Again Karpovich's pleas were ignored. He could only watch in frustration as the captain refocused his attention on the hydrophones.

Valuable minutes passed, and still Dzerzhinsky didn't move. Desperate for his attention, Boris Karpovich reached out and turned the hydrophone volume meter to zero. Flinging the headphones off, the captain screamed, "What has gotten into you, Karpovich? Have you gone crazy?"

Hit with the full force of the captain's anger, Karpovich took a step back. "I'm sorry for that, Captain, but you must give me a second of your time. The minutes continue to tick away and the *Vulkan* continues on to its launch position. Unless the enemy sub can be eliminated, the entire operation will be doomed to failure. Our futures will be doomed! We must stop them now!"

"What do you think I'm doing, Comrade, twiddling my fingers? Believe it or not, we share the same goals. Now, just stand back and leave the operation of this ship to me!"

A look of resignation crossed the political officer's puffy face and the captain instinctively softened. "I know that you mean well, Comrade, but on this

316

bridge I'm not used to being challenged."

"I only wanted to know what's going on out there. Have we lost them for good?"

"No, Comrade Karpovich, they haven't disappeared. Their clever captain has merely pulled them out of their dive as they were approaching their depth limit. This was followed by a quick scram of their reactor. Like ourselves, they are floating silently—somewhere nearby. Certainly, they're in no position to threaten the *Vulkan*."

"But what about the approaching ships of the Yankee surface fleet?" the *zampolit* whined. "Their helicopters were already dropping sonobuoys when we arrived here. We've got to continue our role as an escort, or we risk losing everything."

Dzerzhinsky considered this for a moment. "Though I would prefer to have the Yankees make the first move, there is a tactic I know of that can rout them. Of course, it does entail a certain amount of risk."

"Risk is something that each of us has learned to live with on a daily basis, Captain. Our lives mean nothing anyway if the *Vulkan* fails to reach its launch site."

Dzerzhinsky signaled his senior lieutenant to remove his headphones. "Vadim, the *zampolit* considers it imperative that we eliminate the American submarine threat at once. I concur with him in this instance. To insure that our wire-guided homing torpedoes have a solid target, I propose that we hit them with our active sonar. When the pulse is returned, we will launch our weapons. Before the Americans can react they will be blown to the bottom."

Impressed with the captain's bold plan, Karpovich managed to smile. "The First Deputy himself will know of your unselfish bravery, Comrade Dzerzhinsky."

The political officer's enthusiastic commendation went unnoticed by the captain, who was already deep into the mental calculations that would guarantee their attack's success.

"I can't understand it, Captain. They were there one second, and now there's absolutely nothing."

Callahan's words prompted Cooksey to fit on the auxiliary sensor headphones. After a three-hundred-and-sixty-degree scan, he removed them and said, "They're out there sure enough, Callahan. Most likely they've pulled the plug on their reactor, just like we have. Keep listening. They'll break silence soon enough."

Cooksey checked his watch and solemnly shook his head. Instead of lying there motionless, locked in combat with the Alfa, he knew that he should be continuing to close in on the *Vulkan*. If only he hadn't hesitated earlier, after first tagging them. Yet, with the SOW device down, their conventional torpedoes would have been at or past the extreme limit of their range.

To continue the hunt, the *Triton* would have to somehow shake the Soviet attack sub. The course of action offering the least risk would be to wait them out. The American vessel's superior acoustic capabilities would eventually be the deciding factor. Of course, they could always take a chance and make a run for it. As the minutes continued to tick away, this tactic would appear more attractive. Yet how could Cooksey forget the incident that took place beneath Point Luck? At that time, this same Alfa had easily outdistanced them. The more he thought about it, the more a frantic run appeared to be suicidal.

A gentle hand tapped his shoulder, and Cooksey broke from his ponderings to face his XO. "Just got a final report from damage control, Skipper. All leaks are under control. Weaver has even managed to replace that failed turbine seal. The only system still nonoperational is our garage disposal unit. Chief Bartkowski is down in the galley doing his best, but he thinks it's going to be out of commission for the rest of the patrol."

"Very good, Rich," the captain said softly.

The XO noticed Cooksey's unease and carefully probed. "We'll get back to the *Vulkan* soon enough, Skipper. What's the status of that Alfa?"

"They're playing the same game that we are; our hydrophones pick up no alien engine noises whatsoever."

"We can't stay down here too much longer," Craig said. "How about the old end-run? If we could get on top of the thermocline before they did, there's a chance that their sonar would miss us."

"I thought about running for it, Rich, but right now it's still too risky. Though the smart thing to do would be to keep us pinned down, I've got a feeling that the Alfa is going to try to put a move on us."

"You could be right. Soviet sub captains aren't

known for their patience, and I imagine that this one would just love to take us out with a single shot."

Jolted by his XO's observation, Cooksey reached over and activated the intercom. As he talked into the transmitter, his eyes remained locked on the XO.

"Mr. Spencer, do you still have that Mk-70 MOSS ready to go in the forward tubes? Excellent. How about that pair of ADCAPS? Yes, the stern tubes will be fine. You can seal them up, Lieutenant. I'll be transferring launch command to the control room. If they're needed, the quicker we get those weapons off, the better it will be for all of us."

As the captain hung up, Craig said, "I still wouldn't rule out making a run for it, Skipper. This little lady can give that Alfa a run for its money any day of the week."

"I'm aware of that, Rich. Let's just not be too hasty. Now, how about helping me arm the fire-control panel?"

The exec nodded and followed Cooksey to the deserted armament console. They sat and began the process of routing the launch-access system so that the *Triton*'s torpedoes could be instantaneously fired from their stations. As they finished rerouting, the compartment was filled with the hollow sound of a deafening *ping*. Temporarily startled, Cooksey was pushed into action by the excited cry of Charlie Callahan: "It's the Alfa!"

Without further hesitation, the captain depressed a red-flashing button and launched the contents of their number one forward tube. The sub shuddered slightly as the Mk-70 device, designed to simulate the *Triton*'s sonar signature, surged into the sur-

320

rounding depths.

Before hitting the switches to activate the two stern tubes, Cooksey checked with his sonar officer. "How's the Mk-70 running, Mr. Callahan?"

Satisfied with the sound in his headphones, the freckle-faced petty officer said, "She's proceeding straight and true, Captain."

Cooksey allowed himself a thin smile. Now, if the Russian captain only took the bait, he'd need but a single source vector to confirm the Alfa's precise location. Only then would the two ADCAPs be released. Called to a target they couldn't help but strike, the Mark-48 torpedos would eliminate the Alfa in a blinding flash of explosive fire.

Vadim Nikulin sat expectantly before the *Cheka*'s sonar console. With sensitive, bulky headphones strapped tightly to his ears, the senior lieutenant waited for the return of the powerful sonar pulse they had just released. Though his concentration remained focused on the sounds in his headset, he was well aware of of his shipmates' anxious stares. Captain Dzerzhinsky stood in front of the fire-control panel, a few meters away. It would take only a word from Nikulin to prompt the captain to launch the two homing torpedoes loaded in their bow.

When the distinctive *plink* of the sonar return arrived, Nikulin responded to the distant, roaring surge clearly audible in his headset. "We've got a return, Captain! It sounds like the Americans are running!"

Dzerzhinsky nodded and placed his right index

finger on the torpedo release lever. For a full thirty seconds he remained motionless. This inexplainable inaction prompted an immediate visit from Boris Karpovich, who was monitoring the situation from the room's rear.

"What are you waiting for now, Captain? Finish them off!"

A look of malicious spite crossed Dzerzhinsky's face as the *zampolit* squeezed in beside him. "I'm warning you, Karpovich, this is not the time to interfere. Now get away from here, before I have you thrown in irons!"

Unable to believe what he was witnessing, the political officer flushed with confused rage. Certainly, his hesitance to fire in this instance meant that the man had to be deranged. Karpovich's instincts had warned him of this much earlier. To not fire now was an act of idiotic incompetence. If the Americans were subsequently able to make good their escape, the entire operation would once more be threatened.

As the *zampolit* frantically considered the consequences, a new thought crossed his mind. Dzerzhinsky had proved many times before that he was a capable officer. If this was the case, perhaps his actions were not prompted by insanity. This could mean that their captain inwardly wanted to assure the failure of Counterforce. Allowing the Yankee attack sub to escape now would practically guarantee their failure. Whether inspired by motives of treason or mere cowardice, it was evident that the captain was not the man to complete the job at hand.

Acting on one's instincts was a trait that Konstantin Belchenko had personally taught the *zampolit*. It was this talent that had allowed the first deputy to attain his present position of power. If the operation on which they had worked so hard was not to fail, Karpovich would have to take strength from Belchenko's example.

His course of action suddenly became clear: if the captain wasn't going to launch those torpedoes, he would!

Astounded by his own audacity, Karpovich wiped the sweat from his forehead· and inched his way forward. Peering over the captain's shoulder, he caught sight of the launch button. Without further delay, he adroitly pushed Dzerzhinsky aside and quickly depressed the fateful switch.

The series of events that followed passed in a haze. First, Karpovich was aware of his heart pounding madly in his chest. Then the deck trembled slightly, to a distant hiss of escaping compressed air. Satisfied that the torpedoes were on their way, he readied himself for the inevitable confrontation.

As he had expected, the captain was quivering with rage. With eyes wide and bulging, Dzerzhinsky screamed, "You stupid fool! If the sound we were picking up was merely a decoy, that launch will give us away for certain."

Unable to reply, the *zampolit* expected next to be physically struck. The captain was balling his fists, when the excited observations of the senior lieutenant temporarily diverted his fury.

"We've got them now, Captain! Both torpedoes have a definite sonic lock-on. There's no way that the Yankees will be able to escape this time!"

Dzerzhinsky looked at the cowering figure of the *zampolit*. Though his fists still ached for revenge, he held back as Karpovich bravely offered an explanation.

"I only did it for the good of our mission, Comrade. Counterforce must succeed, no matter the sacrifice. You may do with me as you like. I have only done what my heart demanded."

Dzerzhinsky took a step forward, his face only inches away from that of the trembling political officer. "I'll tell you what you did, Karpovich—you needlessly threatened the lives of the entire crew. A ship can only have one master. To have it otherwise is to invite disaster. If we are fortunate enough to survive this day, I will personally see to your imprisonment in the Lubyanka. Even the KGB must recognize the proper authority of a chain of command."

Sickened by the sweat-stained figure that stood before him, the captain pivoted and addressed his senior lieutenant. "What is the status of our attack, Comrade?"

When Nikulin failed to reply, the captain's gut tightened. Hurriedly, he rushed over to the sonar console where Nikulin was anxiously hunched over the bank of instruments. As one hand shot out to activate various volume gains and filters, the other pressed one of his headphones closer to his ear. Before Dzerzhinsky could don a headset of his own, the senior lieutenant looked up, pale and drawn.

"I don't understand it, Captain. Our bow hydrophone is picking up a pair of high-speed torpedoes headed toward us. Yet they are coming from a

324

portion of the ocean far away from the fleeing Americans!"

The information hit Dzerzhinsky like a fist in his belly. The frantic orders that followed were voiced in pure frustration.

"Engineering, we must have speed! Dive! Dive! Dive!"

The crew valiantly scurried to their stations, but the captain knew it was useless. Vectored in by both the *ping* of their sonar and the sound of the torpedoes launching, the enemy's aim would be fatal. Conscious that his life expectancy could now be counted out in seconds, he focused his gaze on the fat, pathetic frame of the man responsible for this calamity.

Though he would never know for certain what had prompted the *zampolit*'s rash action, Dzerzhinsky got the distinct impression that it was their very system that was at fault. Paranoid and distrustful, Boris Karpovich had been trained to believe in nothing but his own self-importance. It was the strength of a team effort that made a submarine crew successful, and it was the same for a country. Fearful that this was a lesson his comrades had yet to learn, Dzerzhinsky prepared himself for his final dive.

Ninety-three nautical miles due east of the doomed *Cheka*, the *Vulkan* surged onward, ignorant of its sister ship's plight. Acting as the eyes and ears of the 13,250-ton vessel, Lev Zinyakin sat at the sonar panel controls, busily scanning the surrounding seas.

About to conclude his second consecutive six-hour

work shift, the petty officer looked forward to one of Chef Anatoly's good hot meals. Since last night's supper he had eaten practically nothing. When his shift ended he would feast, and then surrender to the call of his mattress.

With a wide yawn, Zinyakin activated the *Vulkan*'s towed-array sensor platform. Reeled out from their stern planes, the device would search the seas behind them for any signs of their elusive enemy. Again he yawned, and pleaded with his weary body to stay alert just a little longer.

To help the time pass more quickly, he allowed his thoughts to wander. As they always seemed to do, his memories brought him back to the beloved land of his birth. Zinyakin lost himself in cherished childhood memories of his family and the seaside cottage in which he had been raised.

Grinning at his recollections the petty officer yawned again and checked the console's digital clock. After calculating that he had precisely twenty-seven minutes to go until his replacement was scheduled to arrive, he looked up to check the towed array's status. As he determined that the tethered platform was indeed fully extended, the thunderous blast of a massive explosion sounded in his headphones. Alertly, he activated the tape recorder and then swiveled to inform the present officer of the deck.

"We're picking up a major explosion in our baffles! Approximate range is one-six-zero kilometers."

Senior Lieutenant Vasili Leonov was the first one at his side. He was soon followed by Ivan Novikov. The cocky political officer commented first.

"So, the *Cheka* has finally eliminated the Yankee attack sub. This is a glorious moment, Comrades."

Vasili Leonov was irritated by this brash statement. "We mustn't be too hasty to jump to conclusions. Comrade Zinyakin, will it be possible to identify the exact source of this blast?"

Zinyakin listened a moment to the distant sound of rending steel then said, "It's all being recorded in the computer, sir. It will take a minute or so to filter out the distortion and pinpoint any background noises."

While waiting for the requested computations, Zinyakin couldn't help but overhear the *zampolit*'s idle boasting.

"I tell you, Comrade Leonov, this means that the final obstacle has been removed from our path. Nothing will stand before us and our dream's fulfillment. We have proven beyond doubt the superiority of the socialist way of life."

Zinyakin's attention was diverted back to the screen as it began filling with pertinent data.

"Well, Comrade Petty Officer, read us the good news," the grinning *zampolit* prompted.

Zinyakin cleared his throat and spoke firmly. "Because of the extreme distances involved, we are unable to determine the source of the blast. But we do have a confirmed analysis of the background track. Clearly audible here is a single surviving sound signature."

"That would be the *Cheka*," Novikov beamed.

Zinyakin's response was flat and grim. "I'm afraid not, sir. The computer shows an eighty-five percent probability that this signature belongs to an American vessel."

327

"That's impossible!" screamed the angry zampolit. "Surely you have mistakenly programmed the computer. Try it again and you'll find your error."

Shrugging his shoulders, the petty officer cleared the screen and again requested an analysis of the hydrophone tape. As the information popped onto the screen, he said, "There has been a slight change, sir. The probability has increased to ninety-three percent that the submarine now trailing us is of American origin."

"I still can't accept this," the *zampolit* said. "Comrade Leonov, surely there's a malfunction in our equipment. Perhaps it's merely a single broken computer chip."

The senior lieutenant somberly shook his head. "That is most doubtful, Comrade. I think it's best to merely accept this tragic news and continue on with our job at hand."

"But it can't be! The *Cheka* was our most advanced attack sub. Her crew was hand-picked from the Rodina's finest sailors. No vessel on this planet was—is—its equal."

"What can I say? We must accept the facts at hand, Comrade," Leonov said softly. "You mustn't forget that strange things happen in times of war. Anyway, I've always said that we have seriously underrated the capabilities of the Americans' Los Angeles-class attack ship."

As the reality of their loss began to sink in, Novikov responded, noticeably humbled. "If what you say is true, this is a black moment for the Motherland. Since we have lost our escort, perhaps we should ascend to launch depth and release our missiles now, before the enemy has a chance to catch up with us."

But the senior lieutenant wanted no part in such a half-baked scheme. "That makes absolutely no sense at all. The only way that our operation can succeed is to eliminate each of the intended targets, totally. In order to be within range of those sites on America's eastern shore, we must attain our preplanned launch coordinates.

"Don't look so worried, Comrade. We are only thirty minutes away from this position. And as for that American attack sub, I think we are more than capable of handling it ourselves."

Turning from the concerned political officer, Leonov issued a solitary command. "Comrade Zinyakin, release the external buoyant thermometer and find me the location of a thermocline."

Then, turning back to the sulking *zampolit*, Leonov said, "Your lack of confidence disturbs me, Comrade Novikov. Don't you think I'm capable of handling our present situation?"

"With the *Cheka* gone, I doubt if even Admiral Sorokin could escape the grasp of the Americans," Novikov replied, his voice heavy with defeat.

"Oh, come now, you continue to disappoint me. This is far from the confident spirit that you showed me in Petropavlovsk. Don't forget, it wasn't so long ago that I was the one who was ready to give up. I'll never forget that it was you who saved me."

The unexpected comment snapped Novikov out of his foul mood. "You are right, Vasili Leonov. I am acting like a foolish crybaby. Please accept my sincere apologies."

From behind them, Zinyakin called, "I've found a thermocline, sir. There seems to be a pronounced band of significantly warmer waters stretching some forty-three meters from the ocean's surface. From that point down it cools abruptly."

"Wonderful news, my friend," the senior lieutenant said as he did some hasty mental calculations.

Puzzled, Novikov asked, "But what does a band of warmer water have to do with escaping the reach of the enemy?"

Leonov winked and said, "Everything, Comrade. By bringing the *Vulkan* up into this layer, the Los Angeles-class sub will be unable to use its sonar to detect us. Because the warmer water is more dense, their sensors will be reflected back into the cold layer, and they will be unable to locate us. In effect, we will be invisible!"

Inspired by the simple logic of this tactic, the *zampolit* managed a smile of his own.

"That's more like it, Comrade Novikov! Now—how about going up there and winning ourselves a war!"

330

Chapter Thirteen

Captain Robert Powell of the destroyer USS *Eagle* knew how rare it was to receive a personal call from the commander of the entire Third Fleet. Of course, he was currently on the strangest mission he had ever been involved with in his twenty-five-year naval career, so the call really wasn't that unexpected.

Admiral Miller had been most firm. With time rapidly running out, he had pleaded, begged, then finally demanded that the captain tag the bogey Soviet sub within the next thirty minutes. Aware of the tragic proportions of the crisis they faced, Powell had assured the admiral that he would do all that he could.

The captain coordinated his efforts from the *Eagle*'s combat information center. This equipment-packed compartment was buzzing with intense activity as he made the rounds of its various stations. Satisfied that the ship's sonar and other underwater sensors were working properly, he joined his XO beside the clear plastic plotting board. On it was a detailed representation of the southern portion of the Emperor Seamount Chain.

"What's the matter, Skipper? You look a bit peaked," said the exec. "Aren't you feeling well?"

Powell responded flatly, "Mr. Morley, what ails me isn't of a physical origin. I just got off the horn with

Admiral Miller. Things don't look good, my friend."

The XO circled the waters to the immediate east of the subterranean mountain range. "If they're out here, Skipper, I don't understand how we could have missed them. Between our own efforts and that of the task force, we've got this sector completely saturated. I've got a feeling that the *Vulkan* is in an altogether different portion of the Pacific."

With both hands on the edge of the plotting table, the captain studied the map intently. "We're going by what the boys in intelligence tell us, lieutenant. With our present time limitations, we've just got to pray that their info is correct. There's certainly no time left to start a new search. What's the status of our choppers?"

The XO pointed to the northern portion of the map. "Bravo team is one hour into its present patrol. They're in the process of resaturating this sector with sonobuoys. We've also got them working their MAD system, dunking hydrophones, and turbulence-wake detector."

"What about Delta team?"

"They came in about fifteen minutes ago, Captain. Not only did they need fuel and oil, but the crew is totally exhausted. After all, they've already completed two full sorties."

"Well, make it three, Lieutenant," the captain replied caustically. "Everyone of us is beat; but as long as that equipment remains operational, we've got to keep it in use. Have them take the southern sector. Of all the remaining areas, that one has been covered the least."

"Aye, aye, Skipper," the exec said, then he went to

make the call that would scramble the weary chopper crew.

Captain Powell continued to study the plotting board. Taking in the positions of the *Eagle* and the other ships in the task force, he wondered if his exec's observation could be correct. Between the *Eagle*, the cruiser *Ticonderoga*, the frigate *Gatewater* and the *John F. Kennedy*, these waters were certainly well covered. The *Kennedy* alone held over eighty planes and helicopters, many of which were specifically designed for anti-submarine operations. And then, of course, there was the USS *Triton*. Commanded by his old schoolmate Michael Cooksey, the Los Angeles-class attack sub was a potent ASW platform. Unsure of their current location, Powell still felt that the *Triton* had the best chance of ridding the seas of the Soviet threat with a single shot.

Balancing himself on the sides of the table as the *Eagle*'s bow bit into a large swell, Powell closed his eyes and offered a single prayer. A little divine help— and a lot of luck—sure would be appreciated.

Two floors beneath the *Eagle*'s CIC, Air Tactical Officer Gerald Grodsky was seated in the destroyer's galley, wolfing down a hearty breakfast. Though he was bleary-eyed and looking forward to a nice long sleep, he had decided on appeasing his appetite before surrendering to the solace of his bunk.

Deserted except for a handful of fellow sailors, the brightly colored galley was Grodsky's second home. Never one to miss a meal, the ATO's full figure was flourishing on the navy's simple yet tasty chow. His present feast was comprised of half a grapefruit, a bowl of oatmeal, a cheese omelette, bacon, sausage, and a trio of thick brown biscuits for good measure. And a mug of steaming hot, black coffee to wash it all down.

Seated opposite him was the Seasprite's diver. Satisfied with only oatmeal and a cup of decaffeinated tea, Wally Simpson shook his head as he watched his shipmate devour the full tray of food.

"I don't know where you put it, Grodsky. If I ate like that, I'd never be able to fit into my wetsuit."

"It's all in the genes," the ATO said between bites of sausage. "Some of us just burn food more quickly than others. My pop was just like me. That guy would put away his three squares a day and never leave out a midnight snack, and you know, he fit into the same pair of pants for twenty years straight."

"That's not the way it is in my family," Simpson replied. "My folks always seem to be on a diet. It's fine with me—I'll most likely live a lot longer without all that sugar and fat anyway."

"Yeah, but it sure as hell tastes good," Grodsky said as he delicately buttered a biscuit. As he took a bite of the bottom half, he looked down and saw his tray shift hard to the right. It stayed on the table because of a protruding steel edge, mounted for that very reason.

"Looks like we're running into some weather," the diver observed. "Wouldn't you know that we'd hit some rough stuff just when we're getting ready for some sack time."

Grodsky scooted his tray back in front of him. "Not even a full-scale typhoon could keep me from winkland now, good buddy."

He burped with satisfaction, then began working on the other half of the biscuit as the destroyer again plunged through a large swell. This time the ATO's hand alertly shot out to make certain his tray remained steady. He was just about to polish off his eggs, when he noticed a familiar face dashing into the mess hall.

Lieutenant Bill Payton was their pilot. Since he was a loner by habit, his presence there could only mean trouble. Without stopping at the chow line, he scurried over to their table.

"Let's move it, gentlemen! The Captain wants us up for one more go at it."

Grodsky looked up in disbelief. "Jesus, Lieutenant, if this is your idea of a joke, I seriously worry about your sense of humor."

"I wish it were a joke, gentlemen, but I'm sorry to let you down. Look, I'm as beat as any of you, but right now there's nothing we can do but get the lead out of our pants. The old man is going to personally meet us outside the hangar, so let's move it!"

With this revelation, Wally Simpson pushed away his tray and quickly stood. Payton eyed Grodsky impatiently, but only after the ATO had stuffed the remaining two biscuits into his shirt pocket did he join them.

Struggling to keep their balance, the chopper crew climbed the two flights of stairs that brought them to the tossing deck. Keeping a hand firmly gripped on the guard rail, they made it to the stern launch pad. Awaiting them was their Kaman Seasprite helicopter and the gangly figure of Captain Robert Powell.

"Sorry to ask this of you, men, but I have no alternative. It's imperative that we put to use every anti-sub device that we have. It's the next thirty minutes that will be the most critical. That's why I'm counting on you to get this SH-2 up and working."

The *Eagle*'s captain took in the chopper crew's disheveled, weary-eyed appearance and explained further. "I know that this will make your third sortie of the day, but if that Delta isn't tagged soon, all hell is going to break loose. That Russian survivor that you pulled from the Pacific has checked out thoroughly, so you can understand why I'm asking this of you. Find that submarine, men, or God help the planet!"

Stimulated by the sincere force of Powell's words, the three-man chopper crew saluted and pivoted to get down to work. After the pilot had some hasty words with the burly, cigar-chomping maintenance chief, they loaded into the Seasprite and switched on its dual turboshaft engines. With a high-pitched whine, the rotor blades began spinning. As they revved up to take-off velocity, the ATO peered out of the plexiglass hatch window and viewed the captain, who still stood stiffly beside the hangar, taking the full brunt of their rotors' downdraft. Having had little personal contact with the captain before this, Grodsky was impressed with the officer's forceful character. The ATO held on as the Seasprite lifted, Powell's somber warning still fresh in his mind. The ship was soon out of sight, replaced by nothing but the surging blue Pacific.

Their course was due south and Grodsky began preparing the various ASW devices that they would soon be deploying. But the ATO's thoughts remained locked on the nature of their current predicament.

When Junior Lieutenant Andrei Yakalov was first pulled from the downed Soviet relay plane, Grodsky had failed to realize the seriousness of their situation. He justified the young sensor operator's mad babblings as being the aftereffects of a trauma-inducing crash.

Though their superiors had yet to brief them fully, scuttlebutt had it that Yakalov's warning tied in directly with the sub they were presently tracking down. This same rumor hinted that a mutiny had taken place on that vessel. Why the United States Navy had been called in to quell what appeared to be an exclusive Soviet problem was still somewhat confusing.

Grodsky knew that the Soviet people were difficult for Westerners to understand. Although he was the grandson of Russian emigres, he had few insights into the Soviet psyche. What he did understand was their love of the land. This was something his grandfather had expounded upon until his death. Paranoid after centuries of constant invasions, the Russian people wanted only to enjoy their fields and forests in peace. As it turned out, the first part of the twentieth century offered them little of that most-precious commodity. With tens of millions slain on battlefields, it was no wonder that they were still so cautious and distrustful.

Grodsky had watched the rapid ascension of Viktor Rodin and had looked to the future with optimism. With their own candidate of peace in the White House, the time seemed ripe for an end to nuclear madness. That was yet another reason why the current crisis was so completely unexpected.

Stifling a weary yawn, the ATO hoped it would all

be resolved with a minimum of bloodshed. After he was certain that his gear was in place, he approached the cockpit.

"When do you want me to get started, Lieutenant?"

From the seat on the left, Bill Payton replied, "We'll be in a position to take our first hydrophone reading in a couple of minutes. Everything ready back there?"

Nodding in confirmation, Grodsky looked out at the Pacific. He had no doubts that their task was a formidable one. More difficult than finding the proverbial needle in a haystack, locating a single submarine beneath those depths seemed utterly impossible. Awed by the challenge, Grodsky ducked back into the Seasprite's central compartment and sat down in front of the sensor panel.

Barely a minute later, his helmet-mounted intercom speakers activated and he received the okay to begin lowering the hydrophone unit. While the chopper hovered some twenty-five feet over the surging swells, the sensitive transducer slowly descended on a sturdy steel cable.

Grodsky replaced his helmet with a set of bulky headphones. Turning the volume gain to its maximum intensity, he took in the sizzling, crackling sounds that were produced as the device plunged under the water's surface. It took only seconds more for him to pick up the alien whining sound produced by a submarine's propellor.

His first instinct was that there had to be some sort of glitch in the equipment. Next, he briefly wondered if he could be imagining the whole thing. Only when the steady whine persisted did he convey this amazing discovery to the cockpit.

"Bingo, Lieutenant! We're sitting right on top of something! I'll bet my next dozen leaves that the sucker is a submarine—and a big one, at that."

The pilot, normally a cool character, answered excitedly "Good work, Grodsky! Are you set up back there to relay this sound signature back to Momma Bird for a definite I.D.?"

"I'm ready when you are," the breathless ATO returned.

Payton switched on the secure radio line back to the *Eagle*. "Mother Bird, this is chick Delta, do you read me?"

A brief crackle of static was followed by a crystal-clear reply. "Go ahead Delta, this is Mother Bird."

"Roger, Mother Bird. Prepare the nest to copy the sounds of your feeding chicks—"

From the Seasprite's sensor panel, the ATO diverted the hydrophone signal so that it would be transferred back to the destroyer via radio wave. In this manner they could take instantaneous advantage of the *Eagle's* massive computer. Their ability to identify the source of the hydrophone signal in a matter of minutes was as important as their ability to find it in the first place.

Though there was always the outside chance that they had tagged one of their own subs, Grodsky felt otherwise. He knew that Bill Payton was thinking the same thing when the pilot sent Wally Simpson back to give him a hand with the arming of their Mk 46 homing torpedoes. The ATO surrendered to the task willingly as they anxiously waited for the analysis to be completed.

Lev Zinyakin couldn't believe how slowly the minutes were passing. It always seemed that way when he was waiting for his shift to change. Though the two consecutive duty segments that he was about to complete had been far from dull, he couldn't ignore the emptiness in his belly and the heaviness of his eyes.

For the last quarter of an hour, the *Vulkan* had been traveling at a rather shallow depth to take advantage of the warm waters of the thermocline. In this portion of the sea, Zinyakin had to focus the sub's sensors on a radically different threat source. Since it was unlikely that they could be spotted from below, what they had to fear most was contact from above. And the American sonar devices were extremely sophisticated. Carried by both fixed wing planes and helicopters those systems had to be respected.

To insure instant detection of such aircraft, such devices as the *Vulkan*'s external buoyant hydrophone were deployed. This neutrally buoyant transducer was presently being towed above them, scanning the ocean's surface for the sound of advancing airplanes.

Since this system was run independently from the *Vulkan*'s hull-mounted hydrophones, a separate monitoring channel was necessary. Analyzing the input from the surface was Zinyakin's current responsibilities.

Steadfastly ignoring the rumbles and groans from his stomach, Zinyakin sat back and listened to the various noises being fed into his headphones. Identifying the swooshing slap of agitated water, the sonar officer determined that the seas were fairly heavy topside. At their current depth the surface turmoil was hardly noticeable, except for this noise.

Aware of his fatigue, Zinyakin was proud of the fact that never once had he fallen asleep while on duty. This was in vast contrast to his shipmates, who generally looked for every opportunity to catch a catnap.

Lulled by the slap of the breaking waves, the sonar officer fought an unsuccessful battle to stay awake. His eyelids clamped shut and he instantly fell into a dream. In his vision he found himself a lad again, sailing from Palanga on his grandfather's battered boat. Though the Baltic Sea had been as smooth as glass when they had started out, the morning sky quickly turned black when an icy northern gale descended in all its fury. Thrown to the deck by the first arriving swells, Lev tried in vain to stand, for his legs would not cooperate. Feeling leaden, nauseous and scared, he looked to the interior of the cabin and saw that nobody was at the wildly spinning wheel. Fearful that his grandfather had been swept overboard, he managed to get to his hands and knees. Continuously pounded by the crashing waves, he found his progress ponderously slow.

Lev made it to the cabin's hatchway soaked and bruised, but try as he might he was unable to make it indoors. Only when the first tears of frustration began falling on his cheeks was he aware of a distant voice, crying over the howling gale.

"Listen to the wind, lad!" bellowed his grandfather. "To the wind!"

Even though his elder was still nowhere to be seen, Lev paid attention to the advice. He closed his stinging eyes and focused his concentration on the boisterous gusts. It was then that he heard an alien chopping sound approaching. The familiar racket merely added to his puzzlement, for how could a helicopter be flying in the midst of such an angry tempest?

A muted electronic tone was ringing in the background when Zinyakin snapped from his dream. His eyes popped open and he swiftly reoriented himself. Slouched before the sonar console, he blushed with embarrassment upon realizing his loss of self-control. Thankfully, only two minutes had passed, and it didn't appear that anyone else had spotted him.

He sat up straight, readjusted his headphones, and was reminded of the end of his dream by a shocking reality. The sound of a helicopter hovering was clearly audible topside! Rubbing his eyes to make certain that he was not still asleep, Zinyakin took a deep breath and reached forward to turn up the external buoyant hydrophone to maximum volume. Assured that the incoming signal was real, he turned and called out loudly.

"Senior Lieutenant!"

Seconds later, Vasili Leonov was at his side. "What is it, Zinyakin?"

"There's a helicopter hovering directly above us!" the frantic sonar officer explained. "Would you like to hear for yourself?"

"No, Comrade, I believe you," Leonov said heavily.

Squeezing in beside the senior lieutenant now was the scrawny figure of the *zampolit*. "What is going on here, Comrades?"

"Our hydrophones have discovered a helicopter

342

above us," Leonov explained.

Novikov seemed relieved. "Then why the look of gloom, Comrade Leonov? Surely such a vehicle can't threaten us."

The senior lieutenant shook his head. "If only that were the case. Because of our present depth, we are extremely vulnerable to their dunking sonar arrays. Not only can they call for help, they can attack us with homing torpedoes."

"Then let's dive for cover," Novikov suggested reasonably.

"It's too late for that. If their sensor operator is the least bit awake, they have already spotted us. Besides, we still have that Yankee attack sub to contend with."

Zinyakin's mind raced for an answer—and found it. "Sir, why don't we utilize one of the new self-initiated anti-aircraft missiles?"

"Of course, the SIAMs!" The senior lieutenant reached out and picked up the intercom. "Comrade Chuchkin, we need the immediate launch of one of our SIAM rockets. . . . I understand that one must first be loaded into a torpedo tube, Chuchkin. Just get it done and launch it at once!"

As Leonov hung up the handset, the puzzled *zampolit* asked, "What is this SIAM?"

"In my haste, I almost forgot it existed," Leonov admitted. "SIAM is a new defensive system that became operational only a few months ago. If Yuri Chuchkin can get one loaded in time, the topside threat will soon be eliminated.

"Now, Comrade Zinyakin, you must keep on the alert for any air-dropped homing torpedoes. If destiny is still with us, we shall pass this final obstacle and yet

343

strike the enemy a crippling blow!"

Two floors beneath the *Vulkan*'s control room, Weapons Chief Yuri Chuchkin hurried his crew into action. "Come on, you shirkers, get the lead out of your pants!"

Moving his portly frame to one side of the cramped torpedo room, he watched the six-man loading team at work. They efficiently pulled a homing torpedo from the number one tube. It was moved back by a hydraulic conveyor and replaced by the encapsulated SIAM presently being drawn up from the magazine.

Except for a single test firing, this would only be Chuchkin's second launch of a SIAM device. Still hot off the drawing board, the new system gave them an unheard of capability. Sounding more like science fiction than fact, the SIAM was one of the Rodina's most ingenious inventions. Anxious to see it operate under combat conditions, Chuchkin shifted his pipe to the corner of his mouth and peered down the unmoving conveyor belt.

"Where the hell is that anti-aircraft rocket?" Chuchkin screamed. "Any more delay and you'll be signing your own death warrants!"

In response to his invective, the belt began to move. From its storage rack on the deck below, a slim, twelve-foot-long, shiny metallic cannister became visible. Without hesitation, it was guided into the now-empty mouth of the number one tube. As his men sealed the tube and prepared it for firing, Chuchkin reflected on the strange course of their current patrol. It was the irony of it all that got to him. Here he was,

344

only a few months away from full retirement, and the Americans had to go and start a war. Deciding it was better to be here than merely sitting at ground zero, he could but apply the years of endless drills and practice alerts. In this way, he would do his part to insure the Motherland's survival.

"Number one tube is sealed, pressurized and ready for firing!" cried the seaman in charge of the loading team.

Quickly, Chuchkin joined him at the console. "Very good, Comrades. Now let us see if our scientists did their homework."

After unlocking the fire-control panel, the chief armed the SIAM and depressed the launch switch. He looked up when a loud hiss of compressed air sounded from inside the tube. This was followed by a noticeable lurch as the rocket shot out into the surrounding waters. Closing his eyes momentarily, he visualized the course this weapon would be taking as it streaked toward its target.

Already the missile should have broken out of its protective capsule. As its engines ignited, the rocket would break the ocean's surface. A split-second later, the SIAM's self-contained radar unit would activate. Steered by a set of aerodynamic fins, the missile would home-in on its target at supersonic speeds. A blindingly bright explosion would follow as the weapon's 30-kilogram warhead triggered, dooming the enemy to an instant, fiery demise.

Chuchkin doubted that they would be able to hear the blast from their present depth. Since they would have to rely on the *Vulkan*'s sensor operators to let them know if the shot was a success, the chief reached

345

for the intercom. He grimaced involuntarily when his call to the control room was picked up by the boat's *zampolit*.

"My, my, you're an impatient one, Comrade Chuchkin," the political officer said. "I imagine that you're calling for the results of the launch."

The weapons chief took his pipe from his mouth and meekly answered, "Yes, sir. I only wanted to know if it would be necessary to load another SIAM device."

Novikov took his time in answering. "Comrade Chuchkin, I'm most upset with you. Don't you have more faith in the Rodina's scientists than that? What need is there for another rocket when this one was more than adequate to do the trick. Lev Zinyakin told us of the glorious results only seconds ago. At that time his sensors recorded a massive series of explosions. This was followed by nothing but the sound of slapping waves. Whatever was hovering above us certainly no longer exists. Good shooting, my friend. Now, please don't disappoint me when the time arrives for the release of our SS-N-18s."

Pleased with their success, yet uncomfortable talking with the *zampolit*, the chief humbly excused himself. As he gave his crew the news, an excited shout of joy followed. He allowed his men several minutes to revel in their accomplishment, then barked out, "Your enthusiasm is duly noted. But are we holding a party here? Reload that vacant tube with the homing torpedo! Then I'm going to want to see the whole lot of you in the *taiga*. The Rodina is going to earn its ruble's worth with you shirkers today, that I can promise you!"

Conscious of his effect on the crew's mood, Chuchkin pivoted and proceeded out the rear hatchway. All in all, they were a good bunch; yet, like any conscripts, they had to be leaned on constantly. This was one lesson he had learned well in his three decades of service.

After placing the stem of his pipe back between his teeth, Chuchkin elected to fill its bowl and have a real smoke. Since the portion of the *Vulkan* he was presently in was off limits to smokers, he headed straight for his cabin. That was where he kept his precious stash of imported tobacco anyway.

Climbing down a flight of stairs, he turned toward the sub's stern. The room that he shared with three other petty officers was located amidships, on the sub's bottom deck. This put him close to the missile magazine in case an emergency called him there in the middle of one of his rest periods.

Though cramped and sparsely furnished with four narrow bunks and two wall-mounted desks, the space at least afforded him a semblance of privacy. Compared to past classes of submarines on which he had sailed, his current quarters could be regarded as nothing short of elegant.

Closing the door behind him, he found he had the entire cabin to himself. This would give him a chance to sort out his confused thoughts. Since the day's events were unlike any he had ever experienced, he decided that he more than deserved the valuable tobacco he was packing into his pipe.

Purchased in Viet Nam while the Golf-class sub he had been stationed on was visiting Cam Rahn Bay, the tobacco was unique. Packed by an English company, it contained the perfect mixture of fine-cut, golden Virginian leaf, vanilla, and just a hint of rum. This produced not only a smooth taste, but a sweet, pleasurable aroma as well. For the past six months he had been rationing the contents of the eight-ounce tin. Because of the current precarious state of world affairs, he decided that he'd better enjoy it now— while he was still alive to do so.

He inhaled the first lungful of smoke, further savoring the taste by exhaling it through his nostrils. While enjoying several more slowly exhaled puffs, his eyes strayed to the desk that he shared with the reactor chief. Here, smiling back at him with a warm, familiar grin was a picture of his beloved mother.

Now, more than ever before, he was sorry that he hadn't made time to visit her during his last leave. How disappointed she had been! Yet, naval matters had called, and there was little he could do about it but wish her his sincere love.

Now he was glad that she lived so far from a large city. The village of Malka was some fifty kilometers from Petropavlovsk. With no military installations to speak of, it would surely be ignored if a nuclear war were indeed taking place. Of course, there was always the chance that the enemy would overshoot its intended target . . . but there was also the nightmare of radioactive fallout to consider. Regardless of location, there was little doubt that if a nuclear war began, her life, and that of every other human being, would be changed forever.

Shivering at the thought, Chuchkin took another deep draw on his pipe and allowed his restless ponderings to settle. For years he had lived in fear of this day—yet, somehow he had fooled himself into thinking that it could never come to pass.

But the launching of the SIAM rocket had proved that they were in an actual state of war. The senior lieutenant had been hinting at this earlier. Passing off their present alert as merely another meaningless drill, Chuchkin had been fooling no one but himself.

The time was rapidly approaching when their own strategic missiles would be released. Few on board were as aware of their destructive capabilities as Chuchkin was. After all, the SS-N-18s were his lethal responsibility. Snuggled securely in their protective silos, the sixteen missiles would account for millions of deaths. Guided by the Rodina's most accurate guidance systems, this single flight of warheads would eliminate targets throughout the entire continental United States. After they struck, America would never be the same.

Chuchkin had no doubt as to who had been the aggressor, for the Soviet Union had sworn never to initiate a nuclear conflict. But deterrence had failed, and their mission would now be one of revenge.

Chuchkin cringed at the thought of the crazed *michman* who had come within inches of wrecking their fire-control system. Though he hated seeing Stefan Kuzmin stopped as he had been, the *zampolit* had been justified. To be stuck in a war situation with a load of missiles that couldn't be released would be the ultimate waste. If the warrant officer had been in his right mind, he would have been most aware of that.

Chuchkin had seen the mad aftereffects of a fever at work before. He had been at his own sister's bedside while she was dying of typhus. Driven insane by an uncontrollable body temperature, she had looked at him like he was a total stranger. Even their own mother had been unrecognizable to her.

When Kuzmin had grabbed Chuchkin by the arm and thrown him into the path of his pursuers, the chief had been sure that this was but another tragic instance of a fever-induced frenzy gaining the upper hand. When Kuzmin then went for the fire-control panel, all the time madly babbling about a mutiny, Chuchkin was certain. The *michman* had crossed that fragile line that threatened not only himself and his shipmates, but his fellow countrymen as well.

Relighting his pipe, Chuchkin wondered about the condition of their captain. For Petyr Valenko's sake, Chuchkin hoped that the fever was not as intense as that of the *michman*'s. Since he heard that the two men had spent time together while they were last in Petropavlovsk, there was no doubt as to where the disease had been contracted. As to who else on board had been infected . . . that was anyone's guess.

It was ironic that the captain had not been around to witness the call to war. Fortunately, it appeared as if Vasili Leonov had more than adequately taken over Valenko's responsibilities. The senior lieutenant was rising to the occasion, and then some. His handling of the SIAM launch had appeared flawless. Only a few days before there had been some concern as to Leonov's mental state. Many of the crew had believed that the abrupt end of his love affair would cause Vasili to go off the deep end—or even to desert. How very wrong they had been.

The chief's pipe was soon empty, and his desk clock

350

indicated that it was time to get back on the job. Mentally and physically relieved, he prepared himself for the speech that he would soon deliver. Even as he sat there, his men were surely waiting for him in the *taiga*. Since their assistance would be invaluable in directing the SS-N-18s skyward, the missile crew deserved to be briefed on their situation as he now understood it. With this task in mind, Chuchkin rose and, after stashing away what little tobacco remained, proceeded out the cabin's hatchway.

Thirty-eight hundred miles southeast of the *Vulkan*, the modified Boeing 747 transport known as Kneecap soared over the crystal blue waters off Baja California. Flying over a portion of the planet far from any potential ground targets, Kneecap cruised southward at a speed of five hundred and eighty-three miles per hour, at an altitude of thirty-five thousand feet.

Viktor Rodin and Robert Palmer had just returned to the plane's conference room after a brief tour of the rest of the aircraft. Beginning in the cockpit, the Premier had been introduced to both the crew and equipment that made Kneecap unique.

As Rodin settled into one of the high-backed chairs that surrounded the President's walnut table, his thoughts remained on the excursion just completed. He was most impressed with the 747's spaciousness, all the while aware of the incredible amount of gear stashed within its walls. This was most evident in the compartments reserved for the battle staff. Dressed in matching gray flight suits, the complement of men and women sat alertly before their consoles. In one cabin the Premier had counted over twenty-four individuals manning their stations. Robert Palmer was quick to explain that this was where the plane's thirteen separate radio systems were monitored. Other compartments held equipment belonging to Kneecap's twenty-five onboard telephones, encryption machinery for secure voice transmission, plus a large bay reserved for the sophisticated power-control system that managed the craft's extremely high electrical demands. Interspersed were several large rest areas, galleys, and, in the nose of the craft, separate cabins with comfortable sleeping accommodations for the senior officials.

All through his tour, the staff had remained cordial and polite. This surprised Rodin, who had expected to find a bit more callousness—especially given their current predicament. The Premier supposed that a great deal of this decorum was prompted by the presence of his host. Everywhere they went, Robert Palmer led the way, always quick with his introductions. Knowing the majority of the crew on a first-name basis, Palmer seemed never at a loss for the light banter that was so effective in making a tense situation more bearable.

His lighthearted attitude also had its effect on Rodin. Infected by the President's charm, the Premier felt instantly relaxed and, considering the situation, generally well accepted. He could just imagine the gloom and doom that would characterize his own command plane if the situation were reversed. In fact, he seriously doubted if his aides would even let Palmer step aboard the flying Kremlin. If they survived this day, Rodin promised himself that he would do his best to eliminate such unnecessary paranoia wherever possible.

The President had been on the phone since they had returned to the conference room. Now he hung up the receiver and met Rodin's curious gaze. "It appears that we're getting close, Viktor, but still no cigar. That was Admiral Miller, commander of the Pacific's Third Fleet. He reports that one of our Kamin Seasprite helicopters tagged an unidentified submarine in the extreme southern sector of the *Vulkan*'s intended launch area. The chopper pilot was in the process of conveying the object's sound signature when the radio abruptly went dead. At present, we're rushing every available anti-sub platform into that sector, on the assumption that what they picked up was indeed the *Vulkan*."

"Do they know why your helicopter broke radio contact?" the Premier asked.

"I'm afraid the Kaman is presumed down," Palmer said heavily. "The way things now appear, I'm afraid that our approaching units are never going to make it in time. If only we had an additional hour!"

Empathizing with the President's frustration, Rodin replied, "Once more, I can't tell you how sorry I am that this whole nightmare came about. I take full responsibility for the entire situation. I know my apology isn't much, but what more can I offer?"

"Easy, now, Viktor, we're not licked yet."

But the Premier's feelings of helplessness caused him to disagree. "The seconds continue to tick away, and what have we to show for it? Our best efforts have netted us absolutely nothing. All this leads up to one more question that I have to ask you, Robert: What will be your government's response if the unthinkable comes to pass . . . and the *Vulkan*'s load of missiles are released?"

Palmer answered directly. "I think the best way to answer that would be to call in my top foreign policy advisors and see what's on their minds. Is that agreeable with you, my friend?"

Rodin nodded and watched the President speak into his intercom.

"Delores, I'd like to see the Secretary of State and Mr. Carrigan at once."

"Very good, Mr. President," returned a high-pitched, nasal voice.

A moment of strained silence followed, as Rodin swiveled around and peered out of the porthole. Since they were in front of the wings, he had a unobstructed view of the land below. He recognized the long, narrow peninsula of barren land visible beneath the cloudless skies as belonging to Mexico's westernmost shoreline. He was the process of scanning the blue waters of the Pacific, when there was a knock on the compartment's door. The Premier turned to see two men enter. One was Patrick Carrigan, the President's National Security advisor whom he had met not long after landing in Los Angeles. The other person was an older, robust, white-haired figure whose frequently photographed face was most familiar.

As always, Palmer was quick with the introductions. "Viktor, you know Mr. Carrigan, yet I believe this is the first time that you've met my Secretary of State, George Michaelson."

The two statesmen shook hands and the Premier

offered a sincere greeting. "It is a pleasure to at last meet you, Mr. Michaelson. Since you have taken your present post, your work has been greatly admired."

Pleasantly surprised by the unexpected compliment, the Secretary of State responded in kind. "The pleasure is mine, sir. Like all of us, I've looked forward to this day with the greatest of expectations. I'm only sorry that it has been clouded by this unnecessary crisis."

"You and I both," Rodin said as he took his seat along with the others.

The President sat forward and initiated the conversation. "I'm sure that you've heard about the Seasprite going down. It's damn bad luck that they didn't get a definite on that bogey, but chances are that it was the *Vulkan*. I just got off the horn with Admiral Miller. He's in constant contact with our task force, which is currently closing in on the last coordinates reported by the helicopter. He's also monitoring the approach of the USS *Triton*, our Los Angeles-class attack sub that had previously tagged the *Vulkan* in this same general area. Unfortunately, the Admiral reports that the surface ships are too distant to close by 2130 hours—the intended launch time. We've got to be realistic: With the *Triton* as our only hope, the odds of stopping the *Vulkan* in time are continually decreasing.

"I've asked you two to join us in an effort to clear the air of all misconceptions. Both of you are free to be completely candid. Trust amongst ourselves is all that we have left.

"The question that we have for you is extremely basic. I know that each one of you has been considering it for sometime now, so here it goes. What course of action do you advise the United States of America to take if the *Vulkan*'s missiles are indeed released? Patrick, why don't you start us off?"

Momentarily surprised by the nature of Palmer's request, Carrigan stared at Rodin suspiciously before beginning. "I think it would be best for me to start with the manner in which we have already reacted to the list of targets that the General Secretary was kind enough to give us. Because of the sensitive nature of the sites involved, we have taken the following actions. Per the request of the Joint Chiefs of Staff, alternative communications systems have been activated worldwide. This includes SAC's Silk Purse, Scope Light, and Blue Eagle flying-command posts, and our minimum, essential emergency communications network. These steps will hopefully insure that military communications will not be totally decapitated.

"When the delicate issue of evacuation was brought up, it was unanimously agreed that the nation's underground command posts would remain on duty. This includes the Pentagon, Cheyenne Mountain, Offut Field, and the various alternative national command centers. The only instances whereby evacuation has been permitted concerns non-essential dependents living in or around the various targeted military installations. To guarantee security, this operation is being carried out under the cover of being just another exercise.

"My biggest concern remains with the residual radioactive fallout created by the blasts and spread throughout the country on the easterly winds; the panic that will ensue once the first warhead explodes;

and, last but not least, the tragedy we're facing in Southern California. A strike by only a handful of nuclear weapons over the Los Angeles basin will produce over one million instant casualties. I fear that our decision not to immediately evacuate the city could be a costly one."

Palmer quickly interjected, "My decision on that matter remains firm, Patrick. I am wholeheartedly convinced that an evacuation at this time, and the resulting panic it would inevitably produce, will cost us more lives than it will save."

Carrigan responded icily. "Even if a few hundred thousand souls could be saved by such a move, my final estimate is that this single attack will cost us twenty-five million lives, at the minimum."

Staggered by the figure, George Michaelson's voice trembled. "Never before in the history of diplomacy has a country been faced with such monumental decisions as we must make. I can only return to Great Britain's decision during World War II to knowingly allow the Nazis to bomb the city of Coventry, resulting in the loss of hundreds of lives. Of course, that was to make certain that the Germans didn't find out that the British had cracked their most secret Ultra code, and, in fact, knew of the attack beforehand.

"Because of the unbelievable loss of life and property that a nuclear strike will produce, it's very hard for me just to turn the other cheek and recommend that we merely ignore the bombs because of the unpremeditated circumstances. Once the first mushroom cloud forms over American soil, my gut instinct will be to side with the surviving public—who will be crying out for some type of hard response to avenge this despicable crime. The number-one priority will be finding the bastards who are responsible for this insanity."

"I agree with you!" the Premier said firmly. "No matter the personal sacrifice demanded, I swear to you that I will focus my every effort into tracking down the conspirators. I have already initiated just such an investigation. Led by a handful of trusted agents, elements of the Soviet Union's internal police force, the MVD, are working around the clock to discover the malefactors. The results of this inquiry are expected shortly.

"It is my guess that we are dealing with a small clique of embittered, sick souls. Since the top-secret information that they acquired lies at the very heart of my command staff, I don't think that I'll have to be looking far."

Allowing himself a calming breath, Rodin added, "Comrade Michaelson, you mentioned that if the bombs do fall, you favor a hard retaliatory response. Do you mean militarily?"

Far from proud of his decision, the Secretary of State somberly nodded his assent.

Patrick Carrigan offered an explanation. "George and I have discussed this subject intensively. Our decision was far from an easy one. The crux of the matter revolves around the general public's initial reaction to the attack. I think it's safe to say, with some certainty, that the citizens of the United States will not sit back and let this strike go unanswered. If we don't react, and react strongly, not only do we face a general insurrection, but also the very real threat of a military coup d'etat. That is why we favor a response based upon the *eye for an eye* principle. For each target that Soviet missiles destroy on American soil, we should take out an equivalent site within the U.S.S.R. Not only will this course of action appease civilian demands, it will also guarantee military parity."

But Robert Palmer could not accept his advisor's decision. "I beg to differ with you, Carrigan. How the hell can you justify killing millions more just to get even? Don't you see—that will only give the ones responsible for this madness exactly what they want! Bomb will follow bomb, and before it's over the entire planet will fall victim to this conflict. You don't really think that a military response is the only answer, do you George?"

Staring the President right in the eye, the Secretary of State said, "In this instance, I'm afraid that I do, Mr. President. It goes against my grain to admit it, but right now I have no alternatives.

"Several months ago, while I was still teaching at Harvard, I chaired a seminar comprised of a select group of the West's top defense analysts. Our own Patrick Carrigan attended. At that time, a nuclear-attack scenario, much like the one we currently face, was presented to the group. Though a great deal of controversial discussion ensued, the panel eventually reached an agreement. No population, no matter how socially conscious, could accept a nuclear attack without any visible response on their government's part. As we learned during the mid-1980's in dealing with the crisis of terrorism, if the guilty parties can be found and isolated, they must be subsequently eliminated. Turn your cheek from this nuclear strike, Mr.

President, and you'll be facing an insurrection that will make the Viet Nam protests seem like a children's birthday party!"

Of all the unlikely places, George Michaelson found support from the lips of Viktor Rodin. "I am certain that if the tables were turned, I would be faced with the very same dilemma. I would not expect my people to allow a flight of Trident missiles into the Rodina and, as you say, merely turn the other cheek. Yet, I fear that a secondary strike on your part will prompt our generals to answer with a counterstrike. I fear President Palmer is correct in his assumption that this is exactly what the conspirators are hoping for. If America can't be crippled by a single first-strike attack, the next best thing would be to accept some casualties and answer with an even larger attack."

"And there goes the ball game!" Palmer concluded succinctly.

His terse comment was punctuated by an abrupt shaking of the cabin, as Kneecap plowed into a pocket of rough, unstable air. As the floor and walls began vibrating around them, a sudden change in the previously steady whine of the plane's engines indicated that the pilot was already seeking a smoother flight path. As the jumbo jet stabilized, a loud chime sounded through the intercom. This was followed by the firm, calm voice of the pilot.

"Please excuse the turbulence, ladies and gentlemen. We're passing on the fringe of a low pressure system that's currently moving into Mexico. The instability extends a bit higher than we expected, so please make certain that your seat belts are securely fastened. We intend to make every effort to reach some smoother air as soon as we are able."

As the pilot's explanation ended, there was a loud knock on the conference room door. Palmer said, "Enter," and the Premier's secretary, Olga Tyumen, poked her head sheepishly inside.

"Do come in, my dear," the President prompted.

The shapely blonde appeared a bit uncomfortable as she surveyed the grim faces before her. Noticing her uneasiness, Palmer said lightly, "I hope that group back in the staff quarters are behaving themselves. It's not often that Kneecap is graced by such a beautiful woman. If anyone gets out of hand, Olga, you be certain to notify me personally."

She blushed and said, "Thank you, Comrade President. But everything is most comfortable. Your crew has been most cooperative."

As the plane was buffeted by another powerful gust of turbulence, Olga found herself thrown off balance. Only the quick reflexes and tight grasp of Robert Palmer kept her from toppling over. Still holding her firmly in his arms, the President gently said, "You'd better get back to your seat and buckle in, my dear. When our pilot gives us these warnings, he's usually not wasting his breath. What was it that you needed?"

Olga took a step back and, holding onto an empty chair, spoke to Viktor Rodin. "I'm sorry to disturb you, Comrade General Secretary, but I thought that you'd want to know about the contents of a strange report I just received from PVO headquarters."

Carefully reaching over the table, she handed Rodin a folded sheet of notepaper. The Premier quickly read it and confusion filled his face. "My, this is an odd turn of events. I certainly did not order it."

President Palmer said calmly, "Perhaps we could be of some assistance."

"Oh, of course," Rodin returned. "I'm not sure what this means, but our national command headquarters reports that the pilot of my personal IL-78 aircraft has just announced that he has taken off from Los Angeles and has requested a flight plan back to the U.S.S.R. Perhaps it's all a misunderstanding, but this is surely not on my authority."

Patrick Carrigan reacted first. "We were informed of the IL-78's request for take-off a quarter of an hour ago. It was assumed that it had been initiated by the General Secretary, so it was routinely approved."

"There must be some rational reason behind this unexpected turn of events," the Premier reflected. "Olga, please be so good as to try to reach the aircraft. Perhaps the pilot can tell us just what is going on there."

"Could this have something to do with the take-over on the *Vulkan*?" Carrigan asked.

Rodin held his response until Olga Tyumen left the compartment. "Right now, I really can't say. All I know for certain is that, at the moment, I can't take anything for granted."

Sensing his guest's frustration, President Palmer said, "This is a most confusing day for all of us, my friend. If somehow the fates are with us, and we see ourselves past this crisis, we must do everything within our power to insure that such a nightmare can never threaten us again. The immediate abolition of all nuclear weapons will be a first step in guaranteeing the security of the planet for the generations that

362

follow."

"You will certainly have my complete cooperation," said the Premier, who now seemed drained of all energy. "I just hope that it isn't already too late."

With this, the President excused his advisors—after accepting a plea on their part for him to keep his mind open to the military options just presented. Alone once more, the two leaders of the world's mightiest nations somberly faced each other.

"Would you really order a nuclear counterstrike if the *Vulkan*'s missiles are released?" Rodin asked quietly.

The President thought for a moment, then said, "Even though my heart says *absolutely no*, I wonder if I will have much choice in the matter. I can only continue to pray that I won't be forced to make such a grave decision."

Rodin swiveled in his chair to gaze out of the porthole. As he did so, the plane shook violently. Tightly grasping the arms of his chair, he peered outside. It took the Premier only seconds to locate the apparent source of the turbulence.

Clearly visible in the skies beyond was a massive formation of swirling black clouds. From within the towering, dark column, the stacatto flash of lightning indicated the storm front's violent fury.

As he watched this raw display of natural violence, Rodin reflected on one disturbing element of the message that Olga had just relayed to him. In fact, so disturbing was its essence that he had been unable to reveal it to the Americans. Admiral of the Fleet Stanislav Sorokin had to have been the one to authorize the take-off of Rodin's IL-78 command plane.

This could only mean that the esteemed naval officer himself was one of the conspirators.

Shocked by this revelation, Rodin shivered involuntarily. Struggling to clear his mind, the General Secretary mentally assembled the evidence that pointed toward the admiral's guilt.

From the very beginning, Rodin had known that the malefactors had to be a small cabal of individuals occupying high positions of power. A thorough knowledge of naval procedures would be a most valuable necessity. Sorokin had been an outspoken opponent of Viktor Rodin's conciliatory position with the West from the start. Fearful of what the world would be like if the current massive military machines were abolished, the admiral must have decided upon a Counterforce strike as a last resort.

Earlier, when the Soviet Kresta-class cruiser had been sunk, Rodin had wondered what had blown the *Natya* apart seconds before its attack against the *Vulkan* was to begin. Since he and the admiral were the only ones who knew of the *Natya*'s attack orders, Sorokin must have notified his fellow conspirators— who in turn had the cruiser conveniently eliminated. The loss of the *Natya* had tragic implications beyond the lives and equipment involved. For, if the warship had been successful, their current predicament would have been resolved.

The Premier realized how shocked Sorokin must have been at being invited on the flight to Los Angeles. Surely he had only accepted so as not to arouse unnecessary suspicion. Knowing full well that the nuclear strike would include a bevy of warheads targeted on Southern California, Sorokin had commandeered the IL-78. His cowardly act would cost the admiral dearly.

The General Secretary stirred when a huge, fiery fork of lightning lit the surrounding heavens. Shaking off his lethargy, Rodin planned the series of directives he would now issue to seal the fates of Sorokin and his fellow traitors. Under a blanket of secrecy, he would authorize his most trusted agents to tap the IL-78's radio transmissions. Each call would be duly monitored and traced. If Stanislav Sorokin was indeed one of those responsible, Rodin would catch him in the act of contacting his fellow conspirators as they gloated over their apparent victory.

Not knowing who else the finger of guilt would point to, Rodin mentally prepared himself for the shock of disclosure that would, hopefully, follow. Catching the entire group would give him great satisfaction. But at the moment he was faced with a much graver problem. In only a few minutes the *Vulkan* would reach its launch coordinates. Oblivious to the real state of political relations, the crew would then carry out the second part of the Red Flag directive and release their lethal load of sixteen SS-N-18s. In response, the Americans would cry for a counterstrike and the world would be plunged into the ultimate horror.

Trembling with anger at the audacity of the individuals who had hatched this insane plot, Rodin knew that, somehow, the *Vulkan* had to be stopped!

Chapter Fourteen

The control room of the USS *Triton* was possessed by a tense silence as the vessel hurried toward the assumed intercept point. Pacing the length of the equipment-packed compartment was Captain Michael Cooksey. Hands cocked stiffly behind his back and eyes focused on the deck before him, he appeared lost in distant thought.

Lieutenant Commander Richard Craig watched his senior officer's slow, monotonous stride, and couldn't help but be concerned. The captain looked as nervous as he had ever seen him. And that included the conclusion of their last patrol, when Cooksey's hair-trigger temper and sullen moods were the talk of the ship.

Looking rested and fit after returning from leave, Cooksey had been just like his old self again. Even his sense of humor had returned. But their confrontation with the Soviet attack sub had quickly changed all that.

While they were in the midst of their crash dive, the XO had caught a glimpse of the captain's face and didn't like what he'd seen. Not only had the lines of tension returned, so had the dark pouches that had previously underscored his bloodshot eyes. Certainly drained by a lack of proper rest and nourishment, Craig wondered how long the captain could keep himself together.

From his position behind the sonar console, the XO scanned the rest of the compartment's interior. With quiet efficiency, the crew went about their individual duties. Conscious of the loud, distant whining of the *Triton*'s turbines, he knew they were pushing ahead at close to top speed.

A muted, electronic tone rang from his wrist, and Craig looked down at his preset watch. As he somberly took in the time, he cleared his throat and addressed Cooksey, who was headed back toward him.

"Skipper, it's 2120 hours."

"I'm well aware of that, Mr. Craig," the captain snapped. He paced for three more strides, then halted and commanded, "All stop! Rig for ultra-quiet."

While his directives were being carried out, Cooksey returned to the sonar station. Without comment, he clipped on the auxiliary headphones and initiated a hasty sensor scan.

"Damn it, they've got to be out there somewhere!" Cooksey shouted as he disgustedly peeled the listening gear off. "Callahan, is this gear working properly?"

The sonar officer responded tactfully. "All hydrophones appear operational, sir. We also show a negative on active search."

"Well, keep on it, Lieutenant, I know they're close!"

Charles Callahan returned to his console, while the

captain quizzed his exec. "What's your opinion of this damned mess, Mr. Craig?"

The XO answered as the familiar whine of their engines dissipated and the *Triton* glided to a halt. "I agree that they can't be too far away. Skipper It wasn't all that long ago that we pinged them. Since our top speed is well over that of a Delta-class boat, they couldn't have gotten too far away—unless they headed out in the opposite direction."

"That's unlikely," Cooksey observed. "They're going to need to attain that launch position as far east as time allows. Those SS-N-18s will be at the extreme edge of their range and they won't be taking any chances. Damn it to hell—I should have blown them away earlier when I had the chance. What was I thinking about?"

"You were only giving them a fair chance to show their colors, Skipper. Don't take it so personally. I would have made the exact same decision."

The exec's words were met with silence. Both men turned their attentions to the green-tinted sonar screen. As Richard Craig watched the pulsing white line, which monitored the surge of high-frequency power being sent out from their bow, an idea came to him.

"You know, Skipper, the *Vulkan* may have taken the chance of ascending up through the thermocline. The last reading of our XBT showed an unusually thick band of warmer water above us. If that's still present, and the Soviets are taking advantage of its veil . . . that could account for their absence on our sensors."

Impressed with this thought, Cooksey nodded.

"You could have something, Rich. Although, that would open them up to surface detection by one of our choppers or aircraft; those Russians might just be trying to pull the wool over our eyes. Launch the XBT and find us that thermocline. Then get the *Triton* ready to ascend. I'd better call Spencer and have him ready one of those ASW/SOWs."

As Cooksey glanced down to check his watch, Craig was already carrying out his directives. As the captain reached out for the intercom, he softly mumbled to himself, "Please God, give me another shot at them. Just one damn shot!"

Seventy-three nautical miles due east of the USS *Triton*, the *Vulkan* silently balanced itself in the cool, dense layer of seawater that signaled the limit of the thermocline. This rather delicate maneuver was being monitored from the ship's attack center, where the sub's command functions had now been transferred. Bathed in a veil of dim red light, the compartment was a smaller copy of the vessel's control room. The main difference was the decreased size of the staff present. A hand-picked complement of selected personnel was all that was necessary to assist the commanding officers in carrying out the *Vulkan*'s primary mission.

Senior Lieutenant Vasili Leonov was aware of this as he quickly checked the individual consoles. Proud that his men had accepted his new position of command without undue questions, Leonov knew that the moment of destiny would soon be upon them.

Continuing down the narrow walkway that circled

the compartment, Leonov passed the seated sonar officer. Lev Zinyakin was completely immersed in his work and not aware of Vasili's presence. Knowing that this was Zinyakin's third consecutive work shift, the senior officer shook his head in wonder. It had taken only a single plea on his part to convince the exhausted sonar operator to follow them into the attack center. After all, this would be the moment when the *Vulkan*'s most talented crew members were needed to insure success. Allowing Zinyakin a quick break to wash his beard-stubbled face and gobble down a sandwich and some tea, Leonov felt more assured just knowing that the brilliant Lithuanian was manning the all-important station.

Next to the sonar console was the navigation plotting board. Peering over the navigator's shoulder, Leonov monitored their progress. Only minutes away from the attainment of their launch position, the *Vulkan* appeared to have the ocean all to itself. A firm hand on his back diverted his attention, and Leonov turned to face the beaming *zampolit*.

"We have done it, Comrade! If it is all right with you, I would like to take a few seconds to address the rest of the crew."

Ivan Novikov's request didn't sound unreasonable, and the senior lieutenant beckoned him to go ahead.

Relishing the spotlight, the political officer took hold of the intercom and situated himself in the center of the room. Novikov's words penetrated every inch of the sub's interior.

"My dear Comrades, this is your *zampolit* speaking. I'm certain that you've all heard the rumors by now, and I'm only here to confirm them. Yes, my friends, we are indeed in a state of war. Since the Soviet Union has vowed never to be the first user of atomic weapons, this tragic state of affairs in which we currently find ourselves must have been sparked by the imperialists. For decades we have watched the greedy capitalists stockpile the weaponry for a first strike. Ever true to their confused bloodthirsty doctrine, the Americans have made the first move.

"Since this most likely means that our beloved Rodina was a primary target of their despicable action, there's no doubt where our thoughts must presently be. Rest assured that we shall avenge the deaths of our loved ones. To your battle stations, Comrades, for the glory of the Motherland!"

An awkward moment of silence followed, punctuated by the excited cries of their navigator. "We've attained our launch position, sir."

Leonov responded in a firm voice. "Ascend to launch depth!"

As the *Vulkan*'s bow planes bit into the surrounding sea, Leonov joined the *zampolit* at the fire-control panel. In unison, both men pulled out the two folding chairs that were attached to the console's steel frame. Exactly two arm's lengths away from each other, they seated themselves. Each man then removed a shiny chrome key, which they had kept around their necks on sturdy chains. Before inserting his key into its proper slot, Leonov triggered the intercom.

"Comrade Chuchkin, are you ready?"

From deep within the *taiga*, the weapons chief reported that he was, and the senior lieutenant beckoned the *zampolit* to continue. In one smooth motion, both men reached forward and unlocked the dual firing panels. Facing them now was a row of sixteen clear-plastic buttons, numbered from left to right. Above this was a large digital counter.

"Initiating release code insert on the count of three," Leonov barked. "One . . . two . . . three!'"

Simultaneously, they dialed in the proper digits. When this was completed, Leonov again spoke.

"Release code insertion completed. Activate arming switch."

A large black button next to the digital counter was depressed and, in response, the sixteen lights began blinking a bright crimson. All eyes now went to the clock mounted above the panel, as the minute hand indicated 2129 hours.

Leonov and Novikov angled their index fingers over the blinking button numbered "one." Thirty seconds before they hit their switches to send the first SS-N-18 skyward, a sharp, shrill buzz broke the tense silence.

"It's the emergency abort system!'" shouted Leonov as he quickly scanned the panel to trace the source of the problem.

Puzzled by this unforeseen postponement, the *zampolit* asked, "Did we do something wrong? Perhaps we have given the improper release code."

Ignoring Novikov, Leonov intently searched the warning panel and finally discovered the malfunction. "We've lost power to our gyroscope! Without it, the warheads will be completely disorientated."

"Let's call Chuchkin and have him check it out," Novikov suggested as he bent toward the intercom.

But Leonov shook his head vehemently. "The missile crew has got its own problems right now, keeping those SS-N-18s ready for instant launch. I'd feel better if I inspected the gyroscope myself."

"Whatever you say," the *zampolit* replied. "But let's get moving!"

Following Leonov's lead, Novikov stood and rushed from the attack center. By the time he had ducked through the hatch, the senior lieutenant was already moving down the metal stairwell. As quickly as he could, Novikov turned to make his own descent. Reaching the proper level, the *zampolit* ran down the hallway toward the *Vulkan's* bow. Barely able to make out the back of Leonov's body ahead of him, Novikov did his best to duck through the series of hatches that now followed. Ignoring the puzzled comments of the seamen who watched their progress from adjoining cabins, the political officer concentrated solely on his forward movement. With heavy limbs and wheezing lungs, he somehow kept going.

He caught up to Leonov at a sealed doorway that blocked their forward progress. Struggling to regain his breath, Novikov watched as Leonov attempted to unlock this obstacle. Mounted beside the door was a small, metallic keypad. Only a proper combination of numerals would allow them further access. As the senior lieutenant rummaged through his pockets, the *zampolit* asked frantically, "What's holding us up, Comrade?"

"I need the code!" Leonov shouted as he searched his billfold. "This section of the ship is so infrequently entered that even I have forgotten it."

Breathlessly, Leonov pulled out a thick plastic card. Holding it up to the keypad with shaking hands, he began punching in a complex series of digits. His haste forced him to repeat the process three times before the door finally slid open with a loud hiss.

Both men immediately ducked inside and the door automatically closed behind them. They found themselves in a narrow compartment that was noticeably different from the rest of the sub. Antiseptically clean, its walls were lined with padded banks of equipment that stretched from the deck to the acoustic-tiled ceiling. A high-pitched hum of machinery sounded in the background as the two officers carefully moved forward.

Surrounding them were the navigational components that comprised the heart of the ship. Without the use of this gear, not only the missiles but the *Vulkan*, itself, would be unable to determine in which direction they were traveling.

Never having been allowed entrance into this portion of the vessel before, the *zampolit* seemed confused. "Now what, Comrade?"

Leonov pointed to the sealed doorway that lay ahead of them. "On the other side of that bulkhead is the gyrocompass. The *Vulkan* depends on that motor-operated device to point out the geographic north pole, from which all navigation is determined. Inside that room is where our problem lies."

"But what could cause it to fail like this?" the political officer whined.

Not stopping to answer, Leonov continued moving forward and cautiously peered through the porthole that was midway up the door's length.

As he peered into the compartment through the reinforced glass, he froze. Without turning, Leonov said softly, "I think this will answer your question, Comrade Novikov."

The senior lieutenant stepped aside to allow the *zampolit* a chance to see. Leonov surveyed the cramped compartment, which was bathed in dim red light and completely lined with thick, sound-absorbent tiles. At its center was a large, circular mechanism, covered by what appeared to be a thick bubble of clear glass. Kneeling beside this device, in the process of removing the protective skirt that encircled the glass bubble, was Petyr Valenko.

As he focused on the captain, Leonov's hand went to his knife. Leonov, his pistol already drawn, held up the plastic code card and began punching a series of digits into the door's security keypad.

Petyr Valenko was completely absorbed in the task before him. Pleased with his progress, he knew that if he could have but a few more seconds, the job would be a total success.

The hardest part of the operation had not been crawling through the cramped air-conditioning duct to escape from his cabin, but rather waiting for the crew change—which was absolutely necessary in order for him to enter unnoticed. Counting the slowly moving minutes from the cover of a storage closet, he had planned the sequence of events that would bring him to his goal. His first move had been to disconnect the gyro's power source. This had been relatively easy to do. Assured that the missiles would now be held back at least temporarily, he proceeded with the next stage, which was to cripple the system permanently. To guarantee this, he planned to complete the removal of the metal skirt, tear out the rubberized sealant, and

375

then break the vacuum needed for the gyrocompass to operate. This would force not only a cancellation of the launch, but also make it imperative that the submarine surface immediately.

Though the removal of the protective skirt had taken him longer than he had anticipated, Valenko knew that the majority of the work was all but over. As he adroitly unscrewed the last of the bolts, he pondered the strange series of circumstances that had prompted his act of sabotage. From the moment that the *zampolit* had originally confronted him in his cabin and revealed their mad scheme, Valenko had had trouble believing that the conspirators were really serious. His first impression was that this had to be some sort of test to check his loyalty and reactions in an emergency situation. Though knocking him out and binding him up gave this theoretical test a bit too much relish, Valenko still wasn't sure of the *zampolit*'s motives until the *michman* interceded. Stefan Kuzmin had assured him that the mutiny was indeed real.

Still not knowing how anyone in his right mind could back such an insane plot, Valenko wondered how his rescuer was doing. Kuzmin had aided him way beyond the call of duty. The blood still streaming from his head wound, Kuzmin had bravely followed Valenko down the cramped duct, displaying a stubborn tenacity the likes of which the captain had never seen.

If the *michman*'s task had been completed, Valenko's piece of sabotage would be superfluous. Yet the results of their failing would be so devastating that this redundant operation was well worth the risk.

Hoping that his friend was currently safe and

sound, the captain removed the remaining screw and the heavy skirt crashed to the deck. Without hesitation, he began searching for the seam in the rubberized strip that was now visible. Just as he caught sight of the spot where the circular gasket was joined together, a heart-stopping hissing noise sounded behind him . . . followed by a familiar, dreaded voice.

"Comrade Valenko, stop your foolishness at once!"

Oblivious to the *zampolit*'s command, Valenko reached out and began tearing the sealant upward. Then he heard another voice.

"Captain, it's Vasili Leonov. I order you to stop this act of sabotage!"

When it was apparent that the captain would not heed their warnings, the political officer cocked his arm and let his knife fly. The blade smashed into Valenko's back with a dull thud. He fell on his side, the blade firmly embedded between his ribs.

Still holding the rubber strip in his hands, the captain forced himself onto his knees and, grunting in agony, continued yanking at the molding. Aware of what he was attempting, the frantic senior lieutenant took careful aim and pulled the trigger of his pistol a single time. The bullet exploded from the chrome muzzle and smacked into the back of Valenko's skull. The captain was dead before his body hit the blood-stained deck.

"Good shooting!" cried Novikov as he ran to make certain that Valenko was out of commission for good. Assured of this, he turned to face the senior lieutenant—and found him standing there, trembling.

"Come now, Comrade Leonov, get hold of yourself! This blow was a most necessary one. Have you already forgotten our glorious mission? One more life lost means absolutely nothing to our great cause."

Unaffected by these words, Leonov was still clearly stunned and shaking visibly. Seeing the senior lieutenant's fragile state, Novikov moved to him. Taking the gun from his hand, the *zampolit* slapped Leonov hard across the face. Like a man awakening from a horrible nightmare, he snapped out of it. His gaze narrowed while he inspected the scene, as if viewing it for the very first time.

"Is the captain dead?"

"He was expired before he knew what hit him," the political officer said smugly. "Can this damage to the gyrocompass be repaired?"

The senior lieutenant inspected the containment seal and sighed a breath of relief. "Yes, Comrade. Fortunately, he had yet to break the vacuum. If that had taken place, we would have been lucky just to find Petropavlovsk again. I will get Yuri Chuchkin and his crew up here to repair the damage and reestablish power. Then, our mission can be completed."

"Thank the fates!" said Novikov with a sigh. Then he thought of something else. "I think it's best that we clean up the blood, cover Valenko's body and stash the corpse in a storage closet for the time being. We certainly don't want the Chief more curious than he already is."

"Good point," Leonov said. "That can be accomplished most readily."

As he turned to initiate this unpleasant task, Novikov was relieved to see that the senior lieutenant appeared to have fully returned to his senses. That was quite a relief, for the *zampolit* would need his expert assistance now more than ever before.

Charlie Callahan remained seated at his console, yet he couldn't help noticing the captain's nervousness as Cooksey paced the deck behind him. Apparently, this restlessness was beginning to get contagious, for now even Mr. Craig, their usually cool-headed XO, appeared unduly agitated. Both officers tensely scanned the control room's stations, vainly doing everything within their power to locate the enemy. Of course, the majority of their attention remained focused on the sonar monitors.

Every thirty seconds or so, the captain would approach Callahan and give him another one of those pleading, inquisitive stares. Since there was nothing new to report, Callahan could only shrug his shoulders and return to his scanners with an even greater degree of intensity. Then Richard Craig would repeat the exact same inquiry; this increased attention was starting to get on the sonar operator's nerves.

More than anything, the captain reminded Callahan of a roommate he once had at the University of Virginia. Both the roommate and he had been enrolled in the naval ROTC program, and were attending a similar schedule of classes. Though they were most compatible for the majority of the school year, toward exam time his roommate became unbearable. Unable to eat or sleep normally, he would restlessly pace the floor for hours at a time, agitated by needless worries. He was an excellent student and received superior grades, yet his nervousness soon took its toll. As Callahan was preparing to accept his commission as a second lieutenant, his poor roommate was being admitted to the university hospital with a bleeding ulcer. That condition had kept him from naval service, and the last Callahan had heard from him, he was working for a civilian computer firm.

Captain Cooksey was headed for a similar physical breakdown if he didn't learn to relax. Their present situation was a critical one, but worrying about it would only make matters worse.

Callahan had learned to pace himself. When the pressures of his job became too great, he would regain control through a series of deep breathing and mental visualization exercises. Once more relaxed and alert, he would then return to his job.

Wanting to give this advice to his senior officers, but knowing he didn't dare, Callahan reached forward and began yet another routine scan with the bow hydrophones. He was conscious of one of the officers breathing down the back of his neck, when the loud, crackling sound of a single explosion rang inside his headphones. Startled by the unexpected sound, he vectored in on its origin and excitedly shouted, "Captain!"

A pair of strong hands instantly squeezed his shoulder, and Callahan knew that Cooksey was standing right behind him. As he rewound the tape recording of the alien noise, Callahan said, "You'd better listen to this, sir. Something out of the ordinary just happened out there."

Cooksey hastily clamped on the headphones as Callahan activated the recorder. Once more, the sharp *bang* could be heard.

"Sounds like a gunshot," the bewildered captain

offered. "Where in the hell did it come from?"

The sonar officer checked his computer monitor. "Big Brother shows an approximate origin in the upper strata of water, some seventy miles to the northeast."

"They've been hiding in the damned thermocline!" Cooksey exclaimed. He signaled his XO to join him. "We've got them, Rich! You were right—those Ruskies have been taking advantage of the warm water. They're still too far to use a Harpoon, so one of those new-fangled ASW/SOWs is going to have to do its thing. Thank the Lord that our prayers have been answered!"

Charles Callahan watched Richard Craig's face light up in response, and felt his own spirits lighten. With practiced ease, he began the task of making certain that the exact targeting data was fed into the fire-control system. From what little he knew of the experimental weapon that the captain planned to utilize, it was of a similar design to the Tomahawk missiles they also carried. Shot from a torpedo tube, the SOW would angle up toward the surface, break the water, then fly to coordinates programmed from the sub. At that point the booster rocket would separate, and a REGAL torpedo would descend by parachute. When it again hit the water, an acoustic array—containing a small computer and a sonar transmitter—would be jettisoned to sink to a preset depth. Meanwhile, the torpedo would propel itself in a slow search pattern, waiting for the array to call it in for a certain strike.

With a theoretical range of up to three hundred miles, the SOW gave them an anti-sub capability second to no other attack submarine on the planet. Aware of this, Callahan did his part to insure that the weapon would not fail.

In contrast to the excited atmosphere inside the *Triton*, the mood of the *Vulkan*'s attack center was most somber, following the lead of the two officers who were seated anxiously before the fire-control panel.

Conscious of each passing second, the *Vulkan*'s political officer looked out with a sour grimace. If it hadn't been for Valenko's interference, their portion of Operation Counterforce would already have been completed, and the first warheads would now be descending to their targets. Frustrated, Novikov turned to address the man seated on his right.

"What is taking Chuchkin and his crew so long, Comrade? Surely they should have completed the repairs by now."

Used to the *zampolit*'s whining by now, the senior lieutenant casually answered, "Have patience, Comrade Novikov. The Chief is one of our most capable technicians. He knows what has to be done, and will call us the second the gyrocompass is back in working order. Until then, we can only bide our time. Fortunately for us, our sonar still shows no sign of the enemy. I can't help but feel that the hand of destiny itself is keeping the Americans away from us."

"If destiny were a bit kinder, this intolerable waiting wouldn't be necessary," said Novikov. "The way I figure it, the warheads would be landing any minute now."

"After all the decades of waiting, surely another half hour won't make any difference," the senior lieutenant reasoned.

"You are right, Comrade," Novikov sighed. "Too often my impatience gets the best of me."

The two lapsed into a moment of silence, suddenly broken by Lev Zinaykin's shouts of alarm. "We show a splashdown in the water above us! I've got active propellor sounds—they could be from a homing torpedo!"

Abruptly broken from his lassitude, Leonov stood and screamed, "Crash dive! Full speed! Take us down, Comrades, for our very lives!"

He ran over to the helmsman as the engines throbbed to full life. "You won't be able to wait for speed. Take on ballast and put those planes down!"

As a roaring torrent of seawater was vented, the angle of the deck steepened noticeably. Holding onto the railing for balance, Leonov made his way over to the sonar console. Here he was joined by the white-faced *zampolit*.

"Can we outrun them?" Novikov asked frantically. "Or are we doomed to failure so close to the completion of our task?"

Ignoring him, Leonov turned to the sonar operator. "Zinyakin, what's our status?"

Lev Zinyakin was gripping the console with one hand to hold himself up, and pressing a headphone to his ear with the other. "Even though we're beginning to pull away, the screw sounds are increasing. I'm afraid it's following us down and gaining quickly."

Out of the corner of his eye, Leonov saw Ivan Novikov tumble to the deck. Not taking the time to

help him, the senior lieutenant picked up the intercom, punched in a series of digits and barked roughly
into the transmitter.

"Who is speaking? Well, listen closely, Comrade
Balashikha—this is the Senior Lieutenant. I know
that Chief Chuchkin is away from the torpedo room at
the moment, but I need you to initiate a launch at
once. Can you do this, Seaman Third Class? Well,
let's hope so, Comrade. Do you know of the cannister
of Zu-23 dye kept stored in the emergency tube?
Excellent, my friend. Release it at once!"

Replacing the handset, Leonov noticed that Ivan
Novikov had returned to his feet. While smoothing
down his crumpled uniform, the *zampolit* gave vent to
his endless curiosity.

"What in the world is this Zu-23 dye, Comrade?
And what can it do to save us from our current
predicament?"

Still struggling to keep his own balance, Leonov
answered, "Believe it or not, this substance is a
synthetic copy of the natural defense mechanism of an
octopus. Veiled in its inky wake, the *Vulkan* should be
effectively invisible."

"Only the Rodina's scientists could have thought of
such a brilliant thing," Novikov replied. "But does it
indeed work?"

"You'd better hope so." Turning away from the
political officer, Leonov shouted, "Prepare to break
descent! Engineering, make ready for a reactor
scram!"

Approaching the *Vulkan* at flank speed, the USS

Triton surged through the turbid waters. From the sub's control room, Charlie Callahan scanned the seas before them in an effort to monitor the hunt they had initiated. With sensitive headphones covering his ears, he adjusted the bow hydrophones to maximum amplification. Even with this additional volume, he shook his head disappointedly.

"I don't understand it, Captain. We were copying them as plain as day a few seconds ago. I even had a definite on the increased propellor whine of our torpedo as it was beginning to close in for the kill. Now, all I'm picking up is a homing pattern, while the REGAL searches out the *Vulkan* once again. It's like the Russians just disappeared!"

"Damn it all!" said Cooksey. "I was wondering if that darn contraption would work or not."

Callahan was quick to defend their high-tech equipment. "It's not the SOW's fault, sir. If that was the case, it would mean our sensors had failed as well. Right now I'm picking up absolutely nothing on the *Vulkan*, while just seconds ago they were churning up the water something fierce."

"Sounds to me like they've scrammed their reactor," the XO observed. "But still, that active sonar array should have pinged them easily enough."

Michael Cooksey rubbed his forehead where a throbbing ache had developed. "The Ruskies could be playing with some sort of anechoic device that somehow deflects our sonar. Although, I don't see why they wouldn't have tried such a trick earlier. All we know for certain is that they're out there, sure enough. If they have scrammed, and in the process of running from our missile have dived below their launch depth, this merely gives us a reprieve, gentlemen. We've got to keep on closing the gap and pray that they eventually show themselves."

Richard Craig nodded and checked his watch: it was 2147 hours. Seventeen minutes ago, the Soviets had been scheduled to empty their missile magazine. By luck and the grace of God, they had so far been unable to complete their mission. Hopeful that good fortune would remain with them, the exec followed his captain over to the plotting table to formulate a final strategy for keeping the SS-N-18s bound to the sea.

Chapter Fifteen

A wave of hushed jubilation sounded through the *Vulkan*'s attack center when Lev Zinyakin reported that the enemy homing torpedo had spent its fuel. Relieved of this threat, the crew returned to their stations and awaited the senior lieutenant's next order.

From his position behind the sonar console, Vasili Leonov grinned in triumph. Beside him, the *zampolit* was as impatient as ever.

"At last we can return to launch depth and complete our mission," Novikov said emphatically.

"We must still wait to hear from Yuri Chuchkin," Leonov said. "And besides, we still have to determine where that infernal homing torpedo came from."

Lev Zinyakin offered an opinion. "It could be from that American attack sub, sir, even though we are no longer picking them up on our sensors. Maybe it's because of our crash dive, which sent us below the thermocline. If the Americans had also ascended into the warmer waters, that could account for our failure to pick them up."

"But surely, we were far enough away from them to be well beyond the range of their Harpoon torpedo."

Leonov reasoned.

"Then perhaps it didn't come from a submarine at all," Novikov interjected. "Isn't it possible that the device was dropped from the air?"

As Leonov considered this the intercom chimed. It was the weapons chief.

"Excellent work, Comrade Chuchkin," Leonov said. "Please be so good as to return to your station to await my further orders."

He hung up the handset and informed his two shipmates that their gyrocompass was repaired. The *zampolit* was the first to respond.

"Well, it's about time. All this endless delay is the hardest part to cope with. Well, what are you waiting for now, Senior Lieutenant? Shall we get on with the launch?"

Leonov balked, still bothered by the unknown source of the attack they had just thwarted. "I don't have to tell you how lucky we were to escape that torpedo. Though ingenious, the Zu-23 dye has been shown to be effective less than fifty percent of the time. We still risk divulging our present location if we break from silent running and ascend to launch depth."

It was clear from the clouded look on his face that Novikov didn't like this response. "Come now, Senior Lieutenant, aren't you being a little too overly cautious? Look at the time, Comrade! Over half an hour has passed since our mission was to have been completed. We are accomplishing absolutely nothing by just sitting here with a full load of missiles in our magazine. If we don't act soon, our strike will be completely ineffective. The Motherland is counting on us, Comrade!"

The political officer strained to control himself. He had to be careful not to alienate the senior lieutenant, for without Leonov's aid he would be practically helpless. Aware of no rational reason why they should delay any longer, he knew that with each passing second the risk of failure increased. No longer was he concerned merely with the Americans. Sooner or later, Viktor Rodin would find out about their little group. Until Counterforce was successfully completed, the Premier still held the reigns of power. Intervention on Rodin's part could be fatal. Not wanting to voice this concern in front of the sonar officer, Novikov could only silently implore his coconspirator to see things his way.

He watched Leonov check the sonar screen and then the console's digital clock. He listened hopefully as Leonov turned slowly to address him.

"I must admit that the minutes do have a way of flying by. Though I still hate to needlessly expose us, there is a maneuver that I know of . . . that could possibly see us out of our current dilemma. One of my instructors at the Sevastopol Higher Naval School is said to have formulated it.

"In a war situation, when a missile boat must release its load of warheads, survival can be greatly enhanced by first launching a decoy. Directed on an opposite course, this specially designed device, which imitates our sound signature exactly, will draw the attention of the stalking enemy. Then we merely have to blow our ballast, ascend to launch depth, and fire away."

These were just the words that Novikov wanted to

hear, and he responded accordingly. "Well then, Comrade, what are we waiting for?"

Conscious of the *zampolit*'s expectant grin, Leonov reached for the intercom and ordered the weapons chief to prepare a decoy.

Thirty-three miles away, the sound of this device's activation was clearly audible to Charles Callahan. The signal was being relayed from their towed sensor sled, which dipped below the warmer layer of water through which the *Triton* was traveling. After hurriedly requesting the computer to analyze the new signal, Callahan turned to inform Michael Cooksey.

"Captain—I think we've got 'em again!"

Cooksey was instantly at Callahan's side. Clipping on the auxiliary headphones, his tense mood lightened.

"That's music to my ears, gentlemen. Get us an exact I.D. and a decent targeting vector."

"Aye, aye, Captain," returned the sonar operator as he expertly manipulated the computer keyboard.

While waiting for the requested data, the XO sighed, "Well, Skipper, it looks like you've got that other shot you've been praying for. Shall I inform Spencer?"

Eyes locked on the blank monitor screen, Cooksey said, "Let's wait for Big Brother to do his thing. Once we get a definite, good-bye *Vulkan*."

The monitor had begun filling with information as Chief Petty Officer Warren Smith, the *Triton*'s navigator, joined them. Callahan interpreted the data for his growing audience.

"There's a little better than a fifty percent probability that it's the *Vulkan*. This thermocline is playing havoc with our sensors, but they can't be more than thirty-five miles distant, and moving to the southeast with their pants on fire."

"So, the elusive Delta has shown itself again," Smith said. "We gonna take them out for good this time, Skip?"

"Just give me the word," Richard Craig said, "and I'll order Spencer to launch that SOW."

Though Cooksey would have liked nothing better, his intuition cautioned him to wait. "Callahan, is there any chance that we can get a more positive I.D. on them?"

After feeding the request into the computer, the sonar operator shook his head. "Afraid not, Captain. Results are the same as before. It's this damn thermocline. I've never seen one so defined."

"What's the problem, Skipper?" his exec asked.

Cooksey met Craig's puzzled stare. "I can't say for sure, Rich, but something's telling me to hold back just a little bit longer before risking that last SOW. I don't know; this new signal could be a decoy. What do you think, Smitty?"

The big-boned navigator ran a hand through his spikey crew cut and thoughtfully replied, "As long as Big Brother tells us the odds are in our favor, I say go for it. The course makes sense. Most probably that Ruskie captain is merely tryin' to hightail it to safer waters. Once they hit their launch depth, it won't take long for them to empty their hold, and then we might as well pack up to see if there's anything left at home."

"I agree with Smitty," the exec chimed in. "We've

391

got nothing to lose, and everything to gain."

Taking in this advice, Cooksey knew that the decision was ultimately his. Minutes ago he had been begging for this second chance, yet something about the situation struck him as not right.

What he feared most was a decoy. If that were the case, and he committed the *Triton* to attack it, the real *Vulkan* would be speeding in the opposite direction. The handful of minutes that it would take for them to initiate a strike would give the real bogey ample opportunity to proceed with its mission. Of course, if this wasn't a decoy, he could be foolishly jeopardizing everything by not immediately launching the SOW.

Conscious of a steady, pounding ache in his temples, Cooksey strained to come up with a firm decision. As his officers waited anxiously beside him, Callahan monitored the bogey's continued progress away from them.

The captain closed his eyes and vainly attempted to clear his cluttered mind. As he sucked in a series of deep breaths, he willed away the distractions that were keeping him from total concentration. Filtering out the hushed conversation of the control room's crew and the distant whine of the engines beyond, Cooksey called for the wisdom to make the right choice. In response, a single, unexpected vision dawned in his mind's eye.

In a heartbeat, he returned to Kauai's Kalalau Beach and the night in which he had experienced his strange, passion-filled dream. Not knowing if it was fantasy or reality, he envisioned the beautiful, brown-skinned native girl who had come to him so willingly.

Remembering her sweat scent and the smooth touch of her lips, Cooksey recreated that magical moment as if it had just happened. He remembered the line of mysterious little people who had watched their love-making, the purple lei she had left behind, and the all-important lesson he had learned that evening. In order to tap his true self he must be relaxed and, above all, trust his instincts. Suddenly he broke from his reverie. As his eyes blinked open and his ears again filled with the normal sounds of the *Triton*, he knew just what their course of action would be:

"Rich, call Spencer and have him ready an Mk-70!"

The XO, who had been watching his captain's plunge into meditation with a bit of concern, hesitantly said, "But Skipper, that's our last MOSS decoy. We'll be practically defenseless without it."

Cooksey remained firm. "Then that's just the chance we'll have to take, Mr. Craig. I'm not going to order an attack until we know exactly what we're facing. If that sound out there is coming from a decoy, then we can fool the *Vulkan* into thinking that we took the bait by shooting our Mk-70 at it. The second that we pick them up ascending to launch depth, we'll release our remaining SOW."

"And if it's not a decoy?" Craig asked.

Cooksey didn't flinch. "Let's just pray that my gut is calling it as it is, Rich. Now, will you get on the horn to Spencer? The sooner we get this whole damned thing over with, the better it's going to be for all of us."

The captain turned back to the sonar screen. There, on the green-tinted glass of the monitor, the success or failure of his desperate ploy would now be revealed.

Important as his responsibilities may have been, Lev Zinyakin knew that he was fighting a losing battle to stay alert. Not only were his eyelids heavy, his entire body was weary and pleading for sleep. When the senior lieutenant had first come to him and asked him to transfer to the attack center, he had taken it as a compliment. Not really thinking about what he was doing, he had too readily accepted. Now, allowed a brief break, he rushed to the head and gratefully relieved himself, then splashed some cool water on his face. He barely recognized the bloodshot eyes and beard-stubbled face that was reflected in the mirror. After a quick, tasteless sandwich and a mug of lukewarm tea, he was soon back at the sonar station, headphones clamped tightly over his ears.

Stimulated by the tea, and the recent approach of the presumed homing torpedo, Zinyakin managed to stay alert. But as the seconds continued to tick away, he seriously doubted that he would hold out much longer.

Whenever he found himself drifting off, he did his best to sit up straight and force more oxygen into his exhausted body. He constantly reminded himself how fatal it could be if he surrendered to his fatigue. The recent incident with the hovering helicopter had proved just how perilous falling asleep on duty could be. It was a minor miracle that he had awakened from his short slumber in time to pick out the sounds of the chopper's engines.

To make matters worse, his present duty was far from stimulating. In the process of monitoring the decoy that had just been launched from their stern tubes, Zinyakin found himself being lulled to sleep by the constant, buzzing drone of the simulator's dual propellors. Because of the *Vulkan*'s silence, and the lack of other audible traffic in the area, this monotonous sound was all that filled his headphones. As he listened to the decoy racing off into the distance, his leaden eyelids gradually closed. No sooner had they shut completely, when the harsh sounds of a sudden argument broke out right behind him. Snapping awake, Zinyakin clearly heard the whining voice of the *zampolit*.

"*Now* what are you waiting for, Comrade Leonov? Since no Americans have yet shown themselves, let's ascend and get on with the launch!"

"We will break our silence when I command us to!" the angry senior lieutenant said. "In my opinion it's still too soon to make any abrupt moves."

"Too soon!" Novikov cried. "We've been sitting here long enough. You've launched your decoy; now, where is this phantom enemy?"

"Comrade Novikov, are you questioning my ability to command this ship?"

Zinyakin failed to hear the political officer's response, for a burst of alien noise echoed in his left headphone. Fully awake now, he activated the computer to determine the sound's source and point of origin. When the answer appeared on his screen, he swiveled around and shouted, "Bogey hydrophone contact, sir! Range approximately four-eight kilometers; heading to the southeast at flank speed. We show a sixty-seven percent probability that it's a Los Angeles-class attack sub!"

"I *knew* they were out there!" Leonov cried. "Now, just as Professor Strelka said, the aggressive Americans have once again taken the bait—hook, line, and sinker."

Reacting to his triumphant outburst, Novikov said humbly, "So, you were indeed right, Comrade Leonov. It only goes to show the brilliant minds at work at our military schools. Now—can we proceed with the completion of our mission?"

In response, Leonov grinned and ordered, "Blow the forward and rear groups! Ascend to launch depth! Comrade Novikov, will you join me at the fire-control panel?"

With a gurgling burst of venting ballast, the *Vulkan* trembled alive once more. Oblivious to the deafening surge of cast-off seawater, Lev Zinyakin strained to hear the playback of the bogey's sound signature. Though he couldn't say what, something about this tape bothered him. It was as if the pitch of the propellor whine was just a bit off. Unable to ignore the analysis of the computer, and the joyous outburst its revelation had generated among the crew, the hydrophone operator decided that it was all a product of his overworked imagination. Stifling a wide yawn, Zinyakin ignored his doubts and listened to the enemy submarine as it sped off on the trail of their decoy.

Hidden in a warm layer of seawater less than two hundred feet below the Pacific's surface, the USS *Triton* plunged ahead due east. Still standing behind the sonar console, Captain Michael Cooksey monitored the progress of their Mk-70 MOSS decoy. As the simulator sped to the southeast in the direction of the still fleeing, presumed enemy bogey, Cooksey wondered if his intuition was wrong after all. As the mystery bogey continued to outdistance them, a proper attack became less of a possibility—if, indeed, it was the *Vulkan*.

Still crippled by a pounding headache, Cooksey pondered his decision. Was he being overly cautious, as Richard Craig had warned? Should it have been the ASW/SOW that was launched in place of their decoy? He had sworn once before that he wouldn't hesitate to attack if the opportunity again presented itself. Why, then, had he held back this second time? Not really certain of what had induced him to choose this tactic, Cooksey prepared himself for the outcome—whatever it might be.

Torn by fear and weakened by doubt, the captain could hardly believe it when Charlie Callahan called excitedly for his attention.

"Venting ballast due east of us, sir. Something massive is presently rising through the thermocline there."

Without a second thought, Cooksey's hand shot out for the intercom. "You may fire that SOW, Mr. Spencer, as soon as sonar conveys the coordinates."

Fifteen seconds later, the control room vibrated as the sub's forward torpedo tube fired a single, encapsulated rocket. Cooksey heard the swooshing sound of released compressed air, as well as the whispered comment of his exec, who stood behind him.

"Well, I'll be damned; the Old Man was right."

Grinning at this, Cooksey calculated the time left for their attack to be a success. To hit the *Vulkan* before it reached its launch depth, they would need a lot of luck and some heavenly assistance.

Ivan Novikov could hardly control himself. Seated at the fire-control panel, with the missiles armed and the sixteen launch buttons blinking before him, he estimated that in less than four minutes their great dream would be realized. Long was the road that had brought him to this present moment. After months of intense planning, Operation Counterforce was about to change the socio-political structure of the entire world.

The *zampolit* wondered if the young man who sat beside him realized the true consequences of their present course of action. Vasili Leonov had been recruited to their cause more on personal reasons than political ones. No matter the motive, Novikov was thankful for his invaluable assistance.

As the senior lieutenant called off their rapidly decreasing depth, the political officer visualized what the new world order would be like. Freed from competition with the money-hungry capitalists, socialism would unite the earth with a single, common goal. The great vision of Lenin would have at last come to fruition. Stirred by his thoughts, Novikov's right index finger itched to depress the first of the blinking missile release switches. Aware of the time remaining before the *Vulkan* attained its launch depth, Novikov inched forward in his seat, with his heart beating rapidly. Expecting to hear Leonov's command to hit the first button any moment now, he froze in horror when the sonar officer's panicked voice rose behind him.

"Sensor contact in the seas above us! I show an active sonar search, and now the signature of another homing torpedo!"

Vasili Leonov's voice broke as he asked, "Are you certain that this is a torpedo, Zinyakin?"

"The propellor whine is exactly the same as that other one," Zinyakin replied. "Estimated contact is in three and a half minutes!"

The senior lieutenant cursed and shook his head disgustingly. "Damn it all, if we haven't been out-foxed! Prepare to crash dive! We must run for the cover of the depths once again."

"No, Comrade Leonov—there's no more time for running!" commanded the *zampolit*, shocked by his own boldness. "By using a ripple fire sequence we can empty our missile magazine in less than one hundred and sixty seconds. That will still give us time to try and evade."

Leonov waved him away. "You don't know what you're talking about, Novikov. If we don't dive now we'll never escape that torpedo!"

Novikov strained to contain his rising anger. "I beg to differ with you, Comrade. Have you forgotten already our little discussion back in Petropavlovsk? At that time you swore to put your life on the line for the sake of the Rodina. Have you abandoned those lofty convictions already, Vasili? Now's the time to prove yourself. Shall you grovel in your own pitiful coward-ice, or stand tall—proud to make your sacrifice a worthy one?"

Without waiting for a response, the *zampolit* shouted out commands. "Belay that order to dive! Continue our ascent to launch depth. Notify the *taiga* to prepare for ripple fire!"

Listening to the instructions, unable to contradict them, was Vasili Leonov. Sweat pouring from his forehead, the trembling senior lieutenant couldn't summon the nerve to intercede. There was no question now as to who was in authority.

"How much longer until we can launch?" Novikov asked firmly.

Hardly able to get the words out of his mouth, Leonov checked the depth gauge and softly answered, "Approximately thirty seconds."

Taking in the information, Ivan Novikov cried for all to hear, "For the glory of the Motherland, we shall prevail!"

Seeing the demonic gleam that lit the *zampolit*'s eyes, Leonov inwardly conceded defeat. Not really certain how he became involved with this insane plot in the first place, the senior lieutenant swiveled around to face the fire-control panel to which his destiny was now unalterably bound.

On the opposite side of the *Vulkan*'s attack center, Lev Zinyakin continued to do his best to monitor the approach of the homing torpedo, all the while absorbing the commotion that was coming from the launch station. There, the *zampolit* and the senior lieutenant were locked in an apparent power struggle. Not certain what had provoked the two officers, Zinyakin knew that if they didn't do something quickly, the

Vulkan would surely be hit.

There could be no doubting the torpedo's intended target. Directed by an independent sonar device, the weapon was advancing toward them at a rapidly increasing speed. Already his initial intercept estimate was no longer accurate. Unless the ship's officers had some sort of last-second maneuver in mind, Zinyakin knew that they were probably doomed.

Strangely enough, he found himself not really fearful of this final confrontation. Death at this depth would be quick and painless. With a vision of his beloved grandfather in mind, he gave full attention to monitoring the advance of the Grim Reaper.

As Zinyakin prepared himself to meet his maker, the *Vulkan*'s senior lieutenant did likewise. Even though it was only fifteen seconds before the first of the SS-N-18s would be released, he was certain that their motions were in vain. At the most, they would only be able to get a handful of missiles airborne. Far from their intended goal, he wondered if the resulting carnage would satisfy the plotter's bloodlust. He listened to the *zampolit* anxiously counting off the remaining seconds as if it really mattered.

"Five . . . four . . . three . . . two . . . one . . . fire!"

Not wanting to make his sacrifice a worthless one, Vasili Leonov managed to depress the first of the blinking switches. Closing his eyes, he pictured the sequence of events that he had set into action.

Deep within the *taiga*, the first of the SS-N-18s received the signal to launch. In instant response, an outer hatch in the *Vulkan*'s superstructure popped open. This unmasked the tube closure—a rigid, dome-shaped shell structure designed as a protective cocoon for the missile. To shatter this closure, a series of linear-shaped explosive charges were detonated. With the SS-N-18 now exposed, a small fixed rocket engine ignited. Its sole purpose was to direct its exhaust into the base of the launch tube, where a pool of cool water sat. The resulting steam pressure would expell the missile from the tube. Only after the SS-N-18 had cleared the ocean's surface would its liquid-fuel boost motor ignite.

The first stages of this complex operation had gone quite smoothly. The tube closure had shattered and enough steam pressure had gathered to begin forcing the missile upward. But as the tip of the SS-N-18 cleared the *Vulkan*'s hull, the *Triton*'s ASW/SOW plowed into the Soviet vessel's sail. This violent concussion was followed by a massive explosion that vaporized the ascending SS-N-18 in a blinding wave of boiling flame. The *Vulkan* imploded in an ear-splitting cacophony of rending steel. Exposed to the ocean's great pressure, the crew had little time to suffer. In a matter of seconds their shredded bodies became one with the depths, as what little remaining wreckage plummeted ever downward.

Nineteen nautical miles due west of this spot, Lieutenant Charles Callahan was the first of the *Triton*'s crew to hear the results of their attack. Warned by the abrupt halt of the SOW's propellor, he ripped off his headphones in time to save his eardrums from the shattering explosion that followed. A fraction of a second later the blast was clearly audible in the interior of the control room itself.

Though a chorus of joyous shouts filled the compartment, Captain Cooksey's words rang out loud and clear. "All stations, General Quarters! Rig for a shock wave!"

A raucous horn sounded throughout the vessel as the crew scurried to secure their equipment and themselves. Callahan had barely braced himself against the edge of his console when a surging wall of compressed water smacked into the *Triton*'s bow. Thrown hard to his left and then to his right, Callahan strained to remain upright. The sound of tumbling crewmates and loose gear broke all around him as the sub's lighting system failed. Disorientated by the sudden plunge into darkness, he found himself once again struggling for balance—when their hull was pounded by yet another series of shock waves. The damage-control panel was blaring loudly in warning by the time the turbulence passed.

Not long after, the lights blinked back on. Turning to check the room's interior, Callahan caught sight of a tangled mess of fallen equipment and several prone seamen. One of the officers slowly picking himself off the floor was the captain. After helping Richard Craig get to his feet, Cooksey snapped into action.

"Someone please turn off that infernal warning buzzer! Damage control, I need to know our status on the double! Callahan, do you have a definite on that explosion's source yet? Is the bogey still there?"

Abruptly called back to duty, Callahan swiveled around and remounted his headphones. Using the utmost caution, he scanned the waters in all directions. The hydrophone search failed to pick anything up but the distant surge of the shock wave.

"All clear on passive, Captain. Can I utilize active?"

"Go ahead and zap them, Lieutenant," Cooksey replied.

As the sensor operator activated the sonar system, the captain and the exec crowded in behind him. Ignoring the incessant buzzing of the ship's intercom, both senior officers studied the sonar screen. For a full minute, they watched the quivering white line that monitored the powerful sound waves being emitted from their bow.

The atmosphere was tense, but Callahan looked up and said matter-of-factly, "Whatever was out there sure as hell isn't there anymore, Captain. We blew them to kingdom come!"

Grinning now from ear to ear, the sonar operator watched the captain and the exec react to the news.

"We got 'em!" shouted Richard Craig triumphantly.

This incited another chorus of cheers from the control room's staff. Taking a few moments to join the celebration, Cooksey then turned to his next concern.

"Damage control, are we still in one piece?"

Warren Smith, the present watch officer, said, "It's gonna take more than a little swell to take this little lady out, Skip. All stations remain dry and secure, except for the galley. The damned seal on the garbage disposal blew again. At last report Chief Bartkowski was up to his knees in seawater and potato peelings, but he'll get a handle on it soon enough."

Relieved, Cooksey allowed himself a real smile—almost as wide as that of his executive officer.

"Well, Skipper, it looks like we did it."

"It certainly does, Rich. How does it feel, knowing that your new family has a reprieve?"

Shaking his head in wonder, the XO asked, "Was it really that close, Skipper?"

Cooksey snorted. "Rich, if even one of those warheads had hit its mark, the world would have been swallowed by a conflict the likes of which your worst nightmare couldn't begin to approach. We got by this time, but we might not be so lucky the next."

Then Cooksey's tone lightened. "Leaving you with that one to think about . . . why don't you chart us the quickest route back to Pearl? I'll handle the communique to Admiral Miller. By the way Rich, how's your golf game lately?"

Chapter Sixteen

From thirty thousand feet up, Viktor Rodin could clearly appreciate the urban sprawl of Southern California. Never before had he seen such a widespread area of population. As they continued on north to Los Angeles, the stormy skies to the south gave way to a blue, crystal clear afternoon. Appreciative of the lack of turbulence, the Premier took in the coastline from the conference room's single window.

Rodin was thankful for the time alone. Five minutes before, Robert Palmer had excused himself to brief his staff regarding the exciting news they had just received from Hawaii. Much to everyone's relief, an American attack sub had reported the destruction of a Soviet Delta-class vessel in the Pacific near Midway. The doomed boat could only have been the *Vulkan*.

With this threat to world peace alleviated, Rodin's initial reaction had been one of pure joy. Yet, his happiness soon faded into melancholy as he considered the innocent sailors who had lost their lives because of this madness. Of course, these deaths were much preferred to a full-scale nuclear war.

But his disillusionment and depression grew as he

surveyed the contents of the top-secret transmission just relayed to him by Olga Tyumen. This message, sent via satellite from MVD headquarters in Moscow, informed Rodin of two relevant phone calls recently made from his IL-78 command plane. Both calls had been placed by Admiral Stanislav Sorokin.

The first had been traced to the Kremlin office of Senior Politboro member Pavl Zavenyagin. Though Rodin had little personal contact with that particular individual, he knew much about the man's checkered career. A thin, balding, beady-eyed figure, characterized by a full drooping moustache and a set of thick, bushy eyebrows, Zavenyagin was one of the last of the old-time hardliners. Still living in the past glories of World War II, it would be just like him to support such a desperate act of treachery.

It proved to be the recipient of Admiral Sorokin's second call that truly surprised the Premier. Konstantin Belchenko had been one of the Soviet Union's most illustrious bureaucrats. Just as much a legend in his time as the admiral, the First Deputy of the KGB was someone who Rodin had always looked up to. With his brave exploits during the Great War a matter of general public knowledge, Belchenko did for their intelligence service what Sorokin had done for the navy.

Rodin wondered if perhaps the sickness that Belchdenko had been fighting the past few months had pushed him to this extreme. Fever could distort a man's perspective in a most subtle way. Although the Premier wished he could blame it on Belchenko's infection, he knew that there had to be a solid motive behind the first deputy's actions. Like Zavenyagin, he must have been still living in the past. Fearful of the new, enlightened world that was dawning, Belchenko had helped instigate the plot in a desperate effort to push back the hands of time. Conscious of the man's position of power, the Premier had made the hard decision to immediately place Belchenko under arrest. Already units of the MVD were moving into the woods that surrounded his dacha on the banks of the Sura.

With him out of the way, there was only one more conspirator to face. Stanislav Sorokin's flight plan made it evident that he was headed for Petropavlovsk. There would be a uniformed "welcoming committee" waiting for him there, courtesy of Viktor Rodin. His decision to place the admiral under arrest had been equally as difficult as that concerning the first deputy, but Rodin had had no choice. To apprehend one of the legends of their time could prove most unpopular, but the Premier knew that he could deal with that problem.

In the new world order that would hopefully follow, Sorokin's talents would have been greatly appreciated. The conversion from a wartime fleet would take a unique vision for which talented sailors such as the admiral were famous. Yet, like his coconspirators, Sorokin had decided to go out with a bang instead of a whimper.

As Rodin's thoughts turned toward the future, he visualized that moment when Robert Palmer had first conveyed the news of the *Vulkan*'s demise. Like young school boys, they had shouted for joy and embraced. Although this day had come close to being the most tragic one the earth had ever known, the hand of destiny demanded that sanity prevail. Out of this black tide of fear and despair would evolve a new era of international cooperation, although neither leader fooled himself into thinking that such a conversion would be easy. Many obstacles would still have to be faced.

First on Rodin's agenda was the reconsolidation of his power back home. Unfortunately, that would necessitate a temporary delay in the present summit. He had gratefully accepted Palmer's offer to use one of the President's command planes to fly back to the Soviet Union. There, he would bring to public justice the madmen responsible for this near tragedy. Then would begin the arduous task of working toward the lofty promises that both leaders had sworn to each other on this most eventful of days.

Looking out at the seemingly endless California city that hugged the coastline here, Rodin shuddered as he contemplated the consequences if the *Vulkan* hadn't been stopped in time. So that such an occurrence could never come to pass again, the nuclear genie had to be contained forever. This was the ultimate purpose to which he would now devote his entire life. Only by banning nuclear weapons from the face of the earth could man's continued existence be assured.

The frigid north wind blew icy gusts, and Konstantin Belchenko halted momentarily to pull the collar of his greatcoat closer to his neck. Peering out toward the narrow footbridge that crossed the surging Sura, he caught sight of the ancient birch forest on the river's opposite bank. Like a fleet of sailboat masts bending in a blustery breeze, the white, shaggy trunks swayed in unison. The sound of the merciless wind rose in a howl, clearly predominating over the steady crash of the Sura's current.

When a raven's harsh cry called in the distance, Belchenko looked up and caught sight of an ominous bank of dark storm clouds, gathering above the woods. Already, the first snow flurries were falling. Soon the total brunt of the advancing storm would be upon them. Oblivious to the threat, Belchenko pushed himself on toward the bridge's tapered span.

Though his nurse Katrina had pleaded with him to remain before the fireplace in the dacha, the call had been much too loud for the first deputy to ignore. Drained by the events of the day just passed, he knew of but a single place where his tangled contemplations would sort themselves out. As they had served for decades past, the birch forest remained his sole place of grace.

Aware of the sheet of ice that was rapidly forming on the bridge's planked floor, he carefully crossed the expanse. Here the crash of the Sura was almost deafening. For an instant, he stopped halfway across and took in the swift current as it tumbled downstream.

Was it really that long ago that he had shared this same view with his father? Aware of the passing years, he remembered a time of glorious innocence when a fishing rod and a picnic basket had been his only concerns. It was during that period that the woods had first spoken to him like a long lost friend. Soothed by its message of primal simplicity, he had never

410

failed to return in the crazed years that had followed.

Even during the Great War he had managed to spend some time there. In fact, it was on this very span that he had conceived the idea which first brought him to the attention of his commanding officer—the legendary Lavrenti Pavlovich Beria. Assigned to an NKVD intelligence batallion, Belchenko thought of a plan to place their agents in occupied towns dressed in the uniforms of the German SS. With instructions to murder, rape and pillage, their agents would always leave behind survivors who could attest to the fact that the Germans were far from saviors. The psychological affects of such an operation had rallied thousands of potential defectors to the Rodina's cause.

Pleased with Belchenko's concept, Beria had given the young officer his own crack unit. Under the direction of the organization known as SMERSH, he had led a squadron of soldiers to the front. Positioned behind their own Red Army units, it was their duty to shoot any of their comrades who tried to retreat in the face of German counterattacks. Though often distasteful, he was well aware of his duty's importance and gave the task his all.

After the war's conclusion, he again returned to Penza, this time as a full-fledged KGB agent. Recruited by General Ivan Alexandrovich Serov in 1954, the year that the KGB was born, Belchenko sought the first Eastern-bloc agents to crack the newly formed imperialist organization known as NATO. Once more, he rose in the ranks.

In April of 1967, under the direction of Yuri Andropov, he went off to Vietnam. With tons of

America's latest captured war gear waiting for them, the KGB had had an intelligence field day.

Promoted to his current position when Andropov entered the Politboro, Konstantin had a free hand to run the KGB as he saw fit. Second to no other operation of its kind, all had proceeded smoothly—until Viktor Rodin's ascension to power. Now, all his hard work was about to go for naught. Stirred by this somber thought, and a biting gust of wind, the first deputy turned from the water and continued on to the birch woods.

As he entered the treeline the crash of the Sura faded, to be replaced by the ever-present howling wind and the creaking of the birch limbs. The snow began falling more thickly now, and he strained to pick out the footpath that would lead him to his goal. Barely visible ahead, he sighted the trail and surrendered himself to its gentle meander.

With the trees acting as a partial windbreak, the going was now much more comfortable. Soothed by the hushed stillness of the forest, his previously distraught thoughts gradually began sorting themselves out. It wasn't all that long ago that he had received the message from their KGB mole in America's military command, informing him of the *Vulkan*'s destruction. At first he had refused to believe it, but then the harsh reality had sunk in.

Not long after, Stanislav Sorokin had called him. Belchenko was surprised to find that the admiral had the nerve to commandeer the Premier's personal IL-78. As Sorokin was relaying his current location, Belchenko watched a small plastic warning light, set into the side of his telephone, begin blinking. The activation of this device could only mean that the so-called secure line over which they were talking was in the process of being monitored.

Although he had already conceded defeat, he had fought the urge to tell the admiral of the operation's failure. Certain that he would find out soon enough, Belchenko had pleaded sickness and broken the connection. But before Sorokin had signed off, he revealed a piece of information that cleared matters significantly for Belchenko.

Abruptly broken from his contemplations by a howling, icy gust, Belchenko ducked his head into the wind. Knifing through his woolen overcoat as if it were made of paper, the cold penetrated down to his bones. A sharp, familiar pain pierced his left side and he found himself seized by a violent fit of coughing. While gasping for breath, he spat up a thick wad of congealed mucus. It wasn't until he saw it land in the snow, that he caught site of the streaks of blood.

Even though the cold had intensified, his forehead was matted with sweat. Caught by a sudden wave of dizziness, Belchenko had to reach out and grab hold of a birch tree to keep from tumbling over.

It proved to be a solitary thought that diverted his mind far away from his physical ailments. Strengthened by a shot of anger-generated adrenalin, Belchenko straightened himself up, caught his breath, and even managed to wipe the moisture from his forehead.

To his shocked dismay, it had been Viktor Rodin who had doomed Counterforce to failure! Sorokin had explained that the Premier had learned of the mutiny aboard the IL-38 relay plane, and the subsequent transmission of the *Vulkan*'s launch orders, from the Americans. Belchenko had been genuinely surprised. Upon learning that Rodin had then asked for American military help in tracking down the Soviet sub, his surprise had turned to loathing.

How dare a Soviet Premier, no matter the circumstances, ask an avowed enemy to eliminate one of Russia's own vessels. Not only was this a supreme act of treason, it was a cowardly move as well. No wonder the operation had failed!

Unable to comprehend Rodin's motives, Belchenko trembled as he thought about what the world would soon be like. After their Premier had sold them out to the capitalists, the Union of Soviet Socialist Republics would be no more. For, once its character was changed by the Westerners' decadent ways, their glorious social experiment would be over.

The snow began falling more thickly now, and the first deputy seriously considered returning to his dacha. At that moment a distant, muted growl sounded distinctly in the distance. Called by this alien noise, Belchenko continued into the forest's depths.

After a few hundred yards, he broke into a large, brush-free clearing. Laying in the center of this site was a fully grown black bear, one foreleg held by the jaws of a rusted steel trap. Conscious of the magnificent creature's weakened condition, he cautiously approached it. As he did so, his eyes fell upon a fist-sized patch of shocking white fur on the bear's right haunch.

"Pasha!" he cried woefully. "What have they done to you, my friend?"

Responding to his plea, the bear opened its reddened eyes and, for a second, their gazes met. With an agonized moan that touched the very pit of his visitor's soul, the bear breathed deeply once, and finally surrendered to the pain that had been its constant companion for the last thirteen days.

Aware of his old friend's passing, Belchenko kneeled beside the creature and stroked its soaked, matted fur. With tears of grief running down his cheeks, the first deputy pondered the message that Pasha had just given him.

Like the bear, Stanislav Sorokin, Paul Zavenyagin and he, himself, were facing extinction. When they passed, their type would be gone forever. The absence of their wild strain would hardly be missed by the strange, alien inhabitants of the world to come. That society would be a place where the ultimate dream of the Rodina's founding fathers would have little relevance. Certain that such a world was not for him, Belchenko curled up beside the still-warm corpse of Pasha, oblivious to the howling winds of change that gusted around him.